To Rayna,
I hope
Catherine's Cross!
Millie West

Catherine's Cross

by

Millie West

gatekeeper press

Columbus, Ohio

Published by Gatekeeper Press
2167 Stringtown Rd, Suite 109
Columbus, OH 43123-2989
www.GatekeeperPress.com

Printed in the United States of America

ISBN (paperback): 9781642375442
eISBN: 9781642375459

Library of Congress Control Number: 2019933496

Book design by Robin Krauss, www.lindendesign.biz
Cover art by Rick Reinert

Dedication

For Tony, Whitney, and Micah
And the gracious people of Beaufort County, South Carolina,
who know how to show a visitor a good time!

Acknowledgments
Catherine's Cross

I would like to thank my editor, Megan Miller, who made excellent suggestions and worked countless hours. My favorite artist, Rick Reinert, of Charleston, South Carolina, who painted the cover of *Catherine's Cross*, just for my novel. I am indeed fortunate to have such a talented, wonderful friend.

I could not have completed the novel without the help of the Sheriff's Department of Beaufort County, South Carolina. Sheriff P.J. Tanner, Chief Deputy Michael M. Hatfield, and Master Sergeant Robert Arbelo were extremely helpful. I wanted my detective hero, Seth Mason, to be authentic. These men showed me great courtesy and professionalism in bringing accuracy to my novel.

I'd like to thank Reverend Chad Lawrence of St. Helena's Episcopal Church for allowing me to use his likeness, and Hilda Upton of the Shrimp Shack for permitting me to reference her restaurant. I look forward to my next shrimp dinner!

Thank you, Dr. Danielle Bernth for sharing your medical knowledge, and Ashley Deming, with the South Carolina Institute of Archaeology and Anthropology, for assisting me with the laws and regulations of the South Carolina Hobby Diver Program.

I'd also like to thank Kelly with Gatekeeper Press.

Each page of this romantic thriller is imbued with the natural beauty of the Carolina Low Country, its people, and its culture. Ms. West weaves its rich and intriguing history, along with the region's distinctive manners and idiosyncrasies into her work. Readers (non-Southerners will need to remind themselves that they are immersed into the pacing of a good Southern tale) will find themselves unable to put down this intriguing southern mystery.

—Chanticleer Book Reviews

CHAPTER 1

The Dark Hours

*J*ust before one in the afternoon, while Jenks was watering her ferns, she felt a strange sensation run through her body, like a chill that went to her bones. She'd had these feelings before. Both Jenks and her identical twin, Gigi, experienced them when they sensed the other was in trouble. Their mother called these instincts a gift. "God has given you two the ability to look out for one another," she would say.

This time the chill gripped her more intensely than ever before. She reached for the telephone, and dialed Gigi's phone. The answering machine picked up. Gigi's cheerful voice said, "Leave a message, and I'll call you back . . ." When she dialed her sister's cell phone, she was forwarded to voice mail. "The owner of this cell phone is unavailable."

Jenks left a short message. "Gigi, please call me as soon as you get this." For the rest of the afternoon, Jenks could not stop thinking of her sister, and her continued attempts to reach her by phone were met with failure.

Just before midnight, the doorbell rang at her home. She cautiously walked to the threshold and asked, "Who is it?"

"Jenks, it's Mom and Gregg. Please open the door."

When she opened the door, fear rushed through her limbs as she looked into her mother's eyes. She knew immediately what was wrong.

"What's happened to Gigi?" Jenks choked as she spoke.

"Baby, can we come inside?" her mother, Linda, asked.

Behind her mother and her mother's neighbor, Gregg Mikell, were two men. They were dressed in suits and both had police identification badges on lanyards around their necks.

Her mother moved quickly to Jenks and took her in her arms. Jenks could feel her mother tremble as she pulled her close. "Baby, I have terrible news," her mother said with a shaky voice.

"Oh, Mama—no."

Her mother stroked her hair back and looked into Jenks's eyes. "Gigi drowned this afternoon in the Beaufort River."

Jenks felt as if the wind had been knocked from her lungs. Her knees buckled, and she collapsed to the floor.

One of the men who had accompanied her mother and Gregg to the house rushed forward and helped her into an armchair.

"Jenks, these are detectives with the Raleigh Police Department," Gregg said, nodding toward the two men. "They were kind enough to come see your mother and me. A Detective Seth Mason with the Beaufort County, South Carolina Police Department contacted them this evening, and asked them for help. Gigi was diving for artifacts with Frank Hiller."

Jenks felt numb to her very core. She had known all afternoon that something was wrong, but not this. She tried taking deep breaths, but her strength failed her. Tears began to well in her eyes, and she nearly choked while speaking. "What happened to her?"

"Miss Ellington, I'm Detective Taylor and this is Detective Turner." Both men looked sad and worried. Detective Taylor continued, "I'm very sorry about your sister. When the lead detective, Seth Mason, called us from Beaufort, he was very concerned about this news coming to you on the telephone. He asked for our assistance. Apparently, Gigi was with her diving partner, Mr. Hiller, when something happened. She became overdue on the dive, and he began to search for her. He called the police when he realized she had to be in trouble." He paused for a moment. "Divers with the Beaufort Sheriff's Department found her this evening. I have Detective Mason's phone number. He said he would like to assist you and your mother, and for you to please phone him."

"Thank you," she said as she choked back tears.

Detective Taylor nodded his head to acknowledge her statement. Jenks looked at her mother, who was sitting in an armchair, staring into space. Tears were rolling down her cheeks and she sat motionless, her face lacking expression. Detective Turner went into Jenks's kitchen and returned with two glasses of water, giving one to Jenks and the other to her mother.

Linda took one sip of the water and then set the glass down on a table. Her neighbor, Gregg, went to her side and softly said, "Linda—the detectives may have some other work they need to do. They can give us a ride back home."

She nodded her head, and then softly said to Jenks, "Would you please call the investigator in Beaufort. I don't think I can."

"Yes, Mama."

Gregg helped Linda from her chair, and the police officer assisted her toward the front door. Detective Taylor turned back and put a couple of business cards in Jenks's hand. "This is Detective Mason's phone number and my business card. We'll help you in any way we can. Don't hesitate to call us."

"Thank you."

Gregg left Linda standing beside Detective Turner, and he returned to speak with Jenks. "Are you going to be all right here?"

"Yes, Gregg, thank you."

"I'll look after your mother tonight, so don't you worry. I'll call you in the morning to let you know what time we'll be picking you up to go to Beaufort. I'll drive."

She nodded as she wiped tears from her cheeks with the back of her hand.

Gregg closed the front door behind him and the room became intensely quiet. Drawing a deep breath, she picked up the telephone beside the couch and dialed Detective Mason's phone number.

It rang a couple of times before a firm voice answered, "Detective Mason."

Jenks had a difficult time beginning the conversation and she choked on her words.

The detective responded after a few moments. "Miss Ellington?"

"Yes, Detective."

"The Raleigh Police Department informed me that they went to see your mother and you. I'm very sorry about your sister, Gigi."

"I just don't understand how this could have happened," Jenks said in a high-pitched voice.

"She was with her diving partner, Frank Hiller. According to Mr. Hiller, they were diving in an area where they had recovered numerous artifacts. An old wharf used to be there. Mr. Hiller lost contact with her, and when she didn't surface, he said he began to look for her . . . when it became clear she was in trouble, he called the police. We searched the river for her . . . I'm sorry, but we recovered her body this evening."

Jenks drew in a deep breath. "Where is she now?"

"She's been taken to the Medical University of South Carolina—for an autopsy."

Jenks could barely get her words out, but she told him, "I'll be riding to Beaufort in the morning with my mother and her friend."

"I'll be available to assist you—the sheriff's department is at 2001 Ribaut Street. Just ask for Detective Seth Mason." The last thing he said was, "I'm sorry. I know how you feel."

As she hung up the receiver, Jenks felt like she was in a daze. Could this really be happening?

She dropped to the floor and slammed her fists onto the hardwood floor. Wails of grief came from deep within her. She sobbed until her body shook. "God no, don't let this be true!"

This was surreal. The shock was debilitating, and she lay on the floor for a long time, unable to move, weeping tears of inconsolable anguish. Her only thoughts—of Gigi and the fear she must have felt as she drowned.

The next morning, Gregg drove the two women to Beaufort. They were too stunned to speak as they made the journey from Raleigh.

Jenks breathed deeply, attempting to calm herself. Ordinarily, the beauty of the South Carolina Low Country would have been exhilarating to her, but feelings of sorrow left her depressed and weak.

Both she and her sister were teaching the third grade; Jenks in Cary, North Carolina, and Gigi in Beaufort, South Carolina. The twins had discovered the beauty of the Low Country when their family began to take vacations to Fripp Island when they were children. Their father was still alive, and they spent countless summers enjoying the beaches, the fresh seafood, and especially the peace and quiet of the barrier islands. When the sisters graduated from the University of North Carolina, Gigi announced that she would be relocating to Beaufort, having developed a deep admiration for the area. She believed she had acquired a strong sense of place for the Low Country and had told Jenks that she couldn't imagine living anywhere else.

Jenks had remained in Raleigh to be near their mother, Linda. After their father's death in a construction accident, her mother had been extremely lonely, but a widower, Gregg Mikell, bought the house next door, and they had both found companionship, if not love. He was there now to take care of her mother when she needed his help the most.

When they arrived at the Beaufort County Sheriff's Department, a young policewoman with dark hair and a thin face was behind the front counter. She slid a glass window open and with a soft voice asked, "Are you the Ellingtons?"

"Yes, ma'am," Jenks responded.

"Please have a seat, and I'll go get Detective Mason. He's been expecting you."

When the door into the offices opened, a tall, dark-haired man came into the waiting room. Jenks thought he looked to be in his early thirties. He was wearing a suit and tie, and an identification badge hung around his neck. She thought him ruggedly handsome. His hair was cut extremely short in a military style.

As he came forward to greet them, his face looked tense, and fine lines of worry formed on his forehead. He first took Linda's hand and told her how sorry he was for her loss. Turning to Jenks, he looked down into her hazel-colored eyes. "Miss Ellington, I am indeed sorry for the loss of your twin sister. Please accept my condolences."

"Thank you, Detective Mason."

After he introduced himself to Gregg, the detective asked them to join him in his office. He explained that they were investigating Gigi's death. There were no signs of a struggle at the landing where her car was parked.

Linda entered his office and placed her arms on the back of a chair to steady herself. The detective noticed her failing strength and helped her sit down. She looked up into Jenks's eyes and said, "You'll have to do this alone, Jenks. I don't think I can talk about this right now." She continued weakly, "Gregg is going to drive me to Gigi's home. Just call us when you're ready to leave."

"I'll be glad to give you a ride, Miss Ellington."

Jenks nodded. "Yes, thank you. That's very kind."

"We'll see you there, honey. Thank you, Detective Mason."

"Yes, ma'am." After her mother departed, Detective Mason offered Jenks a chair in his office. "Can I get you anything from the vending machine? A Coke?"

"Thank you . . . no . . . I'm okay."

The officer cleared his throat, and Jenks noticed that he was staring at her. "Miss Ellington, how close was your sister to Frank Hiller?"

Jenks wiped a tear from her face and the detective handed her a handkerchief from his pocket. "Thank you. Gigi . . . my sister was in love with him."

"Do you know if they were having any problems?"

"No . . . why do you ask?"

"I'm just gathering information. When the autopsy and toxicology reports come back, we'll know more."

"What about her diving equipment?"

"A police diver checked out her gear and said that everything was working fine. She had plenty of oxygen."

"I just don't understand."

"Frank Hiller told me that he and your sister had recovered numerous artifacts from the waterways around Beaufort. He said they had sold many items to collectors. How did they work the division of the assets?"

"Gigi told me once that they split everything fifty-fifty."

"Was your sister a good swimmer?"

"Yes, she was very capable. Frank helped her get open-water certified, and he looked out for her on the dives. She told me so."

"I know he has many years of experience as a US Navy diver."

Jenks wiped more tears away that trickled down her cheeks.

"I've spoken with several divers that knew your sister and Frank Hiller. They all told me they were very close." He paused as he looked at her. "I was told by a couple of people that your sister also dove by herself for artifacts."

"What? I wasn't aware of that. She never told me." Cold chills ran up her spine. "I can't believe she would take such a risk."

"I'm sorry to ask you this, but diving is an expensive hobby. How did your sister afford it on a teacher's salary?"

Jenks looked up into his chestnut-colored eyes. "Our father died in a construction accident when we were teenagers. There was an insurance policy. We both receive $25,000 a year from a trust our mother set up after his death."

He nodded. "I'm sorry. Miss Ellington—did your sister own a boat?"

"Not that I know of."

"How did she get to the diving sites?"

"Some of the locations were accessible from landings. She drove her car to them. I think she told me she went to some sites with Frank in his boat. Why do you ask?"

"She was diving alone at times. Frank told me that he was aware she didn't exclusively dive with him. He said that she was very independent and occasionally leased a boat for diving from one of the local marinas. I checked the records with the South Carolina Boater Registration and she was not a boat owner of record. Do you know anything about her access to boats?"

"No, I don't."

"I spoke with Dave Patterson, who owns a local dive shop, and he told me he did business with your sister and had advised her against diving alone."

"Why are you asking me about her diving alone? She was with Frank when she died."

"I'm just gathering information." He looked at her for a moment and then said, "I'd like to take you to your sister's now."

"Thank you . . . I'd appreciate it."

Detective Mason led Jenks out of the sheriff's department building to a silver-colored police car that was parked at the rear of the building. He opened the car door for her, and she sat down in the front seat of the vehicle. When he started the engine, Willie Nelson's voice crooned the song, "Always on My Mind." He quickly turned the sound system off.

Jenks didn't want to hear music and was thankful that he stopped it. She thought how terribly unfair this was. Gigi had her whole life ahead of her. She thought of all the wonderful times they had shared growing up. Gigi was not only her sister, she was her best friend. Her mind raced to thoughts of their last skiing trip to the mountains of North Carolina and how much fun they had had together. This was just three months ago.

A feeling of numbness descended upon her. They had just spoken a few days before. The conversation had been about a trip Jenks would take to Beaufort during the summer to visit Gigi. As she rode in the detective's car, Jenks could still hear Gigi's voice in her mind. The last words she had said before the conversation ended: "I love you, Jenks."

The policeman drove Jenks to her sister's Port Royal home. Cars filled every parking spot in front of Gigi's house. Many of her friends and neighbors had assembled at her cottage. Gigi's next-door neighbors, the Bernsteins and the Forrests, were on the front porch, and they offered their condolences.

As Jenks and Detective Mason entered Gigi's home, a young woman came forward and took Jenks by the hands. Tears were on her cheeks and she said hesitatingly, "I taught school with Gigi. When I saw you enter the room, I thought you were her."

After Jenks thanked Gigi's friend for coming, she glanced into the corner of the living room. Standing in a darkened corner was Gigi's diving partner, Frank Hiller. Blond-headed and handsome, his towering, six-foot, three-inch frame rippled with muscles. The former Navy diver stood with his arms crossed in front of his powerful chest, and he looked at Jenks as she walked in his direction.

"Frank, thank you for coming," Jenks told him.

As soon as she spoke, his arms relaxed and he hugged her. "I'm sorry about Gigi," he said. "I wish I had known she was in trouble."

"Frank . . . How could this have happened? She told me once that she wore a safety line to you."

"We used the line at first because she was uncomfortable diving in the dark waters of the rivers. On one occasion our safety line became ensnarled in underwater tree branches, and we had difficulty clearing ourselves of it. We discontinued using the line after that."

As the mourners departed, Frank Hiller was one of the last to leave. Jenks knew that Gigi was crazy about him. They had met two years before at the Beaufort Water Festival. He had helped her gain her open-water certification so that she could dive with him in the rivers. A number of eighteenth- and nineteenth-century taverns had been located along the waterways of Beaufort County, and they had had success recovering artifacts and ancient spirit bottles from the sites. They sold their discoveries to antique dealers as far away as Boston, and Gigi had assembled her own collection of antique bottles that she proudly displayed on the shelves beside her fireplace.

As he made his departure, Frank hugged Jenks and her mother and asked if he could do anything to help them. "I'm very sorry about what happened," he said as he went out the door.

Jenks looked in Detective Mason's direction. Earlier that evening, she had noticed the two men talking together. Standing side by side, Frank was slightly taller than the detective, but it was obvious that both men took great care of their physiques. After he had spoken with Frank, Detective Mason had taken a position in one corner and quietly observed the people in the room.

Jenks now noticed the detective give Frank a hard look as he left the home. His light chestnut brown eyes seemed to darken as the former Navy diver passed by.

The next afternoon, Detective Mason came to see Jenks and her mother at Gigi's home.

"I checked with the local marina operators to see about Gigi's leasing of a boat for diving. The owner of the Morgan River Marina, Joe Mitchell, said that he had leased a motorboat to her for several months. He's been out of town for two weeks and was not aware of Gigi's death. He offered his condolences."

"Thank you, Detective," Linda said.

"Joe said that she had used the boat frequently during the spring. The watercraft was set up for operating a GPS, but he said Gigi had her own equipment. It has been removed." The detective gazed inquisitively at Jenks and her mother when he said this.

"I know so little of technology. What is a GPS?" Linda inquired.

"It's a device to measure your position on the earth's surface. It uses satellite signals to triangulate latitude and longitude locations."

Jenks was quiet for a moment before saying, "It would be a method of recording her diving sites."

"Yes, ma'am, she could have done that."

Before the detective departed, he told them that he'd be in touch when the Medical University of South Carolina issued the autopsy report on Gigi's death.

Two days later, Detective Mason came to see Jenks and her mother with the preliminary results from the autopsy. "The cause of death was drowning due to asphyxiation. X-rays proved there were no broken bones and no evidence of barotrauma."

"Barotrauma?"

"Yes, your sister was diving with scuba equipment. A breath of compressed air taken at depth can over expand in the lungs if a diver does not breathe out while ascending. The diver's lungs do not sense pain when the air over expands, but an injury can result. In the depth of water that they were diving, that should not have been a factor. Also, she was wearing gloves, and the check for material under her fingernails did not reveal anything."

Jenks remembered that Gigi had cut her hand on a broken bottle during one of the dives and had started wearing gloves to prevent injury.

"It could take up to two weeks to get the toxicology results, but I have asked the lab to expedite the process."

"I don't understand how this could have occurred."

"Perhaps the toxicology report will reveal new information," Detective Mason said.

———

Gigi had adored the Port Royal community. She told Jenks once that she had heard that the Port Royal of the past was known for three things: bars, fighting, and shrimping. But with the prospect of the port terminal being developed, new businesses had been established. Unfortunately, the port project had failed and during the economic downturn, shops had closed, and some homes were in foreclosure.

Jenks knew that Gigi was proud of her cottage. She had renovated it doing much of the work herself. Gigi had landscaped and decorated her home to be one of the loveliest in the neighborhood.

There were a number of military personnel living in Port Royal since the Marine training base at Parris Island was a short distance away. On the street where she lived, Marine flags flew from the front of a few homes.

Neighbors continued to come by for brief visits to Jenks and her mother. The Bernsteins, who lived next door, brought over casseroles, and they promised to keep a close eye on Gigi's house. The neighbor to the other side of her home, Crawford Forrest, came by twice. Gigi had told Jenks that she had become friends with the Bernsteins, but while the Forrests were cordial, they usually stayed to themselves.

———

Jenks and her mother returned to Raleigh to make preparations for Gigi's funeral. Several days after they returned home, Detective Mason phoned Jenks.

"Miss Ellington, I hope you are well. I wanted to let you know that I have the results from the toxicology tests. The lab was very helpful and got the findings back to me as quickly as they could."

She took a deep breath. "Yes, Detective."

"There was no alcohol or chemicals in her system."

"I would have been surprised if there had been," Jenks replied. "And Gigi was a very capable swimmer. So there's no way to know what happened?"

There was silence on the other end of the phone for just a moment, and then the detective said, "Miss Ellington, there's something bothering me. Frank Hiller is a former Navy diver, and navy divers work with partners or as a team. I know accidents do happen, but with all of Frank's training, I don't understand how he would allow his partner to get into trouble."

"Why would he allow harm to come to her?"

"At this point I don't know."

When they finished their conversation, Jenks hung up the receiver and sat down on the couch. *There is no explanation for Gigi's drowning . . . Perhaps Frank Hiller has some answers.*

———

On a Sunday afternoon, under clear blue skies, Gigi was laid to rest beside her father in a family plot that had been in the Ellington family for several generations. She was just twenty-six years of age. During the service, hot, stinging tears flowed from Jenks's eyes. She felt suffocated, as if the wind had been knocked from her lungs.

Wiping tears away, Jenks locked her eyes on Frank Hiller when she saw him in the crowd of mourners. Standing about ten feet away from him was Detective Mason. When her eyes met with the detective's, he nodded to her. As soon as the service was over, Frank approached Jenks and her mother. He told them again how sorry he was about Gigi.

"Frank, will you take a walk with me?" Jenks asked.

"Yes, I'll be glad to."

They left the group of people and walked about twenty-five feet away to the shade of an oak tree. Jenks felt cold chills envelop her as she began the conversation. "Frank—the autopsy results and the toxicology report have come back on Gigi."

"Yes, Jenks?"

"There is no physical reason for her having drowned . . . no broken bones, no chemicals or alcohol in her system. She was a very capable swimmer."

"Jenks, what are you implying?"

"I want to know what happened to her."

"I don't like where this conversation is headed." Frank's face darkened with wrinkles and he stepped in her direction, towering over her. "I didn't do anything to harm your sister, if that's what you're thinking." He placed his hands on her shoulders.

She immediately recoiled, taking a step backward.

"Jenks—I'll overlook this. I know that you're very upset right now."

"Everything all right here?" Detective Mason said as he stepped toward them.

"Yes, I was just finishing my conversation with Jenks." Frank gave Jenks a quick nod and then turned away. The detective stood by her and they watched Frank leave the cemetery and walk to his car.

"What was that about?" the detective asked.

"I told him I wanted to know what happened to Gigi."

"And what did he say?"

"That he didn't do anything to harm her."

"And you expected him to say otherwise?" He raised his eyebrows and looked at her.

She wiped away a tear. "So what do we do now?"

"I need strong proof of foul play to go before a judge for an arrest warrant. We're going to look for new evidence."

She looked at the metal casket holding her twin sister. A new wave of tears came into her eyes and poured down her cheeks. Choking back the tears, she said, "After the school year is over, I'll be coming to Beaufort to pack her things and put her house on the market."

"You've got my phone numbers. I would like to help you in any way that I can."

"Thank you, Detective."

Besides Jenks, he was the last person to leave.

———

Several nights after the funeral, Jenks began to experience dreams about her sister. The most disturbing thing about the dreams was the acute realism. Gigi's mahogany-colored hair was loose around her shoulders, and her hazel eyes were bright and alive. In each nightmare, Gigi appeared to Jenks wearing a gold cross around her neck. A voice repeated the word *twins*. Jenks would wake in a profuse sweat, unable to get the image out of her mind.

On the third night of enduring the nightmare about her sister, Jenks was awakened by a ringing sound. At first she could not place the sound as she emerged from the darkness of the dream, but as it continued, she realized it was the ringing of her telephone. The time on her alarm clock was four a.m.

Lifting the receiver, she heard an edgy voice on the other end of the line say in a whisper, "Miss Ellington, this is David Bernstein down in Beaufort. I apologize for calling at this hour, but someone has broken into your sister's home. I woke to go to the bathroom, and I saw a flashlight beam inside her house. I have called the police, but I wanted you to know. The police should be here any minute."

Jenks rose from bed and made coffee. There would be no more sleep, but that also meant there would be no more nocturnal visits from her sister that night.

At five a.m. the phone rang again, and David Bernstein was once again on the line. "Miss Ellington, the police are at your sister's, but the place is too much of a shambles to tell if anything is missing. Whoever was in her house turned the place upside down."

"Mr. Bernstein, thank you for calling me. Could you please make sure the policeman on duty calls me? I'll be leaving for work around seven."

"I will, Miss Ellington."

At six forty-five the phone rang, but this time it was Detective Mason. "Miss Ellington, I'm troubled about your sister's home being broken into. There have been incidents of property invasions in Port Royal, and I hate the thought that someone might have been aware of her passing and knew the house was empty."

"That's a horrible thought."

"What bothers me is that there are no signs of forced entry. Mr. Bernstein and his wife are going to look over her place this morning to see if they can determine if any of her belongings are missing. Most of her possessions are on the floor. It's as if someone was searching for a particular item."

"What about her antique bottles on the shelves beside the fireplace?"

"As far as I can tell, the collection has not been disturbed."

"Thank you, Detective Mason. Were you the officer on duty?"

"No ma'am, the officer who received the initial call phoned me at home. He was aware that your sister had recently passed away and that I was in charge of her . . ."

He paused for a moment and Jenks interjected, "Detective Mason, I'll be home around four o'clock, and would it be all right if I call you then? I have your business card."

"Yes, ma'am," he said before saying good-bye.

The news of the break-in had distracted her with intense worry. As Jenks led the class in social studies, she fumbled her words repeatedly, and her hands shook as she wrote on the chalkboard. At recess, one of her students approached her. "Are you all right, Miss Ellington?" Joey Adams asked. "I noticed your hands shaking."

"Thank you, Joey. I have a lot on my mind today." She patted him on the shoulder and smiled. "Go enjoy recess, and I'll see you in a few minutes." He smiled back and then left the classroom.

For the rest of the day, the children were especially quiet except when called upon to answer questions; she concluded that Joey must have mentioned his concerns about her to the other students. Jenks knew that she had not done a good job for them since the death of her sister, but she had difficulty concentrating, and hoped the students would forgive her. There were only a few weeks left before summer vacation, and she wanted to focus on her work well enough to give the students the attention they deserved. Then the painful task of packing her sister's possessions and selling her house would begin.

After school that afternoon, Jenks met with her principal, Dr. Edwin Bishop, and told him about the break-in at her sister's house.

"Jenks, I'm going to allow you personal time and sick leave to go handle what you need to in Beaufort. You've done a fine job with your students and testing is complete for the year." Dr. Bishop was admired by his teaching staff for his fairness and professionalism, and Jenks accepted his proposal and decided to leave after saying good-bye to her students the next day. She placed a phone call to Detective Mason to inform him of her intentions to come to Beaufort and then went home to her apartment to pack.

When Jenks arrived at her sister's home, yellow police tape was wrapped around the front porch of the cottage and Detective Mason was waiting for her on the porch, sitting in a high-back wicker rocker. He rose from his seat, walked to her car, and opened the door for her. After they exchanged greetings, he led her to the house, lifted the yellow tape so they could cross under, and then opened the front door. The living room of Gigi's house had been turned into chaos. Her bookshelves had been stripped and books lay helter-skelter on the floor. Every drawer had been emptied.

"This is maddening. I can't tell if anything is missing or not," Jenks said.

"The Bernsteins noted that one thing is missing—your sister's computer."

"Why would anyone want that?"

"Information."

"What on earth about?"

"We'll have to try to figure that out."

"Were you able to find any fingerprints?"

"The area around your sister's computer table was wiped clean. The fingerprints we did find were run through the FBI's national fingerprint identification system, IAFIS. We found Frank Hiller's fingerprints along with David Bernstein's. The database includes active-duty and former military personnel, plus federal government employees. David worked for the Internal Revenue Service, and Frank is a former member of the US Navy. Your sister knew both of these people, so it's normal that their fingerprints would be found in her home."

"The area around her computer desk was completely wiped clean?"

"Yes—whoever took the computer was smart enough to wipe the surfaces down. There were some other fingerprints, but they are not on record with the FBI."

Jenks stepped over Gigi's possessions gingerly to get to the fireplace, where she inspected Gigi's bottle collection. Not one of the ancient bottles was missing.

"If the burglar was after something of value, he or she could have started with these," she said, pointing to the bottles.

Detective Mason did not respond, but looked around the room.

As she made her way back toward the front door, Jenks noticed a picture of herself and Gigi lying on the floor. She picked up the photo and placed it on a table. They both had a copy of the photograph—it was from one of their favorite experiences together—skiing in the mountains of North Carolina two years before. Their mahogany hair was pulled back behind earmuffs. Gigi had her arm around Jenks, and their faces beamed with brilliant smiles. As she looked at the photograph, she felt bitter tears of resentment well in her eyes. This was so unfair.

Tears fell down her cheeks, and Detective Mason was there with a handkerchief. She thanked him for his kindness and then picked up a book that was lying on the floor.

"*Diving into Glory*," Jenks said, reading the title aloud. "This is about Mel Fisher. I remember that he and his team salvaged the treasure from wrecks of Spanish galleons off the coast of Florida." Jenks thumbed through the pages. "It says here, when Fisher's team was searching for the shipwrecks, he would say, 'Today's the day,' at the start of each work day." She continued to turn the pages. "From these pictures, it looks like they did hit the mother lode."

"They may have hit the mother lode, but I recall he lost his oldest son when a salvage boat capsized," Detective Mason said, shaking his head.

"Salvaging treasure is a dangerous business," Jenks replied as she placed the book back on the shelf.

During this time, a locksmith came to the home and changed the locks. He was a friend of Detective Mason's and had come at his request.

Jenks felt depressed as she continued this arduous task, but the entire time, the detective stayed with her and helped her restore the room to a state of order. After reading about Mel Fisher's treasure discoveries, they spoke sparingly; both seemed to be concentrating on their work. As Jenks picked up the last item from the living room floor, her stomach growled loudly, and the detective looked up and smiled.

"I'm sorry, that was embarrassing," Jenks said.

"No, not at all . . . it just means you need something to eat. Why don't we take a break, and I'll drive you to my favorite restaurant. I need to deliver lunch to a friend of mine."

He helped her put on a light jacket, and when they reached his vehicle, he opened the door for her, making sure she was comfortably seated before closing it.

As soon as he started the engine of the police cruiser, the voice of Willie Nelson emanated from the stereo. He turned the music off, but Jenks interjected, "No, it's okay. I'd like to hear him. I've always liked Willie Nelson's version of 'Moonlight in Vermont.'"

He turned the music back on, softer than it had been playing. "I've liked this album since I was a child."

"Did your parents like the album *Stardust?*"

"My mother did; it was her favorite recording."

"I see," she responded. "Do you live out this way on St. Helena?"

"No, I'm house-sitting for good friends, Dr. Leslie Walker and his wife, Sofia. They live on the Chechessee River, which you cross on the way to Hilton Head from Beaufort. Dr. Walker is on a teaching sabbatical, plus researching material for a book he's writing. They're in Florence, Italy, right now."

Another song started, and Jenks asked, "How did you get to know them?"

He turned and looked at her. "I was one of his students when I went to college, and he and his wife took me under their wing. They're very good friends."

"Where did you go to college?"

"The University of South Carolina."

As they drove through Port Royal, they passed by the business owned by Frank Hiller, Hiller's Barbells. The gym was one of the most upscale fitness centers in Beaufort. After retiring from the Navy, he had opened the facility and made his business a success. A For Sale sign was posted on the marquee.

"Frank Hiller's business is for sale," she said to Detective Mason.

"Yes, I understand he has decided to relocate. I think I heard he was moving to San Diego. There are Marine Corps and Navy SEAL training centers there."

Willie Nelson sang out the lyrics of a Gershwin standard—"Someone to Watch Over Me"—as they crossed the bridge to St. Helena Island.

When they turned onto Highway 21, Jenks started to see the marshlands, and the smell of pluff mud was in the air. She remembered the beauty of the Low Country and the surroundings and sounds that went with it. They were just a few miles from Hunting Island State Park when Detective Mason turned into the parking lot of a rustic restaurant named the Shrimp Shack.

"Have you ever eaten here before?" he asked her.

"No, I don't think so. When we visited this area, we prepared our own meals. Mama said it was less expensive."

He parked the police car and then looked at her. "Let me hear you say Shrimp Shack three times fast."

Surprised by his request, she looked at him, and said, "Shrimp Shack, Shrimp Shack, Shimp Srack." A smile showed on her face, and she even laughed a little.

"I knew there was a smile in there somewhere," he said getting out of the car. He walked to her side of the car and opened the door for her.

As they walked up the stairs to the order window, he said, "Lunch is on me. What would you like?"

"Thank you, Detective. A shrimp dinner?"

"I think I'll have the same."

When he went to the window to order, a middle-aged black woman stepped forward to take his order.

"Mister Seth, how you been?"

"Good, Rose, and what about you?"

"I been real good, ain't gonna do no good to complain no how." She laughed. "What can I get for you today?"

"Rose, two shrimp dinners to eat here—and one to go. I'm taking lunch to Rory Masters."

"How's he doing? I ain't seen that boy in a long time."

"He has his good days, and his bad days."

"I understand why," Rose responded. "Two shrimp dinners to eat here, and one to go," she yelled to the kitchen staff. Seth paid her for their meals, and then she said with a large smile, "You come back real soon."

They went out to a covered porch and sat under a ceiling fan to eat their lunch.

"Are you from Beaufort?" she inquired.

"No, ma'am, I'm from the hills of north Georgia. My brother and I took basic training at the Marine Corps Station at Parris Island. I didn't get to see much of the area during that time, but I liked it here so much that I knew I wanted to come back and live here."

"You sound like Gigi." Jenks suddenly realized what she had said, and she took a deep breath. "What I meant was, Gigi wanted to live here after we finished college. She had a sense of place about this area—she said the Low Country had always been like home to her, although we only visited during the summer."

"I understand what she meant," he responded.

"How long were you in the Marines?"

"Four years—my brother and I joined as soon as we were eighteen. My brother, Steel, decided to make a career of the Marines."

As they finished their dinners, Detective Mason rose from his seat and discarded their paper plates.

"Thank you," Jenks said.

"You're welcome. I hope you don't mind one stop before I take you home?"

"No, not at all."

He extended his left hand to assist her from the picnic table, and she noticed he was not wearing a wedding band.

After leaving the restaurant, they made a turn onto Dr. Martin Luther King, Jr., Drive, passing the Penn Center. Detective Mason asked, "Have you ever been to the Penn Center?"

"Yes, years ago . . . my mother brought Gigi and me here, and we explored the property. She said it was one of the first schools created to teach freed slaves to read and write."

"Yes, a lot of good came out of it. From what I understand, Dr. King visited the Penn Center as a place to relax and write. I read that he worked on his 'I Have a Dream' speech while he was here."

When they reached the end of the drive, they approached a riverside neighborhood called Land's End. Detective Mason turned onto a sandy drive where several mobile homes were situated. A Marine Corps flag flew from the front of one of the homes, and the policeman parked in front. He tapped the horn and a man moved back a curtain and smiled brightly from a window.

Jenks thought him extremely handsome, with sandy blond hair and a beautiful smile. When he noticed her, he nodded back to her and continued to smile.

"Why don't you go in with me? I'd like for you to meet my friend."

"All right," she said, and she picked up the takeaway container from the back seat to take inside.

They walked up a ramp to the front door and it opened as they drew close. Jenks drew a deep breath when she saw that Rory Masters was in a wheelchair and that both his legs were amputated below the knee. She set the container down on the counter and extended her right hand to shake his, hoping he had not noticed the hitch in her breathing.

"Rory, this is Jenks Ellington. I mentioned her to you."

The man took Jenks's hand and shook it warmly. "I'm pleased to meet you. Seth tells me you're from the Raleigh area. I was sorry to hear about your sister."

"Thank you," she responded.

"Seth—thanks for bringing me lunch, and from the Shrimp Shack no less."

"You know I'm glad to do it. Any word on the job you applied for with Taylor Marine?"

"No, not yet. They said it could be a week or more before they would let me know."

"I'll be hoping for you. I have to be at work today at three, but what if I come by tomorrow afternoon? We'll have time to talk."

"Yes, thank you, Seth. Miss Ellington, I've enjoyed meeting you."

"Anything I can get you out of the refrigerator?" Seth asked.

"A Budweiser and the hot sauce," Rory said with a smile.

———

As they were pulling away from the mobile home, Detective Mason said to Jenks, "I'd like to show you something. We don't have time to visit it today, but you may not have seen this before."

He took the drive that fronted the Beaufort River. Houses were set high on stilts to avoid flooding, and some of the newer homes shone with metal roofs and white paint. At the end of the drive, underneath the thick shade of a maritime forest of live oak and pine trees, was what appeared to be the ruins of an old fort. The structure had dark passageways open to the outside, and Jenks felt cold chills run up her arms as she looked at the abandoned structure.

"I don't recall ever coming here before," she said.

"Fort Fremont . . . It was built for coastal defense in the late 1800s. At one point it had two ten-inch guns. It passed into private ownership in the 1930s and was recently purchased by Beaufort County to preserve the site."

"I don't think I can go in there. I'm uncomfortable with the darkness of the grounds." She paused for a moment and then said, "I heard you tell Rory that you had to be in to work at three. I thought you were on duty while you were helping me."

"Oh, no . . . I'm afraid Captain Barrett wouldn't agree to that. I just wanted to help you."

Blushing, she looked into his eyes. "Thank you for what you've done."

He smiled back at her. "You're welcome."

On the way back to Port Royal, Jenks asked, "I don't mean to pry, but what happened to Rory?"

"An IED explosion—there were four Humvees traveling in a convoy in Afghanistan. His was the first in line and was blown up by a roadside bomb. Those bas—the insurgents in Afghanistan were supplied with weaponry when America backed the mujahideen, but they also like to use old Soviet unexploded ordnance."

"Where was he when this occurred?"

"In Kandahar Province—this happened two years ago."

"I'm so sorry."

"Rory was closer to my brother, Steel, but since he's been home, we've gotten to be good friends. I'm worried about him. He was laid off from his job at an automotive supply store a few weeks ago. The store manager said he hated to let him go, but their profits have suffered in the poor economy. I hope he can find another position real soon."

When he walked her to the front door of Gigi's cottage, Detective Mason offered to come back in the morning to help her.

"I appreciate your help . . . tomorrow morning then."

"Yes—Miss Ellington, whoever broke into the house was very aggressive in the search for an item or items. I think you should spend the night with one of your neighbors or sleep at a hotel for the time being."

"I've already spoken with the Bernsteins about coming over for a couple of nights."

"Good. Please keep the doors locked when you're here alone. You have my phone numbers also."

"Yes, sir, I do," she smiled in response.

He waved good-bye as he walked down the sidewalk toward his police cruiser.

As she closed the door behind her, she thought of Rory Masters and what had happened to him in Afghanistan. She wondered how he managed to smile.

———

At eight the next morning, Detective Mason rang the doorbell at Gigi's home. Jenks answered it, and he stood before her in a pair of khaki shorts, a navy polo shirt, and leather topsiders. She could not help but notice his broad shoulders, trim waist, and well-toned muscles.

"Good morning, Miss Ellington. I drove my truck today so that I could help you move anything you might want to give away or dispose of."

"Thank you." She paused for a moment and then said, "I'd like for you to call me Jenks. Most of my friends call me that."

"All right, please call me by my first name, Seth."

They smiled at one another, and then he asked, "Where would you like for me to start?"

"We straightened the living room yesterday. Do you mind helping me in the bedrooms? Whoever was in here made a terrible mess."

They went down the hallway to the bedrooms. Jenks had already filled two boxes for Goodwill. As Seth started to lift one of them, she noticed a large scar on his right forearm.

He took the two boxes out to his truck and then asked, "Anything else, Jenks?"

"No, not for right now."

He picked up several books that were scattered on the floor of Gigi's bedroom. "Do you own your own home in Raleigh?"

"No, I rent. I've been saving my money to buy a bungalow near the North Carolina State campus. That area is more expensive than Port Royal. I want to pay cash."

"Smart girl."

They continued to return the house to order, and after several hours, she made them lunch and they sat on the screened porch to eat.

"Seth, what happened to your arm?"

He took a sip of iced tea and looked at the scar. "A family dispute."

"You got into a fight with your brother?"

"No, with my father."

His cell phone began to ring and he answered. "Detective Mason."

Jenks could faintly hear a male voice on the phone. When he ended the conversation, Seth looked at her and said, "A Methodist minister in downtown Beaufort was robbed at gunpoint. That was Detective Campbell, I partner with him often."

"He was robbed in broad daylight?"

"The minister was walking around the churchyard, reciting a sermon for this Sunday, when a young man jumped out from behind a gravestone and held a gun to his head. He forced him inside his church office and robbed him of his car keys before tying him up. The minister was able to get free and call 911. Detective Campbell and two uniformed officers were at the church quickly, and they found the assailant in the minister's car. When he saw the officers approach, he jumped from the car and ran. He apparently was quite the hurdler, jumping over tombstones like an Olympian." He was quiet for a moment, then said, "These days there is such desperation and disrespect for other people that even clergymen are falling victim to criminals."

"I hope you catch him."

"I do too."

She noticed he did not revisit the issue of the scar on his arm, and she asked, "Seth, how long have you been a policeman?"

"Let's see—six years."

"Do you like it?"

"Most of the time—but I often see situations of lost lives and broken hearts. The job can be very difficult." He paused for a moment. "I've been accepted for the fall term at the new law school in Charleston. They've just received their accreditation, and Charleston is not that far away. My captain has offered me part-time work when I'm not attending classes. I'm really looking forward to it."

Jenks gave him a bright smile and said, "I think that's wonderful. Congratulations!"

He smiled back. "Thank you."

By midafternoon, the home had been returned to a reasonable state of order, and they stopped for a few minutes. Jenks served iced tea on the porch. "Seth—thank you for helping me with this awful task."

"You're welcome. I told Rory I'd come by to see him today, so I'd better be going. Tomorrow afternoon I get off work about five-thirty. I'd like to invite you to dinner. I'll show you the Walker's home where I'm house-sitting. Can I pick you up around a quarter of six?"

"Yes, I'd like that very much. Seth—I noticed you don't wear a wedding band. You are single, aren't you?"

"Yes, ma'am," he said with a smile.

"Why are you being so nice to me?"

"That's easy. I like you."

He waved as he left her house and said, "Don't forget to lock your doors."

After he departed, she stood and looked around the room. She still felt anxious knowing that someone had broken into Gigi's house and that he or she was still at large. The antique bottle collection rested on either side of the fireplace, and she said to herself, *they weren't looking for quick money.* She walked to the shelves that housed the collection and lifted one of the blue-green wine bottles from its resting place. She studied it for a moment before softly saying, "Did you get someone intoxicated two hundred years ago?"

As she started to replace the bottle on the shelf, she noticed a note that had been folded and secured underneath it. When she opened the piece of paper, she read the words "Miss Meta Jane Andrews, Coffin Point."

Retrieving the phone book, she read through the listings for Andrews and came up with only one listing on Coffin Point. It was for an Ida Mae Andrews. Coffin Point was on St. Helena Island, and tomorrow she would go there to see what she could find out.

CHAPTER 2

Coffin Point

t. Helena Island was one of the first areas in the Americas explored by European adventurers as far back as the early 1500s. African slaves were brought to the Sea Islands around Beaufort in the 1700s, and with their labor, rice became a crop that created great wealth for a number of plantation owners. The colonial inhabitants of the Beaufort and Sea Island areas survived Indian wars, hurricanes, mosquito-borne diseases, and the American Revolution.

Early in the Civil War, the Beaufort area was invaded by the Federal Navy in the fall of 1861, and remained in Union hands throughout the conflict. African slaves who were freed by Federal Forces were able to purchase land formerly owned by their white masters. Jenks recalled her mother explaining the history of Beaufort and the Sea Islands when she was a child. Many of the homes of the planter class survived the Civil War because they were used as Union hospitals. Some of the houses were sold at tax sales to freedmen, and in some cases to northern investors.

When she turned off Highway 21 onto Coffin Point, she drove all the way to the end of the road, passing a white cottage-style home with a muted silver-colored roof and blue shutters. In the yard was a sign that read "Spiritual Advisor—Meta Jane Andrews." She went by the home and continued to the end of the lane, where a remarkable, white multistoried house was situated. After she reached the end of Coffin Point, she turned around and returned to the first cottage, which had several cars parked in the yard.

Jenks walked up on the porch. A sign on the screen door said "Come inside and ring bell on marble top table."

The screen door squeaked as she entered, and seeing the bell on the table, she gently rang it. A voice called out from the rear of the house, "I be right dere . . . wait jus' a minute."

Jenks stood in the doorway of the home and glanced around the room. A vase holding a large arrangement of pink roses was sitting on a wooden chest. The fragrance of the roses filled the foyer with a rich fresh scent. Along one wall was an oak hall tree, which held several straw hats, a couple of them with holes in the front. At the top of the hall tree was the face of a woman delicately carved into the wood.

Light footfalls approached the front foyer from a hallway that was partially obscured by a six-panel door. As the door opened, a diminutive woman wearing a dark-colored dress entered the foyer. She was in her late seventies or early eighties, judging by the deep wrinkles on her face and her white hair, which was neatly combed against her head.

As she looked at Jenks a disturbed expression crossed her face. Her eyes became wide with fright, and she began to cross herself. "Lawd—why has you sent a spirit to us? I know Meta talk to de spirit world 'bout every day, but I never see one in full form."

Shocked, Jenks's mouth dropped open, and she stepped back toward the screen door.

The voice of another woman sounded from the rear of the house. "Ida Mae, what you goin' on 'bout?"

"Meta—de Lawd is bringing judgment on us. Come quick!"

A slightly built woman appeared in the doorway that led to the rear hallway. When she came into the foyer, she looked at Jenks and said, "Ida Mae . . . what's de matter with you? You gonna' scare dis chile to death."

"She 'bout to do de same ting to me!" she said in an elevated voice.

The second woman turned to Jenks. "Miss, my name is Meta Jane Andrews. A young lady came to see us several months ago. She bear a strong resemblance to you. I tink you mus' be related to Miss Gigi Ellington. We hear she accidentally drown in de river."

"I'm Jenkins Ellington. Gigi was my twin sister."

"Oh, Lawd," Ida Mae exclaimed.

"Come an' have a seat in de parlor," Meta said.

She and Ida Mae led Jenks to a room off the foyer. Antique furniture decorated the parlor, and a ceiling fan rotated lazily, sending a slight breeze throughout the room.

"The reason I'm here is because I found a note in my sister's home underneath an antique bottle. Written on it was your name, Miss Meta Jane, and the words Coffin Point. I wanted to see why my sister would have kept your name hidden under a bottle."

"Your sister came to see me and Ida Mae 'bout some old diaries we have in our keep. She say dat de librarian at de downtown branch tell her dat we has some of de only recorded history from de Civil War period dat was written by a local resident. You know de white folks flee Beaufort and de Sea Islands when de Federal Navy invade dis area at de start of de Civil War. I hear it called 'de great skedaddle.'" She smiled and chuckled to herself.

"Our great-grandfather learn to read and write when he a little boy even though it be illegal at de time. He have a young master who teach him book learning—I hear dey use de Good Book. My ancestor name Joseph Andrews, and he keep a record of what happen in Beaufort during dat war."

"Do you know what she was interested in?"

"She say she seen a portrait of a young girl in de Gibbes Museum in Charleston with a gold cross round her neck—Miss Iris Elliott."

Remembering her dreams, Jenks blurted out, "A gold cross?"

"Yes, um, she say she hear dat a ship laden with gold and silver sank somewhere near St. Helena Sound during de Civil War. She say dat cross was rumored to be on board de ship when it go down."

"How did she know this?"

"Miss Jenkins, she only say dat she hear about it from other divers."

Meta paused for a moment and picked up a hand fan that had white roses printed on it and began to fan herself. "You know dere were stories dat a lot of de wealth of dis area was carried off to de north while de Yankees was here. My gran'ma tell us tales 'fore bed 'bout de fine possessions dat disappear from de homes around here durin' dat time."

"Did Gigi say she had found the ship?"

"Oh no, Miss, she ask to read my ancestor's journals, and when she finish, she tank us and give us a gift of flowers. We never see her again, but we hear 'bout her death in a diving accident."

"Do you think I can see your great-grandfather's journals?"

"Yes, Miss, but please come back tomorrow around two. I have an appointment in a few minutes, and we have to get de books out of a trunk in de sewing room."

"Thank you, Miss Meta . . . Miss Ida. Please call me Jenks if you'd like."

"Jenkins is a pretty name." Meta paused. "Please try to remember—most of de records dat were kept during dat time was by federal authorities, northern newsmen, and a few white missionaries. Dere may be tings dat de Federals didn't want recorded."

"What kind of things?"

"Dat was a time of war and some of de worst tings 'bout men come out."

Ida Mae was sitting quietly on the settee, and she said to Jenks as she left the room, "I's sorry 'bout my mistake. I's glad you alive and well . . . you as pretty as your sister was."

"Thank you, Miss Ida."

"We see you tomorrow at two," Meta said as she followed Jenks and held the screen door open for her.

As she walked to her car, Jenks thought of the sisters' unique dialect: Their t's were replaced by d's, and there were other distinctive pronunciations. She concluded that they must be descendants of the Gullah people and their language differences went deep into their ancestral roots. Their brogue was sweet and lovely to listen to. What were Meta's words? "'We hear she accidentally drown in de river,'" Jenks said softly under her breath. "Was it really an accident?"

On her way back to Port Royal, Jenks stopped at the Publix Food Market on Lady Island. She was out of almost everything, and she parked her car under live oak trees that shaded the lot.

Inside the store, she loaded her buggy with a gallon of milk, fresh vegetables—most of the produce selections originating from local farms.

An older gentleman with silvery white hair yielded his buggy to her as they came close together at the tomato stand. He looked at her, and with a wry smile he said, "There are women who try to be sexy and others who are born that way."

She was flustered by his comment.

"You are the latter version," he grinned.

"Thank you," she quickly replied.

As he turned the corner of the aisle, he observed, "You are even lovelier when you blush."

Old wolves lurking in the grocery store, Jenks thought.

When she arrived back at Port Royal, she went to the door off the back porch, unlocked it, and then returned to her Jeep to unload the groceries. As she bent into the car, she felt a strange sensation run down her spine, something like a cold chill, but not exactly. Lifting one of the bags, she turned and almost ran into a man who was standing less than two feet from her. He was attractive and appeared to be in his late forties, with salt-and-pepper gray hair; his skin handsomely tanned.

She nearly dropped the bag to the ground but grabbed the bottom, securing the groceries against her chest. Before she could say anything, the man held out his hands and said, "Miss Jenkins, could I please help you with your groceries?" His voice was somewhat garbled, and he smiled at her with a broad grin. "I'm Caleb Grayson. I used to help Miss Gigi with heavy lifting."

Jenks had never heard Gigi mention this man before and felt discomfort under his gaze. "Thank you for your offer to help, Caleb. I apologize, but my sister never mentioned you to me."

"That's okay. She was my friend. I miss her, and I'm sorry about what happened to her."

He extended his arms to take the grocery bag and Jenks released the sack into his arms. "Where would you like me to put this?"

"Why don't you put the groceries on the back porch?"

His speech was difficult to understand, but he smiled at her and started toward the screened porch. Jenks noticed he was wearing khaki shorts and that his calves were well-muscled. He walked with a limp, and he made his way slowly to the rear of the house.

She chose not to enter the home, but instead waited outside while he returned twice more to her Jeep for the groceries. When he finished his task, he smiled broadly.

"Thank you, Caleb," Jenks said as she reached into her purse for a few single dollar bills.

When he saw what she was doing, he raised his hands up and said, "No, ma'am, I can't take your money. It was my pleasure to help you." As he started to walk away, he turned back and said, "I'm glad to have you for my neighbor."

Jenks watched him leave; he had difficulty walking and his left foot dragged to some degree. She concluded that Caleb suffered from both a physical and mental handicap, but his kind heart was evident to her.

Seth knocked on Jenks's door at exactly a quarter of six.

"How was your day?"

"Busy . . . I'll tell you about it when we get home. I mean, to the Walker's house."

He smiled and helped her into the car, closing the door for her. On the drive to the Walker's house, they crossed an expansive bridge across the Broad River and continued in the direction of Hilton Head.

Jenks broke the silence in the car. "While I was unloading groceries this afternoon, a neighbor stopped and helped me."

"Oh, who was that?"

"His name was Caleb Grayson."

"Yes, I know who you're talking about. I know he worked a number of odd jobs for shopkeepers in Port Royal until the poor economy forced many of them to close their doors." A frown crossed his brow. "All I know is that many years ago he was in an accident, and he didn't fully recover from his injuries."

"What kind of accident?"

"An automobile wreck. I'm afraid he suffered a severe brain injury. His family is well to do, and his parents live at The Point."

"The Point?"

"Yes, it's an area in downtown Beaufort with a number of antebellum homes."

Their conversation was interrupted as Seth pointed out a severely deteriorated waterfront building off the highway. "There used to be a business here called the Lemon Island Marina, but it closed down some time ago. I heard that a group of investors wanted to reopen the marina and operate a restaurant as well, but their financing fell through."

When they reached the waterfront structure, Jenks noticed that the building was missing windows and in need of a new roof. Only the dock appeared to be in decent condition. After they passed by, Seth made a turn down a sandy road and followed it past several mailboxes. He turned onto a driveway that led to a magnificent two-story home on the waterway.

"This property belongs to Jacob Spenser. A couple of years ago, he was robbed by three young men who made off with a number of his prized possessions, including a collection of antique firearms and his mother's jewelry. Detective Campbell and I apprehended the young men and retrieved his belongings before they could sell them. Ever since then, he has told me to use his property to access the river any time I want. This is where I meet Mose Lafitte, a local fisherman. I buy fresh fish from him, and this is a convenient meeting place since it's near his home. He calls me when he has fish to sell."

Seth stopped the car near the dock. Tied off to the floater was a worn-out fishing boat with nets and crab baskets resting on the deck. An elderly black man rose from a bench seat at the helm and said, "Lawd, Mister Seth—how are you dis day?"

"Mose, I'm fine. I'd like to introduce Miss Jenks Ellington to you."

He removed a sweat-stained fishing hat from his head and bowed to her. "Miss, I's proud to meet you." He stopped speaking for a moment and then continued. "I's very sorry about your sister. I read about it in de newspaper, and Mister Seth say he been trying to help you out some."

"Thank you."

Mose enunciated his words in the same unique manner as Ida Mae and Meta. He put his hat back on top of his head and smiled at Seth, revealing four yellow, decaying teeth in the front of his mouth. He picked up a sizeable fish and said, "How do you like dis redfish? I caught it about an hour ago, and it's been on ice ever since."

"As long as it's within the legal limit, it's fine with me," Seth replied.

Mose smiled broadly and responded, "Now, Mister Seth, you knows I ain't gonna sell no illegal-size fish to no policeman."

Seth laughed and said, "I know Mose, I'm just teasing you."

Mose put the fish in a large plastic bag and sealed it before handing it to Seth. "How much for your fish?"

"Four dollars—you knows I always gives you a break."

"Thank you, Mose."

"I be back out here tomorrow. I call you if I have a *legal* catch." He grinned when he emphasized the word *legal*.

He handed a business card to Jenks and said, "Miss Ellington, you call me if you like to buy fish." He winked at Seth and Jenks and started the motor of his fishing boat. Jenks and Seth watched as he backed into the waterway and headed toward the Lemon Island Marina.

Seth looked down into Jenks's eyes and said, "Mose is a descendant of Gullah people who inhabited the Sea Islands for hundreds of years. He's fished these waters his entire life."

"Yes, I've listened to other people speak in a similar fashion." At this point, she did not mention her visit to Ida Mae and Meta.

They drove back to the highway toward Hilton Head, and Seth made a turn onto a small rural road that was lined with live oak trees. The window was down on Jenks's side, and she felt the air become cooler under the trees. After several minutes on the sandy lane, they came to a tabby walled chapel. A cross graced the peak of the metal roof, and the grounds were neatly manicured. A sign near the lane read Rabbit Hash Hunt Club.

Jenks read the name out loud and asked, "How did this chapel get to be named Rabbit Hash Hunt Club, and why isn't it utilized as a house of the Lord?"

Seth glanced at her for only a moment and then returned his eyes to the road. "Jenks, most of the people who worshiped at this chapel passed away, and their offspring either moved away for jobs or chose to worship elsewhere. The chapel ceased to operate and a group of hunters purchased the land and turned the sanctuary into a hunt club. They've taken good care of the building, and they're good folks. I joined the club a couple of years ago, and I hunt ducks, dove, quail, and deer on the land. Twenty-three hundred acres and the chapel were purchased at the same time."

"How did it get the name Rabbit Hash?"

"During the Depression, the church put on suppers for people who were in poverty, and a number of local farmers and hunters trapped or shot rabbits to donate for stews—hence, rabbit hash. The chapel was formerly known as French Chapel after Alexander French, who owned the plantation where the sanctuary was situated. The church was at one point a chapel of ease for the planters in the area. After the French family died out, the chapel operated until the 1960s, when it was sold to the hunt club."

As they continued the drive, the lane became even darker with the shade of live oaks and thickets of bamboo that lined the roadway.

"This is beautiful back here." Just as she said those words, they came to a brick entranceway with wrought-iron gates. As the police car neared the gate, Seth picked up an electronic opener and pressed a button. The gate swung open. "This is the Walker's property," he commented.

A magnificent three-story home appeared in the distance, and reflections of light and water danced on the side of the structure. Jenks could see a waterway in front of the home, and she exclaimed, "Wow—this is fantastic. I didn't know college professors earned this kind of money."

"The wealth in the family comes from Mrs. Walker. She inherited three working sugar farms on Trinidad as well as the proceeds from family investments on Tobago. Her ancestors emigrated from Martinique during the French Revolution and became successful planters."

"I'm speechless," Jenks said.

"Wait until you see the inside."

He led her through a ground-level entrance into a large room that housed weights, exercise machines, and a boxer's punching bag.

"Is this equipment all yours?"

"No—only the punching bag is mine; the rest belongs to Dr. Walker and his wife."

In the corner of the exercise room was an elevator, and Seth said, "You get the full treatment today. After this you'll have to walk up the stairs."

He smiled and led her inside the lift. When they stopped on the second story, the door opened and she had to blink at the brightness of the room. He led her into a spacious living room with picture windows that faced an expansive marsh. A grand piano was situated in the middle of the room, and Seth opened a sliding glass door that led to a large covered porch.

"This is fantastic!" she exclaimed.

Deep-green cord grass, pluff mud, and the dark waters of the marsh stretched as far as the eye could see. The marshland was quiet. The only noise she could hear was the wind in the cord grass and the call of a hawk that was flying near an island in the waterway. The scent of pluff mud and the salt marsh brought back fond memories of crabbing with her father on Fripp Island when she was a child.

Seth handed her a pair of binoculars. "I enjoy looking at the wildlife on the marsh. I thought you might like to study the surroundings while I clean the fish. It won't take me very long."

"Yes, I'd love to."

"Oops, almost forgot. Would you like a glass of white wine?"

She put the binoculars down and smiled at him. "That would be nice."

He went into the house and after a few minutes returned with a glass of wine. The sides of the glass were frosty from the cold liquid.

She took one sip. "Mmm—this is delicious. What's the name of it?"

"Montecillo Verdemar Albarino. I hope I said that right."

"Sounds fine to me."

"This wine is one of Mrs. Walker's favorites, so I knew what to buy. I thought we'd have blackened redfish for supper. You can help me with the corn on the cob and red potatoes."

"Just let me know when you want me to come in."

The afternoon was cool for May, and Jenks stood in the afternoon sun for warmth. She thought about her sister and how much she missed her. Tears began to well in her eyes, but she wiped them with her fingers and put the binoculars back up to her eyes. In the marsh, near an island with a rookery of egrets, three dolphins were swimming. Their dorsal fins cut the surface of the water, making a significant ripple. After a few moments, they disappeared into the dark waters of the Chechessee River.

The sound of an airplane engine sounded across the marsh, and Jenks saw a red biplane coming toward the house. The airplane was flying low over the waterway, and as it neared the Walker's property, the pilot rocked the wings before beginning a climb.

"Seth, come look at this biplane." Jenks went to the doorway and called him enthusiastically.

When Seth emerged from the house he was wearing a white apron. He looked at the airplane, which was commencing another flyby. "Hale Branson," he said as he watched the aircraft.

"You know him?"

"Yes, he's a friend. He's a retired Air Force pilot, and he does some volunteer work with the sheriff's department."

"What kind of airplane is that?"

"I believe that's a Pitts Special."

"Wow, he flies well!"

"He sure does. He has several airplanes, mostly for aerobatics, that he keeps at Frogmore International."

"Frogmore International?"

"Yes, that's the old nickname for the Beaufort County Airport. It was named after a plantation on St. Helena named Frogmore. At the outbreak of the Civil War, that plantation as well as Coffin Point were owned by Thomas Coffin."

"Coffin Point? I found a reference to Coffin Point in Gigi's possessions."

The Pitts Special flew by the house one more time. Seth waved at his friend, and then the airplane began a climb and departed the area.

"Why don't you tell me about what you found when we go inside," Seth said. He motioned for her to enter the house. "After you," he said with a smile.

When they went into the home, piano jazz was playing on the stereo. Seth led her to the kitchen. The room was mostly white, with stainless-steel appliances, all of them commercial grade. An island topped by a thick piece of oak was located close to an elaborate gas stove. "I think this is the prettiest kitchen I've ever seen," Jenks said as she ran her hand across the top of the island. Seth smiled at her observation.

The corn and potatoes were on the counter, and she shucked the corn and then washed the ears and the potatoes. "While I was looking at Gigi's bottle collection, I lifted one of the bottles, and underneath it was the name of a lady, Meta Jane Andrews, and the street on which she lives, Coffin Point."

"Ah, yes, Miss Meta—she is known in the Beaufort area as a spiritual advisor. She is purported to be capable of communicating with the dead, and there are a lot of folks who take her seriously."

"I went to see her and her sister, Ida Mae."

He pushed the cast-iron skillet to the rear of the stove and turned to face Jenks. "You did what?"

"I went to see them." She looked Seth in the eye. "I nearly frightened Ida Mae to death. She thought I was Gigi."

"I can understand why she would think that," he said with a smile.

"I asked Meta why Gigi would have had her name tucked away underneath one of her antique bottles. She said that Gigi came to see her several months ago about some journals that an ancestor of hers had kept during the Civil War. Miss Meta said that she asked her about a gold cross that was rumored to be on board a ship that went down near St. Helena Sound." She paused and looked closely at him. "Can I tell you something strange, and you won't think I'm crazy?" He looked at her seriously. "After Gigi died I started to have dreams about her and in the dream sequences was a gold cross. It has red stones in it."

"I don't think of you as being unstable. Jenks, Dr. Walker's specialty is the history of the Italian Renaissance period. However, the semester that I was in his class, he taught a course on Low Country history that explored myths and legends. It was one of my favorite classes. One of the legends that he addressed was a gold cross that was stolen during the Civil War from a Miss Iris Elliott. Her family was one of the wealthiest in the Beaufort area prior to the Civil War. Her father purportedly purchased the cross while on a tour of Europe in the late 1850s. It was supposed to be from the jewelry collection of Catherine the Great."

"They must have been very wealthy."

"Dr. Walker said that the cross and other family heirlooms of the Elliott family were stolen in 1862 and were never recovered. He also said that local lore placed the Elliott family possessions on a ship that sank off the coast of South Carolina—on its way to a northern destination."

"I asked Miss Meta if Gigi had told her she had found the cross, and she said that she had not mentioned locating it." Jenks pulled silk off of an ear of corn. "Seth—do you think she might have found the Elliott treasures?"

"Impossible to say."

"I have an appointment at Miss Meta's home tomorrow to review the journals of their ancestor. I'll call you when I've finished reading them."

Seth opened a Budweiser, took a sip, and said, "All right . . . the water's boiling. Eight minutes on the corn."

The scent of blackening seasoning was heavy in the kitchen, and he opened the windows and doors to the outside to allow fresh air inside. Seth placed the filets of redfish on their plates and they began to eat.

"This is delicious. How did you learn to cook like this?"

"Trial and error—mostly error." He smiled at her and said, "Tomorrow, there will be a newspaper article in the *Hilton Head Island Packet* about the Beaufort minister, Lucius Gregg, who was robbed at gunpoint yesterday. I admire his courage."

"Can you tell me about it?"

"Yes, I think you heard that he was in the churchyard practicing a sermon for Sunday when the assailant jumped from behind a grave marker. He strong-armed the minister and put a gun to his head, demanding money and his automobile. They had to go inside the church office to get his car keys. His wallet was in his car."

"That's very frightening."

"Once they got inside, the gunman removed the minister's belt and tied his hands with it. He then asked the minister to give him three reasons why he should not kill him." Seth looked into Jenks's eyes and continued, "The minister told him that he had a wife and children that he loved deeply . . . that he was in Beaufort to do the Lord's work, and that if he murdered him, he'd have to answer to God. The gunman asked him if he was sure about that."

"That's awful."

"The assailant broke a lamp and tied the clergyman's legs with the cord. Minister Gregg said that he heard the gun click and thought he was about to die. Instead, the gunman left the church, leaving the doors propped open. After he left, the pastor was able to free himself and call 911. A couple of police cars were nearby, and they were at the church within moments. The gunman was sitting inside the pastor's car, and when he saw police approach, he took off across the churchyard, hurdling markers like an Olympian."

"The minister was very brave," Jenks said.

"He said that he was frightened but at the same time felt an inner strength that he knew had come from faith. Pastor Gregg was recording his sermon on a voice recorder and the assailant took it with him. He hopes that the gunman will listen to the sermon, which was on salvation and peace, and that his thoughts will help this man."

"He has faith in the Lord to help this man."

"Jenks—you can only help some people just so much."

They were silent for a moment before Jenks asked, "Do you have an apartment?"

"No—I was renting a furnished apartment in Beaufort when the Walkers asked me to house-sit for them. I didn't renew the lease, and I brought my one possession that I have regular therapy sessions with."

"What's that?"

"My punching bag."

She laughed as she recalled all the workout equipment in the basement. The one item that belonged to Seth: the punching bag.

After dinner, Seth showed Jenks the rest of the home, ending their walk at a home theater. "There's an excellent movie on Turner Classics this evening. It's a favorite of Mrs. Walker's. Have you ever seen *Laura*, with Gene Tierney and Dana Andrews?"

"No, I don't think so."

"Would you like to watch it?"

"Yes, thank you."

He went to the kitchen and poured her another glass of wine. When he returned, they sat down beside each other, and he turned on the expansive screen of the television. He then lifted her hand and put it inside his. She felt the same energy course through her body that she felt any time he touched her. She flushed with incredible warmth.

Seth left her once during the movie, but returned a few minutes later with a bowl of hot popcorn.

After the show was over, Seth drove her home. On the way to Port Royal, they discussed the movie *Laura* and how a detective played by Dana Andrews had become obsessed with the beautiful portrait of Laura—really a painting of actress Gene Tierney. Believed murdered at the beginning of the movie, Laura enters her home and shocks the detective as he sits in her living room, consumed with the beautiful female vision in the portrait.

"I would have never expected another woman to have been murdered instead of Laura." Jenks paused as she reflected on the movie. "You know the detective character really obsesses over Laura's portrait," she said.

"It's easy to obsess over a beautiful woman."

"What do you mean?"

"Nothing." He paused for a moment. "Shotguns can do a lot of damage, and there was no DNA testing back then."

"Who would have thought the murder weapon would be hidden in a clock? What do you like about the movie?"

"I like to look at Gene Tierney." Seth glanced at her. "I'm just kidding. She's really not my type."

"What is your type?"

He smiled at her in the dimly lit automobile.

"How did you know I would like the movie?" Jenks continued.

"Mrs. Walker is a fine, educated lady like you. I can see you two having similar taste."

"Thank you, Seth."

They reached Gigi's home at Port Royal, and without saying another word, he got out of the car and came around to open her door. Accompanying her inside, he slid his arms around her in an embrace and held her slight, five-foot four-inch frame against him. She felt safe and warm in his arms and her body quickly reacted as she felt a surge of fiery energy course through her limbs.

"You're a tiny little thing," he said as he held her.

She placed her head against his chest and breathed in his fresh clean scent—something like mint and citrus. She felt safe as he held her against his body. When he released her from his embrace, she lifted her head up and looked into his eyes. "Thank you for the wonderful evening."

"I've had a great time myself. I'll look forward to hearing from you after you meet with Miss Meta Jane."

Before he left the house, he kissed her on the forehead and then paused in the open doorway. "Lock your doors and use the deadbolt."

"I will," she said with a smile and then leaned her back against the door to catch her breath. She was glad to have his company and his friendship.

The next afternoon Jenks arrived at Meta Jane's home on Coffin Point. She entered the front door and rang the bell on the marble-top table.

A voice that sounded like Ida Mae's called out from the rear of the house. "Miss Jenkins, come on in de parlor. I be dere in jus' a minute."

Jenks sat down on the couch, and within a few minutes Ida Mae entered the room and said, "I's glad to see you today. We got de books you want to look at.

Dey's in de kitchen on de table. Come with me." She smiled and motioned for Jenks to come with her.

Jenks followed her down the hallway into the kitchen. It was a spacious room with high ceilings and a round oak table in one corner. A black pot-bellied stove was situated diagonally to the table.

The books sat on the table beside a plate of cookies and a glass of milk. "We tink maybe you want some refreshments while you read."

Jenks smiled at her, "Thank you, Miss Ida Mae."

"Take your time. Meta has a client in a few minutes, and we'll be in dat room off de kitchen if you need us." She pointed to an entranceway, and then exited into the room, closing the door behind her.

Jenks carefully opened the book on top of the stack. The leather jacket was cracked and worn, and the paper within the journal was yellowed. The writing was hard to read. She turned the pages and found a legible entry from 1860 that dealt with an event at the plantation, Andrews Hall.

> I come up from the fields with the ringing of the lunch bell. Scipio was with me and when we got to the big house there was wild hogs in the yard. They must have come up from the swamp. They black and when they snarl at me, they look like the devil. I had a sickle that I brought from the field. When they came at me, I killed them one by one. Then I see what they done. Miss Adelaide is going to be real upset. They killed her cat, Molly, and her kittens. Their tiny bodies lay all over the yard. I buried them this afternoon before Miss Adelaide return from Charleston. Me and Scipio take the hogs to Maum Gray and Sister Lebo.

"That's horrible," Jenks said as she turned the page. She continued to read through several sections of the journal until she came to this entry:

> We in the fields planting. I with Scipio and Thomas who about nine years old. We working near the woods when I see a coon come out. I know right away that this mean trouble cause ain't no animal of the night going to be out in the day unless they

sick or frightened. That coon run right at Thomas and bite him on the leg before I can get there with a shovel to kill it. We take him to Sister Lebo. I can tell by the look in her eyes that this is bad. She tell folks not to go near that dead coon and she ask me to go down there with her. She burn that animal and then she tell me nothing can be done for Thomas. He will have the madness.

Miss Ida Mae opened the door and stuck her head inside. "You all right?"

"Yes ma'am."

"What you tink of de writings?"

"I think plantation life was very difficult."

"Especially if you one of de ones doing de work," she said with a smile.

"I've learned a little bit about the Coffin family. Where did the name Coffin Point come from?"

"Old Ebenezer Coffin. His house at de end of dis road."

"Yes, I saw it the first time I came to see you and Miss Meta."

"He own over eleven hundred acres of land on St. Helena. His plantation was one of de mos' prosperous ones in de south. When he die, he left de property to his children, but one son, Thomas, he ran tings 'til de Federals take over de Beaufort area. De Coffin family flee Beaufort at de time of de invasion."

"My goodness—they just left it all behind?"

"I suppose dey like de rest of de white folks. Didn't tink dey had no choice."

She took a deep breath. "At one time, de property was part of de Port Royal Experiment. Dere was an attempt to train and educate de freedmen, but dat not last too long. Over de years, de property sold several times and eventually de land was subdivided for houses. Ebenezer's house still lookin' over St. Helena Sound."

Ida Mae started to close the door and step back into the next room. "Let me know if you needs anyting."

"Yes ma'am."

Jenks went back to her reading.

I keep hearing about secession. The white folks talk of it all the time. South Carolina going to leave the United States so they can keep their slaves. Greed is a terrible thing.

An entry from the late fall stunned her by the brutality of the details:

There was a fire on the grounds of Andrews Hall last night. One of the buildings used to store cotton caught fire and burn to the ground. Nathan, Maum Gray's son, was suppose to be tending the fire, but he fell asleep and wind whip up debris that catch fire and then blow into the cotton. All of it was lost. When Jacobs the foreman find out—he take a cane to Nathan and bout beat him to death. Master Preston Andrews, who my age, come out and stop him afore he finish his task. He tell Jacobs not to ever beat anyone like that again. Jacobs remove his hat and say he sorry, but he say Nathan done cost the family a fortune in cotton.

Maum Gray and several women take Nathan away. He hurt bad.

Late that night, Master Preston come down on slave row and bring some medicine to Maum Gray for Nathan. He tell her he sorry about the beating and if it up to him he fire the foreman and send him packing.

When he finish with Nathan, Master Preston come by my quarters and ask me to go for a walk. Preston a fine young man and because of him I can read and write. We walk down to the river and he has tobacco. It real fine quality and while we smoke we watch the moonlight on the water and the current flowin out to sea. Then he tell me. "Joseph I'm going to be leaving Andrews Hall. I've signed up for the army. I hope if there is fightin its short lived and I can come home real soon." Then he say something that I won't ever forget. "Wars have only meant misery to those who have engaged in them. This will be no different." We smoke tobacco until almost first light and he tell me I been a good friend to him and he going miss me. Before dawn a dredfull cry come from the other side of the river and I have the chills. "It's just a screech owl," Master Preston say, but I feel real scared. It sound like death calling out. Then we go back to where we belong—me to slave row and him to Andrews Hall. He say he don't want to get in no fight with his father so he gonna sneak in the back.

Jenks continued to read through the journals until Miss Ida Mae came back into the room to speak to her. "Miss Jenkins, you come back tomorrow if you want to continue to read. Meta would like to speak with you. Come dis way please."

She followed Ida Mae to the darkened room off the kitchen. In the middle of the room was a round table where Meta was seated. "Come in, Jenkins. I'd like to talk with you—please have a seat."

Jenks sat down at the table across from Meta. The old woman looked deeply into her eyes. "Did you find anything in de books dat would help you today?"

"No ma'am. I read through the book that preceded the war. I did find the journal to be quite compelling."

"Dat's good. I's glad you found de writings interesting."

"Yes, ma'am."

Meta looked at Jenks for a moment before she said, "Dere's someting I want to tell you."

"Yes, ma'am?"

"The first time I saw you de aura roun' you."

"What do you mean?"

"I sense your energy, but also dat of another presence."

"You mean supernatural?"

"Yes, Miss Jenkins. When I's around you I keep hearing the word twins over and over. I tink at first it might be your twin, Gigi, reaching out to you, but I's not sure. Also, I hear de words over and over tellin' you to look closer."

"Look closer for what?"

"Of dat, I's not sure."

"That's frightening."

"I do not mean to scare you, but I tink you should know."

Jenks thanked them for their help, and they invited her back at two the next afternoon. When she got outside, she felt flushed and she dialed Seth's cell phone number. He answered firmly, "Mason."

"Seth, this is Jenks."

"How did it go?"

"Can you come by Gigi's? I mean my place after work, and I'll tell you."

"I can get there by seven."

"I'll have a sandwich for you. See you then."

———

When she returned home, Jenks went to the kitchen to get a drink of water. Glancing out the rear window, she saw her neighbor, Crawford Forrest, in her backyard tending her flower beds. She was wearing a large straw hat to shade her face from the sun and capri pants. Jenks went out to the screened porch and said hello.

"Jenkins, how are you today?" she replied.

"I'm fine, Mrs. Forrest, and I hope you are."

"Yes, ma'am. My flower beds needed weeding, but I swear I'm getting too old to bend over like this."

She smiled, and Jenks couldn't help but notice what an attractive woman she was. Crawford was bound to be in her sixties, but she had very few wrinkles. When she stood up from the flower beds, her posture was straight and strong.

As Jenks walked to the picket fence that divided the properties, an angry voice called from inside the Forrest's home. "Crawford, where's my stuff?"

Crawford looked toward the home and then placed her trowel on a bench seat near her flower bed. "Jenkins, I apologize but I need to go inside. Please excuse me."

She turned and walked to her home, opening the screen door. As she entered, the door slammed with a bang.

———

That evening while Seth ate a turkey sandwich, Jenks told him about Joseph Andrews's pre-Civil War writings. She recounted the encounters with the wild hogs and the rabid raccoon, but she had a difficult time explaining what Miss Meta had told her.

"Seth, she said that when she saw me for the first time there was an aura of another presence around me."

"What does she mean by that?"

"She means there is some type of supernatural energy around me. She said she sensed my energy, but also another source. What's really odd is that she said she kept hearing the words twins, and she thought at first it was my sister Gigi reaching out to me."

"What else did she say?"

"She said that the other presence might be expressing this thought about twins." She took a sip of iced tea. "I was told to look closer."

"At what?"

"She doesn't know."

Seth took a deep breath and quietly said, "It couldn't be."

"It couldn't be what?" Jenks asked.

Seth's face became pale, and he rose from his seat and pulled her up. "Let's take a walk to Sands Beach."

"Let me get a Windbreaker," she replied.

They walked to the beach, which was situated along the Beaufort River. The abandoned Port Royal shipping terminal was illuminated in the last rays of sunlight. Its hulking shape dwarfed the rest of the houses and buildings in the community.

"It's a shame that the shipping terminal isn't used."

"There's been more than one attempt to develop the property at the port. A number of businesses in Port Royal closed down in the wake of the developmental failure and the economic downturn."

"That's a shame."

"I understand that another developer is attempting to purchase the property for development."

"Really?"

"Yes, this area will be very different if things work out for them."

When they got to the beach, Seth took Jenks's hand in his. "There's something I have to tell you."

She looked up into his chestnut-brown eyes, which were suddenly very sad. "The night we spoke on the phone about your sister's death, I told you I understood how you felt." He paused and his face darkened. "Like you, I had an identical twin, named Steel. He was my strength and my best friend—he died in Afghanistan two years ago."

Jenks was stunned by his admission and her mouth fell open. "Seth, I had no idea. I'm so sorry."

As night fell, they quietly walked back to Jenks's cottage holding hands. Once at home, she made lemonade, and they sat on her screened porch to talk. Seth opened up about his brother and some of their experiences. "Steel and I did most everything together growing up. We lived in a North Georgia community named Asbury, which had about five hundred residents. One summer, when we were about fourteen years old, my father's sister, Leona, came to visit. She had five of the worst-behaved kids I've ever known. My mother and my aunt went shopping one afternoon while they were there. My father was at work. He was a mechanic, and Steel and I were left in charge of Aunt Leona's five hellions."

"Oh, my."

"We told them several times to stay on the porch and play a board game, which is what Aunt Leona had instructed them to do. Anyway, they decided they weren't going to pay attention to what they had been told, and they were going to go down and explore the creek behind the house. Aunt Leona's oldest son, Frances, was about eleven and the leader of the group. Steel and I climbed up on top of the porch with our BB guns and every time one of them attempted to leave, we shot them in the rear. Frances was shot about a half dozen times. I was surprised that he could handle that many hits."

"My goodness."

"Well, when mom and Aunt Leona got home, her children raised cane about their punishment, and we knew we were in for it." He stopped for a moment and then said, "My father was a strong believer in discipline, and he took a belt to Steel and me that evening. I think I might still have those scars."

"I'm so sorry."

He took a sip of lemonade and looked at Jenks. "Please tell me about you and your sister. I bet you two were like angels growing up."

She smiled at him. "Well, I don't know if I'd say that. I know we took our first steps on the same day. We both twirled our hair when we got nervous. At times, she could be very secretive. And then there was this uncanny ability for each of us to sense if the other was in trouble." Cold chills enveloped her as she thought of the day of Gigi's death. She had sensed Gigi's panic as she perished.

Fear washed over her, and she took a deep breath.

"Hey now, what's wrong?"

"I was just thinking of the day that Gigi died. I knew something was wrong long before I found out about her."

"I understand," Seth said as he took her hand in his and squeezed her fingers. "Tell me about your school days."

"Well, let's see. We always did do our best in school. Gigi was my heroine, but I suppose she was everyone's leader. She had what I think you'd call charisma. We were both on the cheerleading squad in high school; she was the head cheerleader and extremely popular. I think I gained easier admittance to activities because she was so outgoing. One thing is for sure—you couldn't ask for a more loyal friend."

"It sounds like she was a wonderful person."

Jenks nodded. "I remember there was this poor girl in our class that had weight problems. There were these two girls on the cheerleading squad with us that made fun of her." She sipped her lemonade. "I could never understand their cruelty toward her because both of them were very attractive. They were both named Susan. One had dark brown hair and the other was a blonde. To this day, I've never met a more vindictive female than the blond-headed Susan. Midway through our senior year, the dark-haired Susan decided that she was not simply Susan anymore. She changed her name, becoming the illustrious 'Susannah.'"

"Whew—do I detect some jealously issues might have existed between you and those girls?"

"No, they were loathing issues—from my point of view."

"Boy, you're a little fireball . . . go on."

"Gigi found Beryl, that's the girl who had the weight issues, in the bathroom crying. She told her that she had been called hateful names by the two Susans and couldn't help her tears. My sister took those two witches to task over what they had said."

"Witches?"

"Yes. They stopped making fun of her. Unfortunately, there were others who bullied her as well."

"What happened to her?"

"Seth—she committed suicide."

"I'm sorry to hear that," he said, a deep frown passing over his countenance. He looked into her eyes. "What happened to your father?"

"He was an engineer with the North Carolina Highway Department. An overpass was under construction on I-85 near Greensboro and water pipes were being installed along the corridor. The pipes were stacked on a flatbed truck at the site. While a crane was unloading the pipes, one of them rolled forward on the flatbed. As it came off, my father was able to push his assistant out of the way but could not save himself. A five-hundred-pound pipe came down onto his chest. He died instantly."

"I'm sorry."

"I am too. My mother never got over what happened to him, but a few years ago a gentleman moved in next to her. He's a widower, and they became close friends. Gregg Mikell—you met him the day he drove us from Raleigh to Beaufort."

"Yes. I'm glad your mother has someone."

"What about your folks?"

"They split up while Steel and I were at home. As soon as we turned eighteen, we joined the Marines." He paused for a moment. "Jenks, I have to be at work tomorrow at seven. I'll say good night now. Please call me tomorrow after you read more from the journals at Miss Meta's."

She walked with him to the front door, and he took her in his arms. He gently leaned her backwards and kissed her on the mouth. "You smell good—like jasmine and honey," he whispered. She felt her entire existence become fiery hot, and then he released her.

Attempting to regain her composure, she opened the front door and took a deep breath of the cool night air.

As he stepped outside, he said, "Don't forget to call me."

"I won't," she said as she watched him go down the walkway to his car.

⟶

At two o'clock the next afternoon, Jenks rang the bell in the hallway of Meta's home. Ida Mae called out from the back of the house. "Miss Jenkins, dat you?"

"Yes ma'am."

"I be right dere," she declared.

When Ida Mae entered the foyer, she was wearing a floral print dress with pink roses and little white flowers.

"Miss Ida Mae—you look very pretty this afternoon."

She smiled broadly and responded, "Thank you, Jenkins. Meta and I are attending a program at church dis evening." She looked at herself in the mirror of the hall tree and pushed her hair behind her ear. "Come to de kitchen. I have de books set out for you."

Once again the books were on the table along with a plate of cookies and a glass of milk. Ida Mae excused herself into the room where she and Meta met with clients, and left Jenks in the room alone.

The next journal was from 1861, and as with the book from 1860, some of its entries were illegible. She turned the pages until she came to a recording from early April.

> My cousin, Scipio, and me went with Mr. Jacobs to the wharf at Beaufort to pick up Miss Andrews's nephew, Simon, who arrive from Charleston. A freedman name Jessup one of the crew on the ship. He real talkative and says that the Confederates have fired on Fort Sumter and there's sure to be war now. I want to be free but I gets scared with this kind of talk. Scipio and me collect Mister Simon's luggage as quick as we can and start back for Andrews Hall.

During the late summer of 1861 was an entry that began:

18 August 1861

Master Preston has gone with his father to fight in Virginia. Why would they go so far away? He writes to his mother and she read a letter to us. It is not so much about fighting. I think he don't want to scare his mother. The letter about his family and how much he miss everyone. I pray for him every day.

In November of 1861, there was a chilling entry that marked the beginning of fighting in Beaufort.

We hear the sound of big guns all morning at Andrews Hall. Then we learn what the shooting bout. The Yankee navy done destroyed Fort Walker and Fort Beau-gard. Scipio and me went to the river. Ships fill up Port Royal Sound as far as eye can see. The white folks flee Beaufort- not a white man to be found. Missus Andrews pack a trunk and she leave with Miss Adelaide. She tell us to stay on the plantation and she be back when she able. She say she going to her sister in Columbia.

An entry dated two days later read:

For the first time in my life I am free. Scipio and me walk to Beaufort and we see both soldiers and workers in the big houses. What they can't carry off they destroy. We see a piano in the front yard of one house it hacked to pieces. A soldier see us and call out come here nigger. We run for the swamp. When we get back to Andrews Hall the workers is inside Miss Andrews' house. They is stealing and ripping things to pieces. I tell them to stop and they laugh at me–tells me they taking they due.

Ida Mae stuck her head in the door and asked, "Where are you in de journals?"

"I'm to the part where the Federal Navy takes control of Beaufort. Ida Mae, how was your ancestor able to hide these journals and keep them secret?"

"He only work on dem by firelight and he have a hiding place behind some hearth stones. Mus' have been a good hidin' spot 'cause no one find dem."

She smiled as she left the room, closing the door behind her.

Jenks opened the next book, and it began in 1862.

> Scipio has been down to the wharf at Port Royal and says that some of the Federal soldiers are looking for valets to assist them. We both small for our age and he say that we should go down and talk to them. One of them was nice to him. He an officer from New York. The next day we go down to Port Royal and Scipio point out this man and we go talk to him. He say that he and another officer want valets, but he can only pay a little. I get real excited at the thought of wages. The food is running out at Andrews Hall and I think I like this idea of working for pay.

She thumbed through the journal until she came to another legible entry.

> Several days a week ships sail from Port Royal carrying cargo to the north. Scipio and me listen to some soldiers talking on the wharf and we hear one say. "I ship a sterling tea set and whole set of silver to my wife in Massatusets." Then he start laughing. After this when I am not working for Leutenant Jeffrey I watch some of the items being put on ships bound for the north. I see one ship being loaded and I swear I see a fine rug that was in Missus Andrews parlor. I think she call it orental. I consider stealing a sin, but they just beat me or worse if I say sumthing.

In the spring there was an emotional entry about the Andrews family.

> Scipio and I go to Andrews Hall one afternoon after work is finish for the soldiers. The big house is wide open and workers

are living in the rooms. I look in the front door and there must
be twenty folk inside two rooms. I don't even know some of
them. Then I see James. He had gone with Missus Andrews
when she went to Columbia. I ask him what he doing back
here and he say that news is everywhere bout the Federals
being in Beaufort and he want freedom. He say he run away
from Missus Andrews and he say most of the people here are
run aways. Then he takes my hands in his. I see scars from
all the work he has done in the fields and I feels his coarse
skin.

He say Joseph I got something to tell you and it goin make
you real sad. He tell me that Master Preston and his father
was killed in Virginia. I can hardly keep tears back but I thank
him for telling me and then I go to my cabin to cry. There is
a woman with two small children where my famly live and I
tell her this is my home but we can share. She suckle the baby
and go and sit in one corner. I fight the tears I feel for Master
Preston.

Jenks rose from her chair and stretched her muscles. The clock on the
kitchen wall read three forty-five, and she knew that Ida Mae and Meta would
be finishing their work soon. She walked to the kitchen sink and placed the
empty plate and milk glass in the sink. Sitting back down at the table, she
looked through the entries until she came to a recording in August.

There been a gale blowing for the last day and I hear the
soldiers say the winds been steady around twenty knots and
out of the south. The storm come from the tropics. Scipio
and me sleep on the wharf underneath a tarp. We in between
pallets of cargo bound for the north and we stay real dry.
Around mid afternoon we hear two soldiers talking. They
don't know we there so they at ease. I hear one of them say
that Colonel Hubbard shipping some real nice jewelry to his

wife in Boston. The other one says it come from one of the wealthiest plantations in the area on the May River.

After a while they stop and we start to go outside, but we hear a soldier address Colonel Hubbard and he asking them about the readiness of a ship that suppose to be departing the wharf by three. I hear him get mad because a number of soldiers is drunk and asleep on the wharf. He tell everyone of them they should get ready for court martial if they still there in five minutes. We peep from behind the tarp and Colonel Hubbard grab one man by the uniform and pull him up from dock. He slap him and tell him to report to duty. We watch the man stumble from the pier toward a group of soldiers. We close the tarp and move to the back behind the cargo.

After a few minutes I hear Colonel Hubbard tell another soldier to put "it" on board. I don't know what "it" is, but I hear one of the soldiers get excited and tell Colonel Hubbard that Leutenant Jeffrey and General Sherman is on they way to the wharf. The tarp fly open and a soldier place a trunk inside the area where we is hiding. We can hear the soldiers talking and Scipio whisper that he want to see what inside that trunk. I bout scared to death, but Scipio put his hand over my mouth and he say "quiet" real soft like.

There is no lock on the trunk and he open it up. We look inside. There is treasure inside that is probably finer than what the wise men brought Jesus when he stay at the manger. Scipio pick up some of the items and we look close at them. There is silver, gold coins, and jewelry that I never saw the like of. One necklace made of gold with a cross and red stones on it. Scipio say, "This bout the most beautiful thing I ever see."

"This is it," Jenks gasped.

We being real quiet but I think I is breathing so hard that those soldiers can hear me. I knows if they catch us they gonna kill us. He hands me the gold cross and I don't want to touch it cause I scared it gonna brand me. I tell him to put it back in the trunk and close it before those soldiers return. He does and I breathe deeply.

After a few minutes, I hear General Sherman and Leutenant Jeffrey take leave of Colonel Hubbard. General Sherman ask, "When this ship gonna get underway?"

Colonel Hubbard say as long as the rain subsides and winds stay below twenty knots the ship will sail at three. As soon as they gone, a soldier reaches into where we hiding and takes the trunk out. There is a sliver of an opening in the tarp. I see Colonel Hubbard lift that trunk lid. He look inside and feel those pieces like he fondling a . . . My mama would whip me if she know what I was thinking. He turns toward us and I think we had it, but then I see he just kind of staring into space. There is a look of want in his eyes like I never see on a man afore. It kind of scary.

He put a lock on the trunk and then the soldiers load it taking it down to the hold. We scared to move, but some time later we hear a soldier say that ship is getting ready to sail. There is commotion on the dock and we think we can slip out the back and mix in with the soldiers. Just as we about to leave, Scipio part the tarp and we can see down at the other end of the wharf. There is one soldier standing down there and he kind of hiding. We can see him, but from where he is, I don't think the soldiers launching the ship can see him. The ship gets underway toward Port Royal Sound and we see that soldier throw some lit smoking material into the boat as it go by. As he leave his hiding place he have a look of satisfaction kinda like the cat that ate the canary. He the drunk soldier that

Colonel Hubbard slap. After he gone, we lift the tarp and go out between cargo pallets.

Just before dark we sit near Leutenat Jeffrey in his tent. He writing a letter to his wife. All of a sudden there a great commotion at the wharf. A sloop done arrived and say they witness a ship burn near St. Helena Sound. The sails on fire and by the time they get to it the ship done sank and they can't find no survivors. Colonel Hubbard look like he about to have heart failure. His face is gray and he want to know the name of the ship. One of the crew hand him a piece of the hull that has part of the name of the ship on it—it say *Defi*—the ship that sailed with Colonel Hubbards loot was the *Defiance*. Scipio and I make a pact not to tell anyone about this. If we say anything we make an enemy out of someone. Why would they believe us anyway? They thinks of us as niggers.

Jenks took out her notepad from her purse and wrote down the following notes:

"The winds were steady at 20 knots out of the south. The ship left the dock at 3 p.m. The month is August, but does not mention the date. A sloop arrives and brings news of a ship that burned near St. Helena Sound. Does not reference the tides—only sails mentioned as the type of propulsion—all souls lost. The name of the ship—*Defiance*."

She closed the journal and breathed deeply. As she started to rise from the table, Ida Mae and Meta came into the kitchen from the back room. "How did you do today, Jenkins?"

"I think I found what I was looking for."

"Good—good, I's glad to hear it," Meta said.

"I have enjoyed reading your ancestor's journals." Jenks paused as she glanced at the books. "Why don't you donate a copy of the writings to the Beaufort Library?"

"It was very unusual for a slave to read and write. We plan to donate de original journals to de Beaufort County Preservation Society when we pass. Dese writings of our ancestor are part of us. We had plenty of scholars come here to read de journals. We never turn anyone down."

"The General Sherman in the journal?"

"Dat is General Thomas Sherman who in charge of de Federal Navy when dey invade Beaufort—not de General Sherman who like to burn everything down."

"I see. What happened to Joseph and Scipio?"

"The Federals stay in Beaufort for the duration of the War. Joseph and Scipio, dey cousins—dey work around de wharves and earn wages from de officers. De white property owners can't come to pay dere taxes 'cause de enemy hold de town. I's not saying dat was fair . . . I's just saying dat what happen. So many of dem default, and some of de land and houses 'round Beaufort go up for sale due to unpaid taxes. Joseph and Scipio go in together and buy a tract on de May River near Bluffton. Dey know how to farm and dey plant cotton and raise dere families. Over de years, de property pass down through generations by what is called a tenancy in common. Dey all owns a part of de land, but it ain't divided by no survey or deed. It what came to be known as heirs' property."

"Do you still own the land?"

Meta smiled slightly and then said, "No, Miss Jenkins—one of de problems with heirs' property was dat one owner could call for sale of de land to get dere share and dere ain't anyting de other owners could do 'bout it. Developers could get dere hands on property real easy dat way. Dey bribe one person to force de sale of de land and de highest bidder comes in and buys it."

"I'm so sorry. I think that's terrible."

"Yes um. Back in the 1960s, we was still living on dat property. Dere was de most beautiful view of de May River you ever see in your life. Dey tells me water frontage real important to developers and dis property had plenty of it. One of my daddy's cousins, he my cousin too—call for de sale of de entire tract—he say he want his share. No amount of pleading stop him from going through with dis. De sale of de land goes to a Mr. Thurston Harrington III from Princeton, New Jersey."

"Oh, no," Jenks said.

"De family was devastated. About two weeks later, de boy who force de sale of our family land show up in de most beautiful Cadillac I ever see in my life. It about de color of sapphires. All weekend, he go 'round de town showing off and bragging."

"That's terrible."

"We all know dat boy ain't made enough on his proceeds from de sale of de land to buy dat Cadillac. Monday morning, he ain't show up for work at de saw mill. His mama real worried. Days go by, but he never show up." Meta took a breath and then she smiled. "About a year later, some fishermen find dat Cadillac out by Nairne Point. It in several feet of water and if one of de fisherman ain't caught de hood ornament of dat automobile with a fish hook it might still be underwater." She looked at Jenks and laughed ever so slightly. "Dat boy's body was never found. I like to tink he had a visit with a shark."

"Whew! I'm sorry about your family land!"

"You young and sweet. Dis kind of wickedness go on all de time."

"What happened with the land?"

"Dat New Jersey gentleman develop our property and name it some kind of plantation. Plantation life ended about one hundred and fifty years ago, but some white folks still flocking to de plantations. With de proceeds from de sale of de land and his savings, our father bought dis cottage and the de land around it—bout ten acres. He never got over what happened to our family property." She paused for a moment as she folded a tea cloth. "You know I thought about dis many times. I learn to empat'ize with de white folks dat lost dere lands at tax sales during de Civil War."

Meta looked keenly into Jenks's eyes and said, "Dat boy sold out his own people—he got what he deserve."

"Oh, my," Jenks said, stunned.

Before she left, the sisters told her to come back anytime she wanted to read the journals. "We want you to take some more cookies home with you," Ida Mae said as she filled a plastic bag.

"Thank you for your help," Jenks said.

As she started to leave, Meta looked at her closely and said, "You be real careful—especially around water."

Jenks began the return trip to Beaufort and she thought about Rory Masters. Turning onto Martin Luther King, Jr. Drive she passed large tomato farms on the route to Land's End. She parked her car in front of Rory's home, and walked up the ramp to his door. When she knocked on his door, she heard him call out, "I'll be right there."

She waited until the door opened, and he sat in his wheelchair before her. "What a nice surprise, Miss Ellington."

"Please call me Jenks."

"All right, Jenks it is."

"Rory, I was out this way doing some research, and I wanted to bring you some cookies. I didn't make them. The ladies I was visiting with did."

She held the bag up, and he smiled. "That was very thoughtful of you. Can I fix you something to drink?"

"Thank you, but I just finished having refreshments."

"I'm going to have a beer. I hope you don't mind."

"No, of course not."

As he went to the refrigerator, Jenks noticed several photographs on the wall. She moved closer for inspection. Most of the photos were of Rory with other soldiers. In two of them, she noticed Rory beside an attractive woman in a military uniform.

"You had a woman in your unit?" Jenks inquired.

"Yes, Sarah Humphries, along with several other women. She was a special liaison with Afghan villagers."

"She's very attractive."

Rory fell silent and his facial expression looked sad. After a moment he said, "You should have heard her voice. She had such a smooth, mellow voice. The village children used to crowd around her to listen to her sing."

He sat quietly for a few moments before maneuvering his wheelchair onto the deck. "Seth said you were from Raleigh. I've been there a few times. It's a nice town," Rory said.

"Where are you from?"

"California. I grew up in a small community north of San Francisco."

"Do you miss living there?"

"I miss the coldness of the Pacific Ocean and riding the surf. My friends and I were regular beach bums growing up."

"Do you still have family there?"

"Just my mother."

"Well, I probably should go. I just wanted to bring you the cookies. They're really good."

"Thank you, Jenks. I'm going to have you and Seth over for dinner soon." Rory lifted a pocket watch that was attached to his belt by a gold chain. He looked at the time.

"That's a beautiful watch," Jenks observed.

"It was a wedding gift to a male ancestor of mine from his bride to be."

Jenks stepped closer observing the beautiful engravings on the watch.

"See . . . written on the back, 'Forever, Jane.'" A look of sadness crossed his face, and he quietly said, "Only nothing lasts forever."

Jenks wasn't sure what she should say, and she stood quietly waiting for him to continue. He appeared to be in deep thought, but after a few moments, his gaze returned to her and he said, "Thank you again for stopping by. I look forward to the three of us getting together."

"I'll look forward to it as well."

She started down the ramp, and he waved good-bye before entering his house.

When she reached her car, she dialed Seth's cell phone. He answered briskly, "Detective Mason."

"This is Jenks. I was wondering if you could go with me to Charleston in the morning. I would like to see the portrait of a young lady in the Gibbes Museum."

"I'm working with Detective Campbell tomorrow evening, so the morning will be fine. Did you read anything helpful today?"

"Yes I did. I'll tell you on the drive to Charleston."

CHAPTER 3

Miss Iris Elliott

S eth drove Jenks's Jeep to Charleston the following morning. They left the windows down and cool spring air blew through the vehicle. The route of the Savannah Highway between Beaufort and Charleston was beautiful with the lushness of new greenery on the trees and the smell of rich perennial flowers bursting into bloom.

Jenks told him what she had read the day before and showed him the notes she had taken from Joseph Andrews's journals. "Miss Iris Elliott should be wearing a necklace with a gold cross in a portrait that hangs in the Gibbes Museum."

He listened to her recount the history in the journals, and when she finished he said, "Even if we used the information available to us from Joseph Andrews's writings, locating any remnants of that ship would be virtually impossible."

"I want to see what the cross looks like."

"Yes, ma'am," he said with a smile.

"When I left Meta and Ida Mae's home yesterday, I went by Rory's house and took him some cookies that the sisters had made. I hate to see him sitting down at Land's End all by himself."

"I do too. Why don't you and I take him out to dinner?"

"He mentioned having us over."

"Either way, I think he needs to get out more. Taking him the cookies was very thoughtful."

⸻

When the Gibbes Museum opened at ten a.m., Seth and Jenks were the first to be admitted. Jenks spoke with a guide and asked for the location of the portrait of Iris Elliott. The guide gave her a map of the museum and an informational booklet that gave the history of many of the exhibits. When they reached the portrait gallery on the second floor, the painting of Miss Iris Elliott was mounted in the center of one wall that displayed South Carolina residents from the American Civil War period.

"There she is," Jenks declared as they approached the portrait.

The young woman in the portrait was wearing a champagne-colored dress that complemented her golden-blonde hair and rosy cheeks. The dress had a plunging neckline, and around Iris's swan neck was an ample-sized gold cross adorned with red stones. Jenks's mouth dropped open. The red-stoned cross was identical to the one that had appeared in her dreams.

A historical description of the painting was in the brochure.

> Portrait of Miss Iris Elliott, 1860. Daniel Huntington, Artist 1816–1909. Huntington is well known for his landscape works done in the Hudson River School Style. He painted this portrait of South Carolinian, Iris Elliott, at his New York studio after returning from a nine-year stay in England. The necklace in the portrait was purchased by Elliott's father while on a tour of Europe in the late 1850s and was from the collection of Catherine the Great. Designed by artist Aleksi Gregori Kartashkin, whose works were a favorite of the Empress. The ruby-studded and 18-carat gold necklace vanished during the American Civil War.

Jenks paused after she finished the description. "Seth—I swear to you, that necklace is the same as the one that I have envisioned in my dreams."

"That's amazing." A frown crossed his brow as he studied the painting.

"I know I've never seen this painting before." Cold shivers descended upon her as she looked at the cross.

"Have you ever had psychic dreams before now?"

"No. I feel like Gigi is reaching out to me."

"Does that scare you?"

"I am concerned about it—what is she trying to tell me?"

They both gazed quietly at the portrait until Jenks broke the silence. "It says in this booklet that a postcard of the Elliott portrait is available in the gift shop." On their way out of the museum, Jenks purchased the postcard, and they exited onto Meeting Street.

"I'd like to show you where I'll be attending law school this fall. Do you mind a walk?"

"Not at all. Lead the way!"

Seth took her hand once they reached King Street. They lingered in front of some of the stores and went inside several antique shops.

"I like being with you," she told him after leaving a store.

He smiled and responded, "I promise, it's mutual."

When they reached the reception center for the Charleston Law School, Seth opened the glass door for Jenks. As soon as the receptionist saw Seth enter the building, she rose from her seat and came forward to greet him. With a bright smile, she said, "Detective Mason, how nice to see you. It won't be long before classes start."

"Yes, ma'am, I'm looking forward to it. Ms. Berry, this is my friend Jenks Ellington."

The two women exchanged greetings, and Jenks noticed how fond the receptionist seemed to be of Seth. When they left the office, they walked to the location where the classes were held on Meeting Street.

"I'm starting to get hungry. Seth, I'd like to buy you lunch. Where would you like to go?"

"For the best crab cakes in Charleston—Fleet Landing."

"Is that a naval establishment?"

"Come on—I'll show you. The Fleet Landing restaurant is located at the Charleston Harbor in a building that formerly functioned as a US Navy debarkation point for sailors."

As they walked toward the waterfront, Jenks noticed the cranes used for loading cargo onto container ships, towering above the Columbus Street Terminal. They passed a large brick warehouse that housed a shipping firm. Jenks read the name, "Heath Brothers Shipping—wow. They have quite an operation."

"Yes, I've read in Forbes Magazine they are consistently one of the most successful American companies."

When they reached the restaurant, they were seated on the outside deck of the concrete building, which gave them an exceptional view of the harbor.

Seth looked at her closely and asked, "What is it that you plan to do with this information about the cross and sunken treasure?"

"I want to know if Gigi located the *Defiance*. What if Frank wanted everything for himself, and he killed her for what she found?"

"At this time, there is no evidence to prove that Frank had a hand in your sister's death. Listen to me, Jenks—Frank Hiller is a highly trained military expert. Please be careful about sharing your thoughts on this."

"Yes, I'll be careful."

After they finished a lunch of crab cakes and collard greens, the pair walked through Waterfront Park. A child was running in and out of the massive play fountain, and they stopped to look at sailboats racing in the harbor.

"I'm going to start interviewing real estate agents to sell Gigi's home. I know that selling a house is difficult now, so we'll see what happens."

"I hope it takes a long time to sell. I like having you around," Seth said as he put his arm around her.

She was feeling the same way, but she had a teaching job to go to in August, and Seth would be starting law school. There was no doubt she was enjoying his company. His easygoing nature calmed her, and his touch sent deep feelings of warmth throughout her body. She had never felt these sensations before—it was like her insides might melt.

On the drive back to Beaufort on the Savannah Highway, Seth told her he'd like to show her one of his favorite places. "Let's go see the ruins of Sheldon Church."

She nodded, and they branched off the highway, turning onto a rural road to Yemassee marked Sheldon Church Road. The temperature even dropped a few degrees as they entered a thickly vegetated area surrounding the ruins of a church. They parked the Jeep and entered the churchyard. It was enclosed by an ancient wrought-iron fence bent with age. Multitudes of live oak trees shaded the grounds and encircled the remains of the ancient structure. Topped with resurrection ferns, four columns marked the entranceway to the sanctuary, whose brick wall remnants still enclosed the former house of worship.

"It's eerily beautiful, don't you think?" Jenks asked.

"Yes, I visit from time to time."

Jenks stepped to the front of the ruin and read a plaque that was mounted on the front wall. "Church of Prince William's Parish . . . known as Sheldon. Built between 1745 and 1755 . . . burned by the British Army 1779. Rebuilt 1826 . . . burned by the Federal Army 1865." They walked through the interior of the church and went into the rear churchyard. The Southern Cross of Honor medals graced the grave of one Confederate soldier, and a new Confederate battle flag was placed beside the marker. "Died in battle—1864," Jenks read out loud.

"I'm glad to see that fallen soldiers are still honored," Seth said.

"Why do you like to come here?" Jenks inquired.

"This churchyard has known violence, but I have a sense of peace when I visit these grounds."

As they walked around the churchyard, a green manual well pump caught Jenks's eye. "Let's see if the pump still operates."

She led Seth to the well, and in a brick oval pool at the base of the pump was clear water. Jenks bent down and put her fingers in the water, and then Seth began to pump the handle. Within a few strokes, water began to flow from the pump, and Jenks bent over the stream and drank. "Delicious," she said.

After she finished drinking, she operated the pump handle for him, and he drank from the clear water.

"Tastes pure," he said when he finished drinking. "Jenks—I have to be at work in about an hour. I'm going to drive you home now."

They drove back to Port Royal, and Jenks walked with Seth to his police car. She noticed that his suit was hanging up in the back of his vehicle. "Would you like to come inside and change?" she asked.

"No, I'll change at the station."

He walked her to the front door and hugged her. That familiar jolt of energy coursed through her limbs. As he embraced her, she put her head against his chest. "I like your hugs," she quietly said.

He leaned her back and kissed her on the forehead.

"No kiss on the lips?"

"Someone might be watching," he laughed and hugged her once more.

"So what," she laughed softly.

"That's a wonderful sound."

"What sound?"

"Your laughter. I'll call you tomorrow," he said as he walked down the path to his car.

"Seth—Thank you for today."

He smiled and waved as he sat down in his car. She watched him pull away from Gigi's home and then she opened the door to the house and went inside. Closing the door behind her, she leaned her back against it and took a deep breath. She had thoroughly enjoyed her day.

Just as she started to walk into the living room, there was a knock at the door and Jenks immediately opened it, thinking Seth had returned. Standing in the doorway was the powerful frame of Frank Hiller.

He smiled at her, and in his hand was a large shopping bag.

"Hello, Jenks. I know that you were very upset with me at Gigi's funeral, but I hope you no longer are. I have some of Gigi's things, and I wanted to bring them to you."

She felt nervous and stammered for a few seconds. "Frank—Thank you for stopping by." She stepped out onto the front porch, closing the door behind her. Fear surged through her body.

"I've been worried about what you said to me at Gigi's funeral. I don't think that I've conveyed to you how badly I feel about what happened."

"Please have a seat." She motioned for him to sit down on one of Gigi's front porch rocking chairs. Jenks sat down opposite him.

"I saw a For Sale sign on your workout center."

"Yes. I've decided to move to San Diego. There are several old friends of mine who live there. I'm planning to open another workout facility. Plus, it's not nearly as humid in San Diego as it is here."

He turned his attention to the brown shopping bag and said, "I'm sorry— This is why I came over. These clothing items belonged to Gigi. They were at my house. I apologize for not getting them to you sooner."

"Thank you."

"I was wondering if you'd like to go out to eat dinner one evening. I know just the place—Wrens."

She didn't have to think long about a response. "I'm not up to it, but thank you for asking."

He smiled slightly and then handed her the bag.

"I appreciate you bringing this over."

"You're welcome . . . I hope you don't think badly of me. I cared very deeply for your sister." He gazed into her eyes. "Well—I should be leaving. If you change your mind, please let me know."

Jenks stood up when he did, and Frank put his arms around her, hugging her in his powerful embrace. Jenks tried not to let her head rest against his chest. When he released her, he walked down the front path. She watched him go down the lane to where his car was parked at the street. Opening the front door, she stepped back inside. As she shut the door, Jenks felt cold chills run down her spine. She rubbed her hands together and realized her palms were sweating.

CHAPTER 4

Death on the River

*J*enks woke early the next morning and after putting on a bathrobe, she walked to the newspaper box at the street. David Bernstein was outside working in his flower beds and he called out to her.

"Jenkins, I hope you're well this morning."

"Yes, David, and you and Leah?"

"Real good," he responded. "If you don't do this early, it can be too hot to work in the yard in the afternoon," he said as he pointed his trowel toward his plant beds.

"Have a good day," she said as she walked inside.

On the front page of the *Beaufort Gazette* was a headline, "Late Evening Boat Collision Leaves Two Dead."

Jenks took the newspaper into the house and sat down at the kitchen table to read and drink a cup of coffee. As she read about the boat collision, she felt sick. One of the boats had come across the top of another watercraft killing a young woman, Elizabeth Jones, age 28, and her fiancé, Samuel Worthington, age 29. The article stated both victims were in residency at the Medical University of South Carolina. The collision had occurred around ten p.m. on the Beaufort River, and the couple who perished were sitting at the rear of the boat. The article stated that they were with another couple who were at the boat's controls and were spared from the impact of the other watercraft. The operator of the powerboat that had collided with them had kept going after the incident. He had not bothered to come back and check on the passengers on the stricken boat.

Feeling outraged, she said, almost swearing, "I can't believe they didn't bother to come back."

She shook her head and took another sip of coffee before the phone rang. She answered and Seth asked, "How are you this morning?"

"I'm all right, but I am upset by a report in the newspaper. I read about the boat collision on the Beaufort River last night."

"Yes, it's terrible. The son of a—the operator of the boat that went over the rear portion of the other watercraft just kept on going."

"That's horrible," she responded.

"Why don't you and I pick up Rory this afternoon and go to the Shrimp Shack for dinner? I spoke to him a few minutes ago, and he said he'd like to do that."

"What time should I be ready?"

"Four-thirty—five o'clock? I'm really tired. I was up all night working the boat collision with Detective Campbell."

"Get some rest. I look forward to seeing you this afternoon."

After she hung up the phone, she stepped out onto the screened porch. Mr. Bernstein had moved into his backyard and was trimming bushes.

From the home of the Forrests, she heard her neighbor Marvin Forrest yell out, "Crawford! Where is it?"

Mr. Bernstein looked toward the home and then shook his head. He went back to trimming the bush.

Jenks remembered that Gigi had said that the Forrests were somewhat reclusive and she did not see them too often. The Bernsteins had told Gigi that Mr. Forrest had some drinking issues and rarely came outside the house. However, Jenks found Mrs. Forrest to be friendly and wondered how she held up so well living with an alcoholic.

A crash of breaking glass followed and a bottle was hurled into the backyard. Startled, Jenks grabbed the back of a chair, and Mr. Bernstein dropped his trimmers to the ground. "Do you mind if I cross your yard? I'm going to check on the Forrests."

"No, I don't mind at all," Jenks choked out.

He quickly crossed her lawn and knocked at the rear door of the Forrest house.

The door opened, and Mr. Bernstein went inside.

Jenks took a deep breath. The fragrance of fresh perennials was heavy in the air.

At eleven o'clock the first real estate agent with whom she had an appointment, Glenn Moore, rang the doorbell. She invited him inside, and the first words from his mouth were, "I'm sorry about your sister. You explained about her passing, but I read about her drowning in the *Gazette*. Terrible tragedy."

Jenks felt tears begin to well in her eyes, but she quickly wiped them away. "Please have a seat at the dining table," she said as she motioned for him to sit down.

He took the tax records for Gigi's home out of a briefcase and explained that if the house were to sell there might be a loss on the home. "I'm afraid your sister bought the house while prices were rising, and there has been a sharp downturn in property values." He asked her to show him around the house, and she took him from room to room and then to the outside.

"Your sister certainly took good care of the home."

Once they went back inside, he went over a marketing plan that relied on his company's website and magazine to do the advertising. "Do you know what your sister owed on the home?"

"My sister had paid off the mortgage," she responded. Jenks opened a folder and handed him the paid tax receipt from the previous year. He looked at the statement and then brought up a price. Reaching inside his briefcase he removed documents and placed them in front of her. "This is the exclusive right-to-sell contract. Please sign and fill out the information on the bottom of the page."

She took a deep breath and said, "Mr. Moore, I did mention to you that I would be interviewing several people. I'm not prepared to sign a contract at this time."

"My company has led the Beaufort area in home sales for the past five years. You're not going to find a more capable team than mine."

Jenks took a deep breath. "Thank you for your time, Mr. Moore, but I'll let you know something after I talk to the other real estate agents."

He gathered his paperwork and then handed her his business card as he went to the front door.

"I appreciate your coming by," she said as she closed the door behind him. *Whew, a little too pushy.* At one in the afternoon, the second real estate agent arrived. She was wearing khaki pants and a neat pullover polo shirt. "I'm Agnes Manning," she said with a smile, while extending her right hand for a handshake.

"Come in, Ms. Manning. If you'd like, please put your things on the table."

She had a large tote bag, and she set her work materials in the chair beside the table. "I don't want to scratch your furniture." After she placed her tote bag in the chair, she said, "I'm sorry about your sister."

"Thank you, I am too."

They were quiet for a moment until Agnes said, "Why don't you show me the house, and then we'll take a look around the outside."

They walked through each room in the home and then they went around the outside. "Lovely home," she said. As they walked around the perimeter of the house, Agnes commented, "I think it would enhance the curb view if you put some fresh pine straw around the shrubbery."

"Thank you for the suggestion."

When they returned indoors, Agnes pulled out a pair of athletic shoes from her bag and a large tape measure. "Sometimes the square footage of a home on the tax records is inaccurate, so I measure the homes I list for sale." She returned outside and taped the perimeter of the dwelling. When she finished, Agnes used a calculator to compute the square footage. Upon reentering the house she said, "It appears the tax assessor did a good job on measuring this home. I was within five feet of the square footage that appears in the tax records—1,350 square feet."

"Thank you for taking the time to measure Gigi's house."

"You're welcome." After that they sat down, and Agnes showed her a marketing plan that included advertising on her own website, local magazine advertising, open houses, and newspaper ads. Her market analysis detailed the recent sale of homes in the Port Royal area. "I think it would be dishonest for me to give you any type of time frame on how long it might take to sell your sister's home. It's just a tough market right now." She paused for a moment, "You are designated the personal representative in your sister's will, aren't you?"

"Yes, ma'am, and I am authorized to sell property on her behalf. Here's a copy of the will." Jenks had started the probate process and had filed the will with the Beaufort County Probate Court. She showed Agnes where this was documented. Agnes then referred back to her market analysis and gave her a price range. "I hate to see you sell at a loss, but I'm afraid that prices have been declining."

"I prefer your honesty."

"I know you're interviewing other agents, but I'd like to assist you with the sale of the home. I'd really like to have your business."

"Agnes, thank you for coming by, and I'll call you after I reach a decision." She paused and took a deep breath before continuing. "There is one thing I need to tell you. My sister's home was broken into right after her death. It was as if someone was looking for a specific item."

Agnes looked at her intently. "That's a material fact and should be disclosed to the buyer. Is there a police report concerning the break-in?"

"Yes, there is. Only one item was taken—my sister's computer."

A frown crossed Agnes's brow. She paused for a moment, and then her expression brightened. "We'll hope for a Marine drill sergeant."

Agnes picked up her real estate materials and headed for the door. "Here's my business card, Miss Ellington. I look forward to hearing from you."

Jenks felt comfortable with her. Agnes was straightforward, thorough, and friendly—a pleasant combination.

The last real estate agent that she planned to interview would come the next day at ten, and then she would make a decision.

At four-thirty, there was a knock on Jenks's front door, and she quickly walked to it. Using the peephole, she smiled when she saw Seth at the door. When she opened it, he was wearing dark-colored khaki shorts and a white polo shirt. His chest and arm muscles protruded inside the shirt and he took her in his arms. "I missed you today."

She took a deep breath as she admired his handsome physique. "I've been thinking about you too."

"Uh-oh, that could be bad."

"No, I promise it was all good."

He kissed her several times on the face and then asked, "Are you ready to go?"

"Yes, sir, I am."

Just as they got ready to close the door, a loud rumble of thunder sounded close by. "I'm going to get a rain jacket and a few towels, just in case we need them to sit on at the Shrimp Shack." She quickly gathered the items and then returned to walk with him to his truck. He closed the door behind her and said, "After you, my dear."

By the time they reached Rory's home, the winds were picking up and the clouds had turned to a dark shade of silver gray. They ran up the ramp to his house as rain began to fall. Within a few moments, it was pouring. Rory bought out a deck of cards and said, "Bugger your neighbor, anyone?"

"What?" Jenks asked, feeling herself blush.

"It's a card game," Seth laughed. "Rory, watch your language."

"Yes, sir," he said with a smile.

They played cards until the rainstorm passed. Seth pushed Rory's wheelchair out onto his deck. Water was still standing on the wooden boards, and a light mist of rain was in the air. Rory looked up at him. "Will you drive my van?"

"Sure, I'll be glad to."

Seth helped Rory get inside the van. A platform came down on the passenger side and Seth rolled the wheelchair on top of it. When he toggled a switch, the platform came up and Rory rolled himself inside.

On the short drive to the Shrimp Shack, Rory said, "I want to pay for dinner tonight. You bought the last time. You need to be saving your money for law school."

"Why don't we just go Dutch tonight?" Jenks volunteered.

"All right," Seth responded.

Since Rory could not climb the stairs at the Shrimp Shack, Seth went to the window with Jenks to order. There were several men inside the upper screened-in area, and when they noticed Rory, they went down and shook his hand. After Seth finished ordering, he and Jenks went back down to the ground-level screened-in porch and sat with Rory. Rose, who ran the ordering window, came down with their dinners on two trays. There was a stack of cash on the side of one of the trays. She put her arm around Rory and said, "I's glad to see you. You as handsome as ever." She kissed him on the forehead and said, "One of those gentlemen that was in the restaurant paid for all your meals. He says he want to remain anonymous, but he want you to know how proud he is of you."

"Thank you, Rose," Rory said.

She then kissed Seth on the cheek and looking at Jenks she said, "Mmmm . . . you is one lucky woman!"

While they ate their meals, Rory asked, "Seth—do you have any idea who was driving the boat that killed the couple boating on the Beaufort River?"

"No, not yet—the motorboat and its driver disappeared without a trace. The sheriff's department searched the waterways by boat and helicopter today—but no clues."

When they finished dinner, Rory said, "I know there are only a couple of hours of daylight left, but why don't we go to Hunting Island? I haven't been there in a while."

"Let's go," Seth smiled.

They drove to a location in the park where the Hunting Island Lighthouse towered above the ocean. "I love it here," Rory said. "I still miss the Pacific. The water's not as cold as the northern California surf, but it's still beautiful."

"I don't know—the water is pretty cold. It's just May you know." Seth pushed Rory's wheelchair down the concrete walk that led to the beach front.

"Let's go in!" Rory exclaimed.

Jenks brought the towels from the van, and the group looked up and down the beach. On the northeast side of the lighthouse, the beach was littered with scores of dead trees. Their skeletons were a deep shade of gray, in contrast with the golden sands and the ocean's color of green. About a hundred feet away was a group of young men playing volleyball. Jenks observed that they were in excellent physical shape, and a Marine Corps flag was planted in the sand near their volleyball net. The men were there with their families and friends and Seth walked up the shore to talk with them. One young man dropped the ball to the beach, and all at once the group of men came jogging in Rory's direction.

"Sir, we understand that you'd like to take a swim," the spokesman for the group said to Rory.

"I'd love to," he responded.

Several of the volleyball players lifted Rory up to their shoulders, and they ran together into the surf. Several Marines held Rory on their shoulders as the waves crashed around them. The thunderstorm that had recently drenched the area was now several miles out to sea, and occasionally a jagged bolt of lightning would strike the ocean.

Rory laughed as they headed into the surf, and Jenks heard him say, "Quick, get me my surfboard!"

She grabbed Seth by the hand and said, "I know we're in shorts, but let's join them!"

"Watch the waves; there could be dangerous currents because of the storm out to sea."

"I'll count on you to save me," she said as she pulled Seth out into the water.

The swimming group grew larger as the family members of the Marines began to join in on the fun. Jenks wasn't sure how long they were in the water, but every time she looked at Rory, he was smiling brilliantly. He looked so happy.

Jenks put her arms around Seth and floated up to his height kissing him on the cheek. Just as she released her embrace a powerful wave knocked her underneath the water, and she began to feel a strong pull out to sea. She wasn't sure how much time passed while she was caught in the undertow. Lifting her head above water, she cried out to Seth for help. He moved quickly and gathered her tightly in his arms, carrying her to shore.

"Honey, are you all right?"

She was breathing so deeply that she could not respond immediately. After a few minutes, she caught her breath and said, "Yes, thank you for saving me."

He smiled. "You're welcome."

The currents were not affecting the group of Marines in the water with Rory, and Jenks and Seth continued to watch them from the beach.

Several young women who were grilling called to their companions that dinner was ready. They brought Rory back to shore on their shoulders and returned him to his wheelchair. Seth had placed one of the towels in the seat.

"Guys, thank you for the swim. I enjoyed it," Rory said.

Each young man shook Rory's hand.

They all washed off in the fresh water shower near the waterfront and then dried off.

"I don't want a rusty wheelchair."

"I'll dry it off for you," Seth said.

Rory took Jenks by the hand. "I noticed you got out of the water fairly quickly. Too cold for you?"

"No, I got knocked down by a strong wave, and I thought I was being pulled out to sea."

"Seth was there for you." He paused for a moment as through in reflective thought. "He's always been at my side when I needed help too."

She shuddered as she thought of Miss Meta Jane's warning to her when she finished with the journals. "Be careful around water," she had cautioned.

Jenks wrapped herself in the towel, and Seth's arm went around her.

On the way to Rory's home, Rory asked Seth to pull over to the side of Land's End Road near a large oak tree. It was almost dark, and the sounds of the night, crickets, and tree frogs were intense after the engine was shut down. On either side of the road were acres of tomato plants, and Rory lowered himself to ground level on his lift.

"Jenks—I want to tell you a story," Rory said.

He maneuvered his wheelchair under the oak tree. "Come here, Jenks."

She walked close to him.

"Do you remember the ruins of Fort Fremont that are at Land's End?"

"Yes, the fort scares me."

"Why?"

"It looks spooky, even in the daytime."

"Well, speaking of ghosts . . . While the fort was in operation, a fight broke out one night between some of the soldiers and local black residents over illegal liquor. The fight resulted in the death of one soldier named Frank Quigley. He was well known in the Beaufort area because of his involvement with a local baseball team. After he died, a mysterious light began to appear on this stretch of Land's End Road. The locals dubbed it the Land's End Light. I've personally never seen it, but I know several people who have. I'm told that if you stand near this oak tree that the light sometimes appears—kind of floating along the road. See how long the straightaway is here?"

"Yes, I do."

"Why don't we wait a little while and see if we see anything?" Rory said.

Jenks flinched when the call of an owl sounded in a nearby stand of trees. She walked slightly ahead of the two men and Rory called out, "There it is!"

"Where?" Jenks rose on her toes to look down the lane.

Rory quietly rolled his wheelchair behind her and grabbed her hand. She jumped straight up in the air.

"What a terrible trick to play on me!"

"Oh come on, Jenks, it's just for fun," Rory said.

"Yes, at my expense—you two!"

Seth put his arm around her and said, "Calm down now. He did this to me about a year ago. I didn't think it would scare you to death."

"I'm sorry. I think I'm just nervous."

Rory grabbed her hand and said, "Don't be mad at me or Seth. I've had the best time this evening."

When he said this, she smiled, letting go of her anxiety. "I've had a great time myself."

As Seth opened the car door for her, he said, "Do I detect a bit of a bad temper in you?"

"Only when I'm provoked."

When they reached Rory's house, Seth helped him inside and asked, "Is there anything I can get you, buddy?"

"A Budweiser. They're on the door of the refrigerator."

Seth handed him the beer and said, "Now, go light on these."

"Yes, sir. Thanks again."

They said good night to Rory and went outside. Seth opened the door on his truck for Jenks, and he smiled at her. "You know, you scared me tonight."

"What do you think about me? I get into an undertow, and then you two try and frighten me to death."

"Come on, Jenks—he was just teasing you." Seth grabbed her hand and squeezed it. That familiar energy passed between them, and Jenks took a deep breath before she said, "I have the strangest thing to tell you. The last day that I was at Meta Jane's home, she told me to be real careful, especially around water."

"There may be something to her psychic abilities after all."

When they reached her home, Seth walked her to the door. "I'm going to head on home now. I want to get out of these wet clothes."

"I have an appointment tomorrow with another real estate agent to look at the house. After that I'm free. When will I see you again?"

"How about tomorrow evening?"

"I'd like to make you dinner," Jenks offered.

"I can't come until around eight. Is that okay?"

"Yes." She put her arms around him and stood on her tiptoes to try to kiss him. He bent over and kissed her on the mouth, their arms tight around one another. She felt like she might melt.

"I'd better go now," he said. "See you tomorrow night."

The appointment with the third real estate agent, Sally Wilkins, was scheduled for ten a.m. Jenks polished furniture while she waited for her. Ten o'clock came and went. She called the agent's real estate office and the secretary said that she would phone the agent's cell phone and have her get in touch with Jenks. About twenty minutes later, the phone rang and it was Sally Wilkins. She explained that a problem had come up at home, and she apologized for not being able to come.

Jenks allowed her to reschedule for one in the afternoon. However, at one o'clock the same thing happened, only this time Jenks did not hear from her. At one-thirty, Jenks phoned her office and left her a voice message that their appointment would not be rescheduled.

When she hung up the phone, she looked up Agnes Manning's phone number and called her about listing the home. Agnes told her that she looked forward to working with her, and they planned to meet at ten the next morning.

Agnes's suggestion to put out pine straw around the shrubbery came to her mind. Jenks put a tarp down in the back of her Jeep and went to Hancock's Hardware. A young man, who blushed crimson while he talked to her, helped load eight bales of straw into the rear of her vehicle.

She drove back home and began to unload the pine straw. Oddly, she began to feel as if someone were watching her. Jenks glanced up and Caleb Grayson was standing not two feet away.

"I'd like to help you with that," he said with a garbled voice, but his face showed a handsome smile.

"Caleb, you startled me."

"I'm sorry, Miss Jenkins."

"Thank you, yes, that would be very helpful."

He unloaded the bales, and then asked her where she'd like the pine straw set out.

"Caleb, I'll do that later."

"Oh, no, I've got the time, and I'm happy to help."

"Well—let's start over here," Jenks said and pointed to an area of azalea bushes. Caleb untied a bale and reached into his back pocket, removing a pair of leather gloves.

"I keep these with me," he smiled.

As he began to put out the pine straw, Jenks studied his features. He was really an attractive man and his smile revealed perfect, white teeth.

"Where do you live in Port Royal?"

"On Colleton Avenue."

"Have you lived there long?"

"For ten years." He paused for a moment as a frown crossed his brow. "I used to live in The Point with my parents, but I decided I was ready for a place of my own."

Jenks accompanied Caleb around the yard as he carefully placed the pine straw around the bushes. "You're doing a great job," Jenks said.

He smiled again. "Twenty-five years ago, I would not have thought I'd be doing this kind of work, but life throws you some curves."

"What do you mean?"

"I was almost finished with my doctoral degree in Chemical Engineering Practice at MIT when I was in an accident."

Jenks recalled Seth telling her about Caleb having been seriously injured in an automobile wreck. "I'm so sorry, Caleb."

A look of sadness crossed his face. "A delivery truck had a front-tire blowout and my car was hit head on."

"Oh, my God."

"I was paralyzed for almost a year, but my parents never gave up hope. I was fortunate that they were in a position to get me the kind of medical attention I needed." He dispersed the remaining straw around the perimeter of the house. "I wasn't able to complete my studies. After the accident, I couldn't concentrate."

Jenks shook her head. "I am really sorry."

"I'm sorry too, but you just have to do the best you can." He smiled once more. "I think that's got it."

"Can I pay you for your help?"

"Oh, no, Miss Jenkins, I was glad to help you."

She thanked him again and then said good-bye. As she entered the house, she couldn't help but think how uncanny it was that Caleb had a way of appearing when physical labor was needed.

Afternoon sunlight was streaming onto the bookshelves in the living room. Jenks stood and reflected on what Caleb had shared with her and she shook her head over his plight. *The whole world is ahead of you and then with one crippling blow it's in ashes at your feet.* She thought of Gigi. Walking to the bookshelves, she took a photo album from its place. Opening the album, she looked through pages filled with pictures of her, Gigi, and their friends.

Although Gigi and Jenks were identical twins, there were differences between the two. Jenks had always thought that Gigi was more beautiful than she was. At times, she had envied Gigi's charisma, the attention that she received from boys, and her exceptional success in all her endeavors. Most of all, she envied her fearless independence.

The doorbell rang and Jenks placed the album on the coffee table. When she answered it, Crawford Forrest was waiting with a pie in her hand. "I made two apple pies, they're just out of the oven—I thought I'd like to give one to you."

"Thank you—that's very thoughtful. Come in, Mrs. Forrest."

"You are most welcome—but I can only stay a few minutes. I have to get back home."

Jenks started to take the pie from her, but Crawford said, "Dear, it's still a little warm; please hold it with the potholders." Jenks took the pie, holding it with the potholders, into the kitchen. The delicious aroma of cooked apples streamed into the air.

"Please have a seat, Mrs. Forrest. I'll be right back," Jenks said as she walked back into the kitchen. When she returned to the living room, Mrs. Forrest was looking at the open photo album. "May I?" she asked as she reached for the album.

"Yes, most of the photos are of Gigi and me."

Crawford thumbed through the pages and said, "You and your sister are beautiful. I'm so sorry about her, but I promise I do understand about loss."

Jenks nodded and said, "It's so kind of you to bring me the pie."

"Honey, I'm glad to. I didn't get to know your sister very well, but I thought she was a lovely girl."

Crawford rose from her seat and said, "It's been years since I looked at my own photo albums from my youth. If I can find them, I'd like to share them with you." She smiled and started for the door.

"Yes, ma'am, I'd like to see your photo albums."

"There have been many changes since those pictures were taken," she said as a look of sadness crossed her countenance. However, as she said good-bye her smile returned, and she said, "You let me know if I can help with anything."

"Thank you, Mrs. Forrest."

"I'd like for you to call me Crawford."

"Yes, ma'am," Jenks said with a smile.

After Mrs. Forrest left, Jenks went to the kitchen and looked through Gigi's pantry for spices to put on the roast she was going to prepare for dinner. While searching, she came across a bottle of Woodford Reserve on the top shelf behind several containers of sauce. She put spices on the roast and vegetables and placed the roasting pan in the oven to slow cook. When she finished dinner preparation, Jenks retrieved the bottle of bourbon from the shelf and pulled out the stopper. She inhaled the scent of the alcohol and then poured herself a glass. She took a couple of ice cubes from the freezer and dropped them into her drink.

Looking out the kitchen window, Jenks noticed the Forrests in their backyard. This was the first time since Gigi's death that she had seen Mr. Forrest outside. They were seated together on a teakwood bench. She had seen married couples who looked alike in the past. Side by side, the couple bore an amazing resemblance to one another.

Jenks took her bourbon with her back into the living room. She sat down on the couch and began to look through the photo album again. As she continued to sip her drink, uncontrollable tears began to fall down her face. She took another large sip from the glass, finishing the bourbon, and then put her head on a pillow on the living room couch.

Jenks was awakened by a knocking sound at the front door. She sat up on the sofa and looked at her watch. "Oh, my God—it's eight o'clock!" She quickly walked to the door, and using the peephole, saw that Seth was standing on the porch. Opening it, she invited him inside.

She kissed him on the cheek, and he inhaled her scent. "Uh-oh, somebody's been at the hard stuff." He walked her to the couch and sat her down near a lamp. "Your eyes are all swollen. You've been crying."

"I started looking at a photo album this afternoon, and I got upset. After I put dinner in the oven, I had a glass of bourbon." Suddenly she remembered her roast. "The roast—oh no!"

She sprang from the couch and almost lost her balance on the way to the kitchen. Seth stopped her. "Hold on now—you're going to burn yourself. Let me help you."

Taking two potholders, he removed the roast from the oven. Since she had left the oven on a low setting, the roast did not appear overly done.

"See, you did just fine," he told her as he cut into the meat. "I'm going to set the table and get you a plate. One thing is for sure—you need to put some food in your stomach."

"I bought a bottle of wine for dinner."

"No, ma'am, it's time for a glass of water."

After dinner, he led her into her living room and sat her down on the couch. "Lie down and put your head in my lap." She relaxed into his arms.

She looked up into his beautiful eyes. "Seth, how old are you?"

"I'm thirty-two."

"Why aren't you married? I can't believe some fortunate girl didn't swoop you up a long time ago."

"Thank you." He paused and a slight frown crossed his brow. "I was married while I was in the Marine Corps. I wasn't ready for a commitment, and it was my fault that the relationship did not last. I'd like to know the same thing about you."

"I had one relationship that I thought was love, but it turned out to be a disappointment. I got hurt. After that experience, I decided to be cautious about getting involved with anyone."

"I see," he said with a smile.

She gazed intently into his chestnut eyes and ran her fingers down the side of his cheek. "I am being careful. I am waiting for the man who is right for me." Suddenly, she got the hiccups and Seth lifted her up off the couch and placed his glass of water in her hands.

"Hold your breath and take small sips."

"Yes, sir," she murmured.

She took a deep breath and held it while she counted silently to thirty. Letting out the breath, she relaxed back into his arms.

He ran his fingers across her brow and she looked into his eyes. "Can I tell you something personal?"

"Yes, Jenks."

"I'm crazy about you."

He smiled at her words and then responded, "I'm crazy about you too."

"I want to be with you."

He stroked her hair. "Your hair is a beautiful shade of mahogany."

"Thank you—but are you changing the subject?"

He caressed her cheek. "Baby, I'm flattered that you want to be with me, but I think the alcohol could be doing the talking right now." He paused and smiled slightly. "I'm being extra careful with our relationship."

"You are?"

"Yes, ma'am. Now, there's something you must do for me in the future. When you get upset about what happened to Gigi, don't drink alcohol. It just depresses you. I know."

He paused for a moment and then said, "I saw the bottle of Woodford Reserve on the counter. Gigi had expensive taste in her bourbon."

"She had extra money from selling artifacts, and you already know about the insurance policy."

"Yes, I remember."

"When our daddy died at the construction site, there was a significant insurance payout that went to our family. Gigi's house is paid off."

He cuddled her in his arms until she fell asleep.

During the night she woke up with a terrible thirst. She was in her bed with a light quilt pulled up around her. Seth was gone. She went to the kitchen for a drink of water and the dishes and cookware had been cleaned. The remainder of the roast that wasn't eaten at dinner was in the refrigerator, along with Crawford's apple pie, which was covered in plastic wrap and minus two pieces.

She took aspirin, drank her water, and went back to bed.

CHAPTER 5

Nairne Point

*J*enks listed Gigi's home with Agnes Manning's company, Thompson and Thompson Realtors. Agnes put the lockbox on the front porch railing to keep it from hitting the wooden front door, and set out to market the property. Three days later, no one had called for an appointment to view the home. The housing market was struggling, and Jenks realized this. She'd prefer to sell the home before returning to Raleigh for the fall, but she was enjoying being with Seth. They were either together part of each day or spoke by phone.

When she asked him about her behavior the night he came to dinner, he told her, "Anything you did or any secrets you shared with me will forever be safe."

"What secrets? What did I do?"

"Oh—you performed the dance of the seven veils for me on the dining room table, with a long-stem rose between your teeth."

She hit him with a pillow. He playfully wrapped her in a wrestling hold and kissed her on the face. Uncontrollable laughter burst forth from Jenks, and Seth held her tightly, sitting her up in his arms so he could look at her.

"I like that."

"What?" she said as she continued to laugh.

"Your laughter."

As she stopped laughing, a bout of hiccups started. "You must be prone to hiccups. I'll get you a glass of water," he said as he slowly released her.

"Come right back."

"Yes, ma'am."

On Seth's next day off, he invited her to go fishing with him. He gave her the gate code at the Walker's property, and they agreed to meet at two o'clock. When she arrived, he was loading the boat. Seth was working without his shirt. Unable to break her gaze, she looked admiringly at his handsomely chiseled chest and arm muscles. When he saw her approaching, Seth slipped his polo shirt over his head and walked in her direction. "I'm glad you could come. Do you need to go inside before we go?"

"I think I'm fine."

They launched the fishing boat that Seth explained belonged to Dr. Walker. He drove the craft upriver and anchored the boat at the edge of a salt marsh. As soon as he shut the engine off, the sound of jet aircraft passed overhead. Four F-18s from the Beaufort Marine Station were practicing maneuvers, and they passed by in slow flight formation. After the jet fighters departed, the marsh was quiet again. Seth was about to cast his line when his cell phone rang. After a few minutes, Seth closed the phone and said, "That was Mose Lafitte. He says he has something to show me and wants me to meet him on the north side of Nairne Point."

"That's the place where Meta and Ida's cousin's Cadillac was found submerged. You know, the one who betrayed his family over land."

"Nairne Point has an ominous history. The man it's named after, Thomas Nairne, was tortured to death by Yemassee Indians during an uprising. They put slivers of pine under his skin and set it on fire. It took several days for him to die. The Indians felt they were being cheated by the settlers and they were. Tragically, Nairne was one of the few Indian agents who dealt honestly with the Yemassee."

"Oh, that's horrible." Jenks shuddered.

Seth pulled the boat anchor out of the pluff mud and started the engine.

Mose Lafitte was waiting for them on the north side of the point, and he signaled to them as they approached. As Seth pulled alongside Mose's boat, he said, "Mister Seth, I's got something to show you." He paused for a moment and added, "Miss Jenkins, how are you today?"

"I'm fine, Mose."

"Come dis way," Mose said as he drove his boat toward the point.

Once he was near the shore, Mose raised the motor on his boat and slowly landed on the point. He pulled the watercraft up on land and then helped Seth with Dr. Walker's boat.

"It's dis way," he said pointing to his right.

They reached an area of marsh near the point, and covered with a tarp and heavy vegetation was a motorboat. "I was puttin' out crab pots, and I kept noticing how unnatural dat area with de tarp look. See somebody done covered up de boat with willow branches dey cut. I ain't touch nothing. My wife like dose criminal investigation shows so I knows better. I did notice dat de hull of de boat is cracked. I look around de area, and I find where somebody try to bury beer cans. I show you where dey are. I knows de folks dat was killed de other night on de river was run over by another boat dat jus kep' going. I tink dis may be it."

"Mose, the father of the young lady that was killed on the boat has put up a $25,000 reward for information leading to the arrest and conviction of the individuals responsible."

Mose shook his head and frowned, "Mister Seth—I don't know nuttin' 'bout no reward. De folks dats responsible for da wreck needs to meet with justice—plain and simple."

"Yes, you're right, Mose."

"Come dis way, and I'll show you where dey try and bury da beer cans."

Within thirty minutes, two police boats arrived and began to examine the scuttled motorboat and the beer cans. Jenks sat at the controls of Dr. Walker's boat and listened to Seth and Mose answer questions. After an hour, Seth told Jenks he was sorry about the afternoon, but he needed to take her back to the Walker home so she could get her car.

When he let her off at the dock, Seth apologized again and told her he would call her later. Her palms were still sweating from seeing the boat. Blood was on the hull, and she trembled as she thought of the couple killed in the collision.

When she got home, she gathered her notes on the ship *Defiance* that sank in St. Helena Sound and took out her laptop. On the Naval History and Heritage Command website was a listing of the names of United States Naval ships. There were three ships named *Defiance*, and they were all commissioned and decommissioned after the turn of the twentieth century. Under a listing of Civil War ships was a Confederate States ship named *Defiance* that was burned by her own crew in the Mississippi Delta to prevent the ship from falling into Union hands.

Jenks continued to research the website and selected the operational archives for the Naval History and Heritage Command in Washington, DC. The department of archives page stated they had limited staffing and were unable to do extensive research for patrons. However, Jenks composed an e-mail with a lot of detail about the *Defiance* under Federal Navy command at Port Royal during 1862 and the reasons for her inquiry. She sent the e-mail and hoped for the best.

Closing her laptop, she started to go through Gigi's home and put away items. Agnes Manning had explained that while selling a home, only a few personal possessions should be displayed. She'd said several times, "Less is better."

Jenks started with Gigi's bedroom. While putting away some of Gigi's personal items into the bureau beside the bed, she discovered a prescription for birth-control pills in the top drawer. She examined the packet; Dr. Natalie Wray was the prescribing physician. Setting the prescription aside, she reached into the back of the drawer and found an index card box. Jenks opened the lid, and saw a number of receipts. There were invoices for the powerboat that Gigi had leased, diving equipment, and ongoing business with Patterson's Dive Shop. Numerous receipts were for maintenance on diving tanks and refilling them with oxygen. At the back of the box was a receipt for a Garmin GPS. She recalled Seth mentioning that the boat Gigi had leased from the Morgan River Marina had been set up for a GPS unit, but that it had been removed.

The phone began to ring and Seth was on the line.

"Jenks, I've just returned from Nairne Point. I apologize for today, and I'd like to make things up to you. I'm going in to work early tomorrow, and I should be off around five-thirty. I'd like to pick you up and have you over for dinner."

"Seth—I have something to show you."

"Bring it with you when you come."

After she hung up the phone, she examined the prescription for birth-control pills that had been prescribed for Gigi. Jenks's first and only intimate relationship with Alex Connors had ended in heartbreak, and she had vowed to be certain about her feelings before she shared her heart with anyone again.

Jenks knew she had fallen in love with Seth, and she picked up the phone and dialed the office of Dr. Natalie Wray.

Mose Lafitte had a sheepshead fish and stone crab claws to sell to Seth. He looked up from the catch he was bagging for them and said, "Miss Jenkins, how are you today?"

"I'm fine, Mose."

"Dat's good. Mr. Seth, was you able to find out who was de operator of de boat dat I found at Nairne Point?"

"The boat was registered to Gary Donald. His fingerprints and DNA were located on the boat as well as on the beer cans they attempted to bury. When I say 'they,' I'm referring to Gary Donald and another person that was also on board the boat. The FBI database confirmed another set of prints belong to Albert Scott. Both men have been in trouble with the law on several occasions, and warrants have been issued for their arrest." Seth was quiet for a moment. "The victims' DNA was found on Donald's boat and the cans. Mose, I gave your name to Captain Barrett as the person responsible for finding the concealed watercraft. I think you should accept the reward when we bring those two to justice. Without you, we might have never found it."

Mose shook his head. "Reward—dis about justice. Dat man done lost his child. I don't want his money."

Seth paid him for the fish and they watched from the pier as Mose started his engine. He waved to them as he headed toward Lemon Island.

"Mose should accept the reward," Seth said.

"Maybe he'll change his mind."

"I doubt it."

When they arrived at the Walker home, Jenks removed Gigi's card box from her tote bag and showed it to Seth.

He looked through all the receipts. "Your sister was diving a great deal. I already knew from Dave Patterson that Gigi was doing business with his shop." He paused for a moment as he studied the invoice for the Garmin GPS. "She had purchased a state-of-the-art GPS system, but what happened to it?"

"Gigi could be very secretive, though usually not with me," Jenks said, shaking her head.

He looked at her and then pushed an errant curl behind her ear.

"Well, let's get busy. I'll clean the fish and you work on the vegetables."

"Yes, sir."

"Before I go outside can I get you a glass of wine?"

"Absolutely."

After he cleaned the fish, he grilled it over a charcoal fire. When Jenks took her first bite, she said, "I think your trial-and-error method of cooking has paid off . . . this is delicious."

"Thank you."

When the meal was almost over Jenks asked, "Can I ask you something personal?"

"Yes."

"The other evening I asked you why you weren't married, and you said you had been while you were in the Marines."

"Oh, you remember that?"

"Yes, I do. What happened?"

"I think I told you that while I was growing up, my father was a strict disciplinarian."

She nodded.

"Well, that was only part of his parenting style. He could be verbally abusive and controlling. I met Hayden while I was in my second year of the Marines. She was a sweet, young girl with a caring heart. At the time, I didn't appreciate those qualities, and I didn't show her the respect she deserved. I confess, at that point in my life I didn't show any woman proper respect."

"Why do you say that?"

"I'll explain. One evening, Hayden made a special supper for me. I was tired from work and instead of showing my gratitude, I made an unnecessary remark about her dinner. She got up from the table and told me that she could not stand to live with me any longer and she was going to leave me."

"Oh, my."

"You see, the person whose behavior I detested the most was my father's, and I was acting just like him. She left me, and I don't blame her for it. We got divorced, and she wrote me a couple of years later, wished me well, and told me she was happily remarried. I hope she's still content." He took a sip of iced water and then continued. "I learned something very important from my failed marriage. Before I make a criticism, I ask myself two things—is it nice and is it necessary? If the answer is not yes to both questions, then I keep my comments to myself."

"The scar on your arm . . . you said you got it in a fight with your father?"

He looked into her eyes. "When I say my father was a strict disciplinarian, I mean that he inflicted severe corporal punishment on both my brother and me."

"Oh, no."

"My father, Ed—Ed Mason—enjoyed a daily visit with his favorite bourbon. When Steel and I were eleven, Ed drank himself into a stupor and then decided to get angry over a fishing pole that wasn't stored properly. Ed couldn't remember that he had put the pole away, and he decided that either Steel or I were to blame. He beat us both with a belt, and when I begged him to stop, he jerked my arm so hard it came out of the socket. My terrified mother lied to the doctors at the emergency room and told them I had fallen out of a tree. I'm not sure how they missed the belt marks on my legs."

Jenks cringed with his admission. "I'm so sorry."

"When I was seventeen, my father had been on a weekend drinking binge. He became angry with me over a spot I missed while mowing the grass, and he started to hit me. He broke a beer bottle and sliced my arm with it. By then, I was bigger and stronger than him, and I fought back. In fact, if Steel had not pulled me off of him, I'm sure I would have killed him. I was beating his head on the concrete floor of the carport when Steel stopped me."

"Oh, my—please go on."

"As soon as we turned eighteen, we both joined the Marines and left home. My mother—Eleanor—I don't think she could stand to be with him anymore, and she moved to Atlanta to be with her sister. My mother was just fifteen when she gave birth to Steel and me. I think she wanted a new life. She was thirty-four when she got remarried and then had children with her new husband. I think she finally found happiness."

"Didn't she write to you?"

"A few times . . . Steel and I wrote to her often, but usually our letters weren't answered. I think she wanted to push her bad recollections aside, and Steel and I were part of those memories. When I finished college, I invited my mother and father to come to my graduation. I didn't hear back from either of them. Steel was stationed in San Diego, and he came all the way to South Carolina to see me graduate—God, I miss him."

"I know you do. I have the same feelings about Gigi."

They both looked at one another for a moment, but Jenks's curiosity was piqued. "You were going to explain why you didn't show proper respect to women while you were married."

He took her hand in his and gazed into her eyes. "I did some psychological research on my own that caused me to do some soul searching. My mother was intimidated by my father, but she didn't protect Steel and me from *him*." He paused for a moment. "It's true; there were no women's shelters in the Asbury area." A deep frown crossed his brow. "I've tried hard to overcome my personal issues—and my resentment."

"I'm so sorry," Jenks said as she studied his face.

Seth stood up from the table. "Enough depressing talk. Will you please join me in the living room?"

He took her hand and led her into the living room. They stopped in front of the grand piano.

"Steinway. What a beautiful instrument," Jenks remarked.

He sat down on the piano bench and lifted the fallboard. He smiled at her and then began to play a Burt Bacharach song, "This Guy's in Love With You." Jenks sang along to his music and thought, *does he love me?*

When he finished, she clapped. "I didn't know you could play the piano."

"I've been taking lessons for two years. I find playing the piano to be therapeutic."

"I can believe that."

"Do you play?" Seth asked.

"'Twinkle, Twinkle Little Star.'"

He played another Bacharach song and then rose from the piano bench, closing the fallboard. "You should hear Dr. Walker play. He's brilliant."

"I think you performed beautifully."

He took a small bow and then started a CD. Willie Nelson began to sing. Jenks listened to the lyrics and said, "Willie Nelson's rendition of 'Stardust.' You played that in the car for me the first time you took me to the Shrimp Shack."

"*Stardust* was my mother's favorite album. She played it often while Steel and I were young. Usually she was in tears when Willie got to the last song, 'Someone to Watch over Me.'" She needed someone to watch over her. I hope she found happiness."

"I'm sorry," Jenks softly said.

"Me too," Seth said as he stroked her cheek with his hand. Taking her in his arms, he held her tightly and began to slow dance. Whispering in her ear he said, "Don't ask me to try any other dance style. I'm lucky to be able to figure this out."

"There are certain advantages to slow dancing," Jenks whispered back.

"What's that?"

"I'm in your arms."

⟵⟶

When Jenks woke the next morning, the first thought that went through her mind was about Seth. She had never felt the kind of longing she did for him, and she knew that she was falling in love. Whenever he held her in his arms, she felt her entire existence become fiery hot, so much so that she thought she might melt. Another previously unknown sensation enraptured her when he was near: her body ached with desire for him to touch her.

When Seth had brought her home the night before, she had not wanted him to leave. He had kissed her several times, and with each kiss she felt her passions intensify. The words he said to her the evening she overindulged in bourbon were clear in her thoughts: "I am being extra careful with our relationship." He was not pushing her into intimacy. They had only known one another a short time, but Jenks felt such longing for him in her heart, she believed he was the man she had been waiting for.

She rose from bed and put on a robe. After making coffee, she turned on her computer and checked her e-mail. A response from the Naval History and Heritage Command in Washington, DC, was in her mailbox:

Dear Miss Ellington:

I have received your request in regard to a ship named *Defiance* that you believe sank near St. Helena Sound in August of 1862. Preliminary investigation indicates there was not a US ship

commissioned with that title at that time. As you stated from
your research, you determined there was a Confederate States
ship which was operating in the western theatre, mostly in the
Mississippi River Delta. The crew burned that ship before it
could be taken by Union forces.

I too love a mystery, and I will attempt to dig into the archive
records for more information.

Yours truly,
Robert Vance

She replied to the e-mail with a brief thank you and dressed for the day.

The downtown library was bustling with patrons when she went inside. Jenks
saw a group of children who were there for a summer reading program. She
went to the librarian and asked her if there were any historical documents
that might contain information about tides, weather, and sunrise and sunset
information from the Civil War period.

"In our old and rare books collection, there is a record that was kept
by a Union officer who was stationed at Port Royal during the conflict. I'm
afraid the documents are not in the best condition, but I will bring them to the
reference room if you'd like to take a look," the librarian said.

"Yes, ma'am, I appreciate that."

Jenks sat down at one of the tables and the librarian brought a black leather
book that had age cracks in the binder. As she placed the journal on the table,
she said, "You look very familiar. Did I help you with this log before?"

"No, ma'am. You may have helped my twin sister."

"Perhaps that's it." She paused for a moment and then continued, "Sam
Harper was the officer who recorded this information. He was stationed at Port
Royal from the time of the Federal invasion in 1861 to the summer of 1864.
Another officer, Amos Butler, continued recording the data after Harper was
reassigned to another command. It's amazing we have this record. The books
that had been in the Beaufort Library prior to the Civil War were confiscated
by Federal authorities to pay Southern war debt. They were shipped to the

Smithsonian Institution for storage, and the building they were placed in burned, destroying the collection." She shook her head and sighed. "I hope you find what you're looking for."

Jenks slowly thumbed through the journal, and like the recordings kept by Joseph Andrews, some of the writing in the book was illegible. She carefully turned the pages until she reached the summer of 1862. Of the recordings she could decipher, she found Harper's notes to be detailed and informative.

She went through each day until she came to an entry on August 17th. He wrote that a severe storm had come out of the south and heavy rains had fallen all day. The tides were high at 2:30 in the morning, low at 8:45, high at 3:15, and low at 9:30 p.m. on the 18th. Winds were between 20 and 25 knots—sunrise at 5:51 and sunset at 7:10.

On the 18th, Harper notated that the storm was still producing heavy rain and winds out of the south at 20 knots. Jenks concluded that the *Defiance* must have sailed on the 18th because the 19th was fair with light winds. No other severe weather was mentioned for the rest of the month. Thinking back to her notes—the *Defiance* sailed at three o'clock and the ship that witnessed the sinking was in port before sundown, which was at 7:10.

"The *Defiance* sailed with the outgoing tide," she said quietly.

When she finished with the journal, she returned it to the front desk and thanked the librarian for permitting her to read it. As she started to leave, she saw that one group of students didn't have an adult volunteer with them. The young people looked to be around eight or nine years old. Jenks went back to the librarian and asked, "Do you need another adult to assist the children with their reading?"

The librarian's face lit up, and she responded, "Yes, that would be wonderful. Sometimes, we're short on volunteers, and we could use the help."

"I teach the third grade in Cary, North Carolina, and I'm here for the summer. My name is Jenks Ellington."

"Miss Ellington, thank you for the gracious offer. See that young lady over at the table in the corner? That's Ellen Madison. She's the director of the children's summer reading program." She pointed to a young woman who looked to be about her age and was with a group of five children. Jenks went over, introduced herself, and offered to help. Ellen rose from her chair and thanked her. Jenks showed Ellen her credentials and wrote down her principal's phone number.

Ellen led her to the table without an adult volunteer and introduced the students and Jenks to one another. Sitting down with the group, Jenks explained that she was a teacher in North Carolina and she wanted to help them. She listened to each of them read, assisting them as they needed it.

When the students were finished with the reading session, Jenks gave Ellen Madison her phone number and offered to help her on a regular basis.

Ellen was thrilled. "It's hard to get volunteers. Your assistance is greatly appreciated." The children would be back at the library two days later and Jenks told Ellen she would be available to help.

When she went outside, Jenks phoned Seth, and he answered his phone in his usual assertive manner. "Detective Mason."

"Don't you recognize my phone number by now?"

"Jenks, I'm sorry—it's just a habit."

"The library had a log kept by a Federal officer during the Civil War that recorded tide, weather, and sunrise and sunset information. I'd like to show you my notes. Seth—I know I've said this before, but I just can't understand Gigi not telling me about her solo diving."

"Jenks—we can't know everything about our twins."

There was silence on the phone until Seth said, "I'll call you later this afternoon."

After she finished the conversation with Seth, Jenks went to an appointment with Dr. Wray. She had been notified of a patient cancellation and the doctor was able to see her right away.

⸺

That evening Seth came to see Jenks after work. She had made iced tea and they sat on the screened porch to talk.

"Rory did not get the job with Taylor Marine. I spoke to him this afternoon and he was a little down about it. Would you ride out with me to see him tomorrow afternoon?"

"Yes—what time will you come by?"

"Two o'clock?"

"I'll be ready."

CHAPTER 6

Fort Fremont

S everal empty beer bottles were on the kitchen table at Rory's home when Seth and Jenks arrived at his home. He invited them inside, motioning with his arm.

"Detective Mason—how nice of you to come by and bring the lovely Jenks Ellington."

"Rory—I don't want you to have any more of this," Seth said as he held up a bottle of beer.

"Oh, come on, Seth. I'm just getting started."

"No, sir."

"Look at me, Seth—look at me!" he demanded while pointing at his legs.

"Rory—please let me get you some help."

"Help! What kind of help are you talking about? Can you reattach my blown-off legs?"

"I want to get a professional to talk to you—get you involved in a support group. This economic downturn is temporary. There's going to be a good job for you—please don't get discouraged."

"Don't get discouraged! I've spent plenty of time with the shrinks. They can't do a goddamn thing for me."

He started to drink more of the beer, but Seth attempted to take it from his hands.

Rory struggled to keep the beer, and when he saw that Seth was not going to allow him to continue to drink it, he hurled the bottle into the corner of the room. His face became twisted with anger and then he began to weep.

"The nightmares won't stop. I can still hear Sarah's voice. I can hear her cry out for me."

Seth turned to Jenks and said, "Would you mind taking a short walk?"

"No—I'll be back in a little while."

She took a deep breath as she stepped outside onto the deck, and then she walked down the sandy lane toward the waterfront. Jenks could see Fort Fremont in the near distance. Shaded in a dense stand of trees, the fort was surrounded by a chain-link fence. Upon entering the open gate, she began to experience cold chills.

The fort was separated into two sections, and she walked to the right portion of the structure. Openings that looked like caves went into the darkened interior of the fortress, and she walked a few feet inside. Graffiti was painted on the walls, and she stopped her forward progress when she nearly walked into a spider's web. As if guarding the entrance, the enormous yellow-and-black spider sat motionless in position. The spider had bands on its legs that resembled armor. Jenks carefully backed out of the tunnel and returned to the outside. Walking to the front of the structure, Jenks climbed the embankment of an earthen bulwark that protected the water side of the fortress.

She looked down into the now-empty gun turrets that had supported the weapons meant to protect Port Royal Sound. The noise of a passing motorboat caught her attention, and she walked closer to the Beaufort River. As the boat passed downstream, she began to hear the gunfire of recruits performing weapons training at the Parris Island Marine training station across the river.

Jenks stood near the bank and thought of Rory and his fragile nature. If need be, she would take him to a mental-health professional herself.

She waited for an hour before starting back to Rory's home. When she arrived, Jenks gently tapped on the door. Seth let her in and patted her on the shoulder as she entered.

Rory was sitting with his back to her, and as she stepped in his direction, he wheeled himself around. He had stopped crying, but his eyes were red and swollen. He looked up at her and said, "Jenks, I want to apologize for my behavior. I hope that you will forgive me."

"It's all right. We all have bad moments. If you need some help—I'd like to assist you, and I mean that."

A slight smile warmed his tear-streaked face, and he replied, "Thank you, Jenks."

She squeezed his hand, and Seth squatted down on his knees in front of

Rory. "Please don't have any more to drink. I'm going to check on someone for you to talk with. It can't hurt to just talk, can it?"

"I guess not," Rory slowly said.

When the two left his home, Seth was shaken and very quiet. Jenks touched him on the arm. "Sarah is the soldier in the photograph, isn't she?"

"Yes, she was a friend of Rory's who served with him in Afghanistan. She died over there."

"I didn't realize that."

"I'm afraid so."

Seth rubbed his temples with his hand as they drove to Beaufort on Highway 21. As they passed a vegetable stand, Jenks saw that he looked hard at a man who was in front of the tomato baskets. Seth's face darkened. He turned his truck around at the entrance to a sandy lane and quickly returned to the stand.

He jotted down an address on a piece of paper, handed Jenks his cell phone, and said, "Please call 911 and report that an officer needs assistance at this address, and give them my name."

"What are you doing?"

"You see that man over there by the tomato baskets?"

"Yes."

"That's Gary Donald. He was the registered operator of the motorboat that killed the couple on the Beaufort River." He removed a handgun that was strapped to his lower right calf, inside his blue jeans. "I want you to stay in the truck and lock the doors after I go."

He opened the truck door and placed his left foot on the ground.

"Seth—please wait until other officers arrive."

"No—he could attempt to leave."

Without saying another word, Seth got out of the truck and closed the door. Terrified, Jenks watched him cautiously proceed in the man's direction, removing his badge from his back pocket as he went forward. With trembling hands, she dialed 911 and spoke with a police dispatcher.

As he drew closer to the man, Seth pointed his gun and held up his badge. "Gary Donald—Beaufort County Sheriff's Department—you're under arrest for two counts of reckless homicide. Get on the ground and spread your legs!"

As soon as he realized he was about to be apprehended, Donald picked up a basket of tomatoes and hurled them at Seth. The man attempted to run, but Seth tackled him. Donald struggled to get to his feet again, taking a swing at Seth, but with one quick movement, Seth ducked the punch and plowed into the man's torso, knocking him to the ground.

Jenks observed that Gary Donald was a larger man than Seth, but a great deal of excess weight was in an oversized stomach. Seth pounded him with several punches and then forced him facedown into the oyster-shell-and-sand parking lot. He rubbed his face hard into the surface, and the man cried out in pain.

Jenks got out of the truck and ran to where Seth had the man pinned to the ground.

"Let me go, you son of a bitch!" Donald choked.

"There's not a chance of that," Seth told him as he pushed down hard on Donald's elbow, which was bent behind his back.

"You're hurting my arm!"

"Hold still—or I'll break it," Seth growled.

Within moments, a patrol car pulled up at the vegetable stand and an officer helped Seth restrain Donald. Handcuffs were placed on his wrists. As the two officers pulled him up from the ground, Seth began to quote him his Miranda rights. "You have the right to remain silent . . ."

After the man was seated in the patrol car, Seth turned to Jenks. He was sweating from the fight, and he wiped his brow with the back of his arm. "Will you follow us to the police station? I'm going to ride with Officer Fisher to take him in."

She nodded, and then got back in his truck.

He quickly touched her on the cheek and said, "Are you all right?"

"Yes—but remind me to never pick a fight with you."

———

Jenks waited for Seth at the sheriff's department until he finished booking Gary Donald. When he climbed into the truck with her he said, "Someone picked up Donald and the other man who was on the boat at Nairne Point after the accident. Donald wouldn't divulge who that was."

"I was impressed by your bravery."

"It's what I learned in the Marines." He smiled at her and squeezed her hand.

"I want to ask you to do something with me."

"What's that?"

"Can we go see the boat that Gigi was using?"

"Yes, if you want to."

She drove the truck to the Morgan River Marina, and he opened the driver's side door for her. Together they walked to the pier system, and Seth pointed out a red-and-white motorboat. "That's it," he said as he led her to the craft.

"Leave it to Gigi to pick out a red boat."

"Was that her favorite color?"

"Yes. It's often the favorite color of aggressive, daring people with a zest for living."

"I see—those who want to live life to the fullest. Is that your favorite color as well?"

"No—mine is green. People who have green for their favorite color seek harmony and balance in their lives. They tend to be gentle and sincere. What about you, Seth?"

"I like red and so did Steel. I guess you're the only peaceful one in the crowd."

Jenks walked down the ramp to the docking system and stood close to the boat. "I wanted to see the boat she was using."

"Why?"

"I'm trying to understand what she was doing . . . Why the secrecy?"

Seth shook his head, "I don't know."

"She was certainly daring."

She took a deep breath and changed the subject. "Would you like to come over for a sandwich?"

"Yes, ma'am—sounds good to me." He took her hand and led her up the ramp away from the boat.

Over roast-beef sandwiches on the screened porch they discussed Rory.

"Tomorrow, I'm going to make inquiries about a support group for Rory," Seth said. "There are some organizations like Hidden Wounds and Wounded Warriors that I'd like to see him get involved with."

"I'd like to help if he needs assistance in getting to meetings."

"That's very kind of you."

She rose from her seat and went to the kitchen to retrieve her laptop. She checked her e-mail while they ate. A response from the Naval History and Command Archives Department was in her mailbox.

"I've got an e-mail from the researcher in Washington."

"What does he say?"

Jenks read the e-mail aloud:

> Dear Miss Ellington:
>
> I have searched the archives from the Civil War period, and I have not been able to come up with a record of a USS *Defiance* that would have been attached to the Federal Invasion Force that captured the Hilton Head, Beaufort, and Port Royal areas of South Carolina in 1861. Perhaps during the offensive, this vessel was seized by Federal forces along the eastern coast and not officially recorded as a United States ship. That would explain the lack of documentation.
>
> I am sorry that I was not of more help to you, but I wish you the best in resolving the mystery.
>
> Sincerely,
> Robert Vance

"Dead end," Jenks said.

CHAPTER 7

Amanda

W hen Jenks entered the downtown library, students in the summer-reading program were already situated at several tables. Jenks joined the group of pupils she had assisted during the last session, and the children all smiled at her, except for one little girl. She wore her hair parted in the middle with pigtails that were braided and tied with pink hair bows on the ends.

Her name was Amanda Stevens, and when Jenks listened to her read, she found Amanda's shyness seemed to interfere with her ability to communicate. Amanda had difficulty making eye contact. When she finished her passage her tiny face showed a hint of relief.

After the session was over, Jenks took her aside and told her how nicely she had done and that she looked forward to reading with her the next time. She looked shyly at Jenks, but did not respond.

As the children were leaving the library, Jenks approached the librarian, "Mrs. Allen, you helped me recently with a log kept during the Civil War that recorded tides, weather, and sunrise and sunset information."

"Yes, of course, I remember you. How can I help you?"

"I'm looking for documentation on the time that the Federal Army spent in the Beaufort area during the war."

"Well, let's see—there are several histories written about that time period. The authors often used letters and diaries of individuals who were stationed here during the occupation. I think the foremost local authority on that time period would be Dr. Maxim Ware. I try to always attend his symposiums, and I've gotten to know him a bit. Would you like for me to phone him and see if he is available to speak with you?"

"Yes, ma'am, I would appreciate that."

"I'll be just a few moments." The librarian excused herself and went to her office, but returned within a few minutes with a piece of paper. "This is Maxim's—I mean Dr. Ware's—address and phone number. He said that he would be going out of town tomorrow for two weeks, but he has time to see you this afternoon, if that's suitable. He said at two."

"Yes, ma'am, that would be fine. Should I phone him?"

"No, I'll let him know that you're coming by."

Jenks thanked Mrs. Allen and departed the library.

⟶

Just before two in the afternoon, Jenks arrived at Dr. Ware's residence. His property was located off the Savannah Highway, and when she arrived, the gate at the entranceway was open. She proceeded down a sandy lane lined with live oak trees, and at the end of the drive was a magnificent two-story brick home. Jenks parked her car and went to the front door. A bell chimed inside when she rang the doorbell. Within a few moments, a lady who identified herself as Mabel, Dr. Ware's housekeeper, answered the door.

"Are you Miss Ellington?"

"Yes, ma'am."

"Come this way. Dr. Ware is expecting you."

She led Jenks through a richly decorated foyer to a front room with mahogany double doors. "This is Dr. Ware's library. He does most of his research in here."

As Mabel opened the doors, Jenks could just see the top of Dr. Ware's head, as he was sitting in a chair facing away from his desk.

"Dr. Ware, Miss Ellington is here."

He spun the chair around to face them and removed a pair of reading glasses as he stood up. He was perhaps in his mid-sixties, with graying hair, and was impeccably dressed in a dark suit with a red bow tie. He smiled at her warmly, and extended his right hand to shake hers.

"Miss Ellington, how can I be of assistance to you?"

"Dr. Ware—I'm investigating a mystery. My sister passed away recently while diving for artifacts in the Beaufort River."

"Yes—I'm sorry about that," he said as a frown crossed his brow.

"Thank you. My sister had been researching a cache of gold and jewelry that she thought had been stolen from the Elliott family during the Civil War. I've been to the Gibbes Museum in Charleston to see the portrait of Miss Iris Elliott."

"Yes—the Elliott family owned the Petersburg Cross, which was created by one of Empress Catherine the Great's favorite artists, Aleksi Gregori Kartashkin. Some years after her death, the cross and other possessions were sold to European dealers. As you said, one of our local plantation owners, Luke Elliott, purchased the cross in Europe on a grand tour of the continent during the late 1850s."

Dr. Ware took a book from one of his library shelves and opened it to a page about midway through. "This is a painting of Catherine the Great that hangs in the State Hermitage Museum in Saint Petersburg, Russia." He pointed to a necklace the empress was wearing. "Does that look familiar?"

"Yes, sir, it appears to be the cross that Iris Elliott is wearing in her portrait in the Gibbes Museum."

"Yes, it does." He placed the book on his desk and then removed another book, one about jewelry from ancient Greek times to the present. He opened the book and turned to a page that showed the works of Aleksi Gregori Kartashkin.

"Look at the way Kartashkin initialed the back of his works. He inscribes a double curl at the base of the beginning of each letter. His unique way of forming his letters has generally kept forgers from attempting to copy his works."

He closed the book and said, "The Petersburg Cross was stolen from the Elliott home during the Civil War, and is thought to have been taken by Federal occupiers after they invaded our area in 1861. It is well documented that possessions of local residents were confiscated, with many items falling into private hands." He paused for a moment and then continued. "The Elliott treasures are rumored to have been on a ship that sailed from Beaufort in August 1862 and caught fire, sinking somewhere around St. Helena Sound. The best account of this lies in journals written by a former slave named Andrews."

"Yes—I found Miss Meta Jane's name in my sister's possessions, and I went to see her. She said my sister had mentioned the cross, and I read Andrews's account of the sinking of a ship named *Defiance*."

"Miss Ellington, if I were more of an adventurer I might be pursuing the

Petersburg Cross myself. I did some research on the Elliott family. After her marriage to David Cotesworth, Iris died in childbirth with her first child—her two brothers were killed in battle in Virginia during the Civil War. Sadly, the Elliott family died out several generations ago."

"I'm sorry to hear that."

"Yes—terrible shame." He looked intently into her eyes. "I'd like to show you something."

Intrigued by his comment, she stepped closer to his desk.

Dr. Ware again reached to a bookshelf and removed an aged journal, then placed it on his desk. He carefully opened the cracked leather binder, which had cursive writing on the pages.

"I purchased this diary from the great-great-granddaughter of a soldier who served in the Federal invasion force that captured Beaufort. I intend to publish a book from the new information recorded in this journal. She didn't realize it was in their possession until they were discarding some old materials from their home." He paused as he carefully thumbed through the pages.

"Yes, sir, please go on."

"I've been researching the recordings inside this diary, and unfortunately, time has rendered some of Sergeant William Lasko's writings illegible. I was able to determine one entry where he mentions a boat that was seized from a local planter. This ship was used at one time to ferry cargo between Charleston and Savannah, but the planter who owned it was using the vessel to transfer his own cotton from Beaufort to Charleston. The plantation owner named the ship the *Fort Sumter* and it would make sense that it could have been renamed the *Defiance*. May I read this passage to you?"

"Yes, sir."

"'5 December, 1861.

"'Colonel Hubbard ordered us to the Fielding Plantation on the Broad River. There is a sizable ship moored to the wharf at the property. Upon inspection, the ship is fitted with a single screw propeller, but still maintains her sails for long range operations. Colonel Hubbard has ordered the ship confiscated and we are about to get her underway.'"

He stopped speaking and turned the pages. "There is another entry that appears in Lasko's journal:

"'7 February 1862.

"'I have been at the wharf at Port Royal this morning to help load a cargo ship bound for New York. I have determined this to be the same ship that was seized at the Fielding Plantation. The *Fort Sumter* has been refitted with guns and renamed USS *Defiance*.'"

Dr. Ware closed the journal and said, "Just think—this information has been hidden in an attic for almost one hundred and fifty years. I suppose it's possible the Elliott possessions may have been on board the *Defiance* when she burned and sank. With the passage of time, finding those treasures could be impossible—even with this documentation. There are just too many variables to affect where the remnants of the ship might rest—tides, ship speed, winds, just to mention a few."

"You were kind to share this with me."

"Miss Ellington, there is a matter of importance that I would like to discuss with you. When Alexis Allen phoned me this afternoon from the Beaufort County Library, I was a bit startled." He closed the journal of William Lasko and continued, "You see, several months ago, your sister, Gigi, came to see me about this very subject. I read her obituary in the *Beaufort Gazette*, and I recall the announcement mentioning she had a sister. I was saddened to learn of her passing. I'm very sorry."

"Thank you."

"If you choose to pursue this Elliott treasure, please engage an experienced diver to perform the salvage work. I know your sister drowned in the Beaufort River."

———

That evening Seth joined Jenks on her back porch for refreshments. He took off his coat and tie, then rolled up his sleeves and sat down beside her.

Jenks started the conversation. "I went to see Dr. Maxim Ware this afternoon. The librarian told me he is an expert on local history during the Civil War period. He recently purchased a diary from the great-great-granddaughter of a Federal soldier who was stationed here. This is previously undocumented information, and he said that Gigi had come to see him about this subject a few months ago."

Jenks noticed that Seth was watching her intently.

"What is it?"

He slid closer to her and moved a strand of hair behind her ear. "Your eyes are cat-like; the hazel has turned almost pure green. Jenks, what are you up to?"

"Dr. Ware suggested if I wanted to pursue the Elliott treasure I should hire a professional diver to salvage the *Defiance*."

"You'd have to find her first."

"I looked up the specifications for ships during the Civil War period. A number of vessels with a single screw propeller traveled at a speed of about twelve knots." She rose from her seat and opened up the navigational chart of the waterways in the Beaufort area that she had found on Gigi's bookshelves. "I'm trying to calculate how far the boat should have traveled. I know that there were twenty knots of wind out of the south. In the journal of Joseph Andrews, he stated that the crew that witnessed the sinking of the *Defiance* saw her sails ablaze . . . she had been using sails for part of the voyage, and the tide was going out."

"I don't see how you can be precise with this."

"I thought I'd speak to Dave Patterson about helping me."

"Hold on now, Jenks." Seth put his arm around her, and she began to feel warmth from his touch, as she always did.

"Baby—this quest of yours could be expensive and you might still come up empty handed."

"I'd like to try. I think Gigi was looking for the Elliott treasure."

"And you think looking for the *Defiance* could open up new leads?"

"Yes, I do. And Dave Patterson may be able to help."

"Dave is a straightforward individual. Go right ahead."

She was wearing shorts and his hand went down onto her bare thigh. Taking a deep breath, Jenks concentrated on maintaining her composure. "I think it's awfully hot out here. Are you hot?"

"No, I'm fine."

She rose from the wicker couch and turned on the ceiling fan then sat back down beside him. She was quiet for a moment. "I'm going to see him tomorrow."

The next morning, Jenks was waiting for Dave Patterson to open the doors to his dive shop. When he came into his showroom, she knocked on the glass front doors and he let her in with a smile on his face.

"Miss Ellington?"

"Yes, Dave."

"I recognized you immediately. You look just like your sister. I'm real sorry—her passing was a terrible shame."

"Thank you, Dave."

"How can I help you, Miss Ellington?"

"I think my sister was searching for the remnants of a ship with treasure that I believe sank off the coast during the Civil War."

"The waters off the Carolina coast are dark and murky. Visibility at times is near zero. I warned your sister a number of times about diving alone."

"I believe the ship did exist, and I'd like to bring you in as my partner. I'll pay for your expenses and if we can locate the treasure, we'll split everything fifty-fifty."

He picked up a diving mask and relocated it to a nearby shelf. "Miss Ellington, I don't mean to discourage you, but that Elliott treasure has been sought by divers for years. If it even exists, it could be buried in several feet of sand and silt. The hobby diving license that your sister held only permitted searching the ocean floor with your hands. To salvage with equipment requires compliance with the South Carolina maritime laws and we'd have to seek authorization. Also, a hobby diver can only collect ten items per day from a shipwreck site in South Carolina waters."

"What if you find an artifact of significant value?"

"My understanding is that the item becomes the possession of the diver, but regardless of the value, it should be declared to the South Carolina Institute of Archaeology and Anthropology. They're interested in the location of the find and the type of artifact."

"I see. I'll pay you to go down and look for it. I think I have a reasonable idea where the remnants of the *Defiance* might be located."

"Miss Ellington—I'll make a deal with you. I'm going to Savannah for the next several days to clean the hulls of commercial ships. When I get back, we'll go out to where you think this Elliott treasure is located, and I'll dive for it."

"Thank you, Dave," she beamed.

"Now, don't get too excited. I'll go down a few times, but that's it. I'm not about to take advantage of you."

She smiled at him and gave him her phone number before departing his shop.

CHAPTER 8

Rabbit Hash

*H*eavy thunderstorms came through the area on Saturday afternoon, and as they moved out to sea, the air was left cool and damp. Jenks had been with Seth all afternoon at his home watching old movies. He had invited her to spend the weekend with him and attend a cookout at the Rabbit Hash Hunt Club that evening. Rory planned to join them later at the club.

With Seth's encouragement, Rory had become involved in two support groups, Wounded Warriors and Hidden Wounds. Rory's disposition was improving.

After the rain passed, Jenks and Seth set out on foot for the hunt club. Seth brought a flashlight with him, and they walked the mile or so to the lodge, dodging puddles on the sandy drive.

Jenks breathed in deeply. The air was fragrant with rainwater, and she inhaled the fresh, clean scent. Occasionally, water dropped on their heads from overhead branches, and Seth brushed the rain from Jenks's hair. He put his arm around her and kissed her on the cheek. His smile warmed her.

When they reached the club, a large group of people had already arrived, and a campfire had been built in the side lot. Seth took her around and introduced her to everyone, and she immediately felt comfortable in this group of people.

A handsome man with a handlebar moustache and chestnut hair exchanged greetings with Seth. Jenks watched as they shook hands, and then Seth gestured for her to join them. She walked to Seth's side, and he took her hand. "Jenks, do you remember the airplane that flew near the Walker's home the first time you had dinner with me?"

"Yes, I do."

"This is the pilot who was at the controls. I'd like to introduce you to Hale Branson."

Hale took her hand, kissed it, and then looked into her eyes. "I'm pleased to meet you, Miss Ellington."

"I was impressed by your flying skills the afternoon I watched you from the Walker's property."

"Would you like to go flying sometime?"

"I've never flown in a small airplane before; I've just been on airliners."

"Ah, then you've really missed out. Airliners are like buses. I'll take you up, and you can see what flying is really about."

"Thank you, Hale. I'll look forward to it."

"Yes, ma'am. I'll let Seth know when."

Hale excused himself and went to a cooler, removing a beer out of the ice. Jenks glanced around the grounds of the hunt club and noticed several cooking pots with gas burners underneath.

"We're having Frogmore Stew tonight," Seth told her.

"Frogmore Stew—I haven't had that in ages. I can't remember what goes in it."

"Let's see—red potatoes, corn on the cob, sausage, and shrimp. Silver queen corn is being harvested right now, so it's a good time to make the stew."

Seth went to the cooler and retrieved two beers, handing one to Jenks after he opened it.

"I can relax tonight. I'm off duty, and I don't have to drive anywhere."

He kissed her on the lips as he sat down beside her.

Within a few minutes, Rory arrived at the cookout. Seth pulled Jenks up from her seat and they walked together to greet him. Instead of using a wheelchair, he was wearing a pair of prosthetic legs, and he stood as tall as Seth. He used a cane to assist with balance and the three friends greeted one another. "I'm wearing my legs tonight. Kind of hard to move my chair around in the sandy soil."

He put his arm around Jenks and said, "Mmmm, you smell good."

"Thank you, Rory."

He turned to Seth. "How about a beer?"

"Okay, but take it easy."

"I promise I will."

Before the stew was served, the president of the club, Jack Hamilton, led the group in prayer. Rory sat down at a picnic table and had trouble getting his legs underneath. He smiled at Jenks when he accomplished his task, and Seth brought him a large plate of the stew. The threesome sat together enjoying the dinner, and when they finished, Seth helped Rory get a second plate.

Rory turned to Jenks. "I have a job interview with the Johnson Automotive and Repair Shop in a few days. I'm really excited about it."

"I think that's great! I'll be sending you many positive thought waves."

"Thanks, Jenks—I can use them."

She patted Rory on the back and then excused herself from the table. Walking to the entrance of the chapel, she saw that the dark oak pews were still intact. Ceiling fans with schoolhouse globes slowly rotated from the ceiling. In the back of the sanctuary was a lovely stained-glass window of Christ. Except for several tables at the front of the chapel with hunting gear on them, the sanctuary still resembled a functioning house of worship.

When she finished exploring the chapel, Jenks rejoined Seth and Rory at the picnic table. As the sun went down, torches were lit around the chapel, and the group gathered near the campfire for ghost stories.

"It's a tradition," Seth softly said to Jenks.

In the light of the campfire, Jack Hamilton began the first tale.

"This story is about the Colleton Seven. Back during the dark days of the Civil War, there was a large plantation named Schell Hall just next door in Colleton County. Well, when the Yankees invaded our area in 1861, the residents of the big houses evacuated to avoid capture or worse. There was a group of planters' sons who had joined the Confederate Army, and they volunteered to work behind enemy lines to gather intelligence information. They secretly hid themselves in Schell Hall. The son of Rutger Schell, named Harrison, was amongst this group of young soldiers.

"As they were about to turn in for bed one evening, they heard the call of a Union soldier, who identified himself as Captain Marks. He yelled to the young men that he knew they were inside the house and if they didn't come out immediately, he would burn the home to the ground with them inside. The Confederates looked out the window and saw a number of well-armed Federal soldiers holding torches. They made a decision to surrender themselves. As they came outside the home with their hands on top of their heads, Harrison

Schell recognized a former slave from his plantation named Albert. It was well known that Albert was the son of Harrison's uncle, and he bore a strong resemblance to the young Confederate. As Harrison looked at him, Albert glared at him with a look of hatred reserved for only your worst enemy.

"As soon as the young men were outside, the Yankee captain said, 'Anyone else in there? I think I'll see if any more vermin come out.' With that he ordered the soldiers to torch the plantation home, and one by one they threw their torches inside. Harrison Schell and the others watched the mansion burn to the ground.

"These young men were tried for espionage and sent to Yankee prison camps. Over the years, they were released in prison exchanges and miraculously, all survived the war.

"When the scalawags and carpetbaggers were kicked out of South Carolina government in the 1870s, Wade Hampton became governor. These men had bided their time, and one night they met Albert, their betrayer, on his way home. He had been active in South Carolina politics, and he was en route from Columbia—until he met his fate on Orange Road. In the years prior to the Civil War, an abundance of oranges and other citrus had been produced by a planter in that area, but all the trees were destroyed by the Federal occupiers.

"When Albert Schell made his way down Orange Road, he was met by seven horsemen, all wearing black hoods—not the white hoods of the Klan— and each with a fiery torch in his hand.

"One of the riders told Albert that he was about to meet with the Devil for an act of betrayal. Albert couldn't remember how he had deceived anyone of importance to him, but as each rider removed his hood, his memory of the night Schell Hall burned to the ground consumed his thoughts.

"The riders tied a rope around a large live-oak limb and then put a noose around his neck. They slapped his mount, and as the horse ran away, Albert was left to swing from the tree.

"If you venture on Orange Road after dark, be careful when you get to the tree known as the Schell Oak. I'm told that some evenings with a full moon you can see the body of Albert Schell hanging from that tree."

"Oooh," someone in the group said eerily. Then the group clapped for the storyteller and another ghost story began.

When the party was over, Rory said good night, and Jenks and Seth walked with him to his van.

"I've had a great time, Seth. Thanks for inviting me."

"I'm glad you could come," Seth said. He paused before he asked, "Everything all right?"

"Yeah, yeah, I'm fine," Rory said with a smile. He kissed Jenks on the cheek, and then got into his van by way of the lift. They watched as he maneuvered into the driver's seat and waved good-bye to them.

"Are you ready to walk home?" Seth asked.

"Yes, sir—all set."

The two of them started down the darkened lane, which was illuminated only by faint moonlight. Suddenly, a group of deer tore through the thicket along the side of the sandy lane and crossed the road in front of them. Jenks grabbed Seth tightly as the animals disappeared into the marsh. His arms went around her and they kissed.

"Did that scare you?" he whispered after a little while.

"Yes."

"I've got you," he said as he hugged her again.

They held hands for the rest of the walk to the Walker property. When they reached the home, he turned on soft jazz music and he took her in his arms.

"Who are the artists?"

"That's Bill Evans and Stan Getz . . . some of Dr. Walker's music."

"I like it," she whispered as she snuggled her face into Seth's chest.

Holding each other tightly, they gently swayed to the music. Her head rested against his chest, and she felt content in his strong arms. When they began to grow tired, he pulled her onto the couch beside him and rubbed her back. She fell asleep in his arms.

———

When she woke in the morning, the living room was filled with diffuse morning light. The sun was behind a thick cloud cover, and Jenks rose from the couch and looked out onto the marsh. A number of egrets were situated in a large oak tree near the waterway, and Jenks watched them take wing before settling back down into another section of the tree.

Taking a deep breath, she inhaled the aroma of fresh coffee and cooked bacon. She followed the source of the delicious scent into the kitchen.

Seth was standing beside the stove making breakfast, and she walked to him and slid her arms around his waist. He turned and gave her a hug. "Good morning. I hope you like bacon and eggs for breakfast."

"Yes. That sounds wonderful."

She moved close to the stove and saw that a panful of bacon was cooking. "Smells good."

"Just a few more minutes on the bacon."

"Did I fall asleep on you?" she asked.

"I think you just became relaxed and fell asleep."

"You were stroking my face with your fingers. I like for you to touch me."

He smiled and asked, "One egg or two?"

"Just one for me."

After breakfast, Seth asked Jenks to accompany him on a walk through the woods. "I have a special place to show you," he said with a handsome smile.

Seth packed a picnic basket after they cleaned the breakfast dishes. They put on long pants, applied insect repellant, and left the house through the kitchen door. Seth motioned for her to join him at the edge of the lawn adjacent to the woods. A distinct path ran through the maritime forest, and Jenks followed Seth as he led the way. The sun occasionally broke through the cloud cover, casting light shadows on the forest floor. "Deer use this path quite a bit," Seth told her as they walked deeper into the woods.

After walking about thirty minutes, they came to the edge of an open field. "About ten years ago, this part of the forest was burned when lightning struck a tree." There were medium-sized pine trees growing in the field, and they continued their walk on the path. Just as they were about to reenter another section of forest, Seth pointed to a structure that stood near the edge of the trees. An old cabin, which appeared to be in decent repair, was located just at the perimeter of the field.

"This is what I wanted to show you."

"Wow, an old cabin!" Jenks declared excitedly.

Once they reached the structure, Seth walked up a set of stone steps and lifted a latch on the wooden door. "This cabin was the overseer's home when this property was a plantation. The slave quarters were destroyed in the fire, and this is the only building that survived."

Jenks ran her hand along the smooth latch of the door and peered inside. The cabin was in good condition, with a wooden floor and a stone fireplace on one wall. There were collections of old bottles, arrowheads, and farm tools on shelves and hanging on the walls.

"Where did all these old relics come from?"

"Dr. Walker, his wife, and I restored the cabin, and these items were found nearby with a metal detector."

Jenks walked to the arrowhead collection and lifted one of the points from its resting place. She rubbed her fingers across the head and then felt the sharp point. "This could do some damage," she said.

"I suppose so," Seth responded.

She returned the point to its resting place and walked to a shelf that had metal tags lying on it. "What are these?"

"Slave tags."

"What were they used for?"

"Dr. Walker found these tags in the area where the slave cabins were located. Apparently, several slaves on this plantation were sold to the French family from the Charleston area. The city of Charleston collected a tax on slaves that were hired out to perform duties. See, on that tag it says "Servant, No. 184, Charleston," and the year 1832. Slaves wore these tags when they were hired for labor outside the plantations that they belonged to. It was another way slaveholders made money." Seth shook his head, and a frown crossed his brow.

Jenks moved to the shelves with a bottle collection and lifted one of them. "They're clean."

"Yes, we clean items at Dr. Walker's house and then bring them back here."

"South Carolina Dispensary," Jenks read.

"During the administration of Governor Ben Tillman in the late 1800s and early 1900s, South Carolina dispensed her own liquor. That's one of the bottles."

"I like the palmetto tree design on it."

She returned the bottle to its place on the shelf. "This is amazing. I bet collectors would love to acquire these items."

"We think the items belong here with the land they came from."

"Are you making a point with me?"

"Yes, ma'am. Your sister is dead, and your mother does not need to lose her other daughter. I don't want any harm to come to you. Someone tore your sister's house apart looking for something. If they think you've recovered valuable artifacts, you could be in danger."

She looked up into the warmth of his golden-brown eyes. His arm slid around her shoulder, and he embraced her in a hug.

"You smell so good—like citrus," she said as she snuggled against him.

"Are you ready for a picnic?" he said with a smile.

"Yes, sir."

They walked toward the woods, crossing a sandy roadway.

"Where does the lane go?"

"It comes out near the hunt club. We use that road to drive back here."

Seth led her to the edge of the meadow and spread out a picnic blanket on the ground underneath a live oak tree. Opening the basket, he began to set out food he had packed for their lunch.

"What's on the menu?"

"Chicken sandwiches and fruit salad."

Seth removed a bottle of wine from the basket and opened it with a corkscrew. He poured her a glass of wine and then poured one for himself. They clinked their glasses together and he said, "I'm thankful to have you here with me."

She smiled. "I love being with you too."

As they ate, Jenks asked, "How long did it take you to restore the cabin?"

"About a year—we couldn't work on it all the time. I enjoyed the process though."

He was quiet for a moment as though in deep thought. "When Steel and I were young, we often explored the woods near our home in Georgia. We spent hours up in the hills near Asbury. On one of our adventures, we came across an old cabin. It was constructed from hardwood trees and mud was placed between the stacked logs for insulation. The metal roof was still intact, and we were careful not to disturb anything.

"There was an abandoned well behind the cabin, and it was covered with a sheet of metal. We lifted the cover once to look inside, and were amazed at the depth of the well and how wide it was.

"On one of our trips to the cabin we made a mistake and allowed a neighbor to come with us—Chris Lytton. We showed him the cabin, and he promised not to tell anyone about it."

Seth took a drink of his wine before continuing. "Chris Lytton should have been horse whipped. He took a group of boys up there, and they destroyed the cabin. They collapsed the roof by jumping on top of it."

"That's terrible."

"They got their just desserts. Those smart guys decided to look inside the well, and they removed the cover and poured gasoline into it. One of them struck a match and the gasoline along with natural gases that were built up inside the well exploded. A fireball came out of the chasm and set them ablaze—a couple of the boys got burned." A frown crossed his brow. "They had no business vandalizing that property. The cabin didn't belong to them."

"You sound like Meta Jane."

"What do you mean?"

"Her relative—the man who called for the sale of his family's property. Through deceit, he caused his extended family to lose their land on the May River. Remember—his sapphire-blue Cadillac was found submerged by fishermen at Nairne Point."

"Did she have any sympathy for him?"

"No—she said she hoped he had a visit with a shark."

"I have a hard time empathizing with people who commit hurtful crimes against others."

Jenks raised her eyebrows. "Are you allowing me a glimpse into your darker side?"

He frowned slightly. "We all have our dark sides. Some people are more affected—or controlled—by their darker tendencies than others." Jenks squeezed the napkin in her hand and looked into Seth's eyes.

"What happened to Chris Lytton?"

"Steel got his hands on him—but under the circumstances, I thought he went light on him—only a few bruises."

"Oh, my," Jenks said as she shook her head.

"You must remember that we were raised in an abusive household. At the time, solving problems through violence was acceptable to us."

Jenks stared down at her clasped hands before asking, "Tell me more about Steel."

"Growing up he was fearless. I think I told you we did almost everything together, but he was usually the leader. He was the dominant twin, and once he set a goal for himself, he worked at it until he accomplished the task."

"You've just described Gigi."

They both looked at one another for a moment, and then Jenks changed the subject. "How did you get to know the Walkers?"

"You know that I was in his history class, and when the course was complete they invited me to come out here and go fishing. We developed a strong friendship. I can't begin to measure the positive influence they've had on my life. They both have many fine qualities, but I think what I admire the most about them is the kind and respectful manner in which they treat one another." He paused for a moment as if in reflective thought. "I sometimes wonder what it would have been like to have been raised by gentle souls like the Walkers instead of my tyrannical father."

"Did they have children?"

"No, they didn't." He laughed slightly and then added, "When I got out of the Marines, I was a still a country boy from the Georgia hills. I took a job in a grocery store while I was attending college. A lady came in one day and asked me to direct her to the pecans. She pronounced it *pee*-cans and I thought she meant the restroom. I gave her directions to the ladies' room."

Jenks laughed and put her arms around him. After they hugged, he pulled her tightly against him. "I'm crazy about you."

"It's mutual," she responded.

He caressed the side of her cheek with his hand.

"When you go out with Dave Patterson to look for the Elliott treasure, I want to arrange to be off work so I can accompany you."

"Are you worried about me?"

"Yes."

CHAPTER 9

"Where Go the Boats"

*W*hen Dave Patterson returned from Savannah, Seth and Jenks met him at the downtown marina. His wife, Candice, had come with him to serve as his diving partner. Jenks brought out her map of the coastal waterways around Beaufort. She had marked her calculations on the map of the route she thought the *Defiance* might have traveled. Dave studied the chart and said, "Miss Jenkins, I understand how you came up with these estimations. Your technique is close to the Bayesian method."

"What's that?"

"It's a way of calculating the location of shipwrecks." He paused for a moment. "In 1857, the SS *Central America* went down in a hurricane off the coast of the Carolinas. It was referred to as the ship of gold." He glanced at the map. "A little over twenty years ago, a salvage team, the Columbus-America Discovery Group, used the Bayesian theory to locate the ship. They were just about to give up on their search when they noticed some unusual shapes showing up on underwater photos taken by a robot sub."

"What were they?"

"These unusual shapes turned out to be stacks of gold ingots; stacked in the same way that they were when the ship went down. They could even read the mint date on coins they located near the ingots. The wood and iron of the ship had disintegrated, but the gold was there, in virtually the same condition as when the ship went down."

"Wow," Jenks said quietly.

Dave looked back at Jenks's calculations and said, "We know that at the time that the ship got under way, the tide was starting to go out. They would have had an outgoing tide for a portion of the journey, which would have given them greater speed. We don't know when they rigged the sails, since the ship was powered with a screw propeller. The sails would have been the most efficient with the winds quartering from the rear. Your notes state the winds were twenty knots out of the south." He pointed to the chart and showed them where the ship would have picked up the most effective winds.

"I understand that you've estimated the vessel would have had a hull speed of about twelve knots, and you're basing that on similar Civil War era ships that you researched." He pointed to a location on the map. "I see how you reached your conclusions, and we'll try out by Woodward Point. The depth of the water's about twenty-five feet in that vicinity. We'll get out there about the time the tides are turning around, so the current won't be so much of a factor."

When they reached the area off Woodward Point, Dave and Candice prepared for the dive. They inspected each other's equipment. After a final safety check of their regulators, they descended into the murky water, disappearing beneath the surface.

"Jenks, do you remember the minister who was mugged in his own churchyard?"

"Yes, I do."

"Last night, the same assailant attempted to rob a convenience store in Walterboro, but the owner shot him. The minister who had been held at gunpoint made the identification. Afterward, he remained with the man and prayed for him. Detective Campbell was there. He said that the assailant asked for forgiveness."

"I hope he finds forgiveness from the Lord, and I hope he intends to change."

"I'll hope with you. He's going to have a number of years to think about it."

"What happened with the case where the motorboats collided and two people were killed?"

"The girlfriend of the second man who was on the boat that evening came forward and confessed she had picked up the two men near Nairne Point. She said that events of the accident were not disclosed to her and she was unknowingly an accessory. She turned in her boyfriend, Albert Scott, and he later confessed to being a passenger on the boat during the collision. Gary

Donald confessed to being the operator of the boat after the other man signed a confession."

"Dreadful situation . . ."

"I agree. Mose is still refusing the reward."

Jenks shook her head and then stared into the dark waters of St. Helena Sound. She could not see the divers.

Looking back toward the coastline, Jenks asked, "Where did the name Woodward Point come from?"

"Dr. Henry Woodward."

"Who was he?"

"He is considered the first English settler in this area. Woodward is well known for having established trade and relations with Indian tribes such as the Westo. In Dr. Walker's class on Low Country history, the textbook mentioned that Dr. Woodward was responsible for the introduction of rice from Madagascar to this area. However, Dr. Walker said that it's debatable who was actually responsible."

The Pattersons had been underwater for about thirty minutes when Jenks saw the two divers emerge from the water; they were about forty feet away from the boat when they surfaced. Dave was holding a rusty hubcap. She watched them as they approached the boat. He lifted his diving mask to his forehead. "Miss Jenkins, this is the only treasure I found on the bottom."

The couple made one more dive before calling it quits for the day. They found only marine debris on their search, and they returned to the downtown marina empty handed, except for the hubcap.

Jenks arranged another outing with the Pattersons, and then she and Seth walked to the marina parking lot.

"Jenks, how many more times are you going to do this?"

"A few more . . . I have to be satisfied that I tried."

"When are you going out again?"

"Tomorrow afternoon at one."

"I'll be here."

"Seth, thank you."

"Yes, ma'am."

Later that afternoon, Jenks met the children's group at the downtown library. She encouraged the children to each pick out a poem that they enjoyed, and then instructed them to recite it to the group. They read through poetry books and began to make their selections. Amanda smiled ever so slightly at Jenks. This was the first time Jenks had seen the child smile, and she felt warmed by her expression.

"Amanda, have you chosen a poem?"

"Yes, Miss Jenks."

"Who is the author and what's the name of the poem?"

"It be called, 'Where go de—I mean the—boats.' The author be Robert Louis Stevenson."

"Amanda, would you like to read first?"

A nervous expression crossed Amanda's face, but Jenks looked at her ardently and said, "You're doing great." She smiled at Amanda and nodded her head for her to continue.

Amanda looked closely at Jenks and then started the poem.

"Where Go the Boats?" by Robert Louis Stevenson

Dark brown is the river,
Golden is the sand.
It flows along for ever,
With trees on either hand.

Green leaves a-floating,
Castles of the foam,
Boats of mine a-boating—
Where will all come home?

On goes the river
And out past the mill,
Away down the valley,
Away down the hill.

Away down the river,
A hundred miles or more,
Other little children
Shall bring my boats ashore.

When she completed the poem, she took a deep breath, and then sighed. An expression of satisfaction showed on her face.

"Amanda, that was lovely. You did well."

She returned to her seat and then smiled broadly at Jenks.

The other children recited their poems and when the group completed their readings they went to the playground behind the library. Amanda followed Jenks to where she sat down and said, "Miss Jenkins, thank you for helping me."

"Amanda, you read beautifully."

"You just being nice."

"No, I'm not, and I love to see you smile."

She beamed when Jenks said this, and then ran to the swings.

———

Gigi's house was shown to a prospective buyer during the afternoon. Jenks knew only that a Marine Corps lieutenant and his wife were looking for a place to live. When Jenks arrived home, Agnes Manning's business card was on the dining room table. She picked it up and glanced at Agnes's photo. A shadow passed across the back of the dining room wall, and Jenks turned to the window to see who was at the front of the house. She went to the window, but did not see anyone. Walking to the front door, she glanced out the peephole and, not seeing anyone, opened the door. There was no one there.

The phone started to ring inside and she quickly closed and locked the door. When she answered the phone, Agnes Manning was on the line.

"Miss Ellington, this is Agnes."

"How did your showing go today?"

"They were very complimentary of your sister's home. The wife was especially impressed. Her husband wants a house with a garage. It's a guy thing. I don't think they're going to make a quick decision."

"Thank you for your efforts."

"Miss Ellington, you're welcome." Agnes paused for a moment and then said, "I'm sorry there haven't been more showings on your sister's house."

"I understand that selling a home is a challenge right now."

"Yes, it is."

Then they said their good-byes. As Jenks hung up the receiver, she turned and faced the front window of the house. *Has someone been looking in at me?*

Jenks was startled again when someone knocked at the door. She went to the peephole and looked out. Relief swept through her when she saw Crawford Forrest standing on the front porch. Jenks opened the door for her. Crawford was holding several binders.

With a smile, Jenks said, "How nice to see you. Please come inside."

"Thank you, Jenks. I found my photo albums, and I was hoping that you might have some time to look at them with me."

"Of course I do," Jenks replied.

A look of happiness crossed Crawford's countenance as she was shown inside the house. Jenks poured glasses of iced tea for both of them, and they went to the living room coffee table. "Thank you for indulging me this afternoon," Crawford said.

"Oh, before we look at the albums, I wanted to mention that I understand the house behind us has been rented to a young man. I was taking a walk, and I just got a glimpse of him as he entered the house. He was tall and physically fit, but I could not tell much more about him. He was wearing a baseball cap."

"I didn't realize the home was for rent."

"It was for sale for over a year, but the owner finally decided to rent it out."

"I can understand that." Jenks paused and looked down at Crawford's albums, which were sitting on the coffee table. "I'm thrilled to see your photos."

Crawford opened the album on the top. "These photos are from my childhood."

Jenks looked at the beautiful children in the pictures. There were names and dates written underneath the photos and Jenks pointed to one. "Please tell me about the young people in the snapshots."

Crawford pointed to the first one and said, "This is the Forrest family, my three sisters, my brother, and me."

Jenks was puzzled—she had thought Forrest was Crawford's married name.

Crawford turned the page, and there was a photo of a magnificent home with Corinthian columns across the front. A large group of people were sitting on the steps. Underneath the photo was a record of the event: "Thanksgiving, 1964."

Jenks pointed to the photo and said, "You have a really large family."

"My goodness, yes. These are my cousins and extended cousins. Thanksgiving was always a very special time. My parents loved to hold family celebrations at our ancestral home."

"That is a magnificent house. Is it still in your family?"

"Yes, my sister Mary Margaret owns it. It's named Rosalynn after my ancestor, Rosalynn Forrest. She was the first lady to occupy the house after its construction in the 1820s."

"Where is it located?"

"On the May River, near Bluffton."

Jenks continued to look through the family photos. There were many happy faces. "Look at this one—who is this hanging upside down on a tree limb?"

"That's my twin brother."

"I didn't realize you had a twin."

"Oh yes, we did everything together as children. He was my protector—my hero. We were the youngest children in the family having three older sisters." She looked intently at Jenks before continuing. "I did not realize that Gigi had an identical twin sister until she passed away. I confess I am something of a recluse. I should have gotten to know your sister better. It's my fault."

"Oh, no, we all get busy," Jenks responded.

Crawford shook her head and then brought out the next photo album. There were photos of her from her teenage years and early twenties: debutante pictures and cheerleading photographs from her days at the University of South Carolina.

"These are so beautiful of you."

"Thank you, honey."

At the rear portion of the album, there was a series of pictures with Crawford and a young man with blond wavy hair and sparkling blue eyes.

"Who is this with you?"

Crawford smiled and ran her fingers across the photo. "That was Robert Carlisle. My fiancé."

Jenks was afraid of prying, and she turned to the next page—more photos of Crawford with her young man. Crawford pointed to one and said, "That's us together at the Myrtle Beach Pavilion." After she said these words a sudden look of sadness gripped her countenance. She looked intently into Jenks's eyes and said, "That was two weeks before he died."

Jenks was stunned by her admission, and she set the album down on the coffee table. "I'm so sorry."

"He was helping his father in an old storage building on their farm. Robert was wearing his college ring from The Citadel and his hand came into contact with some electrical wires—they were hot. Robert died from electrocution." Tears welled in her eyes and then fell down her cheeks.

Jenks went to the bathroom in the hallway for tissues and returned, handing several to her.

"Thank you, dear. I shouldn't upset you by telling you these things."

"No, I'm glad to listen."

"You see, I've kept many of these painful memories to myself for so long. I hope you don't mind that I'm discussing them with you."

"Of course not."

Crawford wiped the tears from her face and then opened the third album. The photos were of the Forrests as they matured. The people at family gatherings became fewer in number and the happy faces of individuals in earlier albums became less common.

"Here's a photo of all five of us siblings together. This was the last time we were all together." She paused, and with a somber expression said, "My sisters Martha and Olivia were killed in an automobile accident that year."

"Oh no—I'm so sorry."

"That left my oldest sister, Mary Margaret, my brother, Marvin, and me."

Jenks was now thoroughly confused, and because Crawford was being so open about her past she said, "I thought that Marvin was your husband."

"Goodness, no. Marvin is my twin brother."

"Your twin?"

"Yes, ma'am. He had such a brilliant mind; he was a child prodigy. I can still hear him play the violin. Unfortunately, as he aged, he could not control his excesses. He spent two years away at college, but didn't finish. Every job he attempted ended in failure, and Marvin became immersed in alcohol. I've been taking care of him for the last twenty years. Each passing day brings him closer to what will be a long-term suicide."

"Why don't you live with your sister at your family home near Bluffton?"

"We did live there together for several years, but Marvin was carrying off our ancestral belongings and selling them to pawn shops or bootleggers to keep himself supplied with liquor." A wry smile crossed her face. "Miss Hannah Grace Jones. That old lady bootlegger just loved to see my brother coming. He even sold the violin that our grandparents gave him for his twelfth birthday. I tried to get it back, but it had already been sold to a collector in Savannah. It was quite valuable." She sighed and then said, "Mary Margaret told him that he'd have to leave."

She thumbed through the next few pages. "Marvin was my protector and best friend when we were children, and I am his keeper now. I thought you'd understand, having had a twin sibling. I have one failure—I have not been able to get him off alcohol, but you can only control one person—and that is yourself."

———

That evening as Jenks lay in bed, she thought of Crawford Forrest and her unhappy life. *What made her reveal her deeply held secrets and private tragedies?* Before she closed her eyes, Jenks thought of the day she had seen Crawford weeding her garden wearing a large straw hat and capri pants. When she rose from the earth that she tilled, her posture was strong and straight. Jenks drifted off to sleep thinking of Crawford's loyalty to her brother.

In the middle of the night, she was awakened by what she thought sounded like footsteps on the hardwood floors. Fear surged through her limbs, and she took a deep breath as she rose from her bed. She slipped on her robe and took a flashlight from the nightstand.

Leaving the beam off, she went into the living room, but there was only silence. She turned on the outside floodlights and looked around the perimeter of the home. Not seeing anything unusual, she sat down on the couch and waited and listened. The eight-day clock on the mantle chimed three bells.

Jenks decided that she must have dreamed the footsteps and returned to her bed.

———

Seth was waiting at the downtown marina for Jenks when she arrived at one for the next dive by the Pattersons. They returned to a position near the area they had searched the day before. Once again the Pattersons completed two dives, but collected only marine debris. When they returned to the dock, Dave spoke to Jenks, and then she joined Seth in the parking lot.

"Dave says that he'll go out tomorrow afternoon, but he believes that would fulfill his commitment to me. He said if I wanted to continue this search, I'd have to hire another diver."

"I told you he would be candid with you." He took her hand and led her toward Bay Street. "Let's go have an early supper."

"Only if you'll let me buy this time," Jenks said.

"All right . . . but I'm treating you to dinner at the Walker's house tomorrow night."

"That sounds like a fair exchange."

"Where would you like to dine?" Seth asked.

"Let's go to Wren's. Frank Hiller recommended that restaurant."

"You're going to accept his endorsement?"

"He looks healthy to me."

Seth smiled, kissed the back of her hand, and then held it as they walked down Bay Street to the restaurant.

They were seated in a corner table, and since they were dining early, the restaurant had few patrons.

"They are very generous with their portions in this restaurant, so why don't you and I split an entrée and a salad?" Seth said.

"What do you suggest?"

Seth looked at the menu and recommended a seafood medley served over pasta. After the server took their order, Seth smiled at her and took her hand in his. "You're beautiful."

She smiled at him and thanked him for his kind words.

As they dined, Jenks was impressed by how delicious the cuisine was and she said, "Frank made a good recommendation on the restaurant, and you made a wonderful suggestion for our dinner." She was quiet for a moment. "I pray that he did not hurt Gigi."

Seth squeezed her hand and said, "Last year, I saw your sister at an oyster roast at Port Royal."

Jenks felt her stomach tighten with sudden fear. "You've never mentioned that."

"I thought how beautiful she was, and I wanted to introduce myself, but I realized she was with Frank Hiller."

"You were attracted to her?" She felt her face flush as she lost control of her emotions. "Am I her substitute?"

Seth had a look of astonishment on his face, and he picked up her hand and held it tightly. "That's not what I was implying. The day your sister drowned, I helped pull her from the river. I was shocked to see that she was the victim."

Jenks began to feel tears well up in her eyes, and she wiped them away with her fingers before they ran down her face. She felt her face get hot. "What's going on, Seth? Is this like the detective in the movie *Laura* that obsessed over what he thought was the portrait of a beautiful dead woman? Come to think of it, you're Frank Hiller's only accuser . . . and you're basing your suspicions on some military philosophy."

Seth's face darkened. She had never seen the look that descended on his countenance. "Hold on now," he said calmly. "Disclosing my thoughts to you about Frank Hiller was meant to alert you to a possible danger. He could attempt to get close to you in order to . . ." His voice trailed off. "When I found out that Gigi had an identical twin, I knew that I could help you. I felt like there was a bond between us. Only people who lose their twins can understand exactly how it feels . . . how it hurts."

He slid onto the bench seat beside her and put his arm around her. "I stand behind my intuition about Frank Hiller. And your sister . . . I admired her loveliness briefly, and from afar. I think you're beautiful." He put his hand under her chin and lifted her face so he could see into her eyes. "I'm crazy about you."

Feeling her anger beginning to diminish, she wiped a tear off her cheek and squeezed his hand in return.

Suddenly, there was a loud crash outside the restaurant. Seth rose from the table and went out the door. Jenks followed him and stood at the door of

Wren's with the hostess. Two cars were involved in a head-on collision on Carteret Street, and one of the automobiles was on fire. Seth was already at the driver's door, attempting to get the woman out of the burning vehicle, but she was slumped over the steering wheel.

A feeling of horror and helplessness raced through Jenks's mind, and she ran toward the burning car to help Seth.

"Jenkins, get back! The car could explode!" he yelled.

"I want to help you!"

"The car is locked, get back!"

A man came out of an antique store and brought a large fire extinguisher. Seth took it from him and smashed the rear passenger window of the car and then unlocked the doors. He lifted the woman from the driver's seat and ran with her to a nearby park off Bay Street. Placing her on the ground, he took her pulse and then began to perform CPR.

People began to gather at the scene, and several men were using fire extinguishers to put out the blazing automobile. The driver of the other car had been helped to a bench on the side of the street, and two women were applying pressure to a cut on his forehead.

The sound of sirens filled the air, and within moments police cars, a fire truck, and an ambulance arrived. Paramedics took over resuscitating the woman and placed her into the ambulance.

Jenks's heart was still racing and she went to Seth's side. Blood was flowing from his left arm and down his hand. He had been intent on saving the woman's life and was completely oblivious to a serious cut on his forearm.

"Seth—you're bleeding," Jenks said, her voice trembling.

He looked down at his wound, then removed his handkerchief from his back pocket and placed it over the cut. He sat down on a park bench. "I must have injured myself when I broke the car window."

Jenks did not notice a man approaching them until he was standing next to Seth.

"Are you trying to have matching scars on your forearms, Mason?"

Seth looked up at him and responded with a slight smile, "Thomas, how about a ride to the hospital? I think I'm going to need to see a doctor." He paused and turned to Jenks. "This is my partner, Detective Campbell. Thomas, this is my friend Jenks Ellington."

They quickly exchanged greetings and then walked down Bay Street to Thomas's parked car. The handkerchief was red with blood, and the detective removed a first-aid kit from the police car. He put a compress on the cut and then tightly wrapped the wound with gauze. "I hope that will hold you for a few minutes."

He helped Seth into the vehicle and Jenks climbed into the rear. The hospital was less than ten minutes away, and after a short wait, Seth was seen by an emergency room doctor. She introduced herself as Dr. Coleman Petty. As she began to clean and stitch the wound, Jenks walked out to the hallway. Thomas was standing near the nurses' station, and Jenks walked in his direction. He was a tall black man with broad shoulders. His hair was cut short like Seth's, in a military style, and he smiled as he saw her approach. "Miss Ellington, can I get you a drink from the vending machine?"

"No, thank you. I'm fine."

"The lady driving the car that caught fire has been seen by the doctors. They think she suffered a heart attack, which led to the accident. I was told she's in stable condition. She was fortunate that Seth was nearby. The driver of the other car suffered a facial laceration, but he should be released later this evening."

He sipped a cup of coffee. "How's Seth doing?"

"The doctor was stitching the wound. I didn't want to watch."

He smiled at her and then said, "Seth is a good man. I'm proud to have him as my partner."

"Detective, were you in the Marines?"

"Yes, ma'am, for twenty years."

Jenks went back into the room with Seth and waited until Dr. Petty was finished tending his wound. She wrote Seth two prescriptions. After Seth completed paperwork for insurance purposes, Thomas drove them back to their cars at the downtown marina. He offered to drive Seth home, but Seth said he would be all right and thanked him for his help. "Good night then," his partner said as he drove away.

The last rays of sunlight were setting over the bay, and Jenks looked up into Seth's golden-brown eyes. "I owe you an apology. I had no excuse for reacting the way I did in the restaurant."

"It's all right, dear. I understand how raw your emotions are now."

She put her arms around him and settled her face against his chest. "I didn't pay for our meal. I left my purse in the restaurant."

"I'll go with you to settle up."

"Thank you." She raised her head from his chest and looked into his eyes. "You're my hero. You were very brave to save that lady's life without consideration for your own."

He smiled at her words and then took her hand as they began their walk down Bay Street to Wren's.

CHAPTER 10

"At Last"

O n the next morning's edition of the *Beaufort Gazette*, there was a story about the accident. Seth was cited for his heroism in saving the life of the driver, Maggie Reynolds. Jenks was still nervous from last evening's events and embarrassed about her behavior. She cringed as she thought of the accusations she had made against him. She felt fortunate he was still speaking to her. And Gigi—she dearly loved her twin, but at times she had been envious of the ease at which Gigi was accepted and accomplished her goals. Last night, her jealousy had been evident, and she regretted allowing her emotions and poor judgment to show.

The summer heat and humidity was now stifling, and she found that if there were to be any outdoor activity, she needed to accomplish it during the morning. This morning, she weeded Gigi's flower beds, which were planted with an abundance of perennials.

From next door, David Bernstein called out, "Good morning." She put down her trowel and walked over to his yard. Noticing his pink geraniums, she said, "These are lovely. I've never been able to grow them."

"They need a little fertilizer. I've always found that helps."

Jenks inhaled the fragrance of a rose by bending a large pink blossom over to her before saying, "David, I had a visit from Crawford Forrest recently. Gigi thought that she and Marvin were husband and wife, but she told me that he was her twin. Did you know that?"

"Yes, I did. I try to stay out of discussions on other people's business. When I was growing up in Brooklyn, my father set a strict family policy of not getting involved in other people's affairs. He said that you avoid trouble that way."

"I felt badly for her. It's as though she has sacrificed the better part of her life taking care of an alcoholic."

"Jenks—you're just in your mid-twenties. There are harsh matters in life that you will experience as you age. Marvin, no matter what he has done, is her fraternal twin. I'm not sure how she deals with her struggles, and I'm not sure that I could endure what she has. But, I can tell you that I admire her greatly. She could have very easily walked away from here and never looked back, but she didn't. I think she's very brave."

"Yes, sir, I agree."

David trimmed the dead head of a rose from a bush with his garden scissors and then said, "She must feel comfortable with you if she confided in you."

"She said that she didn't realize Gigi had a twin and knew that I would understand her feelings."

"You're both familiar with loss," he solemnly replied.

Before they finished their conversation, Jenks told him that they had a new neighbor. David was unaware that a man had rented the house behind them.

When she finished her work, Jenks looked over the garden with pride and then went inside for a shower. At two o'clock, she met Seth at the downtown marina. He was wearing khaki shorts and a white polo shirt. His left arm was bandaged from the elbow to the wrist.

"How are you today?" Jenks asked.

He smiled and said, "I'm fine, Jenks, and I hope you are."

"Yes, sir . . . and your arm?"

"It hurts a bit."

"I'm sorry."

He smiled, and within a few moments, the Pattersons arrived in their boat. They pulled up to the pier, and Seth and Jenks got on board. They greeted each other, and Dave Patterson came forward and shook Seth's hand. "I heard about the accident last night on Carteret. You were very brave."

"Thank you, Dave."

"Candice and I will be extra careful while diving today. I would hate the thought of your having to come into the water to save one of us. I think the salt water wouldn't feel too good on that arm today."

Before they left the marina, Dave rigged a Bimini top on his boat and they set out for Woodward Point. Once they arrived at the site, the Pattersons prepared for the dive, checking each other's equipment and testing their regulators.

They went into the water and Jenks walked close to Seth's side. They were both under the shade of the Bimini top and she said, "Seth, I feel bad about my behavior last night."

"Jenks, forget about it. We all have bad moments." A slight frown crossed his brow, and then he added, "There were times when I felt jealous of Steel. I think it's normal for siblings to experience that type of emotion. I bet you haven't considered that she was probably envious of you over certain aspects."

She paused as she considered what he had said. "No—I never thought of that—your explanations make me feel better."

"That's what I hope for."

"And my comments about Frank Hiller?"

"Please forget about it," he said as he patted her on the back.

Jenks pointed to an island that was just east of their location. "What's the name of that island?"

"That's Palmer's Island, but it has a nickname."

"What's that?"

"It's called Skeleton Island by locals."

"Why?"

"About twenty-five years ago, an archaeologist uncovered the skeletons of three bodies. They were chained together and staked out. No one knows who they were or why they were treated so unmercifully."

"Those poor people," Jenks responded.

"The facial features of the skulls were reconstructed and scientists determined the bodies were of African origin." Seth shook his head and said, "Slavery was a brutal institution."

They spent the next thirty minutes talking. In the western sky, dark clouds were beginning to build up and a distant rumble of thunder sounded. The Pattersons emerged near the boat and Dave said, "Miss Jenkins, I didn't come across anything new on this dive. We'll go down one more time, but that's it."

He looked to the west and said, "We may have to make this a short dive."

After the couple started the next dive, Jenks put her hand on Seth's shoulder. "Have you heard any more about Maggie Reynolds's condition today?"

"Thomas phoned me and said she was improving. I'm thankful that I was able to get her out of the car."

Another rumble of thunder sounded in the west, and the sky was beginning to take on an unusual deep-green to black appearance.

"I don't like the look of those clouds. The color is strange," Seth observed.

A cool wind suddenly caught the Bimini top, and it flexed up and down in the breeze. The storm was approaching their position from the west. "I hope they come up soon," Jenks said in a concerned voice.

A cloud-to-ground lightning bolt burst from the base of the thunderhead, followed by a loud crack of thunder. Feeling the electricity in the air, Jenks anxiously looked over the side of the boat for the divers. Within a few minutes, they both surfaced, empty handed. They swam to the side of the boat, and Jenks and Seth helped them with their diving tanks.

Dave turned his head to the west and said, "I think we should get off the water."

He drove the boat to the pier at Hunting Island State Park and tied the watercraft off at the dock. The winds were now howling, and rain was pelting them with heavy drops. The foursome ran to one of the bath houses and stood inside as a terrific storm descended upon them. Visibility was next to nothing; the rain was so heavy that Jenks lost sight of the Pattersons' boat.

"Miss Jenkins?" Dave said, raising his voice above the storm.

"Yes?"

"I think somebody's trying to tell you something."

⸺

That evening, Jenks and Seth made dinner together at the Walker's home. They grilled shrimp and vegetables and then sat down at the kitchen table to dine.

"Have you given up on the Elliott treasure?"

"I've concluded that we could look in that area every day for the next one hundred years and never find anything."

"I'm thankful you've realized that."

They looked into each other's eyes for a moment, and then Jenks asked, "Have you spoken to Rory lately?"

"No, not in the last few days. As far as I know, he still hasn't had a job offer. I'm going in to work early tomorrow, and we can go out to see him in the late afternoon. I'll let him know we're coming."

After dinner he played several songs on the piano for her. Then they danced to jazz music until a sultry rendition of "At Last" performed by Etta James began to play.

Seth began to kiss her passionately as they danced. His hands caressed her back, and she became fiery hot.

In a trembling voice she said, "Seth—I'm in love with you. I've been waiting for you."

He tilted her head back from his chest and looked into her eyes. "I'm in love with you too."

She could feel his hardness against her, and she hugged him even closer. "I want you, Seth."

He continued to kiss her repeatedly on the mouth, and between kisses he whispered, "Baby, I don't want to get you pregnant. I'll use protection."

"I went to see Dr. Wray for birth control."

"You've been thinking about this for a while," he said as he ran his hand up and down her back.

She blushed, and her face felt extremely hot. "I have."

With those words he lifted her in his arms and carried her into his bedroom. He gently placed her on his bed. After removing his shirt, he pulled her tightly against him and his hands roamed her body with strong caresses. She cried out with excitement as he pulled her shirt over her head and then fondled her breasts. Gradually, they removed their clothing. She was in the throes of passion as he ran his tongue from her throat to her breasts, gently kissing her nipples. With his touch, she felt deeply moved by desire. She gasped for breath as their naked bodies came together, and she felt the hard muscles of his chest against her own. As she lost herself to him, she cried out his name and wept tears of pleasure. When he stilled against her, he gently wiped the tears from her face and held her until she fell asleep.

Jenks woke in the morning to light tickling on her face and arms by Seth's fingers. She looked into his eyes, which were gleaming golden-brown with the first rays of sunlight shining into the room.

"That feels good," she quietly said.

"I have to leave you soon," he whispered.

She turned and put her arms around him. "I don't want you to go."

He kissed her and softly said, "I'll see you this afternoon. I'll pick you up around five at your house."

"Promise?"

"Yes, ma'am." He paused as he looked into her eyes. "Loving you last night was beautiful."

She brought his fingers to her mouth and kissed them. "I'm certain you're the man I've been waiting for."

He smiled with her words and stroked the side of her cheek. After kissing her again on the forehead, he rose from the bed. Captivated by his well-toned physique, Jenks thought his muscular build reminded her of the statue of a Roman youth she had seen years before, on a trip to the British Museum with Gigi. The youth had a perfect physique and thick curly hair. He was in the course of a hunt and his determination showed vividly in his eyes. *What would Seth's hair look like if he grew it out?*

———

When she returned home, Jenks took a long walk around the Port Royal community. Even in the early morning hours, the humidity was oppressive and sweat ran down her chest and back. *Ladies are supposed to perspire—but this is sweat.* After a shower, she started cleaning Gigi's house, but found that she could not keep her mind off of Seth.

He had deeply stirred the passions within her. During lovemaking, his caresses had stimulated her into breathless desire, and new sensations enveloped her existence with deep pleasure. *There had never been any of this in my relationship with Alex Conners.* Jenks had declared her love for Seth, and she only knew that she wanted to be with him again.

Seth rang the doorbell at five o'clock and when she answered the door, she bounded into his arms. Holding him tightly for a few moments, she leaned her head back and looked up into his eyes.

"I've missed you today."

"I've missed you too," he said as he kissed her repeatedly on her face.

"What time is Rory expecting us?"

"I told him around six."

She let go of him and retrieved her purse. After locking the front door, Jenks held his hand as they walked down the path to his car. He opened the door for her and then closed it once she was seated.

"Seth, do you think we have enough time to stop by and speak to Miss Meta and Miss Ida?"

"We'll have to make the visit a short one."

They drove out to Coffin Point and Seth parked his vehicle in the grass yard near the house. He opened the door for Jenks, and they walked together up the steps. The sound of cicadas in the trees was almost deafening as they stepped to the front door. They went inside, and Jenks rang the bell. Within a few seconds, Jenks heard Ida Mae's voice from the rear of the house. "I's comin."

As soon as she stepped into the foyer, a smile swept across her face and she said, "Miss Jenkins, how nice to see you . . . and who is dis with you?"

"Miss Ida, this is my friend Seth Mason."

"Mmm mmm," she said. "Meta, come to de front of de house!" she called out. "Miss Jenkins has come by for a visit.

"Mr. Seth, nice to meet you. Those were beautiful roses that you sent to us, Miss Jenkins. You didn't have to do dat."

"I wanted to send you the flowers. You were so kind to allow me to read through your ancestor's journals."

Seth came forward and shook her hand. "It's a pleasure to meet you too, Miss Andrews." Jenks noticed how intently Ida Mae gazed into his eyes.

"Come into de parlor," Ida Mae gently said.

They walked into the room and the ceiling fan was operating at full speed, filling the room with a circulating breeze.

"What brings you out dis way dis afternoon?"

"We're going to see a friend, but I wanted to come by and give you an update on the gold cross I was attempting to locate."

"Did you find it?"

"No, ma'am."

Meta Jane entered the room, and she smiled warmly at Seth and Jenks.

"Miss Jenkins, is so nice to see you agin. De roses you sent us were lovely. Who is dis handsome man with you?"

Seth stood and shook her hand. "Thank you, I'm Seth Mason. It's a pleasure to meet you, Miss Andrews."

"Likewise," she responded.

"Meta—Jenkins has someting to tell us 'bout de cross she look for."

"I thought I had calculated the area where the ship *Defiance* went down near St. Helena Sound." Jenks glanced at Seth. "I hired a professional diver to search for any remnants of the ship. He and his wife performed several dives, but all they could find was marine debris."

"It like looking for de needle in de haystack," Ida Mae commented.

"Miss Jenkins, maybe it better dat de treasure stay where it is. It in a place of rest."

"Yes, ma'am."

Meta looked closely at Seth and Jenks. "May I tell you two someting?"

"Yes, ma'am."

"Miss Jenkins, after de first time you come here, I told you I felt de presence of an aura 'bout you. I feels dat same energy round you today, but I feels an almost identical energy from you . . . Mr. Seth. You know live peoples gives off dere own unique energy pattern. Dis is like de energy I sense when I around identical twins."

Seth's face turned pale and he asked, "Miss Meta . . . how could that be possible?"

"De energy in an aura is from de soul of someone who is not at rest. Dey may not have accomplished someting important dat dey's here to finish, or dey may have died violently before dere time. One other reason is—dey's here to protect a live person from harm."

Seth removed his handkerchief from his pants and wiped his brow. Even with the ceiling fan running, the room was warm. He took off his coat and laid it on the settee.

"Let me get you both a glass of ice tea," Ida Mae said.

Seth looked at his watch and said, "I apologize, Miss Ida, Miss Meta, but I told my friend, Rory, that we would be at his house at six."

"Come back when you have more time," Meta said.

"Yes, ma'am."

They walked to the front door together, and Jenks and Seth said their good-byes and started down the steps. They had reached the front walk when

Meta called, "Miss Jenkins, I forgot to tell you someting. Could I speak to you for jus a moment more?"

"Yes, ma'am."

Jenks turned and walked back up the steps. Meta opened the screen door for her, and she stepped back into the foyer.

"I hope I didn't upset your young man. He have a look of shock in his eyes."

"I—I don't know."

"Dere is one more ting I want to share with you. Dere is tremendous energy comin' from de two of you." She smiled a beautiful full smile that showed in her eyes, but said nothing more.

As Jenks descended the front steps, she considered the meaning of Meta's observation.

On the short drive to Rory's house, Seth was silent until Jenks asked, "What are you thinking about?"

"What Meta said about the energy she senses. Her interpretations are disturbing. Did you mention to either of the sisters that I had an identical twin who passed away?"

"No, I didn't."

As they got out of the car at Rory's home, the aroma of garlic and tomato sauce lingered in the air.

"Something smells good," Seth called out as he and Jenks stepped inside the house.

"Lasagna!" Rory exclaimed. He held up the article in the *Beaufort Gazette* that covered the automobile accident on Carteret, where Seth had saved Maggie Reynolds's life. "You're my hero," Rory said with a broad smile.

"Thank you," Seth replied. "Can we help with dinner?"

"You can set the table. Jenks, how are you this evening?"

"I'm well."

They sat down at the table and dined on Rory's lasagna. "This is delicious," Jenks commented.

"I'm so glad you like it," Rory replied. "You know the Beaufort Water Festival is coming up in a few weeks. I'd like to go to talent night."

"Why don't we three plan on attending?" Jenks said.

Seth took his first bite of lasagna and said, "Sounds good to me."

"The start of law school is just around the corner too," Rory commented.

"I'm looking forward to it," said Seth.

Jenks remembered that the start of law school would also mark the time that she would return to Raleigh and start teaching the fall semester. She did not want to leave Seth.

"You know, Jenks, Seth is the darling of every woman's club in Beaufort County."

"What do you mean?"

"I have received excellent support from the community with scholarship funds," Seth admitted.

"You never told me that," Jenks said.

"Now don't get mad, Seth," Rory said as he gestured with his hand toward his friend. "He doesn't like to brag on himself, so I will. He's already been offered a job in the Beaufort County Solicitor's office."

"That's wonderful," Jenks said with a smile.

"The solicitor told me to complete a year of law school, and then I could work part time in their office. I was told that when I pass the bar, I could come on board as a staff attorney."

Jenks squeezed Seth's hand and smiled. "I'm proud of you."

Seth changed the subject. "I found out today that I'm going to be in Columbia for a couple of days for firearms training. I usually attend the class in the fall, but my course has been moved up because of law school."

"When do you leave?" Jenks asked.

"I'm leaving tomorrow, and I'll return Friday afternoon."

"That will give me plenty of time to put the moves on Jenks," Rory said teasingly.

"Nothing doing," Seth said. He put his arm around Jenks and kissed her on the forehead.

"Oh, by the way, Jenks, Seth has a birthday coming up."

"When is your birthday?"

"Next Thursday."

"Why didn't you tell me?"

Seth gave her a shy smile, but remained quiet.

"I want to have both of you over to my house for a birthday dinner!"

"I'll look forward to it, Jenks—thank you," Seth responded.

"I wouldn't miss it," Rory said with a smile.

After they finished eating, they cleaned up the dishes and then played several hands of cards before calling it a night.

As Jenks stood on the outside deck waiting for Seth, she heard Rory say, "I haven't had any nightmares for a couple of weeks. I hope they've stopped."

"I do too, Rory," Seth quietly responded.

They said good night and Seth opened the car door for Jenks and made sure she was comfortably seated before he closed it. They both waved good-bye to Rory, who was sitting in his wheelchair on the deck.

On the way home Jenks said, "I heard Rory mention he suffers from nightmares."

"Yes, he has a recurring nightmare about Sarah Humphries, the young woman who served with him in Afghanistan."

"I'm sorry to hear that."

Not wanting to be nosy, Jenks did not ask what happened in the nightmares. She concluded that Seth would tell her if he thought that further disclosure was proper.

When they arrived at Port Royal, Seth came into the house with Jenks. They began to kiss each other. He disrobed her, and she unbuttoned his shirt as they moved toward the bedroom. Jenks felt a deep ache of desire for him run through her body. They lay down simultaneously on the bed and wrapped their arms around each other. She cried out with pleasure as he made them one again, and she held him close, wrapping herself around him. He was deep within her and he kissed her on her mouth and throat. When he finally relaxed against her, they held each other in breathless exhaustion.

After a period of quietness, Jenks said, "I'm going to miss you while you're away."

"I'll miss you too, but it's just for a couple of days."

She was quiet for a moment. "I don't know what I'm going to do when I have to go back to Raleigh."

"We can see each other on weekends."

"You're going to be working many weekends with the sheriff's department."

"Jenks, we'll make it happen. Please don't worry about our relationship." He raised his head up on his elbow and looked into her eyes. "I love you."

"I want to hear you say it often."

"When I was growing up, I would have never thought myself capable of being close to a beautiful, well-educated lady like you."

"Why do you say that?"

"I thought a lady like you was out of my league."

"That's silly. I think you're wonderful. I meant it when I said you're my hero. I love you too."

He smiled at her. "I have a couple of surprises for you."

"Can you give me a hint?"

"No, but I think you're going to really enjoy yourself."

———

On Thursday, Jenks went to the downtown library to read with the children's group. Amanda Stevens was not present. Jenks read with each child and helped them with the words they had trouble pronouncing. When it was time for the children to adjourn to the playground, she went to the table where Ellen Madison was seated and said, "Amanda Stevens is not here today. Do you know where she is?"

"Her grandmother phoned and said that her car was broken down. She can't bring Amanda until her neighbor has a chance to repair her vehicle."

"Do you think she would allow me to pick Amanda up and bring her to the next session?"

"I'll call her and see if that suits. That's very gracious of you to offer to give her a ride."

"I don't mind at all. When I first started reading with her, she seemed to be shy. We read poetry during the last session. She read well, and then beamed with confidence and satisfaction."

"I'll call you after I speak with her."

Jenks drove to her home in Port Royal when she left the library. The phone was ringing when she opened the front door, and on the line was a real estate agent who wanted to show the house. She explained that she and her client had driven past the house, and they'd like to see the inside. Jenks told them she'd go for a walk, and they could use the lockbox to enter.

She put on a straw hat to shield her from the sun and set off on foot to

Sands Beach. Beads of sweat formed on her forehead and ran down her body. When she reached the beach, she began to hear the Marine Corps trainees at Parris Island practicing firearms proficiency. She listened to the rapid fire of the guns and watched the boat traffic on the Beaufort River. Sitting on the beach, she thought of Seth and how much she loved him. An hour passed, and she believed she had given the real estate agent and her client enough time to look at the house.

On her route back home, Jenks walked through the neighborhood, exploring streets she had never been on before. She was not far from the old shipping terminal when she passed several older cottages. One of the houses was in need of paint and had the look of abandonment. There were a couple of old fabric chairs on the front porch and the screen wire was dark and had numerous tears.

She paused in front of the home. A feeling of overwhelming sadness gripped her as she looked at the aged structure. She also felt as if someone were watching her. Looking around from house to house, Jenks did not see anyone in their yards or sitting on a porch.

Glancing back to the graying, wood-sided dwelling, Jenks's eyes searched the downstairs windows for an onlooker, but no one was there. She noticed the venetian blinds were bent, and some of the blades were missing. As she gazed upward, the feelings of being watched went deeper into her soul, and suddenly she realized the reason for her anxiety.

In an upstairs bedroom window, a young woman with piercing blue eyes and straight golden hair was staring out of the window at her. Jenks felt relieved to see that her intuition was correct, and she smiled and waved to the girl in the window.

The young woman did not return the smile or the wave. Jenks felt an unexplainable sadness as their eyes met. A car was coming in Jenks's direction, and she took her eyes off the girl and stepped into a driveway to stay out of the path of the automobile.

When the car had passed by, Jenks looked back up at the window, but the young woman was no longer there. Cold chills descended upon her as she continued her walk home.

When she reached home, the real estate agent and her client were pulling out of the driveway and they waved to Jenks as they passed by. When she reached the house, the phone was ringing. She quickly unlocked the door and ran to answer it.

Ellen Madison was phoning to tell her that Amanda Stevens's grandmother accepted Jenks's offer to give her granddaughter a ride to the library for the next reading session. Ellen gave her Amanda's address and phone number. The next session would be the following Monday.

That evening, Jenks sat on her screened porch and read from one of Gigi's poetry books. When the phone rang at nine p.m., she dashed to answer it. Seth was on the line, and she was happy to hear his voice.

"I've missed you today," she confessed.

"Yes, I've missed you too. I got most of my requirements out of the way today, so I should be able to leave Columbia by three. Why don't you meet me at the Walker's around six?"

"Sounds good to me."

"I'll look forward to it."

When she hung up the phone, the sounds of the night were all around her. Crickets and cicadas sang out their nighttime melodies. She opened a bottle of wine and sat on the porch thinking of Gigi. She missed her terribly. The thought of Frank Hiller drowning her sister brought anger and thoughts of revenge, but there was no way to prove that he had caused her any harm.

Her thoughts then went to Seth and the love she felt for him. She didn't want to leave him and return to Raleigh. Taking another sip of her wine, she rose from the wicker couch and went into her bedroom to lie down.

She rested her head against the pillow and thought of Gigi once again. Meta Andrews's advice went through her mind: look closer. *But at what?* She pulled the sheet up over her chest and closed her eyes.

———

Jenks was surrounded by darkness. She could hear her sister telling her to wake up. Suddenly, Gigi was standing before her. A deep frown was etched in her brow.

Jenks sat up on her bed. She stared at the place at the foot of the bed where her sister had been standing, but Gigi was no longer present. Jenks looked at the clock on the nightstand. It was three-thirty in the morning. She wiped perspiration from her forehead, and then she heard what she thought were faint footfalls on the hardwood floors.

Picking up her flashlight, she quietly walked into the living room and turned on the outside floodlights. The eight-day clock on the mantle chimed the half hour. She sat down on the living room couch and listened for noises. There were only the night sounds of the crickets. She returned to her bed, but had difficulty falling asleep again.

———

Seth returned from Columbia Friday afternoon, and they spent the late afternoon fishing on the Chechessee River. They stayed on the river until twilight, and then grilled their catch of redfish over a charcoal fire on the grill at the back of the Walker's house.

As they sat down to eat, a distant rumble of thunder sounded to the west.

"How did the firearms training go?"

"It's always good to have a refresher course, and I passed the proficiency test."

"I'd like for you to teach me how to shoot a handgun."

A frown crossed his brow. "Is there something wrong?"

"Several times now I've heard walking in the middle of the night at Gigi's, and a few times I've seen shadows. When I investigate, there's no one there."

The ceiling fan in the kitchen rotated slowly sending a light breeze through the kitchen. Lightning flashes appeared in the windows, followed by the rumblings of thunder.

Seth took her hand. "Why haven't you mentioned this to me before?"

"It's just happened lately."

"I don't want you to ever be frightened. You can stay here with me . . . or I could stay with you several nights in a row to see if we hear anything."

"Thank you. I've wondered if I've been dreaming the walking sounds."

"That's a possibility. I've heard noises in my sleep before that I thought were very real. When I awakened, I discovered the sounds were just part of my dream."

Another flash of lightning illuminated the nighttime sky, followed by a rumble of thunder.

"I had a very odd experience today," Jenks said shaking her head.

"Tell me about it."

"A real estate agent came to show Gigi's house, and I walked to Sands Beach. On my way back, I walked on some streets I had never been on before. I started to have this strange feeling that someone was watching me. I was in front of a house that looked abandoned, and I saw a young woman in an upstairs window looking down at me. I smiled and waved at her, but she did not respond. She only looked at me with such a sad expression."

"What did she look like?"

"She was lovely, with bright blue eyes and straight blonde hair."

"There must have been something troubling her for her not to respond."

Jenks reflected on the experience for just a moment and said, "I bet you're right. I feel badly for her, whoever she is."

Seth rose from his seat and, taking Jenks by the hand, he pulled her up, into his arms. "Let's not talk of sadness anymore tonight." He started a CD player, and they danced slowly to piano jazz in each other's arms. "Bill Evans?"

"Yes, ma'am," he whispered in her ear.

As they held each other, Seth kissed her on the mouth. Jenks could feel her body begin to ache with desire for him, and she whispered back, "Please—I want you."

He lifted her in his arms and carried her into his bedroom.

After making love, Seth gently whispered, "I want to show you a special place in the morning. We'll need to wake early, and get there before the day becomes too hot.

"Is this my surprise?"

"One of them."

"Please give me a clue?"

"You're going to taste something wonderful," he said as he gently stroked her face with his fingertips. Outside, rain was falling, accompanied by occasional thunder. Lulled by the sounds of the storm, Jenks wrapped her arms around him and fell asleep.

———

By six a.m., Seth had prepared a large breakfast for the two of them. She could smell the delicious aroma of bacon when he gently woke her. Pulling her up from the bed, he helped her put on her robe.

"Okay sleepy girl, this way," he said as he steered her toward the kitchen. "We're going to work very hard this morning, so I want you to have plenty to eat." She felt hungry and ate all her breakfast.

After cleaning the dishes, Seth gave her a bottle of insect repellant and told her to be liberal with the application. They both put on blue jeans, and Seth gave her a pail.

"What am I going to need this for?"

"You'll see. Let's head to the path behind the house that leads into the woods."

In the field, near the overseer's cabin, was a large blackberry patch with very ripe fruit. Seth started to pick the fruit, placing the blackberries in his pail.

"Have you ever picked blackberries before?"

"When I was a little girl," she responded.

"Watch the thorns on the bush."

"Yes, sir."

They stood side by side and picked the berries for over thirty minutes. Seth quietly whispered to her, "Look to your right, but make gentle movements."

Jenks turned her head slowly, and standing about ten feet away from them was a doe that was feasting on the berries. The deer glanced in their direction and then continued to eat.

"Looks like someone's having breakfast. I suppose the blackberries taste better than the usual diet of acorns and fresh shoots of plant growth," Seth softly said.

"It's nice of her to share with us," Jenks whispered back.

The doe continued to eat the fruit, and after another fifteen minutes, she walked away in the direction of the overseer's house.

"I can't believe I just saw that," Jenks told Seth.

He smiled at her and continued to pick the berries. When his pail was full, he assisted Jenks until both containers were full.

"Are you ready to make blackberry jam?" he asked.

"Yes, sir."

The rest of the morning was spent making jam and canning the cooked blackberries. By the time they finished, they had made twenty jars of jam, and they smiled at each other in satisfaction.

When the work in the kitchen was complete, Seth said, "Now are you ready for the second part of my surprise?"

"Yes, what is it?"

"Hale Branson said he would take you flying this afternoon. He said for us to meet him at Frogmore International at two."

A feeling of exuberance coursed through her body. She smiled broadly and responded, "Really! That's so exciting. Frogmore International?"

"Remember? That's the old nickname for the Beaufort County Airport. A lot of the locals still call the airport by that name."

Jenks ran to Seth and flung her arms around him. "Thank you for arranging this. Aren't you going up with us?"

"I don't think so. He said he was going to show you what flying was all about, so I expect he'll be taking you up in one of his acrobatic airplanes, which are two seaters."

"Wow, I'm thrilled! I'm ready to go whenever you are."

"All right, young lady, after you," Seth said as he opened the back door in the kitchen for her.

On their drive to Lady's Island, they passed Hiller's Barbells. A large Sold sign was mounted across the top of the For Sale sign.

"It looks like Frank has had success in selling his business."

"Amazing . . . and Gigi's house has only had a few showings."

———

Seth parked his truck in front of a hangar at the Beaufort County Airport. He came to Jenks's side of the vehicle and opened the door for her. Together, they walked in the direction of a side entrance to the building.

Seth knocked, and within a few moments Hale Branson opened the door, greeted them, and invited them inside. The two men began to converse, and Jenks took the time to look around the hangar. Brightly lit with fluorescent lamps, the concrete floor of the hangar was painted gray and appeared polished to perfection. There were several handsome aircraft inside the building; the paint on the airplanes gleamed brightly. Her eye focused on a cherry-red biplane that had a rear tail wheel.

At a pause in the men's conversation, Jenks turned to Hale, "Thank you for offering to take me flying this afternoon."

"Yes, ma'am, I'm glad to do it," he responded.

"All your airplanes are beautiful. What type of aircraft are they?"

"Let's start over here." He led them to a polished red-and-white airplane that had a tail painted like the beams of the rising sun. "This is a Citabria. I fly this airplane in a number of aerobatic competitions in the United States. If you spell Citabria backwards, it spells airbatic."

He ran his hand along the side of the fuselage, and then led Seth and Jenks to the biplane that had caught her eye when they entered the hangar. "This is a Pitts Special. The aircraft was designed by Curtis Pitts and got the nickname Stinker because Pitts put the drawing of a skunk on some of his early designs. Many pilots believe that the Pitts Special is the ultimate aerobatic aircraft for competition."

"Wow, this biplane is gorgeous! This is the airplane you were flying the day you flew near the Walker's property!" Jenks exclaimed.

"Yes, ma'am," he replied.

They looked at a third aircraft that Hale explained was an Aeronca Champ, and lastly at a sleek plane that he said was a Mooney 231 and used for cross-country travel.

"Which airplane are we going up in?" Jenks asked.

"I'm going to take you flying in the Citabria."

Hale raised the hangar door and then went to a wall phone and placed a call. Within a few minutes, two young men wearing mechanic's suits arrived in front of the hangar with a tug and pulled the Citabria out onto the tarmac. Hale thanked them for their assistance, and then Jenks and Seth watched him preflight the airplane. He checked the oil and then ran his hand down the sides of the propeller. Jenks was offered the back seat in the airplane.

Suddenly feeling nervous, she said, "Now, remember, I've never been up in a light airplane before. Please don't do any scary maneuvers."

Hale smiled back at her; his handlebar mustache seemed to curl on the ends. "I'll tell you a saying that I heard when I was learning to fly airplanes. My flight instructor always said, 'There are old pilots and there are bold pilots, but there are no old, bold pilots.'"

He smiled again, and then Seth and Hale helped her into the airplane, fastening her seat belt and shoulder harness. Hale handed her a headset with a mike and then demonstrated how they could hear and talk to one another. After the engine was started, Hale taxied out to a place on the tarmac that he called the runup area and did mechanical checks on the engine. When this was complete, he taxied the airplane out to the runway and announced his intentions to take off on Runway 25.

"Here we go," he said through the headset.

Jenks felt butterflies in her stomach as he applied power to the engine. Rolling down the runway, the airplane took flight in a short amount of time.

She gripped the handles of the seat as the airplane went airborne. Looking over the side of the plane, Jenks marveled at the waterways and marshes, which shimmered in the sunlight. She noticed the town of Beaufort on the right side of the airplane; the structures appearing to diminish in size as the aircraft ascended.

Hale placed a radio call to the controllers at the Beaufort Marine Station. Jenks listened as he told them his intentions and the controller responded that the Beaufort Military Operations Area was *not hot*. After he finished speaking with the controller, Hale explained through the headset that not hot meant there were no military aircraft operating in the practice area. He then said in a reassuring voice, "I promise to be gentle, but it's time to have some fun."

They flew to an area where waterways were underneath them, and then Hale began to do a series of dives, pulling up into a sharp bank above the marsh. With each one, Jenks felt exhilarated, like she was on a rollercoaster.

"Hang on now," he exclaimed before he executed a barrel roll above the waterway.

"Wow, that was outstanding," she told him as they completed the maneuver.

After he finished the aerobatics he had planned, they flew along the coastline. She recognized the lighthouse at Hunting Island State Park, and sunbathers on the beach waved to them as they went past.

When the flight was over, Hale landed the airplane on the runway they had departed on. She felt the right gear touch down first, followed by the left, and then the tail wheel. She still had butterflies in her stomach from the excitement she felt during the flight. Hale taxied the Citabria to the tarmac in front of his hangar, and Jenks saw Seth standing near the building with a smile on his face. He came to the airplane, helped her dismount, and then put his arm around her.

"Did you have a good time?"

"Fabulous!"

"I knew you would," he said as he kissed her on the forehead. His hand went to her back, which was damp.

"Do I detect a bit of perspiration? I hope not from nervousness."

"I was just so excited!" She turned and faced Hale. "I had a wonderful time. Thank you for taking me flying."

"It was my pleasure," he said with a broad smile. "We'll go again sometime."

CHAPTER 11

Twenty Orchid Avenue

*O*n Monday, Jenks drove to Amanda Stevens's residence to pick her up for the Beaufort Library's summer reading program. Amanda's grandmother lived on St. Helena Island, and Jenks found the property in a secluded area along a marsh. The view across the waterway was pristine. A tidal creek ran along the perimeter of the land, and cord grass and pluff mud stretched to a distant bank.

In the yard were old pieces of machinery; an aged motorboat lay partially on its side, and an old seventies Plymouth was sitting on concrete blocks. The yard was full of plastic planters, and a small tomato garden was to one side of a frame house painted a bright shade of blue. Chickens were roaming around the yard, pecking at the ground for food. A large red-and-orange rooster crowed.

When Amanda saw Jenks pull up at the front of the home, she dashed out of the screen door with a beaming smile on her face.

"Miss Jenkins, I appreciate your coming to get me."

"You're welcome," Jenks replied with a smile.

Amanda's grandmother came outside, followed by two small boys who were holding toy cars. "Miss Ellington, it sure is nice of you to come and get Amanda. She hate that she miss the last meeting at the library. I'm Ella Robinson."

Jenks shook her hand. "I'm glad that I could help. Amanda's doing such a good job on her reading."

"She sure do enjoy it."

"I'll have her back here before noon," Jenks commented.

"When you come back, it would give us great pleasure if you'd stay with us for lunch."

"Yes, ma'am, thank you. I'll look forward to it."

Amanda sat in the rear of Jenks's Jeep, and they started the drive to Beaufort.

"Who are the little boys that are staying with your grandmother?"

"They's my little brothers, Samuel and Harry."

"Do you three live with your grandmother?"

"Yes um, my mama works in Hilton Head at a hotel, and my daddy don't live with us. She has to get up real early to get to work, so my Grammie takes care of us."

The morning was getting warm and Jenks and Amanda rolled down the windows, allowing the air to blow through the vehicle. As they crossed the marshlands, the smell of the sea and pluff mud entered the car. Jenks breathed deeply, taking in the salty smells of the coast.

When they reached the library, the children picked out books to read. After they had been given time to read, each student picked a passage to read to their group. Amanda had chosen *Kidnapped*.

"Amanda, I believe you're a Robert Louis Stevenson fan."

"Yes, ma'am," she beamed.

Starting her passage, Amanda read, "The sun began to shine upon the summit of the hills as I went down the road . . ."

When her reading was complete, she smiled at Jenks and the other children and took her seat. Every child read a passage, and Jenks helped them with pronunciations when they needed assistance.

By noon, Jenks and Amanda returned to the home of Ella Robinson. The day had become very warm with high humidity, and Jenks felt perspiration run down the back of her shirt. When they pulled up in the yard, Amanda's grandmother opened the screen door and yelled out, "Lunch is ready. Y'all come on in here and have a seat."

Jenks and Amanda entered the house through the kitchen door and the screen closed with a bang as it shut behind them. A ceiling fan briskly rotated in the room and a feast of black-eyed peas, cornbread, sliced tomatoes, and fried shrimp was on the table.

"Thank you for inviting me to join you," Jenks said. "This looks wonderful!"

Mrs. Robinson smiled broadly. "Oh yes, ma'am, Amanda says you been real nice to her, and we's glad to have you join us. Please, everyone have a seat, and let's join hands in prayer."

Amanda's grandmother blessed the food, and when she finished, the children started passing the serving bowls around.

"Miss Jenkins, I's sorry 'bout your sister. I read 'bout it in the newspaper when she passed."

"Mrs. Robinson, thank you."

"Amanda, please pass the peas, honey," her grandmother said. "Are you planning to stay here, Miss Ellington?"

"Please call me Jenks . . . I'd like to stay here, but I have a teaching job in Cary, North Carolina, to return to next month."

"Honey, if you want to stay here, I'd find a way to do it. Life is too short to be unhappy. You is right 'bout your job though . . . if you got a job is best to hang on to it. There's lots of folks that's unemployed right now."

"Yes, ma'am."

During the meal, the children were quiet and well behaved. When Jenks looked up from her plate, the two little boys would be looking at her. She would smile at them, and then they'd smile back.

When the meal was finished, Jenks thanked Mrs. Robinson for the delicious meal and offered to help her clean up.

"Oh no, Miss Jenks, I'll take care of this after a while . . . I think you inspire Amanda to read. My gran's got someting to show you."

"We have to go outside," Amanda said with a smile.

Amanda and her two little brothers led Jenks toward the tidal creek. The tide was going out and the children went to a wagon and removed sailboats made from bottles and Popsicle sticks. Inside the bottles were rolled up pieces of paper. Amanda removed the cork from one of the bottles and the note slid out.

"This is the poem I read by Robert Louis Stevenson, 'Where Go the Boats?' I wrote my address after the poem so that when someone else finds the boat they can write me. 'Other little children shall bring my boats ashore,'" she said with a smile.

"Amanda, I think this is wonderful," Jenks told her.

"I helped my little brothers with their poems. We wanted to launch them with you."

Jenks smiled as the children took their bottle boats and went to the end of a weathered dock. The children placed their boats in the water, which were quickly caught in a current that took them out to the river.

The foursome watched the bottle boats until they disappeared from view.

———

When Jenks returned to Port Royal, she decided to drive past the house where she had seen the young woman's face in the window several days before. She arrived at the house and saw the screen door was standing open.

Jenks parked her Jeep in the driveway and gazed at the home's deteriorated condition. The screens sagged on the windows, and the wooden siding was in a state of decay. Looking up to the window where she had seen the girl, she saw only a dark background. She thought of her and wondered if she was all right.

From the girl's appearance, Jenks had concluded she was probably in her late teens or early twenties. They could not be very far apart in age, and she thought she could invite the young woman over for refreshments and conversation.

Jenks got out of her Jeep and walked toward the porch. The yard had been mowed, but there were signs that the landscaping was simply being maintained, not properly tended. Weeds proliferated in the daylily beds, and numerous fire-ant mounds were around the foundation of the home.

She carefully walked up the pathway to the house and entered the screen porch. Looking inside the home through the window on the front door, she recoiled and drew a deep breath. To her astonishment, the home was completely empty of furniture. A strong wind came off the river and caught the screen door slamming it shut. She flinched as the noise startled her.

Jenks walked to the door and, examining the latch, realized it was broken. Suddenly, feeling very uncomfortable, she descended the steps and returned to her vehicle.

Without stopping again, Jenks returned to her home, parking the Jeep in the driveway. As she closed the car door, David Bernstein called to her from next door.

"Leah has just made some lemonade. Please join us for a glass."

She felt perspiration trickle down her back. "Yes, I'd love to. It's another warm day."

The Bernsteins rose from their seats as Jenks came up on their front porch. Leah poured her a tall glass of lemonade from a pitcher.

"Have a chair," David offered.

The Bernsteins had a handsome collection of antique wicker furniture on their front porch, and Jenks sat down in a rocker with a chintz fabric cushion.

"Does it ever cool down here?"

"Not until October, and then the days can still be warm. Any interest in Gigi's house?"

"No, I'm afraid we've had very few showings."

"Until the foreclosure epidemic is over in this country, there will be no recovery in the real estate market," David declared.

"I suppose it doesn't help that Gigi's home was broken into recently. If someone was really interested, that could scare them."

"Let's hope not," Leah added.

Jenks rested her head back on the chair and looked up at a ceiling fan that was rapidly rotating above her, sending cooling breezes across the porch.

She sipped her lemonade and then said, "The other day I walked past a house that's a couple of blocks from here on Orchid Avenue. The house is vacant, but there was a young woman staring at me from an upstairs window."

The Bernsteins looked cautiously at one another, and then David asked, "Twenty Orchid Avenue?"

"Yes, sir, how did you know that?"

"Did the girl have long blonde hair and piercing blue eyes?"

A cold shiver ran up Jenks's spine, and she sat forward in her chair. "Yes, how did you know?"

"I believe I have an explanation for the young woman you saw. Her name was Helena Pierce."

"I don't understand what you mean."

"Jenkins—Helena Pierce was murdered in that house in the mid-1950s."

"What?"

"Dear, you're not the first person to see her. She was home alone one evening. Her parents had gone to a movie and someone broke into their house and killed Helena. The killer was never caught. She was just eighteen years old."

"Oh, my God," Jenks said as she rocked forward in her chair.

"She must have been reaching out to you," Leah said.

Jenks was stunned by this information. White-knuckled, she gripped the arms of her rocking chair. "Who owns the house?"

"Helena's cousin, who lives in Maryland. He tried to sell it a few years ago, but was unsuccessful."

"I can understand why," Jenks responded. As she talked with the Bernsteins, one thought would not leave her: Helena Pierce was not at rest because her murderer was never brought to justice. She thought of Gigi and a feeling of dread went deep into her soul.

CHAPTER 12

The Water Festival

*T*hat evening, Seth came to Jenks's home at dusk. So that it would not be apparent that he was spending the night, he parked his car on another street and walked to her home. Concerned about the footsteps that Jenks had heard during the night, Seth had decided to stay with her for several evenings. When he arrived, he pulled Jenks down onto the living room couch and held her in his arms. He lightly touched her face, but his face showed a frown.

"What's wrong?" Jenks inquired.

"You'll read about this in tomorrow's newspaper. This swindler, Robert Mathis, has been posing as a social worker, preying upon vulnerable adults. He would go through veterans' care facilities, looking for tenants to place in his group homes. Jenks, I went into these homes today, and the conditions were squalid. Several of the residents in the group homes suffer from schizophrenia and were not receiving their medications."

"Oh, my," Jenks said.

"Mr. Mathis was having their veteran's and Social Security benefits redirected to himself. Several of the adults were taken to the local hospital for treatment. What a sorry son of a—" He stopped speaking for a moment, but then continued. "When you see horrible situations like this, it makes police work difficult. The houses were filled with trash and rats."

"That's terrible. Why do some people treat others so badly? It just makes no sense."

"Greed," Seth said.

"Unfortunately, I suppose so."

"Robert Mathis should be put *under* the jail," Seth added.

They sat quietly for several moments before Jenks said, "I have something very strange to tell you."

"Go on."

"I told the Bernsteins about the young woman that I saw looking out the window at me with the sad eyes. They said that I saw the apparition of Helena Pierce. She was murdered in a house on Orchid Avenue years ago."

"I didn't realize that you were talking about the Pierce home. I've heard that story as well. Her killer was never apprehended."

"Do you think that's why she doesn't rest?"

"I can't answer that." Their eyes locked. "There are other hauntings—we can be vividly haunted by our memories."

"Seth—"

"Shhh . . . are you thinking about Gigi?"

"Yes, I am. I'm worried that she can't rest."

"Come here," he said as he pulled her even closer against him. He kissed her on the forehead and said, "With your hearing footsteps in this house at night, and now thinking you're seeing ghosts, you're going to scare yourself to death."

"I promise I did see a young woman in the window."

"I believe you. Come on, I'm getting you to bed."

He took her by the hand and led her to the bedroom. Stopping just inside the doorway, he kissed her fervently on the mouth. "I want to protect you, and I intend to take your mind off things that frighten you." He pulled her down onto the bed and stroked her face and neck. While disrobing her, he kissed her all over her body. The feeling was exquisite, and she moaned with excitement as he caressed her into ecstasy.

———

During the night, there were no noises that disturbed her. She was comforted by Seth as she rested in his strong arms, and when she woke in the morning, she was snuggled against him. She opened her eyes to find that he was looking at her.

"Good morning, beautiful," he said. He pushed her hair back and kissed her on the lips. "There were no noises last night."

"I didn't hear anything either."

"I'll stay here a few more nights, and then you can come to the Walker's."

"Don't forget about Thursday. I'm going to make you a cake and a birthday dinner. Rory is going to join us."

His lips turned up into a smile, and then both of them were quiet until Jenks said, "I'm going to stop by the local school district office and check on a teaching position in Beaufort County."

"That's a good idea."

His arms went around her, and she looked at the new scar on his left forearm, caused by broken glass when he saved Maggie Reynolds's life.

Later that day, Jenks went by the school district office and spoke with the administrator, David Simpson. He informed her there were no open teaching positions, but he asked her to fill out a job application, which she did. Before she left, he told her that if she was to remain in Beaufort for the fall, she could count on being a substitute teacher. There was always a need for temporary help.

For the next two nights, Seth stayed the night with Jenks, but there were no nocturnal noises, and she slept peacefully in his arms.

On Thursday, she spent the morning making a German chocolate cake for Seth's birthday. She carefully frosted the cake until she thought it was perfect, licking the spoon with satisfaction after the final touches.

At six, Seth and Rory arrived at the same time and Jenks opened beer for her guests. "That's good," Rory commented as he took a drink of Budweiser. They went to the patio, and Seth helped her grill three steaks before the threesome sat down to dine.

Rory raised his beer in a toast. "Here's to my hero and friend, Seth Mason. Happy birthday and many more!"

They clinked their beers together, and Seth laughed slightly, looking amused.

"What is it?"

"In tomorrow's *Beaufort Gazette*, there will be an article about a case we worked that is now closed."

"Go on," Rory said with interest.

"This guy, Jay Taylor, has been having an affair with another man's wife. Jay Taylor also happens to be married. His married lover is named Mabel Larsen."

"Oh, my," Jenks replied.

"Well, Mr. Larsen happened to come home from work unexpectedly and caught his wife with Jay Taylor. Mr. Larsen threatened him with bodily harm, and Jay Taylor jumped out of a second-story window to get away."

"My goodness," Jenks blushed.

"In his haste, Jay Taylor forgot his wallet and his wedding band. Mr. Larsen took the items to Jay Taylor's wife and told her that her husband had been visiting with his wife and had forgotten some things. He handed her his wallet and ring."

"Oops," Rory said with a laugh.

"Needless to say, Jay Taylor's wife, Emily, didn't handle that information too well, and she threw all of Jay's clothes onto the lawn. When he got home, Emily threatened to shoot him, and a neighbor called the police. When we arrived, she had put the gun away, and her husband was hiding in a neighbor's garage."

"Now—that's what I call leaving evidence behind," Jenks laughed.

Seth opened his presents: a Columbia fishing shirt from Jenks, and a fly rod from Rory. "Happy Birthday" was sung, followed by blowing out the candles and cutting the cake. When the party was over, Rory wished Seth and Jenks a good night and left for St. Helena. The two of them sat together on the screened porch in the darkness, and Seth took Jenks in his arms.

"Thank you for the wonderful birthday party, and Jenks—I greatly appreciate your making me a birthday cake."

"You're quite welcome. It was my pleasure. Was this the first time anyone made you a German chocolate cake?"

He held her hand tightly and whispered, "This is the first time in my life that anyone made me a birthday cake."

"Oh, baby," she said, kissing him on the face as they held each other tightly in the darkness.

———

Seth left her to go to work early the next morning. Jenks planned to spend the day at the Walker property, picking blackberries and sunbathing on their dock. She arrived at the Walker property a little after nine.

Dew was still on the grass and shrubbery when Jenks set off on the path to the blackberry patch. She had collected a pail and a bottle of water from the Walker's kitchen before beginning her hike through the woods.

A red-tailed hawk cried out above her in the treetops. When she glanced up, the massive bird was looking at her. The hawk flew down to a lower perch along the pathway, still observing her. Jenks's gaze met with the hawk's, and they stared at one another as she passed by, continuing toward the meadow.

When she reached the clearing, she could see the cabin in the distance. The morning sun reflected off the metal roof and the glare hurt her eyes as she gazed across the meadow. Her blue jeans and running shoes were wet from dew. Sweat was beading up on her forehead and running down her back.

At the midway point in the meadow, there was a sound like a grunting noise. She stopped in her tracks and listened. The noise was growing louder, and she looked in the direction of the higher grass that was to the right of the pathway.

About thirty feet away, a black boar with tusks that appeared to be about a foot long came into view. She froze. To her horror, several of the creatures emerged from the grass. The black hog that was the leader of the group clawed the ground with its front paws. Suddenly, the beast lowered its head, snorted, and charged in her direction. She threw her water bottle at the hog, striking the animal in the head, but it was undeterred and pursued her.

With all her strength, Jenks ran in the direction of the cabin. There was less than a hundred feet to go. She could hear the grunts of the beast as it chased her through the meadow. During the sprint for the cabin, she dropped her pail but could only focus on the cabin's door. *Please don't let the door be locked.*

When she reached the building, she was out of breath, but she quickly lifted the latch on the door and pushed her way inside. As she turned, the black beast was only several feet behind her. She slammed the door and forced down the latch. Jenks leaned against the door to further secure it. Above her own struggled gasps for air, she could hear the labored breathing of the wild boar just outside the door. A stench pervaded the air in the cabin, and she concluded the foul odor was the breath of the black hog.

Dust particles stirred by the slamming of the door were illuminated in a shaft of light as they floated in the air inside the cabin. Going to the nearest window, she opened the shutters. Several of the beasts were outside the cabin. She put her back against the wall, slid down, and sat in an attempt to catch her breath and calm herself.

Joseph Andrews's Civil War journals came into her mind. He had written an account of wild hogs coming out of the swamps and killing the pet cats of the Andrews family. Even though she was overheated from her run, cold chills enveloped her as she thought of his recordings. She remembered that Joseph had taken a sickle and had slain the beasts as they menaced the farmyard.

Hanging on the wall of the cabin were an ancient pickax and a shovel. She considered returning to the outside and attacking the boar with the pickax, but her mind raced to stories she had heard about these creatures in the past. *Wild hogs will cut a man to pieces.*

She remained seated on the floor of the cabin and tried not to think of her thirst. When Seth came home and could not find her, surely he would look for her. *Why didn't I bring my cell phone?*

She waited—the snorts and grunts of the hogs continued just outside the cabin. By two in the afternoon, she was so thirsty that it felt like her tongue was sticking to the roof of her mouth. The day had turned out to be extremely humid, and the temperature inside the cabin was oppressive. She had not heard the grunts of the hogs for a half hour or so. Despite feeling weak, she slowly rose from the floor and went to the windows, looking out in every direction. There was no sign of the wild hogs. Hopefully, they had gone back into the woods during the heat of the day. She slowly lifted the latch to the cabin door and descended the steps. As she reached the ground level, she heard the snort of one of the hogs and watched the beasts scurry out from a hole in the stone foundation wall of the cabin. Jenks realized that the hogs were taking refuge from the heat underneath the cabin, and she hastily retreated back inside.

Hours passed, and at times she thought of Gigi. She missed her sister and felt bitterness over her loss. Her mind traveled to thoughts of Joseph Andrews's description of the beasts that had come from the swamps: ". . . When they snarl at me, they look like the devil." Because she was completely dehydrated, tears would not even form in her eyes. "Seth, please come for me," she said in a whisper.

There were loud bangs and Jenks thought that a thunderstorm must be approaching the Walker property. She woke from an anxious sleep and glanced at her watch; it was now late afternoon. As she looked in the direction of the doorway, the latch lifted, and Seth was there.

He quickly came to her and lifted her in his arms. "Jenks, what happened?"

"I was going to pick blackberries, but wild hogs chased me. Thank God for the cabin or they might have cut me to pieces. I'm so thirsty."

"I have water in the truck."

He carried her down the steps of the cabin and walked toward his truck, which was about twenty feet away. On the grounds surrounding the cabin were the carcasses of the wild hogs. The first animal she saw was the black boar that had pursued her with a vengeance. Seth had shot them all.

"I'll call Ambrose Gould. He'll collect the hogs and not allow the meat to go to waste."

He opened the truck door and helped her inside. Jenks grabbed the water and drank ravenously.

"Slow down now. You're going to make yourself sick if you drink too fast," Seth told her as he pulled the bottle back from her lips, forcing her to slow her pace.

She did as he instructed.

When they got to the Walker's home, Seth helped rehydrate her by giving her glasses of water. He had suggested she lay on the couch, and he put a cool washcloth on her forehead.

"Thank you for taking care of me. I kept praying that you would come and find me." *Praying for the one I love the most to find me.*

"I'm sorry you spent the day in the heat."

"When I was in the cabin I couldn't get my mind off an account in Joseph Andrews's journal."

"Please tell me about it."

"Joseph recorded a story about wild hogs coming out of the swamps near the Andrews's property. The beasts killed the family cat and her kittens. Their bodies were strewn all over the barnyard."

He squeezed her gently and said, "Nature is in a constant state of change. Even in a place of natural beauty, like this property, there can be dangers. We were recently at the cabin, and there was no sign of the hogs. If you walk this land alone, I want you to be prepared in the future. I'm going to see that you have protection."

⌐⌐⌐⌐⌐⌐

The next morning while the temperatures were still cool, Seth drove Jenks into town to a gun shop, Oakley's. In the rear of the building were lanes designated for target practice. The man who was running the lanes nodded to Seth as soon as he saw him. "Detective Mason, good morning. What brings you to Oakley's?"

"Jerry, Miss Ellington is going to learn how to shoot a firearm this morning."

"Good, do you have a gun?"

"No, I was hoping that she could use one of your Lady Smiths for practice."

"Yes, sir. Good morning, Miss Ellington."

"Good morning," she replied.

"You've chosen a good instructor," Jerry said as he rose from his seat and went to a storage compartment on a nearby wall. Unlocking it, he removed a revolver and then opened the cylinder to check the chambers, which he verified were empty. He handed the gun handle-first to Seth and then went back to his desk, bringing out two boxes. "These are reloads. They're easier to fire than new cartridges. You'll appreciate that after you fire the revolver a number of times," he said to Jenks as he handed her the boxes. "Please use lane eight."

Seth picked out a target and then handed Jenks ear protection and shooting glasses before they entered the lanes. He placed eye and ear protection on himself and held the door to the shooting lanes open for her.

For the next hour, he instructed her on firearm usage, and she practiced shooting at the target. Jenks found that her hand was becoming sore from firing the weapon.

When she finished shooting the two boxes of reloads, Seth used a toggle switch to bring the target to their position. He removed it from the metal hanger, and they exited the firing lanes. Once outside, they removed their eye and ear protection and looked at the target. Jenks had filled the target with holes, and Seth pointed out that she was prone to shoot a little to the left, but they'd work on that the next time.

Before they left Oakley's, Jenks purchased a Lady Smith revolver. "You can keep it in your glove compartment," Seth told her. "But when you're alone on the Walker property, you can wear it on your belt with a holster. I don't want you walking the land ever again without protection," he said emphatically.

⸻

The Beaufort County Water Festival began the second week of July. Many of the festival activities were held at Beaufort's Waterfront Park, and on the evening of the talent competition, Jenks and Seth accompanied Rory to the event. They found a parking place on Charles Street not far from Waterfront Park. The downtown was bustling with people who had come to see the performances. Seth helped Rory to a place in the park where he could view the acts in his wheelchair before setting up lawn chairs for Jenks and himself.

"I've been looking forward to this. Last year, a young lady with a powerful soprano voice, like Mariah Carey, won the competition," Rory commented. The event began, and the first two performers were singers. One of the contestants chanted out a rap song, and Jenks looked at Seth and then at Rory. She noticed both men frown during the performance. When the man finished his act, they clapped for him, but Jenks said to Rory, "I take it you don't care for rap music."

Rory chuckled. "No—not in this lifetime."

The next performer was a tall blonde girl with her hair swept to the side. She sang a ballad that she had written herself, and her voice was deep and mellow. Jenks listened to the lyrics of the song and realized the woman was singing about the loss of a loved one in Afghanistan. The words to her melancholy ballad rang out through the park. When she completed the song, there was loud applause. Jenks looked at Rory whose face had turned pale. Seth noticed his demeanor as well and came close to him to find out what was wrong.

"Are you all right?"

Rory looked at him and tears were beginning to well in his eyes. "Her singing reminded me of someone."

"Do you want to go home?" Seth asked.

"Yes."

On the way back to the van, Rory was silent. Seth tried to engage him in conversation, but finally stopped when he realized his friend wanted to be quiet. They drove to St. Helena, and when they got on Land's End Road, there was a light in the distance. It was like a lantern light floating down the roadway. When they reached the area where the light had been flickering, there was darkness. The only lights along the country road were the headlights from the van.

Seth slowed the van and they looked in all directions for the source of the light. "What was that?" Jenks exclaimed.

Jenks felt an icy feeling descend upon her, but no one commented on the light or its origin.

They continued on to Rory's home in silence, and Jenks could still feel chills from seeing the lamp. When they reached his house, Seth helped him inside, and Jenks joined them in the kitchen. Rory retrieved a beer from the refrigerator, and she could see that he was in tears.

"I don't think you should have that," Seth said.

"Dammit, Seth, mind your own business!"

He drank from the beer. "That girl who sang the ballad, she looked just like Sarah Humphries. Even sounded like her." He reached for her photo on the wall and pulled it down into his hands.

"The girl who died in Afghanistan?" Jenks asked.

Rory took another drink of beer and then wiped tears from his eyes. His face darkened. "She was a wonderful person," he said, looking at her photo. A deep frown crossed his brow. "She killed herself over there."

Jenks looked at Seth and their eyes locked. She could see the worried look on his face.

Seth stepped to Rory, patted him on the back, and then knelt down beside him.

Rory looked intently at him with a grim expression. "I could have stopped it, and I didn't."

"You could not control Sarah's actions," Seth told him.

"I'm not talking about her suicide. I'm talking about the bastards who drove her to it."

Seth frowned and said, "What are you talking about, Rory?"

"She was with our unit to act as a liaison with the residents of Afghan villages. Sarah gave them medical advice and helped them get to doctors if they needed assistance. She had such a good heart. I can still hear her voice. She sang to the children. They would crowd around her and listen to her beautiful voice." He took another drink of beer and continued. "Those two bastards, I heard them talking. I should have stopped them. They raped her. Miles Fisher and David Ross—they're both rotting in hell now. They were in the Humvee with me the day I lost my legs. Both of them were blown straight to Hades, and I should have gone with them." He looked into Seth's eyes as tears rolled down his face.

Jenks sat down in the chair, shocked by what she had learned.

"Dear God . . . Rory, I'm sorry," Seth told him.

"She should have gone to our commanding officer, Major Collins, but she told me she was too ashamed. Don't you see? I should have seen him on her behalf. She didn't feel like she had anyone to turn to, but she came to me, and I didn't have the courage to stand up for her." He stared down at his hands and a looked of desolation descended upon his countenance. "She felt trapped—we should have been looking out for each other—we're our own worst enemies," he said as he sobbed.

Seth put his arm around his friend and held him while Rory wept. His voice shook as he said, "I should have done something." He was quiet for a moment, and then he composed himself and slowly said, "Seth—you understand, don't you? Please . . . I just want to go home."

Seth held his hand tightly and said, "Yes, I understand. You know I do . . . I'll help you get to California."

Rory looked up at him and nodded and then sat the nearly empty beer bottle on the table.

For the next three days, Seth and Jenks spent time with Rory, providing companionship and helping him get to doctor's appointments. His demeanor improved with each passing day and by the end of week he appeared to be in a better state of mind.

On Saturday, Seth took Jenks fishing and they rose at sunrise to get out onto the river. Seth wore his new Columbia fishing shirt that Jenks gave him for his birthday, and he used his new fly rod from Rory to fish for redfish along the marsh grass.

As the morning passed, Jenks found herself relaxing on Dr. Walker's boat. She lay on the deck and gazed at the heavens. The clouds were puffy white against the deep-blue sky. The sky was so intensely blue that she concluded the ocean was influencing the shade of the heavens. She thought of her sister and how much she missed talking with her.

"Do you remember what Steel's voice sounded like?"

He stopped the rhythmic motion of fly fishing and looked at her. "Yes, I experience realistic dreams about him. He saves me from harm. In some of the dreams, he protects me from my father, but sometimes the danger is hidden and he tries to warn me. I can hear him call out to me. It's just as if he were still alive."

He looked at her caringly. "You're having more dreams about Gigi?"

"Yes. You already know about the footsteps I thought I heard. On one of the nights that I dreamed about her, she told me to wake up and warned of a danger. I thought she was in the room with me."

"Our dreams can be vivid at times."

The quietness on the river was broken by the sound of two F-18s from the Beaufort Marine Station. The two fighters passed directly above in formation and then the marsh became almost silent, except for the sound of the wind blowing through the cord grass.

Suddenly, there was a powerful explosion that sounded like a sonic boom. Jenks and Seth looked at one another in dismay while the blast echoed across the waterway.

"What was that?" Jenks cried out.

"I don't know. Those fighters weren't traveling fast enough to make that noise. It sounded as if it originated out in the Atlantic Ocean."

"Do you think it was an earthquake?"

"I guess we'll find out."

When they returned to the Walker property, there were no signs of damage from an earthquake. Seth made a phone call to the police station, and was informed that people from St. Helena all the way to Savannah had reported the booming noise.

In the next day's edition of the *Beaufort Gazette*, there was an article about the boom. Seismographs located in Charleston hadn't registered any earthquake activity. Both the Marine Air Corps Station at Beaufort and the Charleston Air Force Base reported that the boom was not caused by aircraft stationed at either of those locations. The US Coast Guard sent out a message to commercial vessels operating in the area, but none reported feeling an impact from the percussion of the noise.

Jenks read out loud to Seth about the explosion. "The reporter from the *Gazette* says that noises like this are heard from time to time along coastal areas around the world. He calls the noise the Seneca Guns. Legend has it that the blast is made by the guns of the spirits of Seneca Indians in revenge for being driven out of their lands by settlers."

"So no one knows what really causes these booms?" Seth asked.

"Apparently not."

"Some things just don't have an explanation."

"Yes, you're right."

Monday morning, Jenks drove to Rory's home to accompany him to a doctor's appointment in Beaufort. When she arrived, his van was gone, and she went to his door and knocked. There was no answer, and she concluded there must have been confusion in their communication—he must have driven to the appointment alone. Jenks called Seth on his cell phone, and he told her that he had not spoken with Rory that morning.

Before she left St. Helena Island, Jenks drove to the home of Meta and Ida Mae Andrews. There were several cars parked in the yard near their home when she arrived. When Jenks entered the house, three people were seated in the parlor. Jenks rang the bell on the marble-top table. Within a few moments, Jenks heard Ida Mae's voice. "I's comin'," she called out from back of the house.

The door that led to the hallway opened and Ida Mae emerged. As soon as she saw Jenks, the wrinkles on her face changed into a deeply lined expression of happiness.

"Good morning to you, Miss Jenkins. What brings you out our way?"

"I came to help a friend who lives on the island, but he wasn't home."

"You can always come to see us. You know you always welcome."

Jenks glanced to the hall tree and noticed a copy of the *Beaufort Gazette* on the seat. The front page article addressed the unexplained boom heard throughout the Low Country two days before.

"Miss Ida Mae, did you hear that explosive noise on Saturday?" Jenks asked as she pointed to the newspaper article.

Ida Mae frowned and said, "Yes, Lawd. Dat's not de first time we hear dat noise." She took a deep breath and sighed. "I got some ice tea in the kitchen. Why don't you join me for a glass? Dis morning is already hot."

Jenks nodded, then followed Ida Mae to the kitchen. She poured two glasses of iced tea and then invited Jenks to sit with her at the table.

"Meta with two clients dis morning. Dey's troubled by a voice dey been hearing. Dey ain't crazy—dey both hear de same voice. It says one of dere names." She shivered when she said this.

"You said you've heard the explosive boom before this Saturday?"

"Yes, Miss Jenkins. Once when we was children, and another time when Meta and me was in our forties. Both times someting bad happen afterward. De first time, our cousin was cuttin' limbs off a live oak tree. His son 'bout our age, and he came to see his papa cuttin' de tree back. All of a sudden, dis huge limb split off, and it swing down and hit poor Willie in de head. He was dead instantly. I never forget our cousin holding dat little boy and crying."

"Oh, that's terrible."

"De second time we hear it, a neighbor's daughter got hit by a car. She was walking home from Ripley's Landing. It was at dusk, and de driver of de car not see her."

"My goodness," Jenks added.

"We been praying dat nothin' gonna happen dis time."

Jenks took several sips of her tea and said, "I'm worried about my friend. I guess we weren't clear on our communication. I was supposed to help him get to a doctor's appointment this morning."

"Maybe he misunderstand you."

"That must be it." She looked down at her clasped hands before speaking. "I had a very strange experience lately, and I'd like to have your opinion on how to think about it."

"What happened?"

"I was walking past a house in Port Royal, and I saw a young woman looking at me from a second-story window. She had the saddest eyes I've ever seen. A few days later, I went back to the house to meet her. When I went on the porch and looked inside, the house was vacant."

"Did you find out who de girl is?"

"I told my neighbors, the Bernsteins, about it, and they told me that a young girl named Helena Pierce had been murdered in the house in the 1950s."

Ida Mae's eyes grew wide, and she took a deep breath. "She appear to you for some reason."

Jenks folded her napkin and said, "I think she doesn't rest because her murderer was never brought to justice. I'm worried that my sister cannot rest."

"The Pierce girl was murdered."

Jenks looked intently into Ida Mae's eyes and said, "I think Gigi was murdered as well."

Ida Mae drew another deep breath. "Oh, my Lawd. Do de police know dis?"

"There's no proof that Frank Hiller killed her."

Ida Mae shook her head slowly. "If he guilty, justice will be served one day whether in dis world or de next. You can count on it."

Jenks finished her tea and sighed. "Thank you for listening to me."

"I will pray for you and your sister." She crossed herself and then said, "Both Meta and I will pray."

"I know you have clients waiting to be seen. I should be leaving."

"No, Miss Jenkins, you can stay as long as you like."

"I promised Seth I'd make dinner for him tonight, so I'd better get going."

"You welcome here anytime."

She walked Jenks to the front door and waved to her as she descended the front steps. The sound of thunder came from the west and Jenks returned to her car to drive back to Port Royal.

Seth was supposed to come to dinner at six o'clock, but the hour passed and there was no word from him. She called his cell phone twice, but all she heard was the recording of his voice telling the caller to leave a message. By six-thirty, she was nervous about his tardiness, and she phoned the sheriff's department and spoke with a dispatcher. He told her that Seth was on duty and working a case.

Close to eight o'clock, her doorbell rang, and she rushed to answer it. Seth was standing before her. A look of despair was in his eyes, and his face was pale and tear streaked.

Jenks immediately put her arms around him in the threshold. "What's wrong?"

He led her to the couch and pulled her into his arms. His red-rimmed eyes looked into hers. "Rory's dead. He killed himself at Ripley Landing."

"My God!" she exclaimed.

"Some boys went out to the landing to fish this afternoon, and they saw his van parked underneath a stand of live oak trees. The landing is directly across the river from the Parris Island Marine Station. They noticed there was someone in the vehicle, and when the person didn't move for some time, they approached the van." Seth looked into her eyes and choked as he spoke. "There was blood dripping from the driver's door. Jenks—he shot himself."

She wrapped her arms around him and held him tightly as he cried. "I should have done more to help him," Seth said in a trembling voice.

"You did try to help him. He couldn't have asked for a better friend than you." Jenks continued to hold him tightly.

"He left a note in his house. He said we're our own worst enemies and wrote of Sarah Humphries's treatment at the hands of her own comrades. Jenks—he said that he was going home. I thought he meant that he wanted to go home to California. I knew he was depressed. I should have figured this out."

"Please don't torment yourself."

Jenks stroked his head and pulled him close to her. Together, they wept tears of grief over the loss of their friend.

———

Rory was given a military funeral at the Beaufort National Cemetery by an honor guard from the Beaufort Marine Air Corps Station. The chaplain led the funeral service and spoke of Rory's honorable service to his country and the sacrifice that he made on the field of battle in Afghanistan. A team of seven servicemen fired three rifle volleys. Then "Taps" was played, and two servicemen folded the American flag that draped his coffin into a tri-corner shape. Three spent cartridges were put inside the folded flag before it was gently placed in the hands of his mother, Delores. Her back was bent over with grief and tears fell down her cheeks. Seth sat beside her and put his arm around her as her body shook.

The funeral attire of black seemed to absorb the oppressive heat that had descended upon the Low Country in recent days. Perspiration rolled down Jenks's back and chest, wetting her dress. She pressed a linen handkerchief against her face and neck to remove the moisture that dampened her skin.

When the services were complete, Seth stood with Rory's mother. She looked so fragile as tears continued to fall down her cheeks. Rory's friends and former co-workers came by to offer their condolences, and Jenks remembered Rose from the Shrimp Shack as she came forward to speak with Delores.

"Miz Masters, I sure am sorry about Rory," she said, wiping tears from her face. Delores shook her hand and thanked her as another mourner came forward.

Refreshments were served in an air-conditioned sanctuary by Marine Corps personnel. Afterwards, Delores left for her flight back to San Francisco and Seth drove Jenks back to Port Royal. She invited him inside, and he collapsed onto the living room sofa. He held his hand out to her and motioned for her to join him on the couch.

Looking into her eyes he said, "I need to be alone for a couple of days. Please forgive me."

Startled by his statement, she responded, "Are you sure you should be alone right now? I don't want you to leave."

He kissed her on the forehead and hugged her gently. "It's all right. I just need to do this."

He rose from the couch, and she grabbed his hand as he stepped toward the front door. Tears welled in her eyes. "Please don't leave."

He stroked the side of her cheek, but opened the front door. "I'll call you in a couple of days." He walked down the pathway in front of her home to his car. Starting the engine, he pulled away and looked back at her. Their eyes locked, and she observed the sad expression on his face.

When she went back into the house, feelings of frustration and anxiety overcame her, and she picked up a glass flower vase and hurled it with all her strength into the fireplace. The glass shattered with a resounding crash that echoed through the room. She started to remove her damp dress, unbuttoning it as she walked down the hallway.

Once in the bedroom, she placed her clothing on the back of a chair and collapsed on her bed. Her grief over Rory's suicide and the oppressive heat of the Beaufort summer had left her exhausted. She closed her eyes to rest.

———

When she woke the next morning, she felt weak and chose to rest in bed for a little longer. She thought of the events prior to Rory's funeral. His mother, Delores, had arrived in town several days before the services, and she and Seth had gone through Rory's possessions. He had left instructions on his kitchen table as to how his belongings should be dispersed. He wanted to leave Seth his father's military awards from Operation Desert Storm. William Masters, Rory's father, had died in battle while fighting in Iraq in 1991. Jenks thought how painful Delores's memories must be. She lost her husband in battle and now her son to suicide.

Seth refused William Masters's military awards, insisting that Delores take them back home to California with her. As they cleaned out Rory's home, Jenks wept as she thought of having to collect Gigi's possessions for charity. A group of military volunteers from the Parris Island Marine Corps Station had offered Delores their assistance, which she gratefully accepted. Each day, a group of men arrived to help pack Rory's possessions and distribute some of his belongings to charitable organizations.

There was one item that Delores insisted that Seth keep: the gold pocket watch that had belonged to Rory's great-grandfather. The watch was made of fourteen-carat gold and had been a wedding gift to Rory's great-grandfather from his bride. Jenks recalled the inscription carved onto the back of the watch: "Forever, Love Jane."

Jenks watched Seth cry when Delores put the watch in his hand and closed his fingers around it. She held his hand tightly between her own hands and gazed at him. Before she departed, Jenks heard her tell Seth, "I know you did everything you could to support my son. He told me that in one respect he was a fortunate man—he had experienced true friendship with you. Bless you for what you did for him."

She sat up on the edge of her bed. Her thoughts went to Seth. *Where was he?*

———

Two days passed, and there was no word from him. On the afternoon of the second day, Jenks went to the sheriff's department and asked to speak with Detective Campbell. The officer at the reception desk recognized her and asked her to sit down while she went to locate him.

Thomas Campbell came into the reception area and shook her hand. "Please come into my office," he said as he motioned her through the doorway.

He offered her a seat and then closed the door. "Miss Ellington, how can I help you?"

Her voice cracked as she spoke. "I'm worried about Seth. He left after Rory's funeral, and I haven't heard from him since."

"He asked our captain for some personal time, but didn't say where he was going." He looked at her for a moment. "I know he cares for you. He told me so."

Tears welled in her eyes, and she wiped them with her fingertips. The policeman handed her a box of tissues from his desktop, and she removed a couple of them to wipe her tears.

"Please don't worry. He's not the type to let people down—I know he'll be in touch with you."

She rose from her seat and nodded to the detective. He accompanied her back to the reception area and held the door open as she left.

"Don't worry," he told her again as she went down the steps.

She cranked the engine on her Jeep and decided that she would drive to the Walker home to see if Seth was there. As she crossed the Broad River, a rainstorm was moving in from the west. A large crack of thunder sounded, and she turned on the windshield wipers as the rain shower intensified.

She passed the Rabbit Hash Hunt Club and the chapel was almost obscured by the driving rain. Trees swayed heavily in the storm-driven wind. When she reached the entrance to the Walker's property, rain blew into her vehicle as she rolled down the window to press the gate code.

She slowly maneuvered the Jeep down the drive, and she saw the outline of Seth's Ford pickup truck parked near the rear entrance of the home. Jenks parked her vehicle beside his, and despite the downpour, she got out of her Jeep and ran to the basement door.

The window on the door was steamed by humidity and rain. She wiped the glass and inside the basement she could see the blurred image of Seth. He was wearing workout clothes and boxing gloves and hitting the punching bag with fury. As she knocked on the door, a boom of thunder sounded, and she watched as Seth continued to pummel the bag. Jenks hit the door with her fist so hard that her hand hurt.

He turned around and came toward the door, opening it for her. "Come inside, Jenks. You're soaked."

He didn't kiss her, but looked into her eyes. "I'm sorry, I'm sweaty."

His eyes were red rimmed, and either tears or beads of sweat were rolling down his cheeks. Jenks put her arms around him and hugged him with all her strength. "I don't care if you're sweaty. I've been so worried about you."

He did not return the embrace, and she stepped back and looked up into his eyes. "Please tell me what's wrong."

He went back to the punching bag and hit it with renewed vigor. After several punches, he stopped and turned to her. "I should have been paying closer attention to Rory. I knew that he was fragile, and I could have done more for him."

"You were a very good friend to Rory. You told me once that you can only do so much for some people. You could not control his actions."

A bolt of lightning illuminated the room, and thunder boomed from a nearby strike. Jenks jumped from the noise, and chills enveloped her body as she looked into Seth's face, which was contorted with an expression of anger.

"I was too busy thinking about myself and my plans! I was too busy thinking about you!"

"Seth—please . . ."

He turned back to the punching bag and struck it repeatedly with incredible force—in his eyes—pure rage. Her hands were trembling and tears were blurring her vision. She wiped her tears, and looked at him for another minute before turning away. Her feelings deeply hurt, she ran outside.

A deluge of rain was still falling from the storm. She was almost to her Jeep when she heard Seth call out.

"Jenks . . . Jenkins, please don't go!"

Seth ran to her, and took her in his arms, his hands still glove clad. "I'm such a fool. Please forgive me, Jenkins. I love you." His eyes were filled with tears, and he held her tightly against him.

She wept uncontrollably, and he lifted her in his arms, carrying her into the house—both of them drenched from the powerful storm.

⟶

When she woke the next morning, Seth was snuggled against her. Their naked bodies were still intertwined from deeply emotional lovemaking. Tears had been shed by both of them during intimacy.

Jenks gently rubbed her hand across his hard chest muscles. His eyes opened, and he hugged her against him, stroking her hair away from her face.

"Where were you the last two days?"

He propped his head up on his elbow and looked into her hazel eyes.

"I went home."

"You mean to Georgia?"

"Yes, I needed to do something."

"What was that?"

"I went to visit Steel's grave."

"Where is he buried?"

"There's a chapel not far from where we used to live. The hills rise up around the cemetery grounds and Blackstock's Mountain is to the west." He stroked the side of her face. "When Steel and I were kids, we were exploring the mountain, and we found a cave that was concealed by thick vegetation. The entrance was narrow, so we didn't go inside on our first visit. The next day we came back with rope, a lantern, and flashlights. Steel tied the rope around his waist and went in first."

"What did he see?"

"After he got inside, he shined his flashlight and saw the cave had a ceiling of more than twenty feet. Once he lit the lantern, he discovered a stream ran through it, and the walls were painted with numerous Native American drawings. He called out to me to come inside."

His lips quirked up into a slight smile. "I was stunned when I viewed the drawings. One of them depicted a hunting scene, but in the center was the image of a large buck who was smoking a pipe. We wondered what the artist had been doing while he created that drawing."

"Did you ever tell anyone about it?"

"No—after what happened with the log cabin, we chose to remain silent."

"Did you go to the cave?"

"Yes, the last time Steel was home we went there together. I had not been to the cave since his death, and I wanted to visit it."

"Will you show it to me someday?"

"Yes," he said as he pulled her naked body on top of his. "I wanted to see Steel's grave again. I miss him so much."

"I understand."

"I know you do." He stoked her hair and then said, "And now Rory. I just wish I had realized his state of mind."

Seth rose from bed, showered, and dressed. Jenks remained in bed and watched him. He put his Glock in the holster at his waist, and kissed her good-bye.

⟶

That afternoon, Seth was testifying in a narcotics case, and Jenks went back to Port Royal. Gigi's house was to be shown by Simmons Realty to a couple of prospective buyers. She knew she needed to clean up the broken vase that she had hurled in frustration into the fireplace. Her plans were to clean up the glass and make sure the home was tidy before returning to the Walker's property.

She used a broom and dustpan to collect the larger pieces of glass and then vacuumed the smaller particles. As she struck one of the fireplace bricks with the nozzle, she was startled to see the masonry surface move. She got down on her hands and knees and moved a couple of bricks. They were loose, and she carefully jiggled them out of their location. She gasped—a secret cubbyhole was within the fireplace. Hidden inside was a leather journal, a set of keys, and CDs.

She was stunned by her find, and the words of Meta Andrews raced through her mind. *Look closer.* She recalled that Meta's ancestor Joseph Andrews had kept his Civil War era journal concealed in his fireplace.

Her hands shook as she removed the leather binder and CDs from their hiding place. Jenks opened the journal and inside were records of Gigi's dives. She looked over the entries and found that Gigi had kept thorough records. As she read, Jenks noted that her sister had recorded the GPS coordinates, the time of the dive, water temperature, weather, and visibility conditions. Jenks read from the log:

September 18, 2011— I am diving at slack tide in the Morgan
River near Tilden Landing.

After the completion of the dive, Gigi had notated:

Found three artifacts—ancient beer bottles from the river near
the old Morgan River Tavern.

Jenks turned the page and read another entry. Along with the technical
aspects of the dive, Gigi had recorded:

I have collected two wine bottles today. Dr. Henry is going to
be proud of me.

"Dr. Henry—who is Dr. Henry?" Jenks exclaimed out loud. She read
through the entries on several pages and then turned to the back of the book.
There were a number of receipts that were secured into the log. As Jenks read
the receipts, she realized this was a record of the items that Gigi had reported
to the office of the South Carolina Institute of Archaeology and Anthropology.
Jenks looked closely at the records; at the bottom of each receipt was a signed
acknowledgement from Dr. Paul Henry. She put the journal on the desk and
then dialed a phone number.

"Dave Patterson," the man on the receiver said.

"Dave, this is Jenks Ellington."

"Yes, ma'am, how are you today?"

"I'm well. Dave, I was wondering if you could help me with a couple of
questions?"

"I'll try."

"I was looking over some of Gigi's records, and I came across an entry
referring to a Dr. Paul Henry."

"Yes, Dr. Henry. He's the director of the South Carolina Institute of
Archaeology and Anthropology that oversees the records of artifacts collected
in South Carolina waters. You could call him the overseer of the hobby diver
program."

"The hobby diver program?"

"Yes, ma'am. When I went out with you to look for artifacts near Woodward Point, we talked about your sister having a hobby diving license. This type of license permits a diver to collect up to ten artifacts a day from a shipwreck site, and every quarter a written declaration should be reported to that agency."

"I think I recall you saying that the value of the artifact does not make a difference to this agency."

"Yes, that's correct. The agency is more interested in the location where the artifact was found and the type of object."

"I just want to make sure I'm clear about this—as long as the artifacts are declared, the state permits you to keep your discovery, regardless of the value?"

"Yes, ma'am, that's the way I understand it." There was silence on the line for a moment, and then Dave asked, "Miss Ellington, did you find something?"

"Dave, I think so. Thank you for answering my questions."

"Yes, ma'am—have a good afternoon."

Jenks hung up the receiver and then read more in the journal. There were numerous entries concerning Gigi's dives; some of them were with Frank Hiller, but most of them were solo. *Her record keeping is so thorough—she was a budding archaeologist.*

She placed the journal on the kitchen table and opened the CD case. Sliding one of the CDs into her laptop, Jenks was amazed to see it contained video records of the artifacts that Gigi had found. She clicked *Play All* at the computer's prompt, and the first video began. She could see that the video documentation had not taken place at Gigi's home, but had been recorded in a room that had metal countertops and walls that appeared to be a dark shade of concrete. Jenks did not recognize the room where the video had been made.

As she continued to watch, Gigi walked into the frame. She was smiling broadly and displaying a light-green bottle to the camera. Jenks noticed that the camera itself was close to eye level and holding steady.

"Either someone else shot this or you were using a tripod," Jenks quietly said while looking at the computer screen.

When the next video played, Jenks drew in a deep breath. Gigi's hands were holding a box with wooden sides and a wire mesh bottom, and in it rattled dozens of gold and silver coins. On the next video clip, she appeared on the screen holding a magnificent gold artifact. Jenks gasped—Gigi was holding in her hand a gold cross accentuated with red stones. *Iris Elliott*. Gigi kissed the cross, and then held it proudly up at the side of her face.

The sight of Gigi's happy face made Jenks forget about the cross and the coins for a moment. All she could think of was that Gigi looked so vibrant. And then the video stopped, and Gigi's cheerful face was gone. Jenks sat down at the table, stunned from the experience. The journal lay in front of her; she picked it up and read again from the pages.

———

Jenks went inside the Beaufort County Court House. She held a duffel bag that contained Gigi's possessions. Passing through the security station, she looked around the large foyer to find the courtroom where Seth would be giving testimony. One of the police officers working the security detail noticed her. "Miss, can I help you with anything?"

"Yes, I'm looking for Detective Mason."

"Ma'am, he's still in court. If you'd like to sit down in the lobby you can wait for him."

"I'd like to wait for him outside if that's okay."

"I'll tell him—er . . . your name, Miss?"

"I'm Jenks Ellington, and the detective is a friend of mine."

"When he comes out, I'll let him know you're waiting for him outside."

Jenks left and sat down on a brick wall that was situated between the courthouse and another administrative building. Her eye caught sight of two bluebirds that were playfully engaging one another on the lawn. She thought of their rare beauty—so full of life. Then her mind went back to Gigi and Frank Hiller.

Seth had told her he would be in court that day to give testimony in a narcotics case, and a few minutes after four o'clock, he came out of the building. He waved to her when he saw her sitting on the wall. As he approached, a look of concern appeared on his face. "I was told that you were waiting for me out here." He drew closer and a frown showed on his face. "Jenks, what's the matter? You look worried."

"I have something to show you."

"I'm finished with testimony. Would you like to go to my office?"

"Yes—please."

As they walked across the lawn to the sheriff's department, she explained what she had discovered in a secret cubbyhole in Gigi's fireplace. She opened the duffel bag and pulled out the set of keys. "I have no idea what these are for."

When they reached the building, Seth opened the door for her, and then escorted her inside. They took the elevator to the second floor and passed by Detective Campbell's office on the way to Seth's office. Thomas was sitting at his desk filling out paperwork as they passed by. He nodded to them. Seth placed the CD in his computer and intently watched Gigi's video documentation of her artifacts. He frowned as the video continued, and then his eyes grew wide when he saw the gold cross and Gigi's face as she proudly displayed the object.

When the video was finished he turned to Jenks with a stunned expression. Tears had welled in Jenks's eyes and were rolling down her cheeks. Seth was quick to remove his handkerchief and wipe the tears from her cheeks.

"There's more." She removed the journal from her handbag and set it on his desk.

Opening the book to a marker, Jenks read an entry aloud.

> I have been diving for the remnants of the *Defiance*, or should I say the *Fort Sumter*, near Woodward Point for better than two months. I feel certain that I must be close to where the ship would have gone down. I am confident of my calculations. I am determined to continue.

Jenks stopped reading from the entry and took a deep breath. "This is the next entry."

> I have been out to Woodward Point, but the winds have been steadily increasing all afternoon . . . too strong for a dive. I will wait until after the storm has passed to dive again.

Jenks looked at Seth and said, "She recorded that a nor'easter came through this area in the spring."

"Yes, I remember it. It was a powerful storm and late in the season. We normally get storms like that in the winter."

Jenks felt her hands trembling, and she read from the journal again.

> I have returned to Woodward Point. Skeleton Island has been
> torn in two by the powerful tides. The nor'easter that passed
> through two nights ago also appears to have shifted the sands
> and silt of the ocean floor. I am finding coins and artifacts that
> I should have come across before now. Today was the day!

Seth put his arm around her and their eyes locked. "Would you like for me to read?" he asked in a compassionate voice.

She wiped tears from her eyes and gently shook her head. As she composed herself again, Jenks said, "Gigi spent the next two weeks visiting the site." Gingerly turning the page, Jenks said, "This is the last entry."

> I have today found an item of great significance and value.
> The gold object I have discovered in the same location as
> the coins could be the Petersburg Cross. After all these years
> underwater, the condition of the piece is remarkable.

Jenks looked into Seth's eyes and finished the entry.

> I have cleaned the gold artifact, and I am virtually certain of
> its origin. On the back are the artist's initials, AGK, for Aleksi
> Gregori Kartashkin. The double curl on the beginning of each
> letter is there. I can hardly believe it. I will surprise Frank with
> my discovery. His birthday is just a couple of weeks from
> now. He will be thrilled. Together, we will authenticate the
> find, and share in any proceeds that this magnificent object
> might bring. I know he will be proud of me. Fleming would
> never believe what's stored in his old building!!

"She ended the last sentence with two exclamation marks."
Seth's face darkened. "It appears she did find the Petersburg Cross."
Jenks wiped a tear from her face and then reached for the duffel bag. She brought out a sheet of paper. "Look at this list. Gigi documented every item

that was found near Woodward Point—even the cross. She listed herself and Frank Hiller as the salvagers of the items."

"She died before she was able to make the declaration," Seth observed.

"Dear God—she was going to tell him on his birthday."

Jenks wiped her face and looked into Seth's eyes. "I don't understand the last line of the entry. 'Fleming would never believe what's stored in his old building.'"

He looked at her and repeated the name, "Fleming. Where have I heard that name before?"

Seth rose from his chair and motioned for her to come with him. Together, they walked to the doorway of Detective Campbell's office. Seth knocked on the doorframe. "Thomas, I was wondering if you'd help us identify someone."

The detective looked up from paperwork that he was filling out and noticed Jenks's tear-streaked face. "Miss Ellington, I hope you're all right."

"I've just found some documents in my sister's home, and Seth and I are trying to make sense of it all."

"How can I help you?"

"Does the name Fleming mean anything to you?" Seth inquired.

Thomas appeared in deep thought for a few moments, and then he responded, "The only person named Fleming who I can think of ran a fresh seafood business in Port Royal. There was thought that he was involved in a drug-trafficking ring based in the Bahamas, but there was never any solid evidence to prove this. He died several years ago, and his widow closed the business."

"Where was the business located?"

"Not far from the shrimping docks. As you approach the docks, you'll see the buildings on the right—but Seth, they've been locked up for years."

"I think we may drive over to Port Royal and take a look at those buildings."

"Do you want me to go with you?"

"I think we'll be okay, but look for a phone call from me shortly. Thank you."

"Be careful, Seth."

"Always."

CHAPTER 13

The Hiding Place

T he intense heat and humidity of the August afternoon caused Jenks to perspire. She could feel beads of sweat roll down her back and chest. After they parked the police car in front of the former Fleming's Seafood buildings, Seth removed his suit coat and loosened his tie. Rolling his shirt sleeves up, he removed a large silver flashlight from the police car.

A metal fence topped by a barbed wire extension surrounded the buildings. They walked to the gate and found that a chain held the double gates in place with a padlock.

Jenks handed Seth the keys she had found with the journal, and he tried the first key in the padlock. It did not open. He removed the key and tried the next key on the set. The lock fell open as he turned the key in the locking mechanism.

"Oh, my God," Jenks said quietly.

They looked at one another, and then Seth removed the chain around the gate and pushed it open. Sweat beaded upon his forehead, and he wiped his brow with the back of his arm as they walked to the building. The grass inside the fence was high, and weeds had grown up in the cracks of the asphalt parking lot. An old powerboat sat in the corner of the lot; weeds almost engulfed the weathered watercraft.

Seth pointed to fire-ant mounds near the corners of the old concrete building. "Watch your step, Jenks. The bite of those ants can be very painful."

When they reached the exterior door of the building, Seth chose another key from Gigi's set, and this one turned easily. He twisted the doorknob, and with a little force pushed the door open.

"Detective Campbell said that the building had not been used for years, but I can still smell an odor of fish," Jenks commented.

"I suppose that odor is difficult to eliminate."

They looked around the front portion of the building. There was an old table where fish had been filleted. The refrigeration equipment that had held fresh seafood was empty, and the glass windows were cloudy from age.

They walked to the east side of the building where the offices were located. A placard on one of the office doors read "Captain Emil Fleming." Seth pushed the door open. An oak desk sat in the middle of the room. Old photographs of fishing expeditions were on the wall, showing grinning fishermen standing beside their catch. In one corner of the paneled wood office was a file cabinet. Seth slid the drawers out one at a time—all of them were empty.

"This is kind of sad. It's like small remnants of a man's life are still in here."

Seth gave her a hug on the shoulder. "Let's go to the rear of the building."

They walked through the structure to the back section. The concrete floor and walls were a deep gray color, and a couple of steel shelving units were secured against one wall. Sunlight poured into the room from a couple of western-facing windows, brightening the otherwise gray area.

"I think this is the room where Gigi took the videos of her artifacts."

At the same time, they both noticed the refrigerated meat locker at the rear of the room. Above the door a sign read, "Everyone Loves Fresh Seafood, But Fresh Seafood Ain't Cheap." There was a padlock on the steel door handle. "There are two keys left," Seth said. He placed one of the keys in the lock and it opened with little difficulty. Removing the padlock, he placed it on the concrete floor outside the door. Then he pulled the metal handle and the door opened. The stench of fish rushed out of the refrigeration locker.

"Oh, my God," Jenks exclaimed. "It smells like there's something dead in here."

"The locker's been sealed for a while," Seth volunteered.

He turned on an electrical switch and a light in the center of the room came on. Even with the light, the space was dim, and Seth turned on the flashlight he had brought into the building. Diving equipment was stored in one corner of the room. On a steel countertop that ran the length of one side of the compartment was a Garmin GPS unit. "How about that?" Seth said, "Here's the GPS unit." Beside it was a folder. Seth picked it up. "Let's see what this is."

He opened the binder and inside was a lease agreement between Gigi and Leanne Fleming, a collection of water and electric bills—and invoices from a laboratory in Charleston. The address on the lease for Leanne Fleming was Winter Park, Florida.

"It looks like Leanne Fleming is Emil Fleming's widow, and from this stationery it appears she lives in a retirement community. She leased this building to Gigi for a year starting last October, for two hundred fifty dollars a month. Gigi paid her for a year up front. I bet she doesn't know Gigi is dead."

Jenks was silent for a moment while she read a note. "Gigi was apparently worried about her home being broken into, and she had asked Mrs. Fleming if she could lease this building to store her equipment and her artifacts."

Seth looked at the note and Jenks continued to read. "Look at this letter from Mrs. Fleming. She says that she is glad to lease this building to Gigi. It says she admires Gigi's treasure-hunting capabilities, and will only charge a minimal amount of rent on an otherwise abandoned building."

Tears again welled up in Jenks's eyes as she read the end of the note out loud to Seth. "Mrs. Fleming wrote to Gigi, 'You must be a brave young woman, and I wish you the best with your pursuits!'"

"Your sister certainly kept detailed records that she didn't want easily found."

"She must have felt very protective of her discoveries. What work do you suppose Bradbury Laboratories in Charleston did for Gigi?"

Seth studied the invoices before replying. "They performed conservation techniques on artifacts that Gigi had recovered from an underwater ocean environment. I think I've heard of Bradbury Labs before. A few years ago, I read that a team from their laboratory was helping preserve the remnants of a Civil War-era ship that was located in Charleston Harbor."

Jenks turned away from the journal and looked around the room. Hanging on a wall hook was the wooden box with a wire mesh bottom that she had seen holding coins on Gigi's video. In one corner of the room was a camera tripod. She walked to where the tripod rested. Beside it was a digital video camera on a shelf.

Picking up the camera, her hands trembled. "This is what Gigi used to record her findings," Jenks said in a shaky voice.

Seth put his arms around her. "Steady now," he said in a calming voice.

They looked around the rest of the room. On the counter beside a steel sink were brushes, cloths, and bottles of chemicals. A large glass tank, with what appeared to be electrodes attached to it, was situated near one end of the counter. "It looks like your sister had her own laboratory here in Fleming's refrigeration locker."

Seth lifted one of the chemical bottles and read the markings. "This is an acid solution."

"What's the tank for?"

"See this electrical wiring?" he said, pointing to the cables. "Gigi was cleaning some of her artifacts here. I believe the process is called electrolytic reduction."

"How do you know that?"

"One of the police divers for Beaufort County does some hobby diving. He explained the process to me once."

"Then why the need for the lab in Charleston?"

"Perhaps some of the artifacts were in such bad shape that Gigi used a professional lab occasionally."

Jenks looked around the room and nervously grasped the steel counter. "So now—where are her artifacts?"

"Good question. Let's look around. There is one unused key—now, where's the lock?"

Seth shone the flashlight along the base of the walls and over the floor. When he reached the wall with the steel countertops he crouched to shine the light beneath. The beam caught a metal object on the floor below one section. Seth froze the beam and bent down. "It's a padlock," he said hesitatingly.

The padlock was clamped on a narrow handle and clasp on the floor. On inspection, Seth and Jenks traced the faint outline of a trapdoor, flush with the floor beneath the counters. Seth brought out the final, fourth key to try on the padlock. It worked. Seth removed the lock and then opened the trapdoor, revealing a rectangular space, even larger than the door, with a concrete bottom. The hiding space was about six-feet long, two-feet wide, a foot deep, and filled with Gigi's collection of artifacts.

"Unbelievable!"

"Oh, my God," Jenks gasped.

She reached inside the hiding place and brought out antique bottles and then a number of gold and silver coins stacked in containers. "These were minted in the 1850s!" Jenks said as she examined the coins. Seth picked up a small velvet sack. They both stood up to look at the contents of the pouch together. He opened the drawstrings and pulled the bag open. A gold cross with red stones slid out. "This looks like the cross that Iris Elliott wore in her portrait in the Gibbes Museum," Jenks said in a shaky voice.

Seth opened his cell phone. She heard him say, "Janet, could I speak with Detective Campbell?" He stood quietly for a moment and then volunteered, "The phone call has been dropped. I will get better reception out of this unit."

Jenks watched him as he strode to the locker door. Late afternoon sunlight was streaming into the room. A few paces outside the locker, Seth raised his phone, squinting, and began dialing. At that moment, Jenks eye caught the reflection of something metallic—a silver pole—in the rays of the sun. She screamed, and Seth turned sharply to his right, but there was no time for him to react.

The pole flashed across the threshold and slammed into Seth's right leg. A horrifying cry of pain and a bone-splitting crack echoed through the vacant building. Within seconds, the metal pole descended on the back of Seth's back and head. He hit the floor with force and did not move. Then the sound of a heavy metal pipe dropping to the concrete floor resonated throughout the building.

Jenks screamed again with terror and ran to the locker door, but as she crossed its threshold, she was grabbed from the side by powerful hands, turned around, and pushed hard against the concrete wall. The back of her head struck the surface, and in a dazed condition, she looked up into the steel-blue eyes of Frank Hiller.

He pinned her against the wall and his face came to within a few inches of hers.

"Are you a conniving, deceitful little bitch like your sister?" he said in a growling voice. Beads of sweat stood on his forehead before rolling down his cheeks.

"What have you done to Seth, you bastard?"

"I have disabled him."

"Let me go!"

Frank released her and she collapsed to the floor. She attempted to rise, but dizziness overcame her. She saw Frank take Seth's firearm out of the holster and place it in the waistband of his pants. She closed her eyes. When she reopened them, she saw Frank enter the refrigeration locker. Fighting a wave of nausea, Jenks crawled to Seth. The collar of his dress shirt was turning red with blood, and Jenks struggled to turn him over. When she maneuvered him onto his back, she loosened his tie and unbuttoned his shirt. His face was pale, and a moan of pain escaped his lips.

"Seth, it's Jenks, can you hear me?"

He did not respond. As she leaned back up, she noticed Seth's cell phone against the wall, about eight feet away. On her hands and knees, she crawled toward the phone. *Please God, let me get to the phone.* Another wave of nausea descended upon her, and she stopped until the feeling passed, then struggled forward again. The phone was almost within reach.

Her hands were trembling, but she picked up the phone and hit redial. Suddenly, she was jerked from the floor from behind. "What are you doing, you little bitch?"

Frank grabbed the cell phone from her hands and threw it against the far wall. It shattered into pieces. Jenks was terrified and believed she was about to die. He thrust her against the wall again. The wind was knocked out of her lungs, and she started to choke while gasping for breath.

Frank held up the gold cross to her face. "Your sister and I had an agreement that we split everything fifty-fifty. I always upheld my end of the bargain, but she was planning to sell the items from the *Defiance* and cheat me out of my share. I watched her with a telescopic lens several afternoons from Skeleton Island. She had no idea I was there. I saw her recovering artifacts—including what appeared to be a cross. She held it up proudly."

He increased the pressure pinning her tightly against the wall. Struggling to speak, Jenks said, "Murderer—she planned to share everything with you. You drowned her."

"Once the regulator was out of her mouth, she put up quite a fight—but it was no use. I simply held her tightly until she became still." He grinned. "There was not a mark on her. It's almost time for you and your boyfriend to join her." His face came even closer to hers. Jenks could smell the pungent stench of sweat from his body. She mustered every ounce of strength she had in an attempt to fight back, but it was no use. He was just too strong.

He pushed against her even harder. "I've had your sister's home under surveillance since her unfortunate death. I rented the vacant house behind Gigi's, and I've listened to every conversation you've had. I've heard the sounds of lovemaking between you and your boyfriend. I've been in your bedroom while you slept—so close to you that I could hear your breathing."

"You're completely insane," she struggled to say.

Frank Hiller was pressing against her throat, and airflow was being cut off to her lungs. The room became deep amber-brown, and when he released her, she collapsed to the concrete floor. Lying beside Seth, she gasped for air.

Jenks watched as Frank's hazy figure carried a large leather duffel into the refrigeration locker. After a few moments, she remembered that she had left all of the documents that she had found in Gigi's fireplace in Seth's office, except for the last inventory list that Gigi would have turned in to the South Carolina Institute of Archaeology and Anthropology. On that list were the names of Gigi and Frank Hiller as the salvagers of the *Defiance*. She had inadvertently kept it after she and Seth spoke to Detective Campbell about Fleming's Seafood. Jenks rolled to her side and then struggled to her knees. If she could show Frank the list, he'd know that Gigi meant to include him.

Fumbling through her cargo pants pocket, she removed the document just as she was grabbed from behind. Frank jerked her to her feet and then taking her by the arms pulled her close to him.

"I'd find out what you're like if there were more time," he said as he pushed her sweat-soaked hair back from her throat.

Jenks thrust the inventory document into his face and cried out frantically, "She was not cheating you. She was going to surprise you on your birthday. Read this!"

As he looked over the document, his face became ashen, and he released her from his grasp. She collapsed back to the floor.

For a moment, she put her hand on Seth touching him tenderly. The blood was spreading on his shirt.

Time seemed to stand still as Frank read the inventory list. His face was gray. He took a deep breath, and then grabbed Seth by his arm and dragged him into the refrigeration locker. Without saying another word, he pulled Jenks to her feet and effortlessly carried her to the door of the compartment. He pushed her into the locker and she fell hard, striking her head on the concrete floor. There was a sound of breaking glass and then the room went black. She could barely breathe, and her ability to think was failing her. As she lay on the concrete, she felt consumed by the darkness and fear. Her mind went blank.

———

There was a noise like muffled voices and the sudden pounding of what sounded like a hammer. Jenks woke in total darkness, but suddenly the door to the refrigeration compartment opened and someone shined a flashlight inside. The light blinded her, and she could not remember where she was. She heard a voice cry out, "In here, they're in here." The voice sounded like Detective Campbell's.

Other flashlight beams appeared in the darkness, and she heard the voice say with desperation, "Oh, my God—Seth."

She felt someone lift her from the concrete floor and then she was in fresh air. Completely dazed, she closed her eyes as the late afternoon sun blazed into them.

———

The scent of rubbing alcohol was in the air. Jenks looked up at the ceiling of an unfamiliar room. Her head was throbbing, and she felt queasy.

"She's waking up," a voice said.

Someone was holding her hand. She thought it was Seth, but when she turned her head toward the individual, she saw her mother. There were lines of worry on her face, and she gently stroked Jenks's forehead with her fingers.

"Thank God. We've been so worried about you," Linda said in a shaky voice.

Gregg Mikell rose from a settee near the bed and joined Linda at the side of Jenks's bed.

"Honey, we're so glad to see you awake," he said. "Detective Campbell called us yesterday, and we got here as fast as we could."

Jenks slowly realized that she was in a hospital room, and she tried to formulate a sentence, but found she was having difficulty creating her words.

"Baby, don't try to talk. You've had a bad blow to the head."

"Where is Seth?" she said feebly.

Her mother looked at her compassionately, and then responded, "Jenks—I'm afraid he's hurt badly. The doctor said he has a fractured leg and a serious concussion. You've been diagnosed with a concussion as well, although not as severe as his."

Tears welled in her eyes. "He's going to be all right, isn't he?"

"Baby, he's in the intensive care unit. All I know is that the doctors are taking care of him."

Jenks wiped her tears with her fingers as they rolled down her cheeks.

Her mother handed her a tissue, and asked, "Who did this to you?"

"Frank Hiller," Jenks choked out.

"Oh, dear God," Linda whispered as a deep frown crossed her countenance.

"He killed Gigi over artifacts . . . she found a ship that sunk during the Civil War. He thought she was cheating him . . . he murdered her over gold." Her voice was becoming nervous and high pitched. "She wasn't betraying him—she was going to share everything with him."

Her mother wept, and she squeezed Jenks's hand tighter. "Do you feel up to speaking with Detective Campbell for a few minutes?"

"Yes, ma'am."

She closed her eyes and within a few minutes Detective Campbell entered the room. "Miss Ellington, I know you don't feel well, but please tell me what happened to you and Seth."

"How is Seth?"

"His CT scan did not reveal any bleeding, but did show some mild swelling."

"Oh, dear God," she said in a trembling voice.

"Now take your time and please tell me what happened."

"We went to Fleming's Seafood." A wave of pain wracked her brain and she stopped talking. "I'm sorry, my head hurts so much."

"Just take your time."

"We located Gigi's artifacts in an odd compartment in the refrigeration locker. Seth tried to phone you—but the call was dropped. He was going outside to call you again—as he went through the doorway, I saw the glint of a metal bat, maybe a pole. It hit Seth in the leg. There was such a frightening noise from the blow."

"Yes, we found the steel pipe that was used in the assault."

"Then the bat descended on Seth's back and head. He went to the floor and didn't move."

"Who is responsible for this?"

"Frank Hiller, Gigi's diving partner."

"I see," he said as his face darkened with a deep frown.

"He murdered my sister over treasure she discovered off Woodward Point." She wiped tears from her eyes. "Gigi's findings are recorded on a CD and in a journal that I discovered in a hiding place in her fireplace. I left the documentation in Seth's office—except the last declaration she was going to submit to the South Carolina Institute of Archaeology and Anthropology. She had listed herself and Frank Hiller as the divers responsible for salvaging the *Defiance*."

"Yes, we've put everything safely away."

"I showed the list to Frank Hiller. He seemed shocked to find out that Gigi was planning to share the discovery with him—did you find that document in the Fleming building?"

"No, we didn't."

"He told me that he had rented the house behind mine . . . he eavesdropped on all my conversations." Cold chills ran up her spine, and she trembled as she remembered his words. "He said that he had been close enough to me while I slept—that he could hear my breathing."

Uncontrollable tears fell down her cheeks, and in a shaky voice she said, "As he was choking me, Frank told me that he took the regulator out of Gigi's mouth and held her underwater until she drowned."

The creases in Detective Campbell's face deepened. He took her hand and gave it a gentle squeeze. "I'm sorry, Miss Ellington, Mrs. Ellington."

"I thought he was going to kill us—instead he put us in the refrigeration locker. I was so terrified."

"He must have changed his mind—thank God."

Before Detective Campbell departed, he said that the police would go to the house behind Gigi's to investigate for electronic equipment. When he finished interviewing her, Jenks could not control her emotions, and she was sobbing. Her mother gently put her arms around her and whispered, "You just rest, Jenks. Mama's here now."

When Jenks woke again, Linda was sitting in a recliner with her eyes closed. Jenks tried to rise from her hospital bed, but found herself dizzy as she stood up.

"Jenks, what are you doing?"

"I want to go to Seth."

"You get back into bed, and I'll see if the nurses will allow that."

Linda left the room, and Jenks lay back down on her bed. She thought of Gigi and the terror she must have felt in the grasp of Frank Hiller as he drowned her. Tears filled her eyes as she thought of what they had shared as sisters—all stolen by the misplaced revenge of a madman.

After several minutes, her mother and a nurse with a wheelchair entered her room. "Miss Ellington, my name is Sally Hudson. The head nurse, Mrs. Wisdom, says that you can visit with Detective Mason for a few minutes." With their help, Jenks rose from bed and sat down in the chair. Nurse Hudson pushed her out into the hallway.

"Miss Ellington, we're glad to see you are feeling better. The emergency room staff was real concerned about you and the detective when you were brought in yesterday."

"How is Seth?"

"Dr. Lemons operated on his leg. His head injury has caused us deep concern, but we're keeping a close watch on him, I promise."

They entered the elevator and descended to the second floor. At the end of a hallway was the intensive care unit. Nurse Hudson pushed an automatic opener at the entrance and the door opened. They continued down the corridor to a room where Seth was resting. As they entered, Jenks realized that he had two visitors: Detective Campbell and another man. Thomas Campbell was holding Seth's hand.

Both men rose from their seats when the women entered the room. Detective Campbell spoke first in a solemn voice: "Ladies, this is Captain Barrett with the Beaufort County Sheriff's Department. He's Seth's and my boss."

Captain Barrett was a well-built man with thick gray hair, and he came forward to Jenks. He touched her on the shoulder and then lightly patted her on the hand. "I'm sorry about what's happened. An arrest warrant has been issued for Frank Hiller, and the collective levels of law enforcement in South Carolina and neighboring states are on the lookout for him."

"Thank you, Captain Barrett. I hope he's found soon."

"Yes, ma'am."

As he said those words, he looked in Seth's direction, and then drew close to his bedside. Jenks asked to be wheeled to where she could hold Seth's hand. As she took his hand in hers, she gazed at his handsome but bruised face and the bandages on the back of his head. The bed was elevated, placing his head at a higher position than his body, and he was on oxygen. His right leg was in a cast. As she studied his appearance, she could not fight her tears, and they rolled down her cheeks.

She looked up at the heart monitor and watched the rhythm of his heart beating, then laid her head on the side of the bed. Her thoughts went to Caleb Grayson, the brilliant scholar who had suffered severe brain trauma in a car accident and now was only capable of doing menial jobs. *The whole world is ahead of you and then with one crippling blow it's in ashes at your feet.* She said a silent prayer for Seth as she gazed at his beautiful face. Feeling dizzy again, she looked up at her mother and Nurse Hudson. "Please take me back to my room," she said softly.

———

The next morning Dr. Coleman Petty examined Jenks. She was the same physician who had treated Seth when he had cut his arm rescuing Maggie Reynolds from her burning automobile. Dr. Petty did various cognitive exercises with her, and Jenks's reflexes and memory recall were satisfactory. She was still dizzy and suffering from a headache, but she felt better than she had the day before.

After the doctor departed, Jenks stood before the mirror in her room and looked at the terrible welt on her forehead. She pushed her hair back and looked at the bruises on her neck that Frank Hiller had caused while strangling her. Tears came to her eyes, and she wiped them with her hand. She realized that both she and Seth had survived a close brush with death. *Had the inventory declaration caused Frank Hiller to change his plans?*

Detective Campbell came by and informed her that the police had been to the house behind Gigi's and that there was no evidence of surveillance equipment in the home. A photograph of Frank Hiller was shown to the owner of the house, James Barton, and he said that he had rented it to him, but the man had signed the lease "Matt Lipscomb" and paid in cash. Before signing the lease agreement, the owner did a background check that showed that he had no police record and was creditworthy. A frown crossed Detective Campbell's face. "We found that a Matt Lipscomb was one of Frank Hiller's former employees at Hiller's Barbells. Frank had done his own background check on Matt Lipscomb and knew he was completely clean. He even used Matt's social security number. He didn't miss a lick, did he?"

"No, sir, he hasn't yet," Jenks replied.

"I found out that Frank Hiller's parents are deceased and he has one sister, but she said they haven't spoken in two years. One more thing—I contacted Jess Fraser, she's the supervisor at Bradbury Laboratories in Charleston. Those invoices that were in the refrigeration locker were records of work that the lab performed for your sister. Ms. Fraser said that conservation techniques were used on metal artifacts. They did work for Gigi on several occasions, and Ms. Fraser was stunned to learn of your sister's death. She told me she used to tease your sister by calling her South Carolina's female version of Mel Fisher."

Later in the day, Jenks had short visits from the Bernsteins, Crawford Forrest, and Ida Mae and Meta Andrews. Ida Mae said they had heard about what happened at their prayer group. They were very worried about her welfare, and they were astonished to find out that the tall man who had rented the home behind Gigi's was Frank Hiller.

That evening, Nurse Hudson came to her room to check her vital signs and told her, "Detective Mason has been placed in a private room. His condition is improving. I'm very thankful."

"Where is he?"

"He's on this floor, room 312, just around the corner from you."

Jenks fell back asleep after Nurse Hudson left the room. She wasn't sure how long she slept, but during the night she woke. The hospital room was dark, except for a fluorescent light above the sink. Jenks rubbed her head and cautiously rose from her bed, putting on her robe. Her mother was asleep on the settee.

Dizziness overcame her again, and she grasped the bed rail to steady herself. After several moments, she gained her equilibrium and made her way to the door, opening it. There was no one in the hallway, and she placed her hand against the wall to steady herself. Slowly, she walked to Seth's hospital room.

She opened the door and made her way to the foot of his bed. The heart monitor displayed the beating of his heart, and he was still on oxygen.

"Miss Ellington, why don't you have a seat?" a gentle voice said.

"Who's there?"

A woman in a nurse's uniform rose from a chair at the side of the room and came to where she was standing. Jenks smelled roses when the woman approached her side and took her by the hand.

"I'm Bernice Heyward. Please come over here and sit down. I know you aren't feeling well. You probably shouldn't be up."

"I wanted to see Seth."

"Yes, ma'am, I've been praying for the two of you. I know the doctors have been worried about his head injury."

Bernice helped Jenks into a chair beside Seth, and Jenks took his hand in hers. The warmth of his hand comforted her, and she gazed at his bruised face. He had a welt on his forehead where he had hit the concrete floor. She stroked his hand, and then placed it against her cheek.

"Miss Ellington, I work as a sitter for the hospital. I'm going to stay with him tonight, so I don't want you worrying about him being alone." She looked at Jenks compassionately. "The man that did this, he is wicked."

Bernice was silent for several moments and then she quietly said, "I understand you're a school teacher."

"Yes, ma'am," Jenks softly responded.

"My oldest daughter is a fifth-grade teacher in Beaufort. We're real proud of her. She was the first member of the family to graduate from college and her younger brothers want to follow her example. My husband and I work two, sometimes three jobs to save up the money for their education. I'm proud of them."

Jenks nodded slightly, but felt her head throb when she did.

"Honey, I think you best get back to bed. I'm gonna walk you to your room."

Bernice stood up and went to Seth, placing her hand on his leg cast. "I don't usually question the Lord, but you would think that when He was creating our bodies, He would have put some muscle in front of the shin bone rather than just behind it. That's about the worst place to take a bad lick. I'm afraid he's gonna feel this for a long time."

She took Jenks by the hand and helped her to her feet. Bernice supported her as they walked together back to her room. In the light of the hallway, Jenks could see that Bernice was a middle-aged woman with deep-brown skin and graying hair. Jenks felt the strength in her frame as she held her arm. "If we need to stop, you just tell me," Bernice said in a calming manner.

When they reached her room, Bernice helped her back into bed. Her mother woke with the noise and rose quickly from the settee. "Jenks—what are you doing?"

"Mama—I had to see about Seth."

"Here—let me help you back into bed," Linda said as she took Jenks by the elbow.

"Mrs. Ellington, she just wanted to see about her young man. I didn't let her stay too long. Now rest easy, Miss Ellington. I'll keep a close eye on Detective Mason tonight."

Bernice left the room, closing the door behind her. "Jenks—please don't get up by yourself again. You're becoming as independent as Gigi was."

"I just need to check on him."

Her mother sighed. "Please get some sleep."

As Jenks lay in her bed, she prayed for Seth and her sister. She remembered what her mother had just said: "You're becoming as independent as Gigi was." Then she fell back asleep thinking of the scent of roses.

———

Jenks woke to the sound of voices in her hospital room. Her mother was speaking to Dr. Petty. "We're hoping to release your daughter tomorrow. The dizziness she's experiencing should continue to diminish. We'll see how she's doing later today."

"Thank you, Doctor. How is Detective Mason?"

"His condition is improving, but he's going to stay with us for a while."

"Dr. Petty, is he going to be all right?" Jenks asked as she joined the conversation.

"Miss Ellington, good to see you awake," Dr. Petty said as she came to the side of the bed. "The blow to his head concerned us a great deal, and he suffered a fracture to his right leg. I'm optimistic—with the rate of his improvement, he has a good chance of a full recovery—although it may take weeks or months."

She patted Jenks on the hand and then walked to the end of the bed. "You're going to need rest. No activities that require deep concentration and no physical undertakings for a while."

"Yes, ma'am," Jenks said quietly.

She was due to return to Raleigh in the next week to begin preparation for the fall semester. That was now out of the question. She would need to phone Dr. Bishop, her principal, and explain what had occurred, but Seth was her main concern. She prayed that he would be able to fulfill his dream of attending law school, even if his studies were delayed. Jenks knew that she would not leave him, and tears came to her eyes when she thought of how he had been hurt. Seth had accompanied her to Fleming's to search for Gigi's salvaged treasures. Jenks wished that she had never sought the antiquities in the first place.

That afternoon, her mother accompanied her to Seth's room. Linda moved the settee close to Seth's bed, and Jenks laid down on the divan and took Seth's hand in hers. Her mother helped her situate pillows under her head and placed a blanket over her. When she opened her eyes again, she looked at her watch and realized that two hours had passed. She slowly sat up on the settee and looked at Seth.

A voice on the other side of the room said, "Miss Ellington, I'm sorry about what happened to you and Seth. We got here as fast as we could. All the flights from Rome were full, and we just barely made the standby list yesterday. I'm Dr. Leslie Walker and this is my wife, Sofia."

Jenks started to stand up, but Dr. Walker rose quickly from his chair and came to her side. "No, please don't get up. I know you're not feeling well."

The Walkers appeared to be in their sixties. Dr. Walker was of medium height and slight build, with gray combed-back hair and blue eyes that exuded warmth. His wife, Sofia, was about the same height as Jenks, and her sandy-blonde hair was cut short in a bob. Her face had few wrinkles, but her expression showed deep concern.

"Thank you, Dr. Walker. Seth has told me so much about you. I'm pleased to meet you both as well."

"Yes, dear, Seth has e-mailed us many times about you," Sofia volunteered.

"I hope all of his writings were favorable."

"Oh yes, my dear—every word of it." She wiped a tear that was falling down her cheek. "This is tragic. His dreams of attending law school this fall. He may have to postpone his plans. I just hope that he will recover soon."

"Yes, ma'am, I do too."

⸺

The next morning, Jenks went to see Seth as soon as she finished breakfast. She put on her robe and walked to his room. The door was open, and she could hear the voices of Dr. Walker and his wife conferring with a nurse. She tapped lightly on the doorframe and then entered the room.

"Come in, Jenkins," Dr. Walker said.

As she came into the room, her eyes focused on Seth. He was awake. She went to his bed and took his hand. His eyes met hers, and his lips turned up in a slight smile.

"Jenks," he said softly.

"I'm so happy to see you awake."

"Jenkins, I'm afraid the events of the day that he was injured are lost to him at this point. Hopefully, he'll regain his memory," Dr. Walker said.

"Yes, sir, I hope so too."

"I'm so sorry about what happened to Gigi," Seth slowly said.

Jenks took his hand in hers and held it tightly. She could feel tears start to well in her eyes.

"Dr. Walker told me what happened on the afternoon I was hurt. He said that Frank Hiller ambushed us at the Fleming's Seafood building." He closed his eyes for a moment, and when he reopened them he said, "Dr. Walker told me that Frank took the regulator out of Gigi's mouth and held her underwater until she drowned—I'm so sorry."

"Thank you. I am too." She leaned over Seth and hugged him.

<hr />

After Jenks was released from the Beaufort Hospital, she made daily trips with her mother to visit Seth. Dr. Walker and his wife were usually in the room with him, and on each visit he was more alert. However, he was having difficulty remembering new information, and she noticed that she had to tell him some things several times.

Jenks was having trouble with her own cognitive skills; she was forgetful and still suffering from headaches. Her mother placed a phone call to Dr. Edwin Bishop, her principal in Cary, North Carolina, and explained about Jenks's condition. He was extremely worried about her and told her to get in touch with him as soon as she felt like returning to work. Jenks did not tell her mother, but she was considering not returning to Raleigh. She knew that Seth was going to need her, and she wanted to be with him.

<hr />

One afternoon, when Jenks and her mother went to see Seth, Mose Lafitte was in the room. "Miss Jenkins, ma'am, how are you folks today?" he inquired.

"I'm feeling much better. Mose, this is my mother, Linda Ellington."

"Ma'am," he nodded with a slight bow of his head before saying, "I's glad to hear it. We been praying for you and Seth in our prayer group. We been real worried about you two."

Seth was awake, and Mose took his hand in his. "Now, you get well. I miss seeing you for my fish."

"I'll be meeting you for a fresh catch in no time," Seth responded.

"No worries, I'll just look forward to seein' you soon."

As Mose turned to face Jenks and her mother, he grinned at them, revealing a full set of white, clean teeth.

"Mose, your teeth are beautiful," Jenks told him admiringly.

"Miss Jenks, I decided to take some of dat reward money for helping bring dose two men to justice from de boating incident. My wife's been after me for years to do something about my teeth. She says dat dese new teeth are better for my health than de ones I had left. To tell you de truth, dese fits better." He squeezed Seth's hand again. "I asked Mr. Jones—it was his daughter Elizabeth who was killed in de accident—to donate de reward money to my church. Dere's hungry folks in our community and de church need a new roof. I's real sorry though about dat young lady and gentleman dat was killed dat night."

Mose shook both Jenks's and her mother's hands before taking his leave. He told Seth that he would continue to pray for him and expected to see him up soon, even if it was on a pair of crutches.

Over the next few days, several well-dressed ladies from Beaufort women's organizations came to see Seth and wish him well. Jenks remembered that Seth was the recipient of several scholarships funded by local benefactors.

She thought back to the evening that she and Seth had dined with Rory and he told her that Seth was the "darling of several women's groups" that wanted to help him with his educational goals. As she thought of Rory, tears came to her eyes.

When Jenks and her mother entered Seth's room one afternoon, Maggie Reynolds was sitting with him. She introduced herself, and Jenks remembered that she was the lady who Seth had saved from her burning automobile weeks before. "I heard about what happened to you and Detective Mason. I'm real sorry, and I hope you two get well real soon."

Tears welled up in Maggie's eyes and she wiped them with the back of her hand as they fell down her cheeks. She looked at Seth, who was asleep, and quietly said, "When I think of what he did for me I can't control my emotions. I'm sorry for carrying on like this," she said as her voice cracked.

"You don't need to apologize," Jenks responded. "Seth is one of those people who will make sacrifices for others. I know."

"He's my hero."

"Mine too," Jenks agreed.

Before she left, Maggie gave Jenks a card for Seth and asked her to let him know she was praying for him. Maggie looked back at Seth one final time before she left the hospital room.

Later that afternoon, Detective Campbell paid a visit to Seth with news of Frank Hiller. The Savannah, Georgia, Police Department discovered that

Sterling Shipping Company had taken on a passenger on one of their cargo ships, *The Temple of the Winds*, that had disembarked in San Juan, Puerto Rico. One of the dispatchers for the company was a former Navy diver named Richard Martin. He had served with Frank Hiller in the US Navy and had arranged travel for his friend from the Port of Savannah. The police reported Martin's dismay at discovering that his friend Frank Hiller was wanted for assault and murder, and that unbeknownst to him, he had helped Frank escape justice. By the time the Savannah police had researched the shipping departures, Frank Hiller had quietly disappeared in Puerto Rico.

⌐────➤

On the morning of Seth's seventh day in the hospital, Dr. Walker joined Jenks and her mother in Seth's hospital room. Seth had just finished breakfast, and he was watching the morning news out of Charleston.

"Do you mind if I turn down the volume on the television?" Dr. Walker inquired.

"No, sir," Seth responded.

Once the volume was minimized, Dr. Walker said, "I've spoken with Dr. Lawrence. He's the dean of the Charleston Law School. We both started our careers together at Limestone College years ago. He has agreed to allow me to attend classes in your stead until you are able to go by yourself."

"Dr. Walker, I don't want to inconvenience you and put you to a lot of trouble."

"Not to worry. Please believe me, it is my pleasure and that of my wife's to see that you stay on track for your goals. Dr. Lawrence has agreed to allow me to record the classes, and of course, I'll keep detailed notes for you."

"Dr. Walker, I can't thank you enough."

"Son, you already have, many times over," he said as he held Seth's hand.

Jenks watched the two of them together and noticed tears roll down Seth's cheeks. She smiled at him, and then wiped away his tears.

⌐────➤

The day that Seth was to be released from the hospital, Jenks's mother and her friend Gregg Mikell left for Raleigh. Before they left, Linda asked Jenks to sit with her at the kitchen table. "Jenks, do you love Seth?"

"Yes, Mama, I do."

"Are you coming back to your teaching job?"

Jenks fidgeted with a napkin on the table. "Seth needs me, and I want to be with him."

"Does he love you?"

"Yes, he has said so."

Linda was quiet for a moment, and then she said, "Gregg and I will continue to look after your apartment and you can discuss your job with Dr. Bishop. I'll leave that up to you when you're ready." Tears started to well in her eyes. "You've given me a terrible fright—I lost my darling Gigi, and then you—almost." Tears rolled down her face, and then she took her daughter in her arms. "Please be careful."

"I will, Mama."

CHAPTER 14

Revelation

T hat afternoon Seth was released from the Beaufort Hospital and
Detective Campbell came to assist him. Two of the nurses who had
looked after him during his stay helped him into a wheelchair for the
elevator ride down to the hospital lobby. Jenks carried his crutches.

When they left the lobby, Dr. Walker and his wife were waiting beside their
silver Cadillac. Detective Campbell helped Seth into the rear of the car. Before
they departed, the detective nodded to Seth and said, "I think you should talk
to your cell phone provider about dropped calls."

Seth shook his hand while they said their good-byes, but as they pulled
out of the parking lot, Seth whispered to Jenks, "What did Thomas mean about
dropped phone calls?"

She squeezed his hand and responded, "I'll explain when we get you
home."

That evening after dinner, Mrs. Walker showed Jenks to a guest bedroom
and invited her to spend the night. "We would like for you to stay with us."
She ran her hand down the side of the doorway frame, and then said, "Seth
has been like a son to me. I only wish that we had gotten to know him earlier.
He's a dear."

"Yes, ma'am, I agree."

"I hope you'll join us in the living room. Leslie is going to play the piano
for Seth."

When they entered the living room, Seth was lying on the couch with a
pillow under his leg. Jenks sat down in a chair beside him and touched his
brow. His lips turned up in a slight smile before he closed his eyes.

Dr. Walker played his piano and Jenks was captivated by the loveliness of the music. She thought she recognized the song: it was the theme music to the movie *Laura* that she and Seth had watched together on their first date. She thought of her embarrassing behavior over dinner in Wren's, when she had accused Seth of obsessing over her sister. She shook her head, and glancing at Seth, she noticed he was watching her.

"That was one of my favorite compositions—the theme from *Laura*," Dr. Walker said at the end of the song.

He continued to play, introducing each song; first, "Waltz for Debbie," and then, "Some Other Time." She could have listened to him play for hours, but he concluded his performance after a hauntingly beautiful rendition of a composition entitled "Peace Piece."

When he finished, Jenks clapped softly for him. "You play the piano magnificently, Dr. Walker, and I enjoyed each of the songs."

"Thank you, Jenkins. The last three songs were made famous by my favorite artist, the late Bill Evans. He was a fine pianist. The last composition, 'Peace Piece' reminds me of the works of Erik Satie or perhaps Debussy."

Dr. Walker rose from the piano bench and walked to where Seth was lying on the couch. He knelt toward him and softly said, "Son, I'd like to help you get to bed now. Dr. Petty said that rest was crucial to your full recovery." He helped Seth into an upright position and then assisted him down the hallway to his bedroom. Once he was in bed, Jenks went by his bedroom to say good night.

Seth was under the covers except for his fractured leg, which rested on a pillow. Jenks bent over and kissed him on the forehead. His eyes gently opened and he said, "I'm glad you're here. What was it that Thomas said to me today about the dropped phone call?"

Jenks sat down on the bed beside him. "After we found Gigi's treasures in the hidden locker at the Fleming's Seafood building, you tried to phone Detective Campbell to alert him. The phone call failed, and you started to go outside the refrigeration locker to place another one." She squeezed his hand. "As you stepped through the threshold of the doorway, Frank Hiller hit you with a metal pipe."

In the darkened bedroom, Jenks could see a frown cross his face.

"I'm so sorry that happened," Jenks continued. "If I hadn't been so obsessed to discover Gigi's findings, we would not have been ambushed by her killer. You would be about to start law school."

He looked sympathetically into her eyes, and responded, "I want you to understand something, Jenks. What happened to me is not your fault. Frank Hiller is to blame for your sister's death and this." He gestured to the cast on his leg.

Seth then closed his eyes for a moment, opened them again, and gazed at Jenks. "There will be a reckoning. I promise you."

———

During the night, Jenks was awakened by frightening cries; she quickly rose from her bed and went to Seth's bedroom.

Dr. Walker and his wife were already in the room and Seth was in tears.

"Tell me what's wrong," Dr. Walker said as he took Seth's hand.

Jenks noticed how stunned Seth looked as he slowly responded, "I dreamed about Steel. I was trying to save him—get to him before he—" Seth stopped talking and Mrs. Walker stroked his head and then handed him the glass of water that was on the nightstand. He came up on his elbow and took several sips before putting his head back down on the pillow.

"I'm sorry to have scared everyone."

Jenks came forward and took Seth's hand in hers. "Is there anything I can do to help you?"

"No, I'll be all right."

Dr. Walker looked at his wife and Jenks and said, "Why don't you two get some rest. I'd like to talk to Seth."

Jenks went to the kitchen to get a glass of water and on her way back to her bedroom she heard Dr. Walker tell Seth, "Son, I think you need to talk about what's bothering you and get it off your chest. It's unhealthy to keep these thoughts locked inside."

She continued to her bedroom and lay back down in her bed. She had trouble going back to sleep. *What did Dr. Walker mean, "You need to talk about what's bothering you"?*

———

The next morning, Detective Campbell called while Dr. Walker was serving breakfast to everyone in the kitchen. Jenks noticed how tired Seth looked as Dr. Walker gave him the telephone. When the conversation was complete, Seth handed the receiver to Jenks and she returned it to its resting place on the wall.

"Thomas said that he had received a phone call from Detective Sanchez with the San Juan Police Department. The police have been on the lookout for Frank Hiller, but there are no clues to his whereabouts. He's just disappeared."

Dr. Walker placed a plate of cooked bacon on the kitchen table and said, "Mr. Hiller's appearance does cause him to stand out. However, there are dozens of islands in the Caribbean that can be reached by boat from Puerto Rico. The police may not have the manpower to seek out every person who owns a seaworthy craft."

Dr. Walker returned to the stove and lifted a large skillet with scrambled eggs and brought it to the kitchen table. "Now, everyone, help yourselves. There is plenty to eat, so no one is to leave the table hungry." He helped himself and then looked at his wife. "Sophie, dear, would you please pass the tomatoes?"

She gazed back at him and handed him the plate.

Jenks could not help but notice how kind and polite Dr. Walker and his wife were to one another. He often called his wife by a pet name, "Soosy," rather than Sofia. Seth had told her they had been married for over forty years, but they still seemed to be deeply in love.

That morning after breakfast, Dr. Walker helped Seth to the living room couch and then left for Charleston and the first day of law school classes. Jenks made sure Seth was sitting comfortably and had one of his law school books, and then she assisted Mrs. Walker with the breakfast dishes.

"Mrs. Walker, I can't help but notice how kind you and Dr. Walker are to one another."

Mrs. Walker raised her eyebrows. "Jenks, that characteristic in Leslie is what attracted me to him. We met as students at Duke University. While I had other suitors who I thought were attractive, there was no one that I had ever met who showed me the kindness and respect that I have received from him. All I can tell you is that when you are deciding on the person with whom you'd like to spend your life, think about how you want to be treated. That will help you with your choice for a husband."

"Yes, ma'am."

She patted Jenks on the shoulder and said, "Seth would make a fine husband."

———

By midafternoon, Dr. Walker had returned from Charleston, and he joined Seth in the living room. Together, they went over the notes that Dr. Walker had taken, and then Seth listened to the recorded lectures.

While the Walkers prepared supper, Jenks went over the class notes again with Seth, asking him questions. She noticed that he was having difficulty retaining the information, and he was yawning. "Why don't we start back up after supper?"

"I'm sorry. I don't seem to be able to focus on the material." He rubbed his temples and sighed.

"Dr. Petty said that you could have trouble retaining new information for a while. Please don't get discouraged." She closed his notebook and asked, "Is there anything you'd like to talk about?"

Seth was quiet for a moment and Jenks thought he was about to tell her something, but instead he reached for her hand and kissed it.

She looked into his chestnut eyes and said, "I love you."

He pulled her close to him and kissed her on the lips. "I love you too, Miss Ellington."

———

After dinner, Seth fell asleep in his bed while reading over the notes that Dr. Walker had taken for him that day. Jenks removed the study materials and then joined the Walkers in the living room. Dr. Walker was softly playing his piano, and Mrs. Walker was reading Dostoyevsky's *Crime and Punishment*. She motioned for Jenks to sit beside her on the couch.

Mrs. Walker placed a bookmark in her novel and then watched her husband perform on the piano. Jenks thought that each of his songs was rich and beautiful, and she rested her head on the back of the couch. When he finished playing, he closed the piano fallboard. "All we need are bass and drum musicians, and we'll be all set."

"What were the names of the songs you were playing?" Jenks inquired.

"The first was 'Emily,' followed by 'I Loves You Porgy.'"

"George Gershwin from *Porgy and Bess*?"

"Yes, that's correct. Both of those songs were recorded magnificently by Bill Evans."

"I had never heard of him until I listened to a CD that Seth played for me one night," Jenks added.

"You're too young to be acquainted with his work unless you're a jazz fan. He passed away over twenty years ago, a victim of his own excesses. I suppose he committed slow suicide due to his addictions."

Jenks thought back to the day that Crawford Forrest described her brother as brilliant, but ruined by his excesses. "That's terrible," she said slowly.

"Yes, I agree. Sadly, artistic genius is often accompanied by weakness for unhealthy indulgences." He sat down in a chair opposite her and added, "Jenkins, I want you to know that you are welcome here for as long as you'd like to stay. Seth is like a son to me, and I want only the best for him. What he's going through is very difficult, but with all our help he'll succeed. While he was one of my brightest students at the university, he singularly stood out due to his work ethic. I know he'll overcome this."

"Thank you, Dr. Walker," Jenks said as she rose from the couch. She felt tired, and she said good night, checking on Seth before going to her bedroom.

———

Dr. Walker upheld his commitment and for the next few weeks traveled to Charleston, taking notes and making recordings of the law school lectures. Jenks studied with Seth each day. When they weren't working on his assignments, she took long walks around the Walker property. Jenks often ended up at the Rabbit Hash Hunt Club where she studied grave markers from the nineteenth century. Summer was fading into fall, but the days were still warm and the leaves were yet to change color.

On the last Saturday of September, Dr. Walker received a phone call during breakfast. The tone of his voice was oddly morose, and when he hung up the receiver, he looked at his wife. "Sophia, that was Herbert Bradley over on Bray's Island. He said that his granddaughter, Elizabeth, took an overdose of sleeping pills and has passed away."

"Oh, my goodness," she exclaimed. "We must go to them."

"Yes, I agree. My Lord, we attended her high school graduation just a little over a year ago. "

Mrs. Walker rose from the kitchen table and washed her coffee cup out in the sink.

"I'll clean up the breakfast dishes," Jenks volunteered.

"Thank you, my dear," Mrs. Walker said as she left the kitchen.

When the Walkers departed for Bray's Island, Jenks got out Seth's school notes. "Would you like to go over contract law first?"

"Yes, that will be fine," Seth replied. Jenks could see worry lines on his face. For the next two hours they reviewed his notes, but Seth was missing questions.

"Are you all right?" she asked.

"I'm sorry, but I can't concentrate."

"Let's take a break for lunch."

"Okay."

Jenks made sandwiches and as they sat down to eat, thunder sounded in the west. The sky became dark and the winds began to pick up. "Looks like we're in for some bad weather," she said.

Lightning flashed, followed by a large thunderclap, and the electricity went off in the house. Jenks went to the pantry and got several candles out, lit them, and placed them on the kitchen island. Walking to the window, she looked out. "My goodness, it's pouring rain outside. I can hardly see to the edge of the woods." She turned and glanced at Seth—he did not respond to her comment. In the half light of the candlelit room, she saw that he was staring into space.

When the severe weather passed, Seth asked Jenks to help him onto the screened porch. There was a daybed against the outside wall of the house, and she helped him maneuver with his crutches to the settee. He wearily sat down, and then Jenks helped him get comfortable. She put a light blanket over him, and then joined him on the bed.

He looked up into her eyes. "I'm very disturbed by Elizabeth Bradley's death."

"Did you know her?"

"Yes, I met her family on several occasions. Her grandparents are good friends with the Walkers."

"Perhaps her death was an accident."

"Unless she left a note, no one can be certain."

Jenks looked out into the Walker's rear yard. Large puddles of water were accumulating on the grounds, and she noticed a huge turtle making its way across the property. She turned back to Seth and said, "Prior to Rory's suicide, I only knew one person who died that way."

"A friend of yours?"

"I think I mentioned her to you. She had terrible trouble with her weight. This was in high school and teenagers ridiculed her because of her obesity. She took some kind of drug and killed herself one afternoon after class."

"Terrible thing," Seth said as he shook his head.

"I'll never forget her wake. I'm not sure why her parents didn't choose a properly sized casket for her, but she was severely cramped inside her coffin. I felt terrible sadness for her."

"There are many reasons that people are driven to take their own lives. Sometimes, they don't have a choice."

"What do you mean?"

"Sometimes, circumstances are so severe that a person chooses death over other alternatives."

She noticed that he was beginning to have tears well in his eyes.

"What's wrong?"

A painful expression was on his countenance, and he slowly replied, "My brother, Steel, took his own life in Afghanistan."

"Oh, my God. Do you know what happened?"

"Yes, to some degree. Allied forces composed of British troops and US Marines were waging an offensive against the Taliban in the Helmand Province. The area is known as a major producer of opium and was heavily controlled by the Taliban. Steel's unit was in an outpost that came under enemy fire, and the Marines were severally outnumbered. Those bastards . . ." He choked, and taking a deep breath, he said in a sob, "The last communication with his unit confirmed that Steel had been shot twice by enemy fire."

"Please go on," she whispered.

He wiped tears from his eyes and strained to speak. "I was told that his fatal wound was self-inflicted—I believe that he knew that he would be taken prisoner and tortured by the Taliban. They do horrible things to their prisoners, especially the wounded. Everyone in his unit died."

"I'm so sorry."

Tears streamed down his cheeks. "I believe he chose to take his own life rather than have death chosen for him and under tortuous circumstances."

"Oh, baby." Jenks lay down beside him on the daybed and took him in her arms. "This is what Dr. Walker said you needed to get off your chest the night you had the terrible nightmare about Steel."

Seth nodded.

"Why didn't you tell me this earlier?"

"I can barely deal with it myself. Forgive me."

"Shh . . . shh, it's all right."

He gazed into her eyes. "I knew that there was something seriously wrong with Steel on the day he died. I felt an indescribable pain."

Cold chills descended upon her. "The same thing happened to me on the day Gigi was murdered."

"I know," he whispered.

They wrapped their arms around each other and held each other tightly. Jenks could feel Seth's tears against her cheeks, and she leaned back to wipe them from his face.

"After he died, I drank myself into a stupor for several days. But I realized that Steel would not want to see me destroying myself with alcohol. I gained my self-control back by thinking about him. He was a man of courage and will always be my hero. For certain, I lost a part of me when Steel passed away." He wiped tears away with the back of his hand. "I know that you felt the same sensations when Gigi was drowning in the river. God help us," Seth said softly.

"Oh, Seth," she said as she pulled him tightly against her and stroked his face. As they lay together, an occasional rumble of thunder sounded in the distance while the rain continued to fall.

⸺⸺⸺

After his cast was removed, Seth wore a soft cast and walked with a cane. He was having pain in his leg and could only walk short distances before having to rest. Since Jenks had met Seth, she had seen him only with a military-style haircut. He had not been to the barber in weeks and his dark hair had grown out to form wavy curls. Jenks loved to run her fingers through it, and she found him sexier with his thick tresses.

Jenks thought back to the first time they had been intimate. She had mentally compared his physique to the statue of a Roman youth whose steely facial determination and physical perfection had reminded her of her lover. Now Seth's hair matched the wavy tresses of the Roman youth. She recalled wondering at that time what Seth's hair would look like if he grew it out. His hair now covered his scar. *Be careful what you wish for.*

On class days, Seth was now traveling with Dr. Walker to Charleston. He was introduced to performing research in the law library, and Dr. Walker continued to help him in the evenings with his studies. Jenks noticed that Seth still tired easily and was continuing to have some memory problems. While Seth was away at school, she often volunteered at the Beaufort County Library. The children's reading sessions were over from the summer, but there was usually someone who could use help with reading or finding a book.

One evening, when Seth lay down on his bed after dinner, Jenks came in to join him. "I'm so tired. Perhaps I should have postponed law school until the spring," Seth said wearily.

"You're going to be fine. Everyone wants to see you succeed. Just don't put unnecessary pressure on yourself."

He took her hand in his and squeezed it. "I don't want you to lose your job in Raleigh because you're here helping take care of me."

"I've already made a decision about returning home. I want to stay with you. I'm not going back."

Tears filled his eyes, and he pulled her into his arms. "I'm glad you're staying," he whispered.

"I'm going by the Beaufort County School District office to inquire about substitute teaching and to see if there are any openings in the spring."

⟵————➔

The next day, Jenks met with Dr. Anderson at the District office, and she was given the contact information for the principals at several local schools. She phoned each administrator and explained her situation and that she was available for substitute teaching. The principal at St. Helena Elementary asked if she could come to work on Friday. One of their third-grade teachers was taking a personal day for business. Jenks agreed to be at the school early so she could meet the staff and go over the teacher's lesson planner.

———

Jenks looked up from her desk as the children came in to the classroom. She greeted them as they entered. Some of the children had just finished breakfast in the cafeteria, and they were involved in conversations in pairs or in small groups.

Jenks looked down at her roll and noticed a familiar name—Amanda Stevens. No sooner had she read the name than she glanced up to see the happy face of her summer reading friend.

"Our teacher told us you were going to be here today. I was so excited when I found out."

"Thank you, Amanda. I'm glad to be here."

"Miss Jenkins, I've got something to show you."

She removed from her backpack a letter and opened it on the teacher's desk.

"What's this?"

"Do you remember when we sailed our boats from my Grammie's dock back during the summer?"

"Yes, I do."

"This is a letter from the boy who found my boat and read my poem. His name is Charles Cain and he lives near Kitty Hawk, North Carolina. He found my boat in the ocean two weeks after we sailed them."

"Amanda, that's wonderful!"

"Yes, ma'am. We're pen pals now, and we write to each other. One day I'd like to go to Cape Hatteras and see what it looks like. Charles said that the Wright Brothers flew their first airplane from Kill Devil Hills. That's near his home."

"Yes, that's true. I'm so excited that someone found your bottle boat. Now you know 'where go the boats!'"

"He wrote me that Kill Devil Hills got its name from when there were ship wreckers. These bad people would hang lanterns around the necks of nags and walk them up and down the beach. It was dark, so the ships thought the nags were other ships floating in between them and land, so it looked like they had lots of space to sail in. Then they sailed right into the reefs. Nags are the same as mules, that's what they called them then."

"So that's how Nags Head, North Carolina, got its name?"

"I think so. I got a book from the library about it. When the ships got wrecked on the rocks, the bad people would go out and steal the cargo. They stole the rum and hid it in the sand dunes. Charles said that the English called rum Kill Devil so that's why the hiding place is named Kill Devil Hills."

"Wow, you've learned some very interesting history from your pen pal."

Amanda beamed with a tremendous grin and folded the letter, returning it to her backpack.

"What did you write about to Charles?"

"I wrote him about how we came to launch the boats, and I told him about you."

"Really?"

"Oh yes, ma'am, I told him how you picked me up from my Grammie's so I didn't miss my reading, and how you took the time to work with me."

Jenks took Amanda's hand in hers. "I enjoyed every minute of it."

The bell rang indicating the beginning of the school day, and Amanda took her seat in the front row.

As Jenks began their lessons, two boys were talking in the rear of the room. Amanda turned and looked at them. Placing her fingers to her lips, she said emphatically, "You get quiet back there!"

The boys looked in her direction and then became silent as they gave Jenks their full attention. Jenks looked at Amanda; she knew she had a loyal ally in this little girl.

After school, Jenks checked on Gigi's house. There were three real estate agents' cards on the kitchen table. She concluded that the showings had not generated any interest since Agnes had not called her about an offer.

When she reached the Walker's property, Jenks could hear the sound of the piano before she came inside. Entering through the back door off the kitchen, she glanced into the living room and saw that Seth was the pianist. She came up behind him as he continued to play. Before she reached him, he turned around and winked at her.

"How did you know I was behind you?"

"You're too noisy. You'd never make it as an Indian."

She bent over him and kissed him on the forehead. "You were playing so beautifully, I thought you were Dr. Walker."

"They're not here. They decided to visit Savannah this weekend."

"Oh, really?"

"Yes, they have a favorite hotel in the downtown they like to stay in . . . the Mansion on Forsyth."

"Interesting."

"The staff is crazy about the Walkers, and they always invite Dr. Walker to play the piano in the Bösendorfer Lounge."

"Bösendorfer?"

"It's a magnificent piano made in Austria."

"I see," Jenks said as she massaged the back of Seth's neck. She could feel the swollen area where Frank Hiller had slammed the steel pole into the back of his head. "How are you feeling this afternoon?"

"No headaches—third day in a row without any pain."

"I'm so glad."

"How was your day in school?"

"You wouldn't believe it, but Amanda Stevens was in my class."

Seth looked at her with slight confusion. "Jenks, I'm sorry, but who is Amanda Stevens?"

She realized that Seth was still having memory issues and she reminded him, "Amanda is the little girl I helped with her reading this past summer."

"Oh yes, I remember now."

Jenks sat down on the piano bench beside Seth and asked him to continue to play. She watched his strong hands on the piano keyboard and listened to him perform several compositions.

"I see you haven't forgotten how to play the piano."

He faced her on the bench and their eyes met and locked on each other's. "We haven't been intimate since we were both hurt," Jenks said.

"Uh-oh, your eyes are turning green—they're almost catlike. What have you got in mind?"

She ran her fingers through his thick, dark hair and then kissed him on the lips. He put his arms around her, returning the kiss, only with more power.

"I want you so badly," she murmured with deep desire.

"I think carrying you into the bedroom is out of the question right now."

"You don't have to carry me. I can walk," she said, standing up from the piano bench. She helped him up by the elbow and handed him his walking cane.

As she led him to his bedroom, she whispered in a calm voice, "I'll be gentle."

Opening the door, he said, "You promise?"

"Yes, sir."

Once inside his bedroom, Jenks pulled Seth's shirt out of his pants and unbuttoned it. Her hands roamed his chest, massaging his muscles. She placed her tongue on one of his nipples and caressed it vigorously. He gasped for breath and she took his hand, pulling him down onto his bed. Her hands went to his pants and unzipped his blue jeans, continuing to touch him passionately.

"What's gotten into you?" he asked, gasping for air.

"I'm crazy about you," she responded with breathless desire.

A low moan escaped his lips and he whispered, "Just keep proving it . . . just keep proving it."

That evening after dinner, Jenks sat down on the living room couch and motioned for Seth to put his head in her lap. She bent over and kissed him on the forehead while rubbing his temples. Kissing him again, she massaged his head and ran her fingers through his curls. "I don't want you to cut your hair in a military style anymore."

"Why is that?"

"I think you look sexy with the waves in your hair, and I like running my fingers through it."

"I see."

Jenks turned on the television that had been put in the living room for Seth to watch while he rested on the couch. Searching through the channels, she commented, "I thought I saw in the paper that *Casablanca* was on tonight." She picked up the Life and Style section of the newspaper and read through the listings for the evening's television programs.

"Here it is—on Turner Classic Movies." She used the remote control device and changed the channel. The movie had already begun, and the scene was set in Rick's Café Américain.

As Jenks started to put the newspaper down, her eye was caught by the photograph of a beautiful blonde. The caption read: "Italian Countess Maria Gavriella in New York to participate in a fund raiser benefiting refugees in war-torn Sudan."

Jenks stared at the photo and gasped. She tried to catch her breath. Seth sat up on an elbow and asked, "What's wrong?"

"Look at the necklace she's wearing in this photo!"

She handed the newspaper to Seth and his eyes grew large as he studied the photograph. He stared at Jenks. "It couldn't be."

"I think it is," Jenks responded, still in shock.

The Countess Maria Gavriella was wearing a gold cross with red stones that was virtually identical to the Petersburg Cross.

"My God—how can we find out about the cross she's wearing?"

"The New York State Police. Jenks, give me your cell phone. I'm going to call Captain Barrett."

———

Seth found out the next day from the New York police that the countess and her husband were staying at the Plaza Hotel. When questioned about the cross by the state police, the countess stated that she and her husband had recently purchased the crucifix and a gold-beaded necklace from a dealer of rare antiquities in St. Thomas, in the US Virgin Islands. The dealer's name: Frederick Augustin.

Within several days, the countess was shown a copy of the video with Gigi holding the cross beside her face. In conversations with the police, the countess stated that Augustin had authenticated the cross from a series of portraits on display in the State Hermitage Museum in St. Petersburg, Russia, that showed Catherine the Great wearing the same crucifix. The initials of the jeweler were displayed on the back of the cross, *AGK*, for Aleksi Gregori Kartashkin. Augustin further authenticated the piece by showing them Kartashkin's unique method of beginning each letter with a double curl at the base, the defining validation of the artist's work.

The New York State Police, armed with a subpoena, were planning to take possession of the Petersburg Cross, but after their second visit to the countess, she and her husband took the first flight from John F. Kennedy International

Airport to Rome, Italy. After their departure, a Park Avenue attorney by the name of Richard Scarborough contacted the New York State Police and said that he would be the countess's legal counsel in the matter. He explained that the countess was attempting to rectify the matter with Frederick Augustin and since a large sum of money was at stake, she asked for patience in the matter. In an e-mail correspondence to the New York State Police, Scarborough included Augustin's address and phone number in St. Thomas.

When Seth told Jenks of the countess's departure back to Italy, she was livid. "The woman knows that my sister died over the discovery of the Petersburg Cross, but she runs like a coward back home."

"The fact that they paid Augustin over two million dollars for the piece may have something to do with her behavior. I doubt she wants to give it up."

"The cross is of secondary importance to me. I'm going to pay Mr. Augustin a visit. I want to know where Frank Hiller went."

"Please hire an attorney who specializes in international law and let your legal counsel handle this."

"I'm going to hire an attorney."

Seth stared at her before saying, "Uh-oh, I see that gleam in your eyes— your eyes are turning green, Miss Ellington."

"I've made my decision, and I'm going to St. Thomas."

"Not without me, you're not," Seth declared.

CHAPTER 15

Dronningen's Gade

The Boeing 757 touched down at Cyril E. King Airport near Charlotte Amalie, US Virgin Islands. As Jenks and Seth descended the passenger stairs, they heard the sounds of a calypso band in the terminal, welcoming the passengers to St. Thomas; the steel drums reverberated louder than the other instruments. Both Jenks and Seth had carried on backpacks so there was no delay in exiting the terminal. As they left the building, a sultry breeze caught Jenks's hair and blew her tresses around her face. Taking a tie from her handbag, she put her hair in a ponytail.

"This will get my hair off my neck. Whew, it's hot here . . . feels like Beaufort in the summer."

Seth was leaning on his walking cane for support, and Jenks noticed he frowned as he shifted his weight to his healthy leg.

"You should have let me do this alone. You're in pain."

"There's not a chance I would have let you come down here alone. I think the pain is just from stiffness from being on the airliner. I took some Advil in the terminal, so hopefully the pain will diminish."

She stroked his cheek and said, "Thank you for coming with me."

"Yes, ma'am."

When their turn for a taxi came, Jenks handed the address for Frederick Augustin's business on Dronningen's Gade to the driver.

He looked at the address and said, "Yes, I'll have you there in a few minutes. Please have a seat."

They climbed inside the open-air taxi and Seth winced as he sat down in the seat. "Dronningen's Gade. What does that mean?"

"Queen Street in Danish. I looked it up. The Danes controlled these islands for many years until the United States purchased them in 1917."

"You are quite the researcher."

The taxi driver entered the conversation. "Where are you folks from?" he said with an island brogue.

"We're from Beaufort, South Carolina."

"Ah yes, I have been to Charleston. I have a cousin who lives near there. Beautiful place."

"Are you down here on your honeymoon?"

Jenks felt herself blush. She gazed at Seth and responded, "No, we're here to see Mr. Augustin, a dealer in rare antiquities."

"Yes, I recognized his address—I know his family."

"You do?"

"Oh yes, ma'am. They are fine folks."

A cold chill ran up Jenks's spine. "So—he's been in business for many years?"

"Yes, ma'am, and his father before him."

The ride was brief, and they reached the business district of Charlotte Amalie within several minutes. As they got out of the taxi, Jenks paid the driver, and he gave her his card. "If I can take you anywhere else on the island, please call me on my cell phone." He pointed to a phone number and then waved good-bye. "Thank you, Miss."

There were a number of exclusive jewelry shops on Dronningen's Gade, and Jenks and Seth slowly made their way to Augustin's Rare Antiquities. When they reached his shop, there was a Closed sign in the window. There were display cases in the front window of the business, but they were all empty of merchandise.

"Let's look around for a little while and then come back."

"Forgive me, baby, but I'm going to sit on this bench in the shade while you look around. I'll call you on your cell phone if Mr. Augustin shows up."

"You're sure you don't mind?"

He shook his head. "I'll just people watch until you return."

She gave him a squeeze on the hand and went to explore some of the shops. There was undoubtedly some of the finest jewelry she had ever seen in these stores, and she found herself entranced by some of the exquisite diamonds. Gazing into the display cases, she said quietly, "I'd settle for a half-carat."

When she returned to Seth, he was quietly observing passersby and she sat down on the bench beside him.

"See anything pretty?"

"I don't think I saw anything that wasn't pretty."

He raised his chin up and looked at her. "I think you're pretty."

Their eyes locked and Jenks could feel the heat of the energy that existed between the two of them. "Thank you."

She continued to gaze into his eyes. "I'm going to go into the jewelry store beside Augustin's and see if they know anything about why his store is closed."

She rose from her seat and entered the glass doors of Francesca's. A cool rush of air-conditioned air soothed her as she entered the store. An attractive older woman with blonde hair piled on her head and stunning blue eyes approached her. "Is there anything I can show you in the store?"

Jenks knew she couldn't afford anything in the store, so she went straight to the point. "Thank you for your offer to help, but I have some business with Mr. Augustin who runs the store next to yours."

"Was he expecting you?"

"I don't have an appointment for today, but I think he'll be interested in speaking with me." She blushed as she lied.

"He's been ill, and I think he is resting at home," she volunteered. "Miss?"

"My name is Jenks Ellington. Thank you for your time."

Before the woman could ask any more questions, Jenks said good-bye and departed the store. She returned to her place on the bench beside Seth. "The lady in the store says that Mr. Augustin has been ill and is recuperating at home."

"Why don't we pay him a visit? Our taxi driver seemed to know him personally. I bet he knows his address," Seth said.

"Good idea."

Jenks phoned the driver, Charles Sermet, and he responded that he was on a fare but would be able to pick them up within twenty minutes.

When Charles arrived, Jenks engaged him in conversation. "I understand that Mr. Augustin is not well. I have urgent business to discuss with him. Could you please take me to his residence?"

"I see—you have business with him then?"

"Yes, he'll be very disappointed should he miss me." She bit her bottom lip as she told another lie.

"Please come." He got out of the taxi and opened the door for Jenks and Seth.

"What did you do to your leg, young man?"

"It happened on the job."

"You must have dangerous work."

"Occasionally," Seth replied.

Charles took a road into the hills of the island. As they gained elevation, Jenks marveled at the magnificent blue-green color of the ocean. They reached an area of exclusive homes and Charles pulled into the driveway of a stunning white villa that looked over the Caribbean Sea.

"This is Mr. Augustin's residence."

"Thank you for bringing us here. I will be in need of your services again."

"You have my number."

Jenks paid the fare and then turned to Seth. Together they walked to a columned entranceway with French double doors. The interior of the home was completely open, permitting a view to the ocean. Jenks rang the doorbell.

Within a few moments, a young, dark-haired woman in a maid's uniform came to the door. "Miss Ellington?" she inquired.

Jenks looked inquisitively at Seth. "Yes, I'm Jenks Ellington." *How did she know my name?*

"Come in. Mr. Augustin is expecting you. And you too, sir," she said as she looked admiringly at Seth.

Jenks noticed the woman's appreciation of Seth. They followed her through the house, which was richly decorated with Oriental rugs and handsome antiques. Sitting at a desk in a study that opened to a balcony was a gray-haired man wearing a deep-purple housecoat. He stood from his chair, and Jenks noticed that his face was pale.

He did not smile, but extended his hand out to Jenks and then to Seth. "I'm Frederick Augustin, and unfortunately, I know why you're here."

"How did you know we were coming?"

"Francesca, who owns the jewelry store next to mine, phoned me."

Jenks got straight to the point. "I'm Jenks Ellington, and this is my friend, Seth Mason."

"Yes, I know who both of you are. Mr. Mason, I'm dreadfully sorry about the leg and your head. I hope you're feeling some better."

"Yes, sir. I'm taking one day at a time."

Jenks looked at her clasped hands before continuing, "I'm trying to locate Frank Hiller. My sister found the Petersburg Cross along with other artifacts off the South Carolina coast while diving last spring. Frank Hiller murdered her and stole her discoveries. He sold the cross to you."

Augustin rubbed his temples and then a frown creased his brow. "I have heard about this from the St. Thomas police as well as from the irate Countess Gavriella." He sighed and pointed to two chairs in front of his desk. "Please, both of you have a seat."

As Seth sat down he winced with pain, and Mr. Augustin inquired, "Can we get you something for the leg?"

"Thank you. I took Advil a couple of hours ago."

Augustin turned back to Jenks. "I'm afraid that I don't know where he was going after he left me. I paid him a handsome price for the Petersburg Cross. I think I was just so shocked to see one of Kartashkin's creations that I jumped at the opportunity to acquire the piece without asking enough questions." He stopped speaking for a moment and rubbed his temples again.

"I want you to understand that I am guilty of being an overzealous fool, but a charlatan I am not. I'm dreadfully sorry about your sister and what happened to you two when you were assaulted by Mr. Hiller."

He pulled a document out of his desk. Jenks gasped. The sheet of paper he removed from the drawer was the declaration that Gigi had intended to turn in to the South Carolina Institute of Archaeology and Anthropology.

"This document explained how he came to have it in his possession, and I knew immediately that the cross was authentic by Kartashkin's initials on the back of the piece." His face darkened. "I can't begin to tell you how sorry I am."

A cooling breeze blew in from the open patio, billowing white silky drapes that rustled in the wind. He handed the list to Jenks and said, "The police might not appreciate this, but I was saving the document for you. I knew you would come."

Jenks took the document from him and studied it before asking, "Did you acquire artifacts other than the cross from Frank Hiller?"

"No, Miss Ellington—I did not."

"And you don't know where Frank Hiller went?" Jenks knew this was the second time she had asked that question.

"I'm afraid not." Taking a deep breath he continued, "I really didn't care where he was going. I was caught up in my own exuberance." He sighed again. "I'm afraid the countess would slay me if she could. The money that she paid me for the cross was quickly invested into a prime piece of real estate I'd been watching for some time. This is a horrible situation, and I'm afraid it's taken a toll on my health."

He slowly stood up from his desk and said, "I know the police have been checking with yachting services, the airlines, and private airplane charter service for clues. You might want to try speaking with some of the operators yourself."

"Thank you for seeing us."

"Yes, I apologize, but I need to lie down. I hope we can all work toward a settlement over this matter; if we don't it may be the death of me."

———

For the remainder of the afternoon, Jenks hired Charles Sermet to take them to nautical and aviation services that could have provided the means for Frank Hiller to depart the island. Seth stayed in the taxi and stretched his leg out across a bench seat. He had not complained about pain, but Jenks could tell he was uncomfortable by the look in his eyes.

By late afternoon, she had seen most of the operators, but some of the yachting services were on cruises. She gave Mr. Sermet one last address and they went back up into the hills high above the sea.

When they reached their final destination Jenks looked at Seth and said, "This is where we're spending the night."

"Wow, this is beautiful!"

"Most of the hotels were full, so I booked this. It was one of the few places available on short notice."

"You'll have to allow me to help you with the cost."

"No—this is on me. I appreciate your coming with me."

They were staying in a boutique hotel, Guerlin's, which was a white stucco Mediterranean-style building with open-air porches and white drapes that billowed in the wind. The hotel reminded Jenks of Mr. Augustin's villa. The view over the sea was breathtaking.

Jenks thanked Mr. Sermet for his assistance and paid the fare, while making arrangements for him to spend several hours with them the next day.

Before he left, he looked keenly into Jenks's eyes and said, "I know why you are here. Detective Mason has explained about what happened to your sister. Tonight, I will see if I can find out anything else. I get together with many friends on Saturday evening, and I will ask around. Most of my friends drive taxis. Perhaps someone knows something that can be of help to you."

"Mr. Sermet . . ."

"No worries, I will be very discreet. Do you have an extra photograph of Mr. Hiller?"

"Yes, I do."

Jenks removed the photograph from her purse and handed it to him. He glanced at it and then put it in his shirt pocket.

"Thank you. I'll see you in the morning at eight?"

He shook his head. "I'm afraid on a Sunday morning you will find that most people are not at work that early—many are in church. I think nine o'clock would be more reasonable."

"All right."

"Please enjoy your evening."

"Thank you for your help today."

"Yes, ma'am. Until tomorrow." He waved as he departed the driveway in front of the hotel.

When they reached their room, Seth looked around the chamber and whistled softly. "This is going to set you back a few dollars."

"Yes, I know, but it's worth it to find Frank Hiller."

The room had high ceilings, was decorated in white, and had a patio. Jenks opened the French doors to the outside and a strong breeze filled the room. With the setting sun, the temperature had diminished, making the breeze very comfortable. Seth hobbled over to the bed and sat down on the side. He lay back on the mattress and winced as he stretched out completely.

"How are you feeling?"

"Sore."

"I'm sorry." She got him Advil and a glass of water.

"Thank you, Jenks. I'm going to rest for a while." He took the medication, drank the water, and then handed Jenks the empty glass. He looked exhausted as he lay back on the pillows, closing his eyes.

Jenks walked out onto the patio and looked out over the sea. A magnificent sailboat gliding across the water caught her eye, and she focused on the sleek beauty of the watercraft. The spinnaker was set out and the sailboat pitched to one side as it skimmed across the sapphire-blue waters.

"Beautiful," she murmured.

When she walked back inside the room, Seth was lightly snoring. He didn't usually snore, but she concluded his fatigue was causing this condition.

———

At eight o'clock, she woke him, and he was at first startled but relaxed as he looked into her eyes.

"I didn't remember where I was for a moment," he said, taking a deep breath.

"How are you feeling?"

"A bit stiff."

"Dinner is served on the patio."

"My goodness, you've gone all out."

Jenks gave him her hand and helped him into an upright position. He shuffled out to the patio, which was illuminated by torches and candlelight.

Lifting the silver covers that protected their dinners, she said, "Lobster is on the menu. Can I offer you a glass of Pinot Grigio?"

"Yes, ma'am." She handed him a glass and then took a sip of her own. "I apologize, but I already started on the wine."

"Everything looks great."

"I think the staff did a wonderful job of setting up the patio. They wanted to know if we were on our honeymoon."

Seth's lips turned up into a smile. "That would be my dream come true."

Jenks felt herself blush. "Is that a marriage proposal?"

"Yes, it is, but forgive me for not getting down on my knee. I think it might hurt too much."

Excitement surged through her entire body. "I want to hear you say it again. Ask me properly."

He took her hand in his. "Jenks, I love you dearly, and I would be honored to be your husband. Would you please consent to being my wife?"

She didn't have to think about his proposal. "Yes, I would love to be your wife."

With those spoken words, she went to him and crouched down on her knees wrapping her arms around him. He kissed her on the neck and then she gazed into his eyes.

"The lights are dim out here, but I can still tell your eyes are turning green, Miss Ellington. What have you got in mind?"

"I'll tell you after dinner," she said in a whisper.

———

At nine the next morning, Mr. Sermet was waiting for them outside Guerlin's. A warm tropical breeze was coming off the ocean and the wind caught Jenks's hair and blew it around her face. She immediately tied it back.

As Jenks and Seth approached the open-air taxi, Mr. Sermet opened the door for them and Seth gingerly climbed into a middle seat.

"Good morning. I hope you are both well today," he said in his deep island brogue.

"We're fine, and I hope you are."

"Oh yes, ma'am."

Curiosity was driving Jenks mad. "Were you able to find anything out last night?"

"I'm not sure."

"What do you mean?"

"I showed Mr. Hiller's photo to a number of my friends. One of them thought he may have taken a man who resembled Mr. Hiller down to the wharf. He said that the man had dark hair—he was not a blond." Mr. Sermet held up Frank Hiller's photo as he said this.

"Do you know where he took him?"

"Yes, to the Red Hook ferry. First, we'll go there."

"Thank you," Jenks said as she climbed into the taxi.

After Mr. Sermet climbed into the driver's seat, he turned around and said, "My friend, Albert, dropped this man off at the Red Hook terminal. A scheduled ferry runs between St. Thomas and St. John at that location. We'll talk to the captain."

When they arrived at the terminal, the ferry was parked at the wharf and passengers were going on board. Mr. Sermet opened the door for Jenks and Seth.

"Come, I will go down to the ferry with you."

A tall black man in naval attire was in charge of the operation and Mr. Sermet walked in his direction. When the man saw him, he grinned, and they shook hands. Mr. Sermet waved to Jenks and Seth to come forward and he said, "Lawrence, this is Miss Ellington, and her friend, Mr. Mason."

Jenks noticed that he did not introduce Seth as Detective Mason and she extended her right hand for a shake. Seth followed suit.

"Lawrence, Miss Ellington would like to know if you remember seeing this man." Mr. Sermet held up Frank Hiller's photograph and Lawrence took the photo in his hand. He studied it for a few moments and then shook his head. "I can't say that I recall seeing him." Lawrence called to two other employees and showed them the photograph. They both shook their heads as they studied the picture. He started to hand it back and then said, "Wait."

He went on board the ferry and after a few minutes he returned with a young woman also dressed in naval attire.

"This is Tyra. She thinks she may have seen this man."

She stepped forward and said, "It would have been a few months ago, but I remember I thought him very handsome, tall, you know—well built. The man I remember had dark hair, but his face . . . it could be the man."

"Where did he go?"

"He was on the ferry to Cruz Bay."

"Do you have any idea where he was going after that?"

"No, ma'am. I'm sorry, but I do not."

"When we get to Cruz Bay, I'll introduce you to Gunnar Lund. He's the harbor master. Just wait for me at the rear of the ferry when we dock," Lawrence said.

She thanked Mr. Sermet for his help and paid him for the fare. He gazed into her eyes and said, "Call me if you need further assistance. I am very sorry about your sister. I hope I have helped you in some way."

"You have—thank you."

Before he departed, he shook Seth's hand and then looked keenly at the two of them. "Be very careful." With these words, he turned and walked back to his taxi.

———

The trip to Cruz Bay was brief. Jenks admired the clear, sapphire-blue waters and the volcanic islands of the British and US Virgin Islands. When they arrived at St. John, the ferry pulled to the wharf. After several moments, the passengers disembarked the boat. Jenks and Seth waited in the aft portion of the ferry for Captain Lawrence to finish his duties.

"Our plane leaves at four-thirty, so we can only stay here a short while," said Jenks.

"We could stay longer if we need to."

"No, I don't want you to miss classes because of this."

"I've already spoken to my professors and explained that I had police matters to handle and may miss some of my classes. They told me I could make up any missed work."

"Yes—they've been very helpful, but let's hope we can find something out today."

Within a few moments Captain Lawrence joined Jenks and Seth. "Let' go see Gunnar Lund. I'll show you the way."

They descended the ramp from the ferry to the dock. Lawrence noticed that Seth was limping and using a cane for support and slowed down his gate. Pointing to Seth's leg he said, "I'm sorry. I will walk slower."

He led them inside a building that was adjacent to a pier. There were numerous oil-stained engine parts on the floor, and the air smelled heavily of grease and saltwater.

"Gunnar, are you here?" Captain Lawrence called out.

"Yes, back here. Be right with you," a voice responded from the rear of the building.

Within a moment, a man with deeply tanned skin and large blue eyes emerged from a back room. He was as tall as Seth and rugged looking.

"Lawrence, how are you today?" Gunnar asked.

"I am very well, and I hope you are."

They looked at one another while Gunnar rubbed his hands on a grease-streaked blue cloth.

"What can I help you with?"

"This young lady is looking for the man in this photograph." He motioned for Jenks to show it to him.

"No, I don't want to touch it. I'll get grease on it. Just hold it up for me."

He gazed into Jenks's eyes and said, "What'd he do?"

Jenks drew a deep breath and replied, "He murdered my sister."

The two men looked at each other warily, and Jenks saw that Seth was studying their reaction.

Gunnar looked back at the photo and said, "Maybe. A few months ago, there was a man with darker hair, but similar facial features, who waited for several hours for a yachting service to pick him up."

Jenks took a deep breath as she heard this news. "Do you know where he went?"

"No, ma'am."

Thinking they had reached a dead end, she sighed with disappointment—but then he continued. "You see that red, double-masted sailboat down at the end of the wharf, the *Alhambra*? Her Captain, Lucas Soto, may be able to tell you."

A young man was sitting on board the deck of the handsome watercraft. "Good morning," he said as Seth and Jenks approached.

Jenks's heart was racing, but she acknowledged the ship's mate, who appeared to be a youth of about twenty years. His dark hair was unruly, and he blushed as he looked at Jenks.

"Good morning to you too," she replied. "We're looking for Captain Soto. Is he here?"

"No, ma'am, he's—er . . . visiting with a friend."

"Do you know where we can find him? It's very important."

The young man replied, "I don't think he'd appreciate my discussing his whereabouts when he's off duty."

Determined, Jenks removed the photo of Frank Hiller from her pocket.

"We just spoke with the harbor master, Gunnar Lund, and he thinks that the man in this photo chartered the *Alhambra* some weeks ago."

"Let me take a look at it. I'm Rhett Alexander."

Handing him the photograph Jenks introduced herself. "I'm Jenks Ellington, and this is my friend Seth Mason."

He studied the picture and then raised his head up and looked in Jenks's eyes. "Yeah, he looks like the guy we took to Belize."

"Belize? That's a long way from St. John."

"Yes, ma'am, it is."

"Do you know where he was going?"

"No, ma'am. The guy kinda kept to himself. He had dark hair—not the blond in this photo."

He handed back the picture. "Did he do something wrong?"

"He murdered my sister."

The young man's mouth dropped open and a look of shock went across his face. "Jesus Christ," he murmured. "Can you come back later today after three? Lucas—I mean Captain Soto—will be here then."

"No—our airline flight leaves this afternoon from Charlotte Amalie. Please!"

He was quiet for a moment, and then he said, "Captain Soto's gonna have my ass, but hang on a minute, and I'll give you the address where you can find him."

They waited only a short while at the taxi stand in Cruz Bay before an open-air taxi pulled up beside them. "Good morning," the man enthusiastically called out in an island brogue. "Can I take you somewhere?"

"Yes, we need to go to this address," she said, handing him a note card.

"Ah yes, it will take us only about fifteen minutes." He got out of the driver's seat and opened the rear door for Jenks and Seth. "Bad leg?"

"Yes, I'm afraid so," Seth replied.

As Jenks climbed into the taxi, she studied the man's features. He was probably in his forties, his hair was cut very short, and he had perfectly straight white teeth.

"You have a wonderful smile," Jenks told him.

"Thank you, ma'am. It is in my family's blood roots. My name is Elias and welcome to St. John."

Just as Elias had said, the drive took about fifteen minutes, and they parked at a hillside home that overlooked the ocean. "Jason Brinkley's residence," he murmured.

Jenks heard his comment and said, "Wait for us, please."

"As you wish, ma'am."

Jenks got out of the taxi, and Seth slid out behind her. "Let me go first," he said.

He went ahead of her to the home and knocked firmly on the door. Within a few minutes, an attractive brunette came to the door and looked at Seth and Jenks. Jenks noticed that her eyes lingered on Seth. "How can I help you?" she inquired.

"We need to speak with Captain Lucas Soto."

She had a shocked look on her face, and she responded, "I'm afraid you have the wrong address."

Jenks felt a heated rush of energy caused by fear and anxiety course through her limbs and she responded, "Please! Captain Soto took a man to Belize several weeks ago. That man, Frank Hiller, murdered my sister."

The woman looked stunned, but then walked away leaving the door slightly ajar. Within a few minutes, a handsome, sun-tanned man with dark hair and wearing only shorts appeared at the door. He was well built, and he looked at Seth and Jenks. "How can I help you? I'm Lucas Soto."

Jenks introduced herself and Seth to him. He came outside and led them to a secluded sitting area in the yard. Jenks handed him the photo of Frank Hiller, and he studied it for a moment. "The hair was darker, but that's his face. James Jefferies. He had a Belizean passport."

"A Belizean passport?" Jenks asked with surprise. "His name's not James Jefferies, it's Frank Hiller, and he's a US citizen."

"I can only tell you what I saw. He kept to himself. Didn't say too much."

He handed the photo back to Jenks. "The guy paid me cash and with the economy being the way it is, I was glad for the business."

"Where did you take him in Belize?"

"Miss Ellington, I don't know if you're familiar with Belize, but there's a reef system that runs the length of the country. The *Alhambra* runs too deep in the water to get past that reef. When we were off San Pedro, he called a water taxi that picked him up and took him to shore. He said 'thank you' and that was it. I figured it was his responsibility to handle any business he might have had with immigration services."

Jenks took a deep breath and said, "Thank you for talking with us."

"He murdered your sister?" he said as a deep frown crossed his countenance.

"Yes, he drowned her."

Lucas's face darkened, and he replied. "If you pursue him to Central America, use extreme caution. I saw that he was a powerful man."

"Yes, he is."

When they returned to Cruz Bay, Elias dropped Jenks and Seth off at the Red Hook ferry. Opening the door for them, he pointed to Seth and said, "Take it easy on the leg."

Seth nodded.

"Thank you for your help this morning," Jenks said.

"Oh yes, ma'am . . . you never know what you'll discover on a Sunday morning."

Jenks knew what he was referring to.

"I mind my own business. I stay out of trouble that way," he beamed.

She paid the fare and rewarded him with a generous tip. He looked at the payment, grinned at the two of them, and said, "It is nice to be nice," in a sweet island brogue.

On the flight back to the United States, Seth was seated in an aisle seat and Jenks sat in the center. He stretched his leg out and winced slightly as he settled in for the flight. He then took her hand in his and kissed her knuckles.

"I insist that you let me help on the cost of this trip. It's not every day a man gets engaged."

"No—I'm going to use a little of the money that I was saving to buy the bungalow in Raleigh. That's no longer in my plans."

He leaned back in the seat and frowned slightly.

"How are you holding up?" Jenks asked.

"Other than law school, I hope there are no pressing matters for the next several days. I'm tired."

"I'm sorry."

She sat quietly for a moment before saying, "Why would he pick Belize?"

"Remember what Lucas Soto said. There is a reef system that runs the length of the country. Frank Hiller is a diver. World-class diving conditions would be of interest to him."

"You're smart."

"Thank you, Miss Ellington."

"But how did he get a Belizean passport?"

"I'm only guessing of course, but it's possibly a very good forgery. When we get our hands on him, we'll find out precisely."

"How are we going to find him, and what did he do with the other artifacts he stole from Gigi?"

"The Federal Bureau of Investigation has a legal attaché in San Salvador that covers Belize and other Central American countries. As far as the other artifacts, that question can be answered by Mr. Hiller."

"It sounds like he's attempting to disguise himself by darkening his hair, but his physique is hard to mistake," Jenks said.

"There's no way to be sure he stayed in Belize. I'll start the investigation process tomorrow."

Seth was in touch with Captain Barrett from the Beaufort County Sheriff's Department early the next morning. When he finished his conversation, he came into the kitchen, where Jenks was making coffee. "My captain is going to contact the FBI office in Columbia, and they'll get in touch with the legal attaché in San Salvador."

"What we need is a break," Jenks answered. "Maybe I should hire a private investigator."

"Let's see what happens with the FBI legal attaché, and then you can decide what to do."

"Good morning, Seth and Jenks," Dr. Walker said as he entered the kitchen. "I'd like to hear about your trip, but first, I'm cooking eggs and bacon. Can I make you breakfast?"

"That would be nice," Jenks declared. They had not eaten dinner the night before, and she found herself extremely hungry and tired from the trip to the Virgin Islands.

"Dr. Walker, we have something to tell you," Seth said.

Dr. Walker turned to both of them, giving them his full attention. "Jenks has consented to be my wife," Seth said proudly.

"How wonderful," Dr. Walker said, clasping his hands together. "Sophie, where are you? Come into the kitchen, dear!"

Within a few moments she entered the room, her white linen shirttail hanging out of her lounge pants. Jenks was surprised to see her so casually attired. She was normally dressed to perfection.

"What is it?"

"Seth and Jenks have decided to become husband and wife. Isn't that wonderful news?"

Her face erupted into a brilliant smile, and she came first to Jenks and hugged her. She then went to Seth. "I am so happy for you. I think you two are perfect for each other."

Jenks could barely control her emotions and tears welled in her eyes.

"Have you decided on a date?" she asked, her eyes twinkling.

"No, ma'am, not yet," Seth replied.

"We can host the wedding here at our house. It would give Leslie and me great pleasure if you would allow us to do that."

Jenks felt herself blush with excitement and appreciation. "That would be wonderful!" She spoke without consulting Seth, but when she looked in his direction, he nodded his head in agreement.

"This is wonderful news. I'll make you dinner tonight, and we can celebrate," Dr. Walker said. He turned back to the stove and removed a large stainless-steel frying pan from the pot rack.

"Now, tell me how things went in the Virgin Islands. I hope you found helpful information."

Seth took a sip of coffee and told the Walkers details of their findings.

———

After breakfast, Jenks read the *Beaufort Gazette* and noticed an article concerning an upcoming exhibit in Columbia featuring artwork from Hudson River School artists. She thought of the portrait of Iris Elliott that hung in the Gibbes Museum in Charleston. Her portrait had been painted by Daniel Huntington, who was known for his contributions to the Hudson River School movement.

Seth was preparing to leave with Dr. Walker for law school, so Jenks quickly showed him the notice concerning the art exhibit.

"I'd like to go to this show in Columbia. Would you go with me this weekend?"

He looked at the article and gave it a quick read. "As long as you drive." And then with a brief kiss to her lips, he headed out the door.

CHAPTER 16

The Course of Empire

*T*he Columbia Museum of Art was in a modern building on Main Street with walls of glass that permitted sunlight to fill the vestibule. As they approached the front desk, a young woman acknowledged them.

"Are you here for the Hudson River School Exhibition?" she asked Seth. Jenks cleared her throat and the young woman looked in her direction.

"Yes, we are."

"That will be twelve dollars each."

Jenks paid the price of admission, and they walked to a gallery within the building that displayed the exhibit. Numerous paintings filled the walls of the rooms, and Jenks walked from canvas to canvas studying the artwork.

There was an antique sofa with intricately designed woodwork around the edges in the center of the first exhibit room. Seth took a seat on the couch and stretched out his leg.

Walking back to him, Jenks quietly asked, "Are you all right?"

"Yes, I'm going to admire the paintings from a distance. You go right ahead and look. Take your time."

Jenks's eyes were drawn to a large placard that described the Hudson River School philosophy:

> Nature was the image of the Creation and God was to be found within it. Painting the land expressed hope for the future in America where natural wonders were plentiful.

She roamed from one exhibit room to another admiring the beauty of the artwork. Finally, at the last room, Jenks came to Thomas Cole's *The Course of Empire*. This was a series of five paintings that depicted the transformation of a wilderness area into a state of glory and then, due to human intervention, into a wasteland. The first painting showed a magnificent view of the wilderness landscape while the second depicted the same location, but in a pastoral state: man and nature in harmony. The third painting illustrated civilization in a golden period, followed by a fourth: the violent destruction of the magnificent city at the hands of an unknown enemy. Lastly, the once-majestic empire had been returned to a savage state, but—without humanity.

Chills ran though her body as she viewed the paintings in sequence. Returning to the front exhibit room, she walked up behind Seth and placed her hands on his shoulders. "I want to show you something. Please come with me."

Jenks extended her right hand. Seth took it, and as he stood he pulled her against him and kissed her on the forehead. "You smell like honey," he whispered.

Jenks noticed that a couple was looking in their direction, and she took his hand in hers. "This way," she said. He used his cane to steady himself as he shuffled to the Cole exhibit.

Once in the room, Seth went to each painting and read the placard describing the symbolism in each work of art. The most disturbing of the portraits depicted the empire under attack; the citizens being murdered by an unidentified adversary. "It says on the placard that Cole was comparing the rise and fall of the Roman Empire to the rise of America. He questions if time is running out for civilization."

She thought back to what Rory had said about Sarah Humphries and her rape by her own comrades.

"Seth—do you remember what Rory said about what happened to Sarah Humphries?"

He sighed and squeezed her hand. "Yes, he said, 'we're our own worst enemies.'"

"We need to be looking out for one another rather than preying on one another for the purposes of exploitation," she said softly. She thought of Gigi. Frank Hiller had attacked and murdered her sister for an ornament of gold. *All-consuming greed is a horrible vice.*

Seth stood at her side and put his arm around her. The last placard she read detailed how Thomas Cole opened the exhibit of *The Course of Empire* in 1834. He advertised the exhibit in a newspaper using a portion of a poem written by Lord George Byron:

> There is the moral of all human tales;
> 'Tis but the same rehearsal of the past.
> First freedom and then Glory—when that fails,
> Wealth, vice, corruption—barbarism at last.
> And History, with all her volumes vast,
> Hath but *one* page . . .

"'Hath but one page' means there is only one story for all civilizations: the rise and fall," Jenks said as she read from the brochure on the exhibition.

She felt coldness descend upon her: *Our destruction comes from within: We're our own worst enemies.* Jenks thought of the inner torment that Rory had experienced. He had felt that when Americans prey on each other we're heading for our own demise. She then thought of Frank Hiller. His misplaced greed had led him to murder Gigi. *Barbarism at last.* She whispered, "One page . . ."

She looked into Seth's eyes and hugged him closely to her.

CHAPTER 17

Thanksgiving

*D*r. Walker prepared a feast of turkey and dressing for Thanksgiving. The day was cool without a cloud in the sky. He led the prayer over the meal, giving thanks for the beautiful blue sky and the heavens. "We're only stewards of this land—here to take care of His creation while we're on this earth." He thanked God for Seth's and Jenks's recovery. Before he finished, he asked God to continue to watch over Seth and Jenks. Jenks knew that he was concerned about her consuming desire to bring Frank Hiller to justice.

Seth's final examinations were coming up, so instead of watching the traditional game of football after the meal, Jenks and Seth went into his room and pored over his studies. Seth was having almost no trouble recollecting the material, and after several hours of study they took a break.

"How would you like to take a walk?" he asked.

"Do you feel strong enough?"

"Yes, ma'am, I thought we'd walk to the hunt club. It's such a beautiful day."

As they left the Walker's house, Jenks noticed that Seth was not using his cane. He walked without a limp. The autumn air was cool and a light breeze blew falling leaves across the sandy lane. Seth held her hand during the walk and occasionally pulled her hand to his mouth, kissing her knuckles. They spoke of his law school exams until they reached the Rabbit Hash Hunt Club.

Seth motioned for her to sit down on one of the picnic tables. As she sat down, the wind caught her hair and blew it around her face. Seth pushed it back and, pulling her close, kissed her repeatedly on her face. "Miss Ellington, you are beautiful."

"Thank you, Detective Mason."

Her mind flashed back to the last time she had sat at one of the hunt club's picnic tables. Rory had been with them then.

"What are you thinking about?" he gently asked.

"Rory."

"Me too."

They both looked into each other's eyes and Jenks rested her head against Seth's shoulder. "I miss him," Seth slowly said.

"I do as well."

He took Rory's gold watch out of his vest pocket and looked at it—his expression unreadable.

They were both silent for a few moments and then Jenks brought up Frank Hiller. "We haven't heard any news from the FBI legal attaché in San Salvador."

"Captain Barrett said they are in regular contact with the police in Belize City. This is just going to take some time."

Jenks picked up a stick and drew a face in the sand. "I want Captain Barrett to find out the names of private investigators in Belize. What we need is a break. This could drag on for ages."

"Patience, my dear."

"I'm trying. I just can't stand the thought that he's free and my sister . . ."

"I know, baby."

The sun was getting low in the western sky and Seth stood up from the picnic table. He pointed up to the sky. "Look—the moon's already up. Let's start back home."

"I have something I want to tell you."

"What's that?"

"I've made a decision about Gigi's house."

"Go on."

"When the listing expires at the end of the year, I'm going to take it off the market. Eventually, we're going to need a place to live. I thought we could stay there for a while—just until you finish law school."

"Are you sure?"

"Yes. I have many memories, both good and bad, associated with Gigi's house, and I'd like for us to have a home that we choose together. I don't think we have to rush it."

"I believe you have a good idea."

"I intend to reimburse Agnes for her expenses. I know she's tried hard."

"Good girl," he said kissing her on the lips.

On the way back to the Walker's, Jenks noticed that Seth had started to have a slight limp with his right leg, but he did not complain.

———

On Seth's last day of exams, Jenks drove him to Charleston. She spent the morning Christmas shopping on King Street, but had an irresistible urge to visit the Gibbes Museum and revisit the portrait of Iris Elliott.

Once inside the museum, she went to the second floor, to the display on the Civil War era. Jenks's eyes locked onto those of Iris Elliott as she stood in front of her portrait. She admired her lovely features: rosy cheeks, golden hair, and swan neck with the gold cross around it.

"You had no idea what you were in for, did you, Iris?" Jenks said softly.

She imagined the severe changes that had abruptly altered Iris's life after the painting of her portrait: the tragic effects of the Civil War, her home being looted by Union soldiers, the death of her two brothers in battle, and then her own tragic death in childbirth. "You are so lovely and look so innocent," Jenks spoke softly, out loud, to the portrait. "It's good that you didn't know. You wouldn't look so content." She spent a few more moments studying Iris's delicate features before speaking again. "You came to know sacrifice and loss, but I wish your jeweled cross had never been found. Oh—how things would be different," she said as tears welled in her eyes.

Leaving the museum, she walked back to the Charleston Law School. Seth came out of the building after his last exam and wrapped his arms around Jenks. "Have you been waiting very long?"

"No, sir, I just arrived. How did it go?"

"I think everything went well. I feel good about all the exams."

"Wonderful—lunch is on me!"

They walked several blocks to a diminutive café, Jestine's Kitchen, where they waited in line for a table. "I hear this is a great place to eat."

Jenks was feeling melancholy from visiting Iris Elliott and from thinking of Gigi. She stared at the ground and was quiet.

"Is there something wrong?" Seth asked as he lifted her chin up to look into her eyes.

"I went to the Gibbes Museum and had a conversation with Iris Elliott."

A slight smile came to Seth's face, and he responded, "Did she have anything to say?"

"Oh Seth—don't tease me!"

He bent down and kissed her on the lips. "What are you thinking about?"

"Gigi. I want you to ask Captain Barrett to get a recommendation from the FBI legal attaché in San Salvador or the Belize police for a private investigator who can search for Frank Hiller. I intend to find him," she declared with determination.

"Miss Ellington, your eyes are turning green."

———

Captain Barrett was able to get an endorsement for a private investigator from Detective Alvarez with the Belize City Police Department. A semiretired Belize City Detective, Richard Price, was highly recommended. Alvarez explained that Price had been the Chief of Detectives for fifteen years, and still assisted the police on special operations. Price was knowledgeable of all the districts of Belize, and possessed strong political connections.

When Jenks contacted Price, she explained the details of her sister's death and how they had tracked Frank Hiller to Belize. She found the detective to be patient and reserved in their conversations, and very thorough with the questions he asked her.

When Jenks had secured his services, he told her, "Miss Ellington, I will start with the cays since Mr. Hiller is a diver, but if I were attempting to hide, I would probably choose a rural location to sit comfortably until I felt enough time had passed by. Belize has thousands of acres of jungle and forest land with sparse settlement, except in the cities and the cays." He stopped speaking for a moment. "It is good that Belize has an extradition agreement in homicide cases with the United States—and we always do our best to cooperate. Of course, we cannot be sure that he is still here."

"Mr. Price, how could he get a Belizean passport?"

"I will investigate this—a very good forgery possibly." She remembered that was exactly what Seth had said.

She thanked him for his help and he asked for patience. He told her he would be in touch when he had an update.

———

Before Christmas, Seth received his grades from the Charleston Law School. When the transcript arrived, he insisted that Jenks look first. Carefully, she opened the envelope and studied the grades.

"Well?"

She hugged him. "One strong B that was almost an A—all the rest are solid A's. I'm so proud of you."

He picked her up and twirled her in his arms. Holding her tightly, he kissed her on the face.

"See—I told you you'd do great."

They kissed each other fervently, and he led her into his bedroom.

"The Walkers are in Beaufort this afternoon—let's celebrate," Seth said.

"I'm ready!"

"You're always ready."

"I adore my teacher and the lessons!"

———

That evening before dinner Dr. Walker opened a bottle of Schramsberg Blanc de Noirs to celebrate Seth's highly successful semester in law school. He toasted Seth and praised him for his hard work. "Son, I'm so proud of you."

"Thank you, Dr. Walker. I couldn't have done it without you."

"I promise you it was my pleasure," he said, patting Seth on the shoulder.

For dinner, Dr. Walker had prepared a meal of filet mignon, grilled vegetables, and salad. During the meal, he explained that he and Sofia would be returning to Italy immediately after Christmas. They wanted to celebrate the New Year in Rome, but would be back from Europe by spring to help with Jenks's and Seth's wedding.

Seth and Jenks had decided on an early June wedding date and Sofia Walker had discussed several events that she'd like to host for them, including the nuptials.

After dinner, Jenks and Seth cleaned up the dishes while Dr. Walker played a soft jazz piece on the piano. "I'll load the dishwasher, if you'll bring me the plates," Jenks said.

Seth handed her the dishes. "I must have done something right to have the Walkers and you in my life."

She looked at him, and saw his eyes brimmed with tears.

He kissed her on the lips before returning to the dining room for more of the plates.

———

On Christmas Eve, after dinner, Seth invited Jenks to accompany him out onto the Walker's front porch. White lights decorating the porch twinkled in the darkness. The night air was cold and the scent of pluff mud and salt air was strong in the evening breeze.

Jenks felt chilled and she wrapped her arms around Seth, pulling him close to her. "Merry Christmas—I love you."

He kissed her on her forehead and then on both cheeks. Suddenly, he dropped down on one knee and took a small box out of his coat pocket. Jenks was thrilled as she gazed down into his eyes.

"Miss Ellington, I am honored that you have consented to be my wife." He took a diamond engagement ring out of the case and slid it on her left ring finger. She held her hand out and gazed at the fire in the stones created by the white Christmas lights.

"Thank you, baby."

"The Walkers went with me to Charleston to pick it out one day after class."

"I had no idea," she said blushing.

"Well, it was supposed to be a surprise."

"I love you, Detective Mason." With those words, she dropped to her knees and hugged him tightly against her. "You've made me so happy!"

"Have I?"

"Yes, you have," she said with blissful delight.

They both stood and danced to the slow jazz music that Dr. Walker was playing on his piano, the melody only slightly muffled by the closed doors.

Please don't let this ever end.

———

Two days after Christmas, the Walkers left for Italy. Jenks was taking down some of the Christmas lights when the phone rang. Seth was assisting at the sheriff's department that week, and Jenks picked up the phone.

"Walker's residence," she announced into the receiver.

"Miss Ellington, please. This is Richard Price calling from Belize."

"This is she."

"Miss Ellington, I'm not sure yet, but I may have a lead on the whereabouts of Frank Hiller. I have a nephew who works in the city office of the town of Orange Walk. He has told me of a man who some weeks ago leased a home in the Orange Walk District that formerly belonged to the British Honduras Mahogany Company. It was used by their company elite until their operations ceased. The home is now owned by a Canadian couple who have attempted to sell the property with little success. I checked to see how any utilities are listed, and the electricity is still in the Canadians' name."

"I see."

"The property is backed up to the Rio Bravo Conservation Area."

"Rio Bravo?"

"Yes, ma'am—it is one of the most abundant wildlife sanctuaries in the world—with many unexcavated Maya sites. All in all—a very private location."

"I see."

"Miss Ellington, I will try to find out more about the man without contacting the Canadian couple who owns the house. You never know how they might react. If this man is Mr. Hiller, I don't want him alerted. When I know more, I will be in touch."

"Thank you for your help, Mr. Price."

"It is my pleasure, Miss."

When she finished her conversation with him, she anxiously phoned Seth at the sheriff's department. He was helping Detective Campbell with a case file when she got him on the line.

"I've heard from Mr. Price in Belize!" she said, barely able to catch her breath from the excitement. "A nephew of his who works in the city office of Orange Walk says a man who resembles the description of Frank Hiller leased a home in the Orange Walk District . . . near a nature preserve named Rio Bravo."

"Hmmm . . . I thought that was the name of a John Wayne movie," Seth interrupted, deadpan.

"John Wayne? Would you please be serious?"

"Baby, you sound terribly nervous. Calm down now. Take a deep breath."

She inhaled deeply and tried to calm herself. After a moment, she said, "I'm better now."

"Okay, young lady—I'll see you in a few hours."

That evening several photographs were e-mailed to Jenks from Mr. Price. The pictures were of a physically fit man with brown hair and a beard, sitting on the front porch of a handsome white two-story home. Due to the distance from which the photos had been taken, it was difficult to confirm if the man was Frank Hiller.

Jenks e-mailed him that she was simply wasn't sure if the man was Hiller. He replied that he would try again for a closer shot.

The next afternoon, Mr. Price sent two more photos of the same man, taken from a closer distance, while he sat in a lounge chair in the yard. There was a striking resemblance between the man and Frank Hiller, but she wasn't certain.

Jenks phoned Seth at the sheriff's department and he immediately came on the line with her.

"I received two more photos of the man who Mr. Price thought could be Frank Hiller."

"And what do you think?"

"I'm just not sure if it's him."

"I can go down to Belize to identify him."

"He murdered my sister. I want to be the one to identify him. We'll go together."

"Are you sure that I can't talk you out of this?"

"No, sir—absolutely not."

CHAPTER 18

Little Bird

T he drive from Belize City to the Orange Walk District took about an hour on the Northern Highway. Once they left the main highway and traveled on rural roads, the surroundings became dense with jungle flora. The roads were unpaved and so pitted that Jenks felt like her teeth were about to be knocked out.

They passed by some dwellings that looked barely habitable. There was no electrical wiring connected to the shacks, no telephone poles, and clothes hung on lines to dry. Instead of doors, a section of cloth hung in the doorways of several dwellings. Children played naked in front of some of the huts.

Mr. Price had picked Jenks and Seth up when their flight landed in Belize City for their drive to the Orange Walk District. In person he was just as he had been on the telephone, reserved and polite. He was almost as tall as Seth and wore a white linen shirt and khaki pants. He had dark, serious eyes and graying hair beneath a straw fedora.

When they reached the area where the Canadians' house was located, Mr. Price pulled the car off the road and parked behind a stand of bamboo near a stream. "We will walk in from here," he said as he handed them both insect repellant. "Mosquitos," he commented dryly.

They walked along an old roadway that had thick vegetation on either side. "This is an old logging road," Price said quietly. "When the British Honduras Mahogany Company was in operation, they were very active in this area." He pointed to the thickness of the jungle that encroached on the trail. "It doesn't take very long for the wilderness to take over."

He continued, "There are many unexcavated Maya sites in this area. The jungle is so dense that most of the locations are covered by centuries of plant growth."

Seth held out his hand to Jenks and pushed some branches out of her path. "What happened to the Maya?" Jenks asked.

"Their society flourished for many centuries, but by the time of the Spanish Conquest, the Maya civilization had collapsed. The cause of their decline is uncertain, but I have heard some scholars put forth the theory that deforestation led to their demise."

"How did that happen?" Seth asked.

"The jungle was cleared for farming, but strong storms caused the washing away of the fertile soil. They were unable to grow enough crops to support the population. I have also heard that perhaps deforestation led to long-term drought. There are many theories."

"History hath but one page," Jenks said softly as she thought back to the Thomas Cole series of paintings, *The Course of Empire*.

"Miss?" Mr. Price looked at her quizzically.

Just as Jenks was about to explain, a slight movement of something on the trail in front of them caught her eye. She was behind Mr. Price, and Seth was following in the rear. She grabbed Mr. Price by his arm. "There was something moving . . . just ahead."

All three of them stopped in their tracks as they studied the trail. *"Mi Dios!"* he exclaimed, crossing himself. "Good eye, Miss Ellington—now watch yourselves . . . yellow-jawed tommy goff," Mr. Price put his arm out to stop their forward progress.

"Big female from the looks of it," he continued.

They all stood motionless as a brown-and-tan snake with triangle designs on its body moved in a serpentine across the trail. "Back up . . . give it a wide berth."

They slowly retraced their steps, giving the snake plenty of room to move into the jungle.

"Poisonous?" Jenks choked out the word.

"It is not the most poisonous snake, but it can be very dangerous. Mostly, it is nocturnal—we may have disturbed it from rest. It is a pit viper . . . also known as the fer-de-lance. There are a number of bites in Belize each year, mostly occurring while farmers are tending their fields."

"Can you die from the bite?"

Mr. Price removed his fedora and wiped his forehead with a handkerchief. He looked intently into Jenks's eyes before saying, "Oh yes, Miss. If untreated, the bite can be fatal. Belize is a very rural country. Doctors are mostly in the cities, so a bite victim may have many miles to travel for treatment."

"Oh, my."

"Just to let you know—I have heard that the Maya built their cities in locations where these snakes were prevalent, to ward off intruders."

After a moment, the snake disappeared into the jungle, and Mr. Price motioned for them to continue.

"Perhaps that's how the Maya civilization collapsed," Jenks murmured softly to Seth.

He squeezed her hand and gave her a wink as they went forward.

———

After another fifteen minutes of walking, Mr. Price pointed through an opening in the jungle to the house formerly owned by the British Honduras Mahogany Company. The structure stood out like a white jewel in contrast to the background of greenery that surrounded it.

The threesome moved as close to the beautifully manicured lawn as they could while still staying out of view. Many lush tropical plants were included in the landscaping. Hummingbirds were darting around red flowering plants and multitudes of butterflies were fluttering above a fountain in the yard.

"This place is like a vision of paradise," Jenks whispered. *What is Frank Hiller doing in paradise?*

Mr. Price removed a telescopic lens from a camera bag. They drank from water containers and took positions to watch for the tall man who had leased the property.

Thunder faintly sounded in the distance and as time passed grew louder and more frequent. Rain started to fall, lightly at first, but after a few minutes they were drenched by a downpour. The threesome got underneath the boughs of a large tree in an effort to stay dry. Jenks snuggled close to Seth, but after several minutes in the deluge, she was soaked.

Even though they were in a tropical climate, Jenks felt cold chills, and she realized she was trembling. She snuggled close to Seth in an effort to stay warm.

Mr. Price noticed her shivering and said, "We can come back tomorrow if you like."

Determined, Jenks replied, "No, I've been waiting for this for some time. I'll be all right. Let's wait."

"Come closer," Seth told her as he hugged her against him.

They waited. Several hours went by. Mosquitos descended upon them and were humming in their ears. Jenks took her jacket off and put it over her head.

Eventually the rain passed, and multitudes of birds, some very colorful, alit on the lawn in front of the magnificent white house. "I've never seen so many different types of birds in my life," Jenks said softly.

The quietness was suddenly shattered by extremely loud growls and howls.

"What was that?" Jenks said in shock.

"Do not worry. That is the call of the howler monkey. Their cry can be heard for miles."

The calls continued and Jenks huddled close to Seth.

The sun was getting low on the horizon, and Mr. Price spoke up after a long silence. "We have only a little light left in the day. I have made arrangements for us to stay at a jungle lodge not far from here. I think we should call it a day. I prefer not to be on the logging trail after dark."

Just as he finished his last sentence, the sound of a car engine became audible in the distance. A white Range Rover came into view from the jungle road and parked in front of the house.

Mr. Price handed Jenks the telescopic lens and nodded his head for her to take a look at the vehicle's occupant. She quickly raised the lens to her eye and stood motionless.

The driver stepped out of the Range Rover and came around to the passenger side to remove two shopping bags.

"Can you tell if it's him?" Seth asked.

She quietly studied the man for a few moments before saying, "Yes, I can. It's Frank Hiller. I can see his blond roots from here."

She handed the lens to Seth so that he could take a look. An expression of deep determination crossed his face as he studied the man. "That's him, all right."

They watched as Frank got back into the vehicle and drove into a garage.

A few lights came on inside, and the white house glowed warmly against the deep green of the jungle flora.

⤙⟶

That evening from the Chan Chich Resort, Seth and Mr. Price made phone calls to the police in Belize City and to the FBI legal attaché in San Salvador. Detective Campbell would fly to Belize to accompany Seth when they returned to the United States with Gigi's killer.

Detective Alvarez would be going before a magistrate in the Northern Court Sector of Belize the next day to obtain an arrest warrant for homicide for Frank Hiller. Then the combined forces of the Belize Police, the FBI, and the Beaufort County Sheriff's Department would serve the warrant. Jenks was told there would be at least six officers to make the arrest.

"Do you think that's enough?" she inquired.

"Yes, I think so," Seth replied.

"Mr. Price—thank you for all your help with this," Jenks said.

"Miss Ellington, I plan to see this through with you. A good detective doesn't abandon the case until it is complete. If you'll excuse me now, I will retire for the evening. I will see you two at breakfast . . . at eight."

"Yes, sir," Jenks responded.

Seth put his arm around Jenks and gave her shoulder a gentle squeeze. "Would you like something to drink?"

"I'd love some white wine."

Seth went into the bar and when he returned he had a bottle of Chilean Chardonnay and two wineglasses. They left the lodge and walked across the torchlit grounds of the resort to their cabana.

Jenks collapsed onto the bed and Seth opened the bottle of wine and poured her a glass. "Here you are young lady," he said handing her the wine.

She sat up and took a sip. "Mmmm . . . I don't think I've ever had Chilean wine before."

"How are you feeling?" Seth asked.

"I'm exhausted. Thank you for holding me during the rainstorm today."

"My pleasure." He gazed at her for a moment and then a slight frown crossed his brow. "When we serve the warrant on Frank Hiller I want you to stay here at the resort. I've already spoken with the manager, Elder, and he'll arrange transportation for you to Belize City for the flight back to the US."

"I'm coming with you. I want to see him arrested."

"If you're present, then I'll have to worry about you as well as making the arrest."

"I'll make a deal with you. I'll ask Mr. Price to stay with me, and we'll observe the arrest from a distance."

"Jenks, the other officers may object to your presence as well."

"I'll think about what you've said." She took another sip of her wine. "I'm tired, but I'm so anxious about Frank Hiller being caught, I don't know if I can sleep."

"You'll have no energy tomorrow if you don't sleep. Let me help you."

He climbed onto the bed beside her. "Lie on your front."

She did as she was told and Seth massaged her shoulders. "Why don't you take a shower, and then I'll continue this."

"You're so good to me."

"It's easy to be good to you."

After her shower and Seth's back massage, Jenks fell into an exhausted sleep.

———

When she woke the next morning, she was alone. Her body was stiff from the exertions of the previous day, and she slowly rolled out of the bed. Taking a few moments, she studied her cabana, admiring the thatched ceiling, tile floor, and the warmth created by lamplight. She had been too tired to admire the petite lodge the night before.

Seth opened the door carrying two large mugs of coffee in his hands. She could smell the delicious aroma of the drink as he handed her a cup. "Here, baby, this will get you going."

She took a large sip. "Mmmm . . . tastes great. It's strong."

"I was told that the coffee beans are grown nearby at Gallon Jug."

"Gallon Jug?"

"Yes, I was told by the hostess, Irma, that when the British arrived to harvest mahogany, they found old gallon jugs left by the Spanish centuries before—hence the name, Gallon Jug."

He looked at his watch. "Thomas will be arriving in Belize later this morning. The police will be picking him up from the airport for the drive up here. Two federal officers with the FBI will be flying to the airstrip at Gallon Jug this afternoon from San Salvador. We will be meeting here to make our plans."

"I see."

"Jenks, get dressed. I've been out exploring while you slept. I want to show you the grounds around the lodge. This place is remarkable. I was told that the lodge is built on a former Maya site, and *Chan Chich* means *little bird*. I don't think I've ever seen so many species of birds in my life. After we meet with Mr. Price for breakfast, let's take a walk around."

After a delicious breakfast of sausage, eggs, biscuits, and fruit, Seth and Jenks set off on foot to explore the grounds. Mr. Price declined to join them, as he had visited the lodge on several occasions.

Seth took Jenks by the hand. "We'll start with this pathway. I was told that there is an undisturbed Maya site along this trail."

As they ventured into the jungle, a group on horseback passed by them. Greetings were exchanged before the party on horseback disappeared around a bend in the pathway. Eventually, they reached the Maya site. The jungle was cleared away to some degree and a wall of limestone surrounded what appeared to be an ancient temple. "One of the guides said this site dates to approximately seven hundred BC."

"It's simply amazing," Jenks replied. She studied the structures at the site. There was movement in the trees above them, and a group of large brown-and-black monkeys congregated in the tree limbs above.

"I was told that we might encounter howler monkeys. They're looking at you like they might carry you off."

Jenks gazed at the monkeys for a moment and then looked at Seth. "I'm nervous."

"I won't let the monkeys grab you."

"I mean about Frank Hiller."

"I know. I'm just teasing you. I plan to keep you busy today so that you don't have time to think about him." Seth put his hand under her chin and tilted her head up to look at him.

"Everything's going to be all right. Just calm down and take a deep breath."

She complied with his command and then they continued their walk. "I understand that a couple sighted a jaguar in broad daylight a few days ago along this path."

He took her by her hand and led her back onto the trail. The monkeys continued to let out deafening growls and howls.

⟵⟶

Late that afternoon, the combined law enforcement officers met in the lodge at the Chan Chich Resort. Detective Alvarez had secured the arrest warrant for Frank Hiller from a magistrate earlier in the day. Accompanying him was a young officer, referred to only as Lopez, from Belize City. Seth introduced himself and Thomas Campbell. Then he introduced Jenks to the group of officers.

The two FBI agents from San Salvador were physically fit men in their forties. The higher-ranking officer was named Warren Simpson. The other agent, Antonio Castillo, had a deep scar just at his hairline and remained quiet most of the time.

Seth drew out a sketch of the property with Mr. Price's help. The two police officers from Belize City agreed to go in before nightfall to watch the property and verify that Frank Hiller was there and that the warrant could be served at first light. Satellite phones and side arms were provided by the FBI. Due to Belize's strict gun control laws, special permission had been obtained from the police commissioner in Belmopan to bring the weapons into the country. Seth and Thomas would serve the warrant and the other officers would provide support. Jenks couldn't help but think how much she wanted to see Frank Hiller's face when he was placed under arrest.

Before the meeting concluded, Mr. Price said that he would remain off the property with Miss Ellington at a safe distance to observe and to help with surveillance. "Extra sets of eyes can only help," he said.

Due to Price's reputation with both the FBI and the Belize police there was little argument. Jenks stood and thanked the men for their efforts to bring Frank Hiller to justice. She looked in Seth's direction after speaking, only to see him glaring at her with a dark scowl on his face. Thomas took a look at Seth, and then came to her patting her on the shoulder. Jenks looked up into his eyes. "Thomas—thank you for coming down here to help with the rendition process."

"Yes, ma'am. I'll be glad to see this guy brought to justice."

Mr. Price joined Jenks, Seth, and Thomas. He looked at Seth before saying, "I do not want you to worry. I am not only a private investigator, but I am still an employee of the Belize City Police Department, and I often work in security details as a bodyguard. I will look after Miss Ellington." He nodded to the group and then said good night.

The two FBI agents were the next to leave the room. On the way back to the cabana, Jenks and Seth passed the two men as they sat on an open-air porch, smoking cigars. Their conversation was being conducted in Spanish, but when they noticed their presence they switched to English and said good night.

Seth followed her into the cabana. Jenks could see on his face a rare look of contained anger. "Did you ask Mr. Price to stay with you during the arrest? The truth, Jenks!"

"I'm always honest with you. Look, Seth—I need to do this for Gigi."

"Anything can happen, and I don't want you to get hurt."

"I think Mr. Price knows what he's doing."

"That's not the point."

"Seth . . . Please, no more discussion. I intend to see that bastard put under arrest." She held up her hand to stop him from saying anything else.

During the night, a severe storm descended upon the area. The winds blew with such ferocity that Jenks feared that the roof might come off their cabana. She snuggled close to Seth, and she realized he was awake as well. He kissed her repeatedly on her cheeks and lips.

"Are you worried?" she whispered.

"I am about you."

She didn't respond, but put her arms around him and held him tightly. "I love you."

"Miss Ellington, I love you too."

Before dawn, the police officers who had staked out the property overnight phoned the FBI agents to confirm that Frank Hiller was at home and to say that the road leading to his home was blocked by trees downed in yesterday's storm. The officers approaching the property would have to park a short distance away and walk in. The downed trees also meant that Frank Hiller had no effective means of escape—except on foot.

At first light, the group of law enforcement officers took their agreed-upon positions around the home. Jenks and Mr. Price were positioned just off the roadway to the property, in a location that made the viewing of the arrest possible.

The winds were still strong and Jenks pulled her hair back with a tie to keep it from whipping into her face. Mr. Price looked at her. "I was told this morning that the weather we experienced last night is coming from a tropical disturbance off the coast of Belize. We may be in for some more bad weather today . . . late in the year for it though."

Jenks was so nervous that she had begun to twirl her hair with her fingers—a motion that was noticed by Mr. Price.

"Do not worry. We will soon have Mr. Hiller in custody."

Jenks gave him a slight smile, and he returned it. He then handed Jenks a pair of field glasses before putting the telescopic lens up to his eye. Together, they watched.

Jenks's breathing hitched as she watched the officers take their positions around the house. Seth and Thomas went to the front door. Jenks could not hear what they were saying, but without hesitation they entered through the screened doors at the front entrance. Just as they went inside, movement caught Jenks's eye off to the right of the house. She quickly realized that a portion of a large tree had broken off during last night's storm, and someone was moving within the large boughs that lay across the lawn. "Frank Hiller," she hissed.

Pointing quickly to the area, Jenks declared, "He's there . . . inside the boughs of a downed tree."

The sound of chopping wood could now be heard above the whistling of the wind. Mr. Price laid his lens on its case and used his cell phone to alert the other officers. Jenks could barely breathe as she watched Seth and Thomas come back outside to the front of the house and then quickly race to the side with the downed tree limbs. She tried to lick her lips, but there was no moisture in her mouth.

The other officers appeared from other vantage points, and she could still see the torso of Frank Hiller. His lower body was obscured by the branches of the tree.

Within seconds, he was surrounded by the officers, and she watched as his hands went up into the air.

Then—almost as if some unknown force had intervened, another large bough broke off the partially downed tree and came careening to the ground. Jenks watched in horror as the limb descended upon the men. Frank Hiller was untouched and ran toward the jungle behind the house. For a moment, the story of Meta Andrews's relative losing his son when a large limb broke from a tree he was trimming, striking the child dead, flashed through her mind. Mr. Price put down the telescopic lens and removed a large black handgun from a holster underneath his linen shirt.

"The man has incredible luck," Mr. Price murmured. "Miss Ellington, stay here," he said, looking her in the eye.

He moved quickly in the direction of the house and she made a decision. Right or wrong—she was following Price to the home. She prayed that none of the officers were injured from the falling bough. *Dear God, let Seth be all right.*

Her heart was beating fiercely when she reached the downed tree. The young officer, Lopez, who had accompanied Detective Alvarez, had been struck by a bough and was bleeding from a contusion to his head. Alvarez and Mr. Price were administering first aid. Jenks caught her breath, and Mr. Price looked up at her with a look of warning. "Miss Ellington, stay here. Do not go any further."

"Mr. Price, I have to see about Seth."

Jenks ran toward the back of the property. She could see on the damp lawn the trail of footfalls that led toward the jungle. As she neared the edge of the lawn, the path split in two. She could tell that both trails had been taken. *They've split up. What trail to take?*

Suddenly, the sound of a gunshot rang out. Then a noise that was surreal filled the air. It sounded like the beating of the wings of thousands of birds. She was frozen in place as the sky went black ahead of her.

The wave of darkness descended upon her, and she realized the origin of the beating of wings. *Holy Lord Jesus, bats, thousands of them.*

She dropped to her knees and covered her head with her arms as the creatures engulfed the air around her. Just how much time passed as she crouched on the ground, she could not be sure. The fluttering noise of their beating wings dissipated, and she cautiously lifted her head up. The sky was still obscured by the multitudes of bats disturbed from their rest by the gunshot.

Taking a deep breath, she continued her trek down the trail. At a bend in the pathway, there was a man lying face down. Jenks ran as quickly as she could to the individual and turned him over. "Thomas, are you all right?"

He only made a slight moan and did not wake when she shook him. Thomas had a serious welt on his forehead, and Jenks attempted to revive him, but to no avail. *Seth, where are you?*

Jenks felt like her heart might burst as she ran with all her might further into the jungle. It was obvious to her that the path had recently been used by others. Above her own frantic breathing, she heard the sounds of a struggle just ahead of her.

She entered what appeared to be a small clearing, and in front of her were Seth and Frank Hiller in hand-to-hand combat. Moving quickly, Jenks ran in their direction. On the ground in front of her was Seth's handgun. She picked it up and pointed the gun toward Frank Hiller.

Terrified that she might accidentally shoot Seth, she stood by as the two men battled one another furiously. In a split second, Frank hit Seth hard across the face, and he fell to the ground.

She raised the gun and pointed it at Hiller. He took only one step toward her—his expression unreadable.

For just a moment thoughts of Gigi flashed through her mind. *Don't hesitate—he killed Gigi—he'll kill you and Seth as well.*

"Jenks—protect yourself! Shoot him!" Seth cried out as he raised himself from the ground. "Shoot!"

Without warning, the ground underneath Frank Hiller gave way, and he disappeared off the side of the plateau. Jenks looked around her and realized they were standing on a partially cleared terrace. They were on the site of a Maya ruin.

From the hollow into which he had descended, Hiller made a chilling cry of pain, guttural, almost inhuman. Jenks had never heard a sound so frightening in her life. Seth slowly got to his feet and carefully made his way near the edge of the terrace. He held his hand out, signaling for Jenks to stop. "Don't come any further."

A deep frown crossed his face. "What are you doing here?"

"I had to see about you!" she cried.

At that moment, one of the FBI agents and Mr. Price emerged on the pathway. "Where's Hiller?" Agent Simpson asked.

Seth pointed over the side of the embankment. "My partner's helping Detective Campbell out of the jungle. Nasty blow to the head," Simpson said.

Mr. Price inched closer toward the edge of the terrace, and Jenks watched as he took a deep breath and his eyes grew wide. He crossed himself as he had done when they saw the fer-de-lance on the logging trail.

Jenks noticed that none of the three men were making an effort to descend from the terrace for Hiller. She could hear struggled breathing and after several moments, he crawled back onto the terrace from the precipice into which he had fallen. Jenks covered her mouth in shock as she realized Hiller had several small snakes still on his body.

"Tommy goff," Mr. Price murmured. "In this case, a mother and many small ones."

Hiller's facial expression showed deep agony, and he yanked the remaining snakes from his body and flung them back into the jungle. Looking completely spent, he dropped to his knees and then forward onto his elbows. After a moment, he rolled onto his back and stared up at the sky.

"The closest medical clinic is at Blue Creek Village, but it is some distance away. We must try to get him there," Mr. Price said.

Seth and Officer Simpson lifted Frank Hiller from the ground. They put one of his arms around Seth's shoulder and the other arm went around Simpson's. They struggled with his weight and began the trek out of the jungle. Hiller's feet were at times dragging the ground.

Even through both men were in exceptional physical condition, they had to stop twice to regain their breath and strength as they carried the full weight of the man. By the time they reached the edge of the jungle, the other FBI agent, Castillo, joined the two men in carrying Hiller.

When they reached the house, they placed him on a lawn chair that was on the rear patio. His face was contorted with pain, and he was having spasms throughout his body.

"Water," he begged.

Castillo went inside the house and returned with a bottle of water, opened it, and handed it to him. Mr. Price was speaking to someone on the telephone. He turned and looked at the group. "I have called the medical clinic at Blue Creek Village. I spoke to the doctor's wife. He left yesterday afternoon with his nurse to handle an emergency delivery for a woman in Rosita. She says that he has not returned. We must take him to Orange Walk."

"We'll use his Land Rover. We can probably get over the downed trees in it," Seth commented.

"I'll see if I can find the keys to it," Castillo volunteered as he went toward the house.

Hiller could hardly manage to drink from the water bottle and Jenks helped him take sips. She looked into Frank Hiller's eyes and realized he was staring at her. Their eyes locked.

He struggled to speak. "Gigi, I'm—" He didn't finish his sentence as a surge of pain gripped him.

"Frank, why?" Jenks implored him.

He started to speak again, but a wave of agony washed over him, and he shook with a seizure.

The sound of an approaching vehicle was audible as Castillo drove the Land Rover onto the lawn, stopping near the patio.

Frank started to speak again. "Gigi—" Again, he was consumed by pain.

"Let's get him into the truck," Simpson said.

The men started to lift Hiller into the back of the Land Rover, but Mr. Price held his hand up in a fist, signaling for them to stop. Jenks looked down at her sister's killer, and his eyes were fixed and unmoving, staring straight at her.

Mr. Price felt for a pulse on his neck and then closed Hiller's eyes. He stood above Hiller and crossed himself again. "Too much venom," he said dryly.

Jenks looked at Seth. He had red marks on his face that she knew would turn to bruises, and he was sweating heavily from the chase and then from carrying Hiller's full weight through the jungle. Tears started to well in her eyes and fell down her cheeks.

Frank Hiller lay dead a few feet away from her; during all the times she envisioned him brought to justice, she had expected Hiller to spend his life in prison. Justice had been dealt, but she felt only remorse. She wished that she still had her precious sister.

Seth put his arm around her and led her away. He winced as he took a step, limping on the leg that had been broken.

"Are you all right?" Jenks asked him.

"Just sore, let's go see about Thomas and Lopez."

"He thought I was Gigi. He was trying to tell me something." She wiped tears from her cheeks. "He didn't attempt to take the gun away from me."

"I know."

"Why do you think he didn't?"

"That—we will never know."

The deafening cry of howler monkeys filled the air as they made their way toward the others.

CHAPTER 19

Blackstock's Mountain

"I'm afraid to come in there."

"You afraid—no way!" Seth called out to her, his voice echoing from within the cave. "Just hold on to the rope and crawl in. You have nothing to fear."

Jenks shimmied across the ground. She felt claustrophobic as her head bumped the top of the tunnel. She took a deep breath and cautiously crept the remaining feet to the entrance of the cave. The lanterns that Seth had lit illuminated the grotto, and when she emerged, she gasped at the wonder of her surroundings.

The cave was at least twenty feet high and a small stream ran through the rear portion. The stream gurgled and the light of the lanterns cast shimmering reflections of the water on the walls of the cave.

"Wow, this is amazing." Her voice echoed.

"Yes, ma'am, it is that."

Seth took her by the hand and led her close to one wall. "Take a look at this drawing," he said, holding a lantern close by.

"Oh, my goodness—it's a buck smoking a pipe. It actually looks like that deer is smiling."

"Could be." Seth chuckled.

"And to think, you and Steel could be the only ones to have found these drawings since they were created. Thank you for taking me here."

"My pleasure."

They spent another thirty minutes studying the rest of the artwork before exiting the cave. When they came out into the fresh air, the glare from the sun on a landscape of snow blinded them, and they put on their sunglasses.

It was early January, and Seth had brought Jenks to Asbury to show her where he had grown up. After they arrived, five inches of snow had fallen in the hills of north Georgia. They played in the falling snow Saturday afternoon into the evening and walked around the small community—Seth recounting stories of adventures he had shared with Steel growing up.

Despite the snowfall, they rose just after sunrise and left the bed and breakfast, Asbury House, to drive up into the hills near Blackstock's Mountain. The four-wheel drive on Jenks's Jeep worked effectively.

Putting their gear back into her vehicle, Seth told her, "I want to show you something."

He took her hand and led her up a hill to a plateau. In front of her lay a cemetery; snow covered the graves and created drifts on top of the markers.

There was not a single noise except their breathing.

"It's so quiet," Jenks whispered.

They stood in place and observed the serene surroundings. The hills and the mountain were covered with snow. Suddenly, the lone cry of a hawk sounded nearby, and the large bird flew above them, looking for prey.

"Come this way."

He led her to a grave marker that was covered with snow, and a small American flag was displayed near the stone. He dusted it off with his gloved hand.

Steel Mason was the name on the marker.

Jenks huddled close to him as they stood together quietly.

She wasn't sure how much time passed by, but finally she broke the silence. "What a peaceful place to be at rest," she said as she looked around her surroundings. "The flag looks brand new."

Seth looked as if he were returning from somewhere far away and then turned to gaze at her. "I think it is," he said as he examined it closely. "God, I miss him."

"I understand."

He looked down into her eyes and then hugged her.

Thick clouds were moving in and began obscuring the sun. Snow began to fall again, flurries at first, but quickly changed into large fluffy flakes.

"I love you, Miss Ellington."

Jenks hugged Seth close to her and then stood on her tiptoes in her hiking boots to kiss him on the cheek. "I love you, too."

He unbuttoned his coat and took his gold watch out of his wool vest. Looking at the time, he commented, "We should still be able to get breakfast at Asbury House. Are you ready to go back?"

"Yes, sir."

As they walked away from the cemetery back to Jenks's Jeep, she asked, "How's Thomas feeling?"

"Much better—he's stopped having headaches. The Lopez kid spent a week in a Belize City hospital, but I was just told he's doing better."

Jenks dusted snowflakes out of her hair. "Seth, do you think any of the artifacts that Frank stole from Gigi will ever be recovered?"

"As we both know, Mr. Price is very capable, and he's doing research in Belize. Your lawyer, Mr. Delamere, in Charleston, is investigating as well. And of course, you have the Beaufort County Sheriff's Department and the FBI still investigating. I think you're doing as much as you can."

"And that cross—I wish Gigi had never found it."

"Yes, but she did."

"I hope that a settlement can be reached over it without some type of court action."

"Have patience."

"I am—I'm cold. I want you to make me a hot chocolate when we get to the Asbury House."

"Let me warm you." Seth wrapped his arm tightly around Jenks and looked down into her eyes. "It will be my pleasure, Miss Ellington."

The End

Thank you for reading *Catherine's Cross*. Reviews are very helpful and important to authors. Please post a review on Amazon, Goodreads, or your favorite book seller's website.

Many thanks! Millie West